CONTENTS

DECEASED: THE LAST VAMPIRE

by

T.A. Bound

DECEASED

The Last Vampire

Paperback: 979-8-9853936-5-1
Ebook: 979-8-9853936-2-0

First paperback edition September 2022.

Cover art by Photographia
Cover Model: Caroline Fowler
Photographs by Photographia

PART I

Bloodlust

"One of the artifices of Satan is to induce men to believe that he does not exist."
John Wilkinson, *Quakerism Examined,* 1836

WELCOME HOME (SANITARIUM)

1987

"Yea, though I walk through the valley of the shadow of death, I will fear no evil: for thou art with me; thy rod and thy staff, they comfort me."

The squeak was neither loud nor overly distracting. To most seated in the quaint sanctuary, it went unnoticed, and those who heard paid it no heed. Of the hundred-odd mourners filling the pews to near capacity inside the diminutive church, those reciting the Scripture with closed eyes saw nothing, while others reading along in the prayer book intent on following the words of the Psalm. Only one head turned.

In the second pew, Aunt Barbara wiped her eyes with a starched linen handkerchief behind two identical cascades of extravagant orange curls in the front pew, the one reserved for the closest family members. The billowing, colorful mop in her direct line of sight spun, revealing the pale, freckled face of her niece lured to glance over her shoulder. Brilliant violet eyes focused beyond her, toward the door at the rear of the sanctuary. A color so rare and striking, the twins' eyes inspired admiration and awe since they were infants.

More annoying to Aunt Barbara than her inattentiveness was the shamelessness of the teen's pristine makeup. Not a streak in her eyeliner. Way too much eyeliner, at that. Woeful impropriety for the funeral of her grandfather. Attempts to communicate her disapproval of the teenager's disrespect by clearing her throat three or four times went unacknowledged, so the elderly woman tried signaling her by waving a soggy, wadded handkerchief toward the casket and the minister up on the pulpit behind it. If the teen noticed the surrender flag, she ignored it.

Curious what diversion had captured her niece's attention, the woman also turned toward the main entrance in time to see a tall, wiry young man with tousled blond hair taking his seat in the last pew. Dressed all in black, handsome —although Aunt Barbara did not recognize him, he bore a striking resemblance to several members of the Brown family, enough for her to conclude he must somehow be kin. Strange, for she knew everyone in the family. Few were still alive.

"Everyone turn in your hymnals to William Brown's favorite hymn, *It is Well With My Soul*, and stand as we sing."

In the front pew, Angelique turned to her twin. "Did you see him?"

"Who?"

"The eye-candy who wandered in late."

Celeste, seated on the twin's other side appearing tired and emotional, turned to her daughters, piercing eyes of absinthe green flashing with anger. "Do you need a hymnal?"

Angelique confirmed her hymnal's existence by lifting it a few inches, cradling it while her sister flipped to the proper page to the sound of the organist launching into the opening bars. "He must be our relative. Looks like one of us," she said in her softest voice, enticing her sister to turn so she could take in her sister's eye candy for herself. From way in the back, the stranger flashed a brief smile, acknowledging their curiosity before returning his attention to the pages and joining in the singing.

"My sin—oh, the bliss of this glorious thought. My sin not in part, but the whole..." the sisters sang together in one voice, waiting for the brief musical interlude leading into the second verse to steal another glance over their shoulders. Turning as mirror images, the blue eyes of the stranger met them across twelve rows of pews. The girls' heads jerked back to the page. Having lost her place, the smitten one gave the other a side-glance, a helpful neon pink nail pointing her to the proper line. Their shoulders bumped together, exchanging a grin, although Angelique's came easily and more enthusiastic. Her sister had taken their grandfather's death much harder.

At the conclusion of the service, family, friends and neighbors surrounded the Brown family, offering their deepest condolences. Lost in a crowd too lofty to peer above despite her two-inch heels, she craned up on tip-toes, lifting her narrow heel off the ground, struggling to locate the stranger who had disappeared. The assemblage of bereaved dwindled, all heading outside to the adjacent graveyard.

"Let's go, girls." George placed an arm across Angelique's shoulder, steering her toward the double doors on the side, the direct route reserved for family to avoid delay. The same doors through which the deceased leave feet-first on their one-way journey to the grave waiting especially for them. Their mother ventured nowhere near him, so this gruff firmness gave away that he had not missed their distraction during the funeral, either. Outside, she again reconnoitered for the mystery man. Only when the coffin hung suspended above the fresh rectangular hole in the ground, the preacher reciting more rote words over their grandfather's corpse, did Angelique spot him.

There, standing alone in the old section near headstones worn smooth by generations of rain, snow and hail, in the now-full plot containing the graves of her ancient Brown family ancestors. Must be a hundred feet distant, though observing with keen interest from afar. An elbow jabbed into her twin's side, followed by a swivel of her eyes, directing her attention to the man. Watching. Even at this distance, the sisters realized his stared back at them. Hard to believe, but the way the late spring light lit them, blue irises reflected the sun back toward them.

"Earth to earth, ashes to ashes, dust to dust," the preacher said. The solemnity of the moment drew the twins' attention, despite themselves. "In sure and certain hope of the Resurrection to eternal life, through our Lord Jesus Christ; who shall change our vile body, that it may be like unto his glorious body, according to the mighty working, whereby he is able to subdue all things to himself."

"Amen," the assembled mourners spoke in unison. The instant they finished, Angelique hurried past the circle of huddled bereaved surrounding the grave toward the old cemetery and its historic Brown graves.

No one was there. A frantic scan of the flat, open ground of the graveyard confirmed her fears.

The stranger had vanished.

In the few seconds the preacher distracted her attention with his concluding words at the graveside, where could he have gone? Her family and neighbors regarded her with curiosity, wondering what had so captured her attention, but that did not faze her. In fact, she hardly noticed.

"Ashes to ashes, funk to funky, we know Major Tom's a junkie," sang the more tempestuous twin under her breath as she scanned the surroundings. "Why does that song get stuck in my brain at every funeral?"

"Daddy hears you singing that at Grandpa's funeral and there will be something else sticking from your brain." Images of David Bowie costumed as a spacy Pagliacci had infected her mind as her sister launched into the tune.

Wind tossed curls across their faces as they lowered their grandfather into the ground. The twins slipped away unnoticed through a slight haze of dust the sudden breeze kicked up. Upon reentering the church, a lone deacon gathered up discarded funeral programs in an otherwise empty building. Dejected at the handsome specter's disappearance, they made their way back outside. "Missed your chance," her sister taunted her.

"Who do you suppose he was?"

"Some stranger? The kid who mowed Grampa's lawn ten years ago? Who knows?"

"But we knew everyone who worked for Grampa."

"Whoever he was, he's gone now. Come on, they'll be heading to the house soon." Together, the twins rejoined the dispersing crowd to find their family. From a distance, dressed in identical short black dresses and walking with elbows locked together, even those who knew them best could not tell them apart.

†

Seemingly insignificant events can irrevocably alter destiny.

Simple decisions often steer the ultimate course of history. Every crashed plane contains at least one empty seat meant for a passenger who missed their flight or decided on the spur of the moment to grab an earlier one. What's one more beer before driving home? Lincoln chose to attend a play. Even a decision whether to answer a firm knock on the door carries enough potential to change the world.

Celeste fought against her instinct. Not that she was too busy mincing onions in the kitchen. Instead, it was the anger. At that moment, she did not wish to speak to anyone, let alone someone who felt the need to knock. The only face she wished to see was one who could help get this mess ready. Bernie was at baseball practice, and Lord knows where the twins were. George called to say he was running late. Timed to reach the answering machine when he knew she was out. After everything else that had gone on, that cold, tinny voice on a micro-cassette that made it sound even more phony set her off. Too cowardly to speak to her, because he knew how upset every late return home makes her.

But the insistent knocking drew her as a magnet to iron.

"Hi. By any chance, are you Mrs. Brown?"

For a moment, she wondered if a Mormon missionary

had dropped by. The young man standing there looked about college age, devilishly handsome, blonde hair pleasantly unkempt and bordering on need of a haircut, and he might have had the most piercing azure eyes she ever saw. One side of his mouth lifted in an arresting crooked smile. Had he been wearing a short-sleeved white shirt with a black tie, she might have slammed the door in his face. Judging by the preppy white oxford shirt, olive green chinos and penny loafers sans socks, he must be a frat boy calling for one of the twins.

"Now is not a good time. The girls aren't home yet. Leave your name and I'll let them know you dropped by."

"Oh, no, ma'am. I'm here to see you—and your husband, if he's here."

"Honey, whatever you are selling, we ain't buying. If I don't get back to stirring, my sauce will catch on."

"I'm sorry. It's just that—I'm Eddie Brown. Edwin, actually. I believe we're distant cousins. Well, your husband is, anyway, and I'm passing through and took a chance to stop by to meet you. Someone in town told me this place is still in the family."

Horrible as his timing might be, she could not turn away a relative—even one she never heard of. Her mother raised her better than that. He looked harmless enough and, now upon closer inspection, a family resemblance was undeniable. In fact, the similarity to George's father was rather remarkable. "Okay, come in. But I'm afraid I can't offer much company right now. Seems I bit off more than I can chew with this new recipe."

"Perhaps I can help? I know my way around a kitchen. In fact, sauces are a bit of a specialty. Don't let the summer I spent studying culinary arts in France go to waste."

"Let me find you an apron." Celeste, smiling for the first time, closed the door behind the handsome visitor.

†

Bernie returned first. Celeste introduced him to his new, long-lost cousin, but after a brief conversation, her son rushed off to shower before dinner. Eddie sure knew how to cook, but even had he been a novice, a second pair of hands to slice and stir unburdened hers. Charming, too. And funny. When her husband arrived, she did not hear him at first, because Eddie was right in the middle of a hilarious story about getting lost on the New York City subway earlier this summer on his way up to Rhode Island.

George missed the joke and found nothing at all humorous about his wife yucking it up with a handsome stranger in the kitchen. "Am I interrupting something?"

"Oh, there you are! Eddie, this is your cousin, George."

George's eyes narrowed. "Cousin? I have no cousin named Eddie."

After a quick hand-wipe on a towel, Eddie extended his with a wide grin. "Distant cousins. Celeste and I tried to figure it out. What did we decide? Second cousins three times removed?"

"Third cousins, twice removed," she corrected him. The last traces of her anger had melted like a tablespoon of butter in a pan while they cooked together, her tone cheerful.

George hesitated, but took the offered hand, gripping like a vice when he did. "We don't have many cousins. We're a small family. How do you figure we are related?"

"Our great grandfather, Edwin Brown, Jr. Our grandfathers were brothers. My grandfather was Ernest Brown."

"Ernest? He disappeared. No one knows what happened to him."

"Eddie does," she said with a wink. "It's a fascinating story, although I only got part of it. Doesn't he look like your father?"

Now that she mentioned it, he did. The shape of his face, the nose, his eyes. "Maybe a little. I'd be interested in hearing that story."

"The whole thing is too long," Celeste said. "But since your cousin is staying for dinner, there will be plenty of time for him to explain the entire family tree. Dinner will be ready in five minutes or so."

With a puzzled expression, George asked, "He will?"

"If you don't mind. I came to Exeter on a quest to meet you."

"Of course he doesn't mind, do you, dear?" The iciness of the tone indicated the only acceptable response was to give his consent.

"No. No, I am interested to hear all about this."

"Oh, it is interesting, alright," she said.

"This family has plenty of interesting stories, if nothing else!" Eddie added, then turned toward the rest of the house. "Your wife says the front of this house is the original dating from the early 1800s, but you added this whole rear section?"

"Well, my father added some, but we built it out. My mother was still alive and staying with us, and we had three young children, so we needed to add a few rooms. Renovated the entire interior, too." George beamed with pride.

"From inside, you could never tell it is that old. The front, though, it looks... original."

"The town is big on retaining its historical charm. They would have blocked us if we tried to change the appearance. Every few years there is talk about designating it an historical landmark. Like our little family home is historically significant enough for that!"

"You should be proud," Eddie said, still intently inspecting the ceilings and floors.

"Oh, we are. Never really considered changing the exterior, but the old part of the house looked like a barn when I grew up here. Could not wait to update everything. Drywall, new hardwood floors, updated wiring and A/C-heat." George showed him around. This kid had a way of making you feel at ease. Few people struck George that way. Must be some family connection.

"Celeste says you have other work in addition to running the farm. What business are you in?"

"I own a Shakey's Pizza franchise up in West Warwick."

Eddie nodded. "Player pianos and picnic tables. Sure. They started up in Sacramento, not far from where I'm from."

Pleased with himself, George said, "That's right. Best pizza around, too."

"How is business?"

"Good, good. Future looks unlimited, although we're currently going through a rough patch. Requires some travel, particularly these days. They're always having meetings at the regional office, if not the home office. Lots of competition. The economy's tough all over."

"Too bad."

"Yeah, the farm is not much of a money-maker these days. We decided to turn much of it into a Christmas tree farm a few years back. Low overhead, but it cranks out a small yet steady profit, if only for about six weeks."

"Still have some fruit trees, I see."

"A few. The apples and one of the pears date back to before the turn of the century. Might need to get rid of them. The girls used to sell their fruit by the roadside when they were kids, but outgrew that long ago. My son never had an interest."

"Be a shame to lose such ancient trees," Eddie said.

"Nostalgia is a poor business strategy. How much apple pie can a man eat? Know what I mean?" George patted a plump stomach straining his belt. "Money's tight, and we cannot pick them. I'm not hiring Mexicans to pick only a few trees. Besides, they're Greenings. Too tart to eat, and cooking apples just don't sell. So, most of it goes to waste."

"Don't Greenings apples make excellent cider?"

"Who knows? Back in the day, they say the Browns made cider, so it does make sense. Can't stand the stuff, myself. Give me an Old Milwaukee and I'm happy. I suppose you decided to stay for dinner since you helped Celeste with it? The twins better be home soon or they'll miss it."

"She invited me, if you do not object."

"Object? No, I already told you, seeing how we're family."

Minutes later, the sound of Madonna blasting from an approaching car ended abruptly near the kitchen door. "That will be the twins," Celeste announced as she dished the last of the meal onto serving platters. Eddie had finished setting the table while George watched Vanna turn letters on *Wheel of Fortune* on TV, beer in hand.

The four had just taken their seats when the front door opened. Deep in conversation with one sister trailing a few steps behind, in they breezed, oblivious to Eddie standing there. Their mother said, "Girls, come meet your cousin Eddie."

The twins stopped dead in their tracks, one's eyes comically wide with her jaw hanging open. Neither one spoke.

"You look like you've seen a ghost," her father said.

"I know you. At Grampa's funeral a few days ago."

"Yup, that was me. Had I known who you were, I would have introduced myself. As it was, I had pressing business that required my attention before the service ended, or else we would have properly met. That and my Irish propensity to burn after only a few minutes in full sun. Please accept my apologies for such unforgivable rudeness."

"I did not see you there," Celeste said.

"He sneaked in late," her daughter explained.

"I only planned a quick visit to town that day, and when I got here heard tell that a distant relative's funeral was being held that morning. I underestimated how long a determined preacher can eulogize."

"Everyone, sit down before the food gets cold. Your cousin Eddie helped me cook."

Up close, the girls' fine features created the impression of matching china dolls, impossible to tell apart. Only slight differences in facial expressions gave any hint they were not, in fact, some clever trick with mirrors. Transparent alabaster complexions complimented brilliant hair cascading several inches past slender shoulders, with full rosy lips, faint wisps of eyebrows and narrow, turned-up noses that—if partial to freckles—might well be perfect. But it was those eyes of delicate lilac that were capable of ensnaring the unwary.

"Hello, Cousin Eddie, I'm Angelique," the talkative one said, her warm hand taking his in what passed for shaking, which she held longer than necessary. His eyes followed her as she walked past, a gaze she returned by swiveling her head. "Sit next to me so we can get to know each other. Josette, sit over there." She pointed to the spot across from their cousin.

The other twin offered a much more formal handshake. One of Eddie's eyebrows raised high. "Josette?"

"Mother didn't tell you? She named her twin babies after her two favorite characters on *Dark Shadows*."

Crimson spilled down Celeste's heart-shaped face towards her neck. "When I was their age, I was a huge fan. And with our family history... They are pretty names, though."

"Beautiful," Eddie agreed.

Face settling in a pink deep as blush wine, Celeste continued, compelled to explain. "I loved the names!"

"We put our foot down when she tried to name our baby brother Barnabas," Angelique said. "That's how he got stuck with Bernie—it's as close as we allowed."

"Hey," her mother laughed, "I'll have you know, the mansion they show in the opening is right over in Newport. Blame you grandparents—they took me to see it because of my addiction to the show."

"No need to explain," Eddie smiled with a jocular wave. "They truly are lovely names."

Josette gave him fair warning. "Don't make the mistake of shortening hers to Angel. She hates that, and will hate you for it if you do."

"Got it," he said with a wink, although curious why. Maybe for the obvious reason, but with the sense of humor her mother claimed she possessed, shouldn't any juxtaposition strike her as a fun play on her melodic name?

"Strange names run in the family," George blurted out,

flailing for relevance in the conversation. "Honey, tell our cousin your full name."

Her pupils flared into green flames, the color of burning copper. "First, there is nothing strange about my name, George. Second, if I recall correctly, you didn't state any qualms about our daughters' names when we put them on their birth certificates." Tense brows relaxed when she turned to their guest. "My full name is Mary Celeste, as in…"

Her husband completed it for her, twisting the knife. "The ghost ship."

More than a century before, back in 1872, a passing vessel found the infamous Mary Celeste drifting derelict in the Atlantic hundreds of miles from the nearest land. Other than minor damage to her sails, the ship otherwise appeared in perfect normal order when another ship came upon her. Only when the other vessel drew close did it become clear that this ship was anything but normal. The crew and passengers were gone, vanished without a trace, and for no apparent reason. In the hundred years since, investigators have found no satisfactory solution matching the documented evidence, creating one of the most baffling and enduring seafaring mysteries.

"Okay, what you need to understand is the Brown family —well, my branch of it, at least—has a long history of naming their daughters Mary, then calling them by their middle name. So, my parents intended for me to be called Celeste, not Mary Celeste."

Eddie grinned. "It's a lovely name. If I'm not mistaken, isn't it Latin for heavenly?"

A satisfied smirk on her face, Celeste aimed the green torches back at her husband.

"That story about Brown women's names? I've heard that before," Eddie continued. "Mary Olive, Mercy Brown's sister, is a classic example. Did you know no one ever called Mercy by her first name, either? To those who knew her, she was Lena, so even the most famous woman in our family followed that tradition."

Angelique placed her napkin in her lap, a formality unseen in their home, and prodded the table in a new direction. "Tell me all about yourself, Eddie. Where are you from? What brings you here? Why haven't we heard of you before this surprise visit?"

"I'm from Coloma, California. Home of the Gold Rush. I made the trek East for the summer, to see where my family originated. As for why you haven't heard of me, most likely for the same reason I never heard of you and Josette. Old family secrets involving a grandfather everyone here believed was dead, but instead went West to seek his fortune. Cut off from his family."

"Sounds mysterious," Josette said.

"He's already told your father and I the story, but it is a peach. Maybe you can tell the kids after dinner?"

"Ooh, I cannot wait," Angelique said. "Family secrets sound so... naughty!"

"And I suppose they are. Darker than naughty, perhaps. Why don't you tell me about yourselves? I traveled all the way across the country to see the Brown farm, never dreaming to find long-lost relatives still lived on it."

Bernie took it all in, not saying much as he devoured a pile of food on his plate. His expression almost concealed a hatred of being around his sisters while they flirted. Especially Angelique. The sickening way she acted around the popular guys in school inspired him to express how eagerly he awaited their graduation, so he needn't be subjected to it daily. Then they ended up attending the University of Rhode Island at Kingston, which, the way she told it, was better than Yale. The fact that the twins were top students despite hardly trying filled Bernie with the urge to puke. "May I be excused?" Without waiting for an answer, he picked up his plate, took it to the kitchen, and hurried upstairs.

"Nice talking to you," Josette called up after him.

"Oh yeah, nice to meet you," Bernie called down from the

stairs.

"He's such a twerp," Angelique said.

"That's enough!" George's voice came out as a shout. Controlling himself, he continued, "Your cousin did not come all this way to hear your constant sniping at each other."

"He's the one who ran off without saying a word to our handsome guest," Angelique said, defending herself. Upon hearing the flirty compliment, George glared a warning at his daughter, but thought twice about yelling again. After clearing the table, the five of them sat in the living room, chatting. Celeste brewed coffee.

"I hope this won't keep you up all night," she said, placing a cup of their lovely heirloom china in front of Eddie. Staring at it, Eddie's entire countenance changed, his pleasant expression draining away.

"No, it's... I'm a night owl."

"Where are you staying, Eddie?"

"I have reservations at a bed & breakfast over in Pawcatuck, the Morgan Inn."

Celeste's eyes lit up. "Impressive—spoken like a true Rhode Islander. Most visitors have no idea how to pronounce it."

Angelique snickered. "Tourists normally make it sound like a dirty word."

"That must be twenty miles from here," her sister said.

"Thereabout," he confirmed.

Angelique asked innocently, "Hey, why don't you stay here?"

"Oh no, I cannot possibly impose upon you like that."

"It's no imposition," Celeste said. "Is it, George?"

"I'm sure he would prefer some peace and quiet. Some privacy."

"Nonsense." It was Angelique again, her interest transparent. "He is family! And he came all this way to see the farm; why not let him stay at it for a few days? He can sleep down in the guest room."

Celeste beamed. "What a wonderful idea! Yes, why don't you? It will give us all a chance to get better acquainted, won't it, George?"

His face refused to belie the fact that having this stranger staying under his roof would not only be an imposition, but a burden. "Well..."

"Listen, I will not dream of it," Eddie said. "Unless you will allow me to pay. The same as the bed & breakfast is charging. It's only fair, and I will not take no for an answer."

This offer sweetened the deal and brightened George's receptiveness. "Well, if you insist..."

Celeste objected, but Eddie held firm, so the deal was struck. "Let me retrieve my things from the room, and I will be honored to stay here in the Brown ancestral home."

An hour later, Eddie returned with his luggage. One small decision to answer the door led to a new family member. A paying guest even George welcomed.

†

Someone must have left the light burning for their guest in case he got up in the dead of night. This realization slowed Josette's descent, bare feet slapping quietly against the old wood of the stairs. When she awakened, their visitor slipped her mind. For an instant, tempted to return for a robe, but thirst compelled her onward. A tall glass of chilled water from the filter pitcher her mother stored in the fridge did the trick, sending chills through her body in the process. Two steps from the stairs, a rustle from the living room made her jump and spin toward it.

"Sorry, didn't mean to startle you." Her cousin sat in her father's comfortable chair in the corner. A beam aimed at him from halogen track lights cast his face in harsh light and shadow, distorting his features into an unrecognizable sight.

Heart pounding crazily, she let out a deep breath upon catching sight of an open book in the crook of his crossed leg.

"Shit! Don't do that!" Then, lowering her voice, she pointed toward the ceiling. "My parents' room is right there."

"That's why I didn't say anything. Figured you might scream. At least you aren't armed." The shadows contorted his grin into a Jack-o'-lantern grimace. "Care to keep me company? I was just reading." A vague wave toward the bookshelf in the corner, where a gap stood out like a snaggletooth from the removed book.

"No, I was just...," then stopped, realizing his spot in the corner offered an unobstructed view through to the kitchen. That's the moment she wished she was not half-naked, wearing only a thin tee-shirt emblazoned EWG Knights Cheerleading, one size too big, so it hung just long enough to cover her panties. Not appropriate for a conversation with a male stranger she met hours ago who claimed to be a mystery cousin, even before chilling her body with ice water. But curiosity took over. "What did you find to read here?"

"Somebody keeps a fascinating collection of Reader's Digest Condensed Books here in your parlor," he explained, closing the book and holding it up to read from its spine. "*Captain of the Queens*, *Beloved*, *In My Father's House* and *The Last Hurrah*, all in one volume!"

"My father's. Claims he's read the classics when all he reads are Cliff's Notes for lazy adults. Which one were you reading?"

"*In My Father's House*. It's not what I hoped for."

"What were you hoping for?"

With mock seriousness, he answered, "The kind of thing Reader's Digest doesn't publish."

"Stop it! They'll hear us laughing and come downstairs to see what we're up to."

"Then come sit down over here where we won't have to shout to each other." His head shifted, the shadows under his brows and nose now less sinister.

"I'm not exactly dressed for hanging out with a guy I just met."

Shadows lengthened as his head angled down toward her feet, then back up. "Ever been to the beach?"

Since the shirt did cover more than a bikini, Josette chose a chair facing the same direction to avoid offering him too good a view, stifling a humorous realization to avoid answering what struck her so funny. Something about her cousin could charm the pants off her—if she was wearing any. "We've got better books upstairs. My father's taste is, shall we say, lacking. My sister and I read. Proper books, not condensed."

"What about your mother?"

"She is literate, but not much of a reader. Never had time for it with three kids, I guess."

"Your brother must have plenty of time to read, being a mute and all."

"Oh my god, wait till I tell Angelique that one! She'll think that's the funniest thing ever. No, his best conversation is when he is cursing out Nintendo. There is nothing worse than teenage boys."

"I can think of a few worse things. A broken leg, acne…"

"Wrong. So, what's your first impression of our little branch of dysfunction in your family tree?"

"Honestly? The women seem friendly, intelligent. Sure are pretty."

Warmth on her face only suggested the color at his compliment. "And the guys?"

"Well, they don't seem to take to me all that well. Your sister can be a bit overpowering…"

"That's one word for it."

"At least she is funny."

"All the guys say so—the reason she's so popular—well, one of them. Stay on her good side, though. Her sense of humor can turn biting like that." A snap of her fingers made the point clear.

"Noted. Not that a little bite ever scared me off."

Was he flirting with Angelique while she wasn't even

here? "No, I don't suppose it does."

"You, though," he pointed, lowering his head like sighting a gun at her chest still chilled from her drink, "the quiet ones are who you need to watch out for. Taking everything in, analyzing, intelligent enough to know sometimes stillness can be ruined by words. Deep. And they say, the deeper the water, the more dangerous it is. Don't know if it's true."

It came out as a question unasked, his intense eyes bearing a physical presence, real as a hand reaching out, touching her. Reaching inside her. A shudder ran through her, further tightening her skin, so she crossed her arms over her chest. "It's late, and someone will hear us if we keep this up. Let me go back upstairs," she said, standing, pointing unnecessarily toward the second floor while tugging the tail of her shirt to belatedly cover where it got hung up on one side of her bum when she stood.

"Well, I'll stick around for a while. I'm curious to find out what happens *In My Father's House*," he said, even the shadows unable to disguise his smile as wry. "Goodnight!"

"'Night," she said, scurrying up the safety of the staircase.

AND SHE WAS

For a few blissful moments after George left for work and the kids headed off to school, time belonged to her and her alone. It may not be the most enjoyable part of the day —at least not every day—but the most reliably peaceful. No one around to ask anything of her, no rigid schedule. Another pot of coffee, at least one cup watching the *Today Show* or, on a warm morning such as this, on the porch just enjoying colorful songbirds flitting about the trees. Blissful leisure. Splayed fingers run through her bed-head pushed it off her face as she wandered back to the kitchen to brew that second pot, her mind quiet. Blocked by a handful of hair, a sudden movement to her right startled her enough to launch her feet six inches off the floor with a little "Oh!"

Maybe more than a little one.

"Sorry, didn't mean to startle you. Figured you might want some more coffee—I sure do. Hope you don't mind." Finished pouring into a mug, Eddie held up the fresh pot to her as an offering.

Tense fingers pressed against her upper chest to push her heart back inside, where it belonged. "Oh, Lord—for a second, I forgot you were here!"

"Wow, that forgettable, huh?" He snatched another mug from the shelf and filled it while she recovered. "Let me guess: you like it sweet."

"Jesus, you scared the crap out of me. Yes, sugar. Extra extra sugar."

He handed over the mug. "I better let you cut it yourself. I take it black, so I tend to underestimate when I make it for others."

"Thank you." She shoveled into her mug from the bowl on the table. "Care to join me on the porch? That's where I drink mine on days like this."

"After you." Summer birds chirped in every direction as a family of robins plucked hapless worms from the small patch of grass before the first row of fruit trees. "It is peaceful here. No wonder you enjoy it."

"Sorry I screamed at you. This is my usual alone time."

"I can leave you be and finish mine inside..."

"Don't be silly. It will be nice having someone to chat with. Calm after the storm."

"Missed most of it. Not much of a morning person, myself."

"Me, either. Not naturally. When I was your age, I was still a night owl. Kids and a husband who leaves by eight have a way of changing that. Particularly kids. Enjoy it while you can."

"Oh, believe me, I do."

Was that a wink? Low sun peeked over a tree to hit their faces, causing both to squint. Not that winking would be out of line, right? Strange how a virtual stranger already acted with such familiarity. Suddenly aware her discomforting gaze lingered on him for too long, she turned to the family of robins.

"What's the matter with Angelique?"

"What do you mean?" Hurriedly, she sipped on her sweet, dark tan drink.

"Well, her hair almost hides her neck. At first, I assumed she had a rash; then I saw her toenails sticking out of her slippers when she was going to bed. She's ill, isn't she?"

"Probably shouldn't talk about it behind her back."

"You're right." He took a sip from his steaming mug. "Was going to ask her about it, myself, but she doesn't let on, does she? Not the type to show any sign of weakness, that one."

"No, she is not."

"You've got it, too, don't you? That little spider-web rash

below your throat." One hand shot up, squeezing shut the gap above the top button. This time, it was his gaze which held too long in hers. Her mind whirled how to respond.

"Zinsser-Engman-Cole Syndrome. Quite a mouthful, isn't it? We just call it DKC, a billion percent easier to say since no one can pronounce its other name, Dyskeratosis congenita. Took me about a year of practice to pronounce it correctly. The doctors say I may have ten, twenty years. Some people live to sixty with it, and I'm not quite forty, so who knows what treatments they will come up with in that time?"

"And Angelique?"

"She's already got scarring on her lungs. The doctors say her case is the severe kind. It affects your bone marrow—what that has to do with your lungs and skin, I haven't a clue. She refuses to let it slow her down any."

"What causes it?"

"Oh, don't worry—it's not contagious. It's genetic."

"Since they are identical twins, is Josette afflicted by it, too?"

"So far, not yet, thank the Lord," she rapped knuckles on the arm of her rocking chair. "They can only diagnose it by the symptoms, and so far, she has shown none. But it keeps me awake at night, terrified she's going to wake up some morning with a purple neck or chest."

"I'm sorry."

"How did you notice? Does anyone on your branch of the family tree have it, too?"

"Not that I know of. To tell the truth, never heard of it before. Might have thought nothing of it, just a rash, some cracked toenails. Sometimes I can sense things, is all."

"Funny how a stranger picks up on it right away, yet her father is oblivious to it."

"Since this is new for me, how serious is DKC?"

"Deadly serious."

"I'm so sorry. Is there anything I can do?"

"There isn't much anyone can do. My death certificate

will likely say, *cause of death: bone marrow failure*. Since its already in her lungs, the doctors worry about Angelique. Worries me more, too; I've already lived, had children…" A long sip allowed her to shift gears. "Know what sucks most about it? One symptom is premature aging. I've been dying my hair for years. It's my natural color—or was. Now it's almost completely gray. And all these wrinkles? None of these were here two, three years ago. Vain as it may sound, death doesn't bother me half as much as growing prematurely old!"

A quick laugh slipped out. "Sorry, it isn't funny, but your attitude is amazing."

"I admire Angelique's. Frustrating as she can be—and trust me, she's enough to drive me gray without DKC—she's going to have a lifetime of fun before this thing gets her. She knows she's on borrowed time, but instead of letting it control her, she's going to go out like a rock star. Did you know Jimi, Janis and Jim Morrison—all were 27 when they died? Brian Jones of the Rolling Stones, too. Angelique might not even have that long, but she's going to have as much fun as they did. Sometimes I believe she couldn't care less about growing old. Can't say I blame her for that."

"The moment I met her, I wondered what it was about her. Betrayed by her eyes—the eyes of a wild animal."

"The disease didn't do that to her—that's how she was born. If she had her sister's personality, so introverted and gloomy, she'd have handled it much differently. Wildness is a gift when handed a life sentence like hers, that's for sure. Seriously, I envy that. Look at me—the wildest I can manage is dye my hair my natural blonde. Can't believe I told you that. Nobody knows, outside the family."

"Well, I am family, so…"

"Listen, don't breathe a word to her, okay? She'll be furious if she finds out I told you. Makeup hides that mark well, but she must have taken it off last night thinking you'd never pick up on it."

"Your secret is safe with me. All of 'em." He leaned

forward and, with two fingers, pushed the part running down the center of her hair wide. "You do a good job with this; looks totally natural."

"Well, you should see my purple chest—not that you will, because this is the last time I wear a V-neck around you. It's disgusting."

"That I seriously doubt."

†

From somewhere outside, country music swelled to an obnoxious volume. An unfamiliar song, country being not at all his style, although the way it rattled the speakers or some ill-fitting body panels did a decent job distorting it to near-unrecognizable. A late model Camaro kicked up dirt in the driveway. A big, ugly monstrosity, its slab shape a far cry from the sensuous curves of classic models. The passenger door opened, and one twin shoved the front seat forward to squeeze out of the rear seat while the other continued chatting with the driver. The engine cut off, a belated mercy killing of the music. Both the remaining twin and a pretty boy in a school letter jacket exited their sides at the same time.

Up close, Eddie recognized Josette when she came in ahead of her sister and the jock. "Oh, hi."

"I hear you got a ride home."

"Ugh. Swear to God, if I ever hear Eddie Rabbitt again, I am going to ralph. Don's trying to get into my sister's pants again, which explains the ride home."

"Don, huh?"

"He's a dork, a total wannabe. Who still wears their high school football jacket a year after graduating? Spent four years trying to score with her, and finding out colleges have no interest in quarterbacks with lousy grades can't discourage him from still trying. For some unfathomable reason, she tolerates his crap." The door opened. "There they are. Don, meet our cousin, Eddie. I need to go wash up."

"Hey, buddy," Don grabbed his hand in a macho display, squeezing way too hard. Eddie returned it, grinning as the quarterback's eyes narrowed, then flinched and pulled back. "Dude's got a good grip."

"Don was nice enough to give us a ride home."

"How thoughtful."

"What brings you here, Ed?"

"Just visiting. And it's Eddie."

"Whatever. Hey, babe, what are you doing this weekend? Bill Simms is throwing a party. Hey, Ed, do you party?"

"Depends."

"Why's Bill having a party?"

"He moved into an apartment up in North Kingston. Christening the place with a keg."

Angelique turned to her cousin. "What do you say, Eddie?"

"Sure. A keg sounds good."

"Cool beans," Don said. "Look, I gotta bolt. Call me later."

"Okay," Angelique answered. Don leaned to kiss her, and she turned her head to offer a cheek for him to kiss while smiling at Eddie.

†

Forty or fifty kids must have squeezed themselves into the apartment. Michael Jackson blared from the stereo, but no one was dancing. Another jock with longish, wavy brown hair hugged the twins, then looked at Eddie. "Let me guess, you're the cousin."

"Good guess. Bill?"

"My man! Beer's out on the deck." From the looks and size of him, Bill had been Don's gridiron teammate. "Plenty of chicks here; have fun!"

"Always do," he answered.

Don appeared like a fly at a picnic, bee-lining straight toward Angelique, so Eddie asked Josette, "Want a beer?"

"I'll come with." She clung to the back of his shirt as he elbowed a path through the mob, stopping to say hi and introducing him to several people until they spilled out onto the deck. There, two more former teammates stood guard over the beer, one with his foot on the edge of the ice tub. Seeing Eddie, they stepped back, one waving his hand as an invitation to tap the beer. He poured two red Solo cups full and handed one to Josette.

"Should we head back inside?"

She glanced through the glass door before replying. "What's the rush?"

"Don't like crowds, do you? I saw the look on your face in there."

"It's that obvious?"

"Pretty much."

"My sister loves being packed in like sardines. I mean, most of these people are friends from high school, but I don't need to see every one of them at once. Know what I mean?"

"Oh, yeah."

"See any girls you are interested in?"

"A couple."

"Let me know if you want an introduction."

"What happened to staying out here for a few minutes?"

"You don't have to babysit me; I'll be fine."

"Oh, I have no doubt. Beer's good."

"Narragansett," the eavesdropper with his foot on the tub informed him.

Eddie raised his cup to him as a toast, then whispered to Josette, "So much for privacy."

"Right?" At that moment, a couple of pretty girls stumbled out, one with teased out blonde hair squealing and running to hug his cousin.

"So good to see you! Is this the cousin?"

"It is."

"Oh, isn't he adorable?"

"And he is not deaf. Eddie, meet Bernadette and Nina."

The prettier of the two, Nina, offered her hand, but Bernadette, the exuberant one, hugged him, making sure to press her boobs into his chest. Another invitation.

"Are all the women in Exeter beautiful?"

Bernadette laced her arm through his. "I adore your cousin already! You don't have a girlfriend, do you?"

"Not tonight."

"Oh, you are a devil, aren't you? We're going to get along just fine! Josie, where have you been keeping yourself? Haven't seen you in ages." She maintained her hold on Eddie, staking her claim while catching up with Josette. Nina, whose short, black hair cut a stylish asymmetric slash, maintained occasional eye contact while ceding possessory rights to Bernadette, chatted away. Eddie drained his beer and drew another Narragansett.

Don came out and slapped him on the back. "Hey, is that beer cold?" He stuck his finger in and sucked foam off. "Sure is!" He cackled at his joke as he filled two cups and disappeared back inside. Visible through the sliding glass door, he handed one of those cups to Angelique inside. A space invader, his cousin continuously leaning back or side-stepping to maintain some distance—however small—as Don hugged and touched and bumped against her. Like watching a game, Angelique defended the goal against Don's constant efforts to score, and every bit as entertaining as watching the Celtics vs. the Lakers in the final.

"What do you say, Eddie?" Insistent tugging on his elbow brought him back to his own game. "What movie are you looking forward to most this summer? Nina bets it's *Fatal Attraction*, but I bet you're more into *Predator*."

Turning to his cousin, he asked, "What's your guess?"

"Definitely *Lost Boys*."

A smile, a raised red cup, and a wink. "She's got an unfair advantage—you two just met me tonight."

"I can see that," Bernadette nodded along with Nina, who also agreed how wrong they had guessed.

Sudden movement through the sliding glass door caught his peripheral vision. Inside, his cousin backed violently away, mouth formed into an O, eyebrows low. Don laughed, stepping forward, palms high in mock surrender. Glass and *Beat It* blocked the sound, but her lips needed none to read with clarity.

No! What is wrong with you?

When he reached to prevent her from backing away through the crowd, she violently parried his arm and tried to turn, but Don was quick, grabbing hold of her wrist and yanking her toward him.

"Wait here."

The three girls on the deck watching in disbelief, he barged through the massed throng, forcing several kids to jump out of his way, but one guy didn't give an inch, so Eddie went through him, knocking him a step back.

"Let go of her!"

The look on Don's face, total shock at someone charging him through a crowded room, but that was his only reaction. Only when a palm in the center of his chest shoved him back with tremendous force did he let go of her arm. "What's your fucking problem?"

"Eddie, it's okay—let it go!"

"I said, what's your problem?" Football buddies appeared alongside to back up the retired quarterback.

Rather than answering, he asked his cousin, "You alright?"

"I don't need your help!"

"The hell you don't!" Josette showed up a few steps behind.

"I've got it under control."

Nearly chest to chest, the two gladiators glared at each other, neither making the first move while the twins bickered. One of Don's buddies asked, "You aren't going to take his crap, are you?"

Still, Eddie remained motionless, staring down the other

man with an intensity that visibly shook him. In frustration, Angelique turned her attention from her sister to him. "Let it go. This party sucks anyway. Let's get outta here."

A small, insistent hand tugged on his left elbow, the opposite of the one Bernadette had been holding onto. As Eddie started to turn toward Angelique, Don picked that moment to salvage his reputation. A tight, well-aimed punch streaked toward Eddie's face.

It happened so fast no one could recall afterward how, but the punch somehow missed. Instead, this time with two hands, Eddie shoved the larger guy with enough force to toss him through three of the friends behind him. Four bowling pins hit the floor as another hand hooked Eddie's right elbow and the twins dragged him out, yelling in synch, "Let's go!"

"Macho asshole!" Angelique shoved him toward her sister, then she laughed. "Jesus, two grown men fighting over me. What a show!"

Josette glared at her mirror image. "What the hell was that all about?"

"Nothing. Macho asshole here saved a damsel in distress from a total asshole."

"You should be thanking this macho asshole."

"For what? Embarrassing me in front of everyone we know?"

"Oh, my god!" Josette took her sister's hand and held it up to the streetlight. Already, an angry, brownish hand mark was forming around her slender wrist. "Look what he did to you!"

She laughed it off, jerking her arm free. "You know I bruise easily. It's just a side-effect of..." She caught herself and glanced at their cousin.

"Be glad Eddie stopped it when he did."

On the drive home, all three crammed onto the bench seat with Josette in the middle grilling her sister about what the uproar had been about, her valiant defense crumbled. "The asshole wanted us to do a threesome with him. There, are you happy now?"

Incredulous, her twin said, "What the hell?"

"Right? Out of the blue, he asked, 'How many beers do you think it will take to get your sister to join us for a three-way?' I couldn't believe it. He doesn't want to sleep with me, he wants to sleep with *us*!" Craning forward to address Eddie across her sister, she said, "I haven't slept with him, if that's what you are wondering—thank god!"

"That's not what I was wondering."

"Well, I haven't—and sure as hell won't now—knowing what he's really after."

Josette's voice trembled. "He's such a tool! How many times have I told you that?"

"Eddie, you're a guy," Angelique started.

"Glad you noticed."

"Yeah, acting like a gorilla back there clued me in. I'm not your territory, by the way."

"Noted."

"Anyway, speaking for guys, what makes you think we are into having orgies just because we are twins?"

"Please don't ask me to speak for guys like Donnie boy."

Josette asked, "So, not every guy wants to screw twins?"

"Is that a trick question?"

Angelique, voice dripping with sarcasm, confronted him over the contradiction. "What happened to not wanting to speak for all members of your sex? Now you admit all you guys think we are just dying to have threesomes with every guy we meet?"

"Wanting something is not the same as assuming someone else shares your fantasy. Search me why any guy might assume twins would want to jump into bed with him. Seems pretty arrogant to believe that. But, seriously, do you have any conception of how beautiful you two are?"

"What does that matter? If a guy meets two beautiful girls—friends, for example—do you immediately assume they are both going to screw you?"

"Probably not—I never have."

Josette joined the pile-on. “Then why do you all treat us like sluts just because we are twins?”

“Wow,” he chuckled as he turned off the highway toward their house. “That’s the thanks I get for preventing a guy from snapping your little wrist like a twig—now I’m treating you as sluts.”

“Not you,” Josette backtracked, “you guys.”

“Other guys,” her twin jumped in to help.

“To set the record straight, I don’t think you are sluts. In the few days that I’ve known you, it never crossed my mind that you would do that sort of thing.”

“Tell us the truth,” Angelique said. “You haven’t fantasized about the two of us?”

“Angelique! Christ, he’s our cousin!”

“He’s a man, isn’t he?”

Her face earnestly sincere, Josette said, “Don’t answer her!”

“No, that’s cool. You may be my cousins, but I’m not blind. Have you ever wondered why so much of what goes on inside your head does so totally outside your control? That doesn’t mean I’m going to assume anyone else is thinking the same thing any more than it means I am going to blurt out every thought that crosses my mind. Are you women any different?”

Angelique answered. “Sometimes I hate the thoughts swirling around my brain, but try as I might, they refuse to go away.”

“Okay, answer me this: if I had shown up with a twin—Eddie and Freddy—would your mind have imagined…? Sorry, don’t mean to put you on the spot. Would Bernadette or Nina have fantasized about the two Eddies, or would each grab one of us for their own?”

“Oh, great,” Angelique said as the car slowed to turn into their driveway, “how am I supposed to sleep tonight with cousins Eddie and Freddy running around inside my brain?”

All three laughed at her unexpected audacity, together

releasing tension built up by the night's drama. Once it subsided, as she opened the door, Angelique turned back to her cousin.

"Thank you."

"For what?"

"Don't make me explain myself." Her arm slipped through his to lock elbows together. "Who needs Freddy when we've got Cousin Eddie?"

DON'T STAND SO CLOSE TO ME

Few tasks in life are harder than cutting a squash.

Celeste split the first two enormous acorns with great difficulty, but they sapped the strength from her fragile arms before forcing her to concede defeat to a third. For a moment, the prospect of taking the cleaver to it brightened her mood. She knew better, though. Images playing in her head of the damn thing hacked to pieces all over the cutting board and counter stopped her. Instead, she relied on an old, final desperate measure monstrous squash yield to. First stabbing deep as her arms allowed with her trusty foot-long knife, she then raised the impaled squash a foot into the air and hammered it on the cutting board.

"God damn it!" Using a kitchen knife to try hacking through wood might yield better results. Swinging the heavy squash depleted her energy almost as fast as her patience. Once more, she put what little weight her body had into the effort, pressing down on the knife one hand on the grip, the other palm evening out the pressure near the tip of the blade protruding beyond the dark green hull of the stubborn squash.

Those loud, repeated thuds drew Eddie from the guest room. More curious than expecting trouble, the increasing tempo conveyed a growing rashness all the way back to the guest room. Or anger. There in the kitchen, Celeste leaned on tip-toes, shoulders forward, hair hanging down, engaged in a struggle against something on the counter. Her straining body obscured her enemy. As he opened his mouth to speak, she let out a little shriek and jumped back, followed by an impressive string of obscenities.

Eddie asked, "Are you okay?"

"Oh, shit!" She turned toward him with one hand wrapped around the fingers of the other. Her cheeks glistened with tears. "I forgot you were here."

"What's wrong?" Blood stained her fingers, although where it came from impossible to tell, held tight as they were. All he knew for sure is she injured herself as he entered the room a second before—her outcry left no doubt—yet the tears down her cheeks ran the full length to her chin. Obviously, those tears were there before she hurt herself. "Oh, hell—you're bleeding!"

She shot a glance toward the counter and the squash with a lethal-looking knife embedded in it. "Damn squash!"

"Let me look at it."

"No, I'll be fine."

"Celeste, blood running down your arm tells a different story." A stream already trickled halfway down her forearm on its way to her elbow. He extended his hand to her, palm up. Head tilted forward to give her an up-glance, Eddie insisted. "Let me see it."

An angry slice in the webbing between the thumb and index finger was the source of the blood. Glancing at the half-split squash offered scant information about how she might have cut herself in this unusual place. Thumb firmly on her palm, he turned it around to see how deep the cut was. "Don't think you'll need stitches—if we can stop the bleeding. Here, let's get some cold water on it."

Obediently following, Eddie led her by the hand to the sink, thumb and forefinger pinching the gash as direct pressure. The way he held it, the tips of his other fingers rested on the inside of her wrist, with hers doing the same to his. When flowing cold, Eddie held her hand under the faucet while still applying pressure, using the other hand to wipe blood from her hand and the delicate, white skin the length of her arm. She offered no resistance. Up close, the green in her eyes glowed against bloodshot whites, eyelids puffy and pink around them. She tried to turn away, but kept returning his unbroken gaze until he turned his attention back to her hand in his.

"Give me the other hand." Despite making no particular sense, she did as he asked, allowing Eddie to hold it under the flow for a few seconds to rinse away an accumulation of blood from holding the wounded hand, then wiped that hand dry. "You did quite a job on that hand. Why didn't you call me? I'd have been happy to cut that for you."

"Guests don't prepare dinner. Not in this house."

"Guest? Are you forgetting I'm family? Or my stint as your sous chef two minutes after we met? Let's check if the bleeding has let up." It had, although not completely, so he held it under the flow of cool well water again. Capable of doing it herself, Celeste allowed him to administer first aid. "If I was to speculate on such things, I'd guess you were distracted. Need someone to talk to?"

A vigorous shake of her head, she answered, "No."

"You sure? I might be a good listener."

"I'm sure you are," she said as his thumb rubbed a red spot from her wrist while holding the cut under the flow. "Nothing you can do about it if I did."

"Sometimes it helps just to have someone to talk to. Someone who won't breathe a word of it to anyone."

Again turning away to focus on her hand, she brushed off his offer. "How can you tell? We may be family, but we've just met."

"Is it George?" Her eyes locked onto his and confirmed his suspicion with a barely perceptible nod. "He strikes me as a challenging husband."

"Oh, it's that obvious?"

Eddie smiled. "Keep it under the water for a minute while I finish gutting the squash." This time, she voiced no objection. The rock-hard vegetable yielded to his muscular arms and the weight he put behind it. "Where do you keep your seeds?"

With a gesture of her head to the corner, she answered, "Usually in the garbage can."

"Heck, no, we're keeping these. Plant 'em again in the spring. Or toast them—they're a delicious snack." After scooping the seeds onto a plate and spreading them to dry, he glanced down and asked, "How's the hand?"

Removed from the flow, the gusher had stopped, and she held it up for his inspection. "The hand is fine," she said, turning back to shut the spigot. Then her chin fell, and she braced herself on the sink with both hands. Her shoulders rocked with silent heaves.

"I'm here for you," he said, placing a comforting hand on her shoulder. Looking back over her shoulder, eyes full of tears, she gave a weak smile before turning away. Eddie rubbed her shoulder, and her head tilted into it. Increasing in pressure, it went from consoling to light massage. Her head flopped back as taut muscles relaxed, her hair brushing against his forearm. "Feeling better?"

"Mm-hmm." It came out as a moan. "Getting better all the time."

"I worried it might be... too personal."

"If you get too personal, I will let you know." Her head rocked from side to side with this rhythm. "Did I mention my dream the other night?"

"Not that I recall. What sort of dream?"

"Probably not the kind I should tell you about."

Eddie dug his fingers in to elicit a response. "Sounds like the interesting kind."

"Mm-hmm. Very interesting. Strange, too—and a little naughty."

Now digging into her muscles hard enough to send a message, he said, "In that case, I must insist."

"Ow! Okay, but promise not to tell anyone."

"It will be our little secret."

"You were there, in my room, watching me sleep. There, feel better now?"

"Sounds a little creepy."

"No, not creepy. It felt a little exciting. Oh, I can't believe I admitted that to you, but it's true. And you asked—forced me to tell you about it."

"Tell me more: what did you do?"

"That's just it—I did nothing. Just lay there, watching you watching me. I wasn't wearing much, a silky nightgown, but I didn't even pull the sheets up. Sounds much creepier now when I put it into words while you are standing here looking at me than while dreaming."

Without another word, he stepped closer, into her space, and cupped his hand on the curve of her hip. Rendered lightheaded, Celeste leaned back against his chest. Ever so slowly, his hand crept forward, up across her stomach; his other hand stopped squeezing and, instead, caressed her shoulder. With the slightest of gentle pressure, he pulled her back against him. Once again, her head fell back until it came to rest on his muscular shoulder.

In his hands, she grew limp and her stomach moved with measured inspiration, deep, as if sleeping. Only when his thumb hit the underside of her bra, a mere breath from her breast, did he stop.

"Eddie, I'm old enough to be your mother."

A feeble attempt lacking conviction, spoken only because it was necessary. "Hardly. Who are you trying to convince?"

Without moving away, she turned to face him. There was nowhere to go, the way he had her trapped against the sink and cabinets, but she could have tried stepping to the side. Instead, she placed the palm of her unlacerated hand on his chest and drummed his taught muscles with extended fingertips. "When you first arrived, you know what I thought?"

"Tell me."

"Which one of my girls is going to fall for this handsome man? Or more accurately, which do I need to worry about him trying to seduce? Even before they came home that night, I knew what they would think of you."

Their unblinking eyes were close, on the edge where focus fades and begins losing detail. "What would they think?"

"Inappropriate thoughts for a cousin to have."

"Like what?"

"Kissing cousins." With a little laugh, she hid her face by resting her forehead on his sternum.

"You're my cousin, too."

"Isn't one of them more interesting to a handsome young man like yourself than a married woman pushing forty? They are so beautiful and young, and my prediction was spot on—I know how my girls think."

"Don't you realize?"

"Realize what?"

"How beautiful you are?"

She did not move. Could not. His large, firm hands slid up her back, not stopping at her bra strap this time, but to her shoulder blade. The slightest of pressure, on the edge of perception, urged her forward toward his lips, already moving to hers. His slightly parted when they met. Soft, and she felt his breath on hers. Still, she could have pulled away, should have pushed him back, taking her last chance to escape. But his lower lip fit so well between hers. Eddie pulled her to him again, this time with one hand down over the waistband of her jeans, forcing their hips together.

He watched her, but her eyes were closed. She responded when he opened his lips to plant a deep kiss, and when she returned it, holding his cheeks between her hands, he let both hands drop, following the curve of her round bottom—still small and tight through mom-jeans, despite her protested age. Arms wrapped around her shoulders, holding her up as he leaned forward, forcing her to bend backward over the sink.

"We should go upstairs—someone may come home."

"What if that someone is your husband?"

"He won't be back until late tonight, remember?"

Like a gentleman, or a young boy raised well by his parents, Eddie led her upstairs by the hand, not letting go until he closed the bedroom door behind them.

†

"Which of the girls did you expect me to try seducing?"

With a laugh and a hand on the bare, almost hairless chest, Celeste answered, "Angelique, of course. Josette is too... aloof, too dark for a guy like you."

"Like me? What am I like?"

Sheets spilled off the bed in a frozen cotton waterfall, one pillow taken with it lying on the floor alongside. "Full of life. On the outside, you may look sweet as a Mormon missionary knocking on the door during summer break, but inside..."

"Inside?"

"A wild child. Just like Angelique. Why me? Why not one of them?"

"They are girls; you are a woman, full of substance and passion. Passion pent up inside, waiting to be released. Ready to burst out of you!" He smacked her little bottom hard enough to make a slapping noise.

"Oh, you are so cute. I could just eat you up!"

"Again? Should we put those squash that almost cost you a thumb in the oven? Then we can come back here and eat each other up."

"You stay right here. Do not move," she said as she tugged her jeans up with a series of little jerks, causing her still-firm breasts to bounce, then slipped her shirt back on. "Better take care of dinner. Then we can work up our appetites together." With that, she bent down to kiss him, fighting his pull back toward the bed, rushing out the door. Her bare feet slapped on each stair all the way to the bottom, loud enough for him to follow her progress. A wicked smile crept over his lips as he rolled onto his back.

Downstairs, Celeste rushed to get the food cooking. She, too, was smiling, but for a different reason. He never suspected the lie she told him. In the dream, he watched her—for a while. Then he came to her. Today was much more vivid, more physical, yet no less intimate than that dream. The truth had to remain unspoken, buried deep inside, because confiding would appear too aggressive. Men enjoy the pursuit. This she remembered. Predatory creatures, men—and like most predators, they flee when something charges toward them. Predators don't know how to handle being prey.

What if she had dreamed of something else? Anything else? A nightmare, or one of those nonsensical dreams about enormous snakes chasing her through the house? Without that dream, would she have dared inciting him the way she did?

†

At dinner, George's announcement that he would leave early in the morning and spend tomorrow in Warwick went unacknowledged.

"This squash is delicious," Eddie said. "How did you prepare it?"

Celeste beamed. "Why, thank you! I spiced it up by adding a little 5-spice and ginger. I'm glad you approve."

"It is good this way, Mama," Josette agreed.

Angelique's squash sat pristine upon her plate. "I'm not a big fan of squash."

"This might change your opinion," Eddie said to encourage her.

George said, "I'm with Angelique. I still don't know why we grow the stuff. But this way isn't too bad."

Bernie said little, but finished his, so Eddie counted him as somewhere in between. "Well, I am glad some of you like it," Celeste said, directing her comment to their guest.

When finished, Eddie gathered the plates and carried them into the kitchen, where Celeste had already begun washing and loading the dishwasher. Brushing up alongside, he asked, "Need some help?"

Rather than answering, she took a plate from him by placing her hand over his, then running it around to the side while locking her eyes onto his. Sidled up to him, her hip and shoulder against his gave the plausible appearance they squeezed together into limited space in front of the sink out of necessity.

"Let us help Cousin Eddie wash those for you, Mama." One twin spoke behind them, causing Celeste to jump and ease an inch to her right to give some daylight between them. Eddie suspected Angelique, but so hard was it to imagine her sounding so excited about dishwashing, it may well have been Josette.

Celeste rolled her eyes at him before yielding her spot to her daughters. "Good luck," she said, voice quiet enough that the girls may not have heard it.

"Do you always do the dishes?"

"Only to help when our guest of honor is washing them." No doubt Angelique. He wondered if she always went braless, or if it was something special for tonight? Far as he could tell, Josette always wore hers, a simple way to differentiate them, pleasant as it was accurate. Sandwiched between the twins, Eddie washed and handed off to Josette for rinsing; on his left, Angelique handled her simple task of handing him dirty cooking implements and dishes. Like their mother, each daughter ensured a safe hand-off with plenty of hand-to-hand contact. Josette surprised him with the frequency of her touch.

"It's been a very long time since I've had two such beautiful women help me wash dishes."

"It's been a long time since Angelique has volunteered to wash the dishes," her twin joked in that way twins have, received as much more benign than it sounded.

"How was I supposed to know how fun housework can

be?" Shoulders, elbows, forearms and sometimes hips meeting, along with their fingers, yet the sisters acted with an innocent nonchalance. Every few moments, Angelique gave the game away with a side-glance of those enormous pupils of polished amethyst. Then she leaned past him to address her sister. "You know what we should do?"

"Bonfire down by the pond?"

"Bingo," Angelique answered her clairvoyant twin. Spontaneous as it sounded, it had the slight ring of choreography. "Do you enjoy bonfires on a summer night?"

"Do dogs like their bellies rubbed?" Eddie smiled, turning from one to the other. "Funny, neither of you seems like the bonfire type."

"One thing you will learn about Exeter: there isn't much to do," Angelique said.

Her sister picked up the sentence, and had he not been looking, with their indistinguishable mezzo-soprano voices, might have assumed the same one continued. "So, you learn to make your own entertainment."

"A person could go crazy from boredom here."

"Many of them do."

"Lucky for us, we have someone to keep us sane."

"That's the best part of twins. Two people..."

"One brain," they finished in unison.

Their back-and-forth style of speaking, which he had yet to experience, reminded him of Run-DMC, completing sentences the other began, one speaking a few words only to hand the rest off to the other. Laughing at a joke one twin said that he did not understand.

"You've done that routine before, haven't you?"

"Maybe a time or two," Angelique admitted.

"Is it true that twins know each other's thoughts without needing to speak? Like you are two halves of one brain? Two different people, yet one?"

"Sometimes. Angelique tries desperately to keep secrets from me, but I know. I always know." For a moment, Josette took on the mischievous expression of her sister.

"Let me guess which of you is the right half of the brain and which is the left?"

"That shouldn't be too hard," Josette answered, her face returning to its usual practiced scowl.

"She's a textbook left brain," Angelique said.

Eddie asked, "Are you a textbook right brain?"

"Ab-so-lutely," she answered with a slow wink.

Her sister asked, "Which is your dominant hemisphere?"

"Now that you mention it, I never really thought about it. Which do you think it is?"

The twins regarded him for a moment, turned to each other, then said together, "Left."

"To me, you are a perfect example of yin and yang," he said. "A duality; identical, yet opposite. The same shape and form while totally different."

Josette asked, "Which is the yin?"

Her sister snarkily added, "And who is a yang?"

"In China, the yin represents the moon or clouds. The dark half. The white side, the yang, is the sun. The light."

Josette sighed. "Let me guess, my sister is the sunshine; I am the clouds."

Somewhat counter-intuitively, Eddie answered, "I prefer the translation of yin as the moon. The beauty and the light of the night. To tell the truth," turning back to Angelique, he continued, "I see the moon in you. People see your light, even though you are a creature of the night. Wild, possibly dangerous. Certainly luring the unwary into danger."

Then he handed a tea glass he had wiped someone's lipstick from for Josette to rinse. "You suspect everyone sees only the darkness in your spirit, and I suspect most do. What I see, though, is virtue. It shines from you, hard as you try to conceal it from others."

Josette responded, "You're weird." But while she kept her face aimed down at the sink, her eyes flickered back to him several times and the tiny muscles under the soft, white skin of her face flickered to stifle any hint of a smile.

"Looks like the three of you are having fun." Celeste leaned against the doorway, arms crossed tight just below her breasts. Although he could not be sure, her expression hinted of annoyance—or was it something else? The expression of someone left out, missing the fun. George came in, turning sideways to squeeze past Celeste. Before he got to the fridge and his beers inside, he realized all the laughter and the voices he heard from the dining room came to a crashing halt. In the awkward silence, rain began pelting the window. Huge drops that struck with intent.

"Don't stop the party because of me." No one spoke, so he scanned from face to face. "Go ahead. It sounded like you were having a great time until I interrupted."

"We were just doing the dishes, Daddy." Angelique spoke in a strange tone, one she had not used since Eddie arrived.

"Doing the dishes. Funny, I don't remember the two of you doing the dishes before. Nor do I recall hearing anyone yucking it up while cleaning up after dinner. Seems having a cousin around causes a lot of changes around here, doesn't it?"

"Sorry, George," Eddie said to smooth suddenly rough waters. "It's all my fault. We're just getting to know each other."

"Eddie, let's have a talk." His hand had been on the refrigerator handle for a while, which he finally opened to grab a beer. "Alone."

Celeste rolled the back of her shoulders against the door frame to spin slowly away, arms crossed even more tightly now, eyes going from George to Eddie, but the visitor did not see it, focused intently on George. The twins ghosted behind their mother out of the room.

"Look, I did not mean to cause any trouble..."

After a swig, George put his arm around the guest and turned him toward the window over the sink, rain obscuring any view. "When I allowed you to stay here, I assumed you understood I meant as family. Our family," he said, waving the beer in an inclusive circle, "not *your* family. Do you understand what I mean?"

"Sure do."

"Funny, but I don't believe you do. Just because work keeps me away from the house does not mean I don't know what goes on here."

George was twice his age, soft, with a slight paunch and two inches shorter. No match for Eddie. Nevertheless, he asserted his dominance in his home and over his females like a silverback.

"What do you think goes on while you are away, George?"

"Don't assume I miss the way you look at my twins. Or the way they look at you. When I said you can stay in our guest room—as my guest—you are aware I meant alone, right?"

"George, I have not touched either of your daughters."

"Keep it that way." He gave Eddie a few condescending pats on the shoulder before letting go. "If it turns out you take advantage of my hospitality—a family member, no less—well, let's just say neither of us wants to find out what happens."

Eddie watched him walk through the doorway, then he turned back. "Strange how we never heard of you before you showed up at our door. Not a phone call, no Christmas cards. No family members have ever heard of you. I know; I asked around. Why is that?"

"I explained all that the other night."

"Yes, you did. I've got some calls out," he said, tapping his palm on the door molding. "The only reason I believed you at all and allowed you to stay with us is you look like a Brown. A hell of a lot like a Brown. Don't know what it is yet, but something—there's something not right about you. And I will find out what it is."

"I am family, George. That is the truth. We are blood."

One finger pistol pointed at him. The cocked thumb fell against George's knuckle. Then he turned to saunter back into the rest of his house, leaving Eddie standing alone in the kitchen.

POLICY OF TRUTH

Long before Celeste arose, Eddie left a note for her on the kitchen table.

Will be out sightseeing today.
See you at dinner!
Eddie

The previous night's downpour by morning lingered as a miserable, chilly drizzle. A truly awful day for sightseeing. If not for a mood dreary as the weather, his poor timing might have prompted a laugh.

Only two sights in Exeter qualify as sightseeing attractions worthy of any visitor's time: Tomaquag Indian Memorial Museum, operated by the Narragansett and Wompanoag Tribes, and the ski park a few miles north of town. During the summer, it doubled as a water park, its pool and slides drawing kids and families from across the state. Bernie and the twins practically grew up shooting down its twisting blue chutes.

Weather like this rain might just make visiting a water park even more miserable than spending time with George.

A third sight, though—one Eddie already has seen—draws curious visitors from all over the globe, although why it attracts them always puzzled her.

The graveyard out at Chestnut Hill Baptist Church.

They come to the Brown family's graves, including their cousin's namesake's, who died at the tail end of the New England vampire panic. Next to her husband's namesake, too. But the grave they come to see belongs to another of their ancestors, the accused vampire Mercy Brown.

Before they met, Eddie had already been there. On the day they buried Grampa, when the weather was much more conducive to a visit. Since he had already made that pilgrimage, why return in this wretched rain? On a better day, Eddie seemed the type who might spend the day hiking up trails at the state park, but with this miserable weather, he must have driven over to Newport or made the trek up to Providence where legitimate tourist sites capable of entertaining visitors can be found.

George walked in and filled his car tumbler with coffee. "The kids aren't up yet?"

Celeste ignored him, so he returned the favor. Noise upstairs announced the kids' progress readying for school. Over a bowl of cereal, George asked with a smirk, "Seen our house guest this morning?"

"His name is Eddie. Congratulations, you succeeded in driving him off. He left a note that he's gone sightseeing." The tone she used to emphasize *sightseeing* conveyed her skepticism.

"Hmph," he answered, glancing through the window at the steady rain. "Nice day for it."

Since their discussion the night before, when Celeste launched her silent treatment, this was the first time they had spoken of it. "After the way you treated him, I wouldn't blame him if he never returned."

"You saw him blatantly flirting with the twins. Don't deny it—I saw the look on your face when I walked in on them last night. He's their goddamn cousin, for chrissakes, and I will not sit back while some...," he lowered his voice so no one else could hear, "while some stranger claiming to be their cousin waltzes into our house intent on screwing our daughters right under our noses. Is that what you want? Huh? Is it?"

Rather than answer, she spun around and left the room, giving George plenty of peace to eat his breakfast. When finished, he set off looking for her, only to discover she had vanished. The kids came down; the twins joining in with their own cold shoulders, an effective demonstration of whose side they took. Great day to be up in Warwick, for what he was looking forward to—and who he would see in a few scant hours.

At least Bernie acknowledged his goodbye when he left ten minutes later.

†

A day later, the rain let up, ushering in warm sunshine and dry air that removed all exterior traces of two miserable, dreary days. Inside the Brown home, though, remnants of stifling tension hung in the air whenever George returned. Celeste dissuaded Eddie from taking a room at a bed & breakfast in North Kingston, but his impending departure cast a pall over the Brown women. The twins uncharacteristically assisted when she prepared a fancy dinner featuring a selection of produce the farm still produced, a pot roast with turnip mash and steeped greens.

Over a dessert of peach pie, made from early peaches ripening on the one remaining tree out back, Eddie sprang the news. "I've got reservations at a spot up in Providence."

Celeste's fork rattled on her plate. "Oh, really? When?"

"I'll be leaving Friday."

Angelique's visage clouded. "Why so soon? We've been so busy with school and all we've barely had a chance to get to know you."

He smiled, but a melancholy one. "I know. But it's time. At least we had these few days. Now that we know each other, we'll keep in touch. Thank you for welcoming me into your home and for allowing me to stay with you. Who knows, perhaps someday I can lure you out to northern California to return the favor?"

George did not try to conceal his giddiness with the news. The thanks, pointed barbs aimed at him, rang with unmistakable sarcasm. “Providence is a friendly town; you’ll enjoy it there.”

Bernie’s apathy went unabated.

“We never had that bonfire we talked about, with all the rain,” Josette said, mirroring her twin’s disappointment with his announcement.

Eddie’s eyes brightened. “Well, what’s wrong with tonight?”

“Has the rain stopped for good?” The prospect of a rain-out gave George a brief glimmer of joy.

Confident as a sea captain, Eddie answered, “It’s passed. Sure looks that way.”

“Didn’t you watch the weather forecast on the local news?” George asked.

“I never watch local news. Do you suppose the wood has dried out enough?”

“There’s plenty of dry firewood in the barn,” Celeste offered, earning her a glare across the table from her husband. She added, “You don’t mind if they use some, do you?”

With a begrudging frown, he consented. “I suppose we have enough.”

“Great.” Eddie dabbed his napkin on the corners of his mouth. “Bernie, why don’t you join us?”

“Naw. I’ve got an English paper I need to write tonight.”

“That’s too bad,” Eddie commented without a detectable hint of insincerity. “George, what about you?”

“Why don’t you young people have your fun tonight? Besides, Celeste and I have some things to go over, don’t we?”

She appeared puzzled. “Like what?”

“With all the excitement over the last few days, you haven’t shown me the books for last month. We can go over the numbers while the kids have their fun.”

Decision made, Eddie stood with his plate. “Ladies, thank you for the delicious dinner. Your pie was amazing! Let me gather up some wood and split it so we can start a fire before it gets too dark to see what I’m doing out there.”

†

Flames crackled, spitting sparks bright as stars high into the crystal-clear sky. A column of smoke rose, filling the night with the warm scent of an old-fashioned winter's fireplace. The twins laid out an old red and black plaid blanket to sit on. For a while they watched the flames spread while exchanging sporadic small talk, but news of his imminent departure cast a pall the blaze's glow failed to penetrate.

"Beautiful night," he said. "It's not too cold out here, is it?"

Shadows flickered across Josette's face. "The fire gets any hotter, we'll burst into flames if we don't move the blanket back a few feet."

"Is this how you two spend summer nights?"

"When we were younger." Angelique's voice lacked its usual boisterousness. Flames reflected from the pond's surface and from her eyes. "It's been a year or two since we had one."

"Two," said Josette, changing position to lie prone, chin propped up by both hands on planted elbows. "Are you leaving because of our father?"

Eddie considered for a moment before answering. "Not entirely. Little did I suspect when I knocked on your door that I'd stay this long."

"He was a real asshole the other night," Angelique said. "We heard most everything. It's an old house. The way sound carries in there; secrets are hard to keep."

"Oh, he's not so bad," Eddie said. Then he chuckled. "Well, maybe he is."

"Believe me, he is," Josette said.

"Hey, let's brighten this soiree up—tell ghost stories or spill our dark secrets by the fire." From the sound of her voice, Angelique wished to move on and enjoy the night. "Any suggestions?"

Eddie asked, "Have either of you played Truth or Dare?"

Angelique regarded him like he was a fool, orange light dancing across her face. "We may not be from California, but we aren't from the Sticks."

"Well, I am from California, and from my town you need to drive twenty miles on twisty mountain roads to even get to the Sticks. Civilization is at least an hour further. I dare you to play."

A shiver ran through Josette. "They made a movie called *Truth or Dare* a year or two ago. A slasher flick. Ever since, that game has skeezed me out."

Her sister said, "I didn't see that one."

"We have very individual tastes in movies. Surprise, surprise. Left brain likes dark films: horror, old black and white noir. Right brain over there prefers comedies."

"Hey, I like Gremlins!"

Josette cast a dismissive eye-roll at her sister. "See? That's a comedy, not a proper horror film. Anyway, in the movie, some guy plays Truth or Dare and ends up mutilating himself, slicing his face off piece by piece with a razor. Turns out he is a serial killer, and when he gets released from the asylum takes turns murdering people then slashing off more bits of his face. You aren't a serial killer, are you?"

"Josette! You cannot accuse our cousin of something like that!"

"Why not?" She focused on Eddie. "We know next-to-nothing about you. Until a few days ago, we never even know you existed. It's possible you went over the fence of a mental institution last week and ran here to murder us."

"It is possible," Eddie agreed.

Josette made a face at her sister. "See?"

"I'll give you a free Truth before we start the game, but you must promise to keep it a secret. Just between the three of us."

Josette answered, "I promise."

"Me, too."

"I am a serial killer, one who's never been locked up in an

asylum. But, the truth is, even if I was a serial killer, the last two people I would dream of hurting are you. The safest place you can be on earth is right here, because no harm will come to you here with me tonight." Silence hung heavy, broken only by the crackling fire reflecting in two identical sets of eyes.

Josette alternated flickering eyes between them. "What happens if someone lies?"

"We won't," he answered. "If someone does, we will know… and there will be a penalty."

"What kind of penalty?"

"Oh, I don't know. Death is a bit too extreme, so let's call that the limit."

Angelique shattered the moment of quiet. "Do you smoke pot?"

Eddie laughed. "Has the game started already?"

A playful grin came over her face. "Why not?"

"Did you bring some, or are you teasing me?"

"I would never tease you," she answered, producing a rolled joint and butane lighter hidden somewhere in the dark, which she lit, then passed to her cousin. After he exhaled a cloud of smoke, he handed it to Josette, whose sensuous fingers wrapped around the tips of his fingers to take the blunt from him.

Eddie pulled a flask-shaped bottle from the back pocket of his jeans and asked no one in particular, "Want a drink?"

Angelique responded, "We're not old enough," then snatched the bottle from his grasp. A quick, tentative sip, then she said, "So that's what was bulging in your pants."

"Oh, Lord," Josette groaned in disgust.

"It's rye."

"Oh, that's what you call it?" She leaned to hand the bottle to her sister, who took a bigger slug, which Eddie matched when she passed the rye back to him. The joint followed the bottle around the triangle.

Following a long, theatrical exhale of smoke with his head tilted back, Eddie said, "I guess it started with me. Who's next?"

"Truth," Angelique volunteered.

"Okay, I've got one," he said. "Do you flirt with every guy as aggressively as you've been flirting with me?"

"No."

"Why not?"

A laugh, followed by a toke of the shrinking joint, gave her a moment's contemplation before answering. "I've already answered one question. Truthfully. I guess you'll just have to wait for your next turn. You can go next."

"I will go with Truth, too."

Before Josette could respond, her sister asked, "Do you have a girlfriend? Honestly?"

"Not anymore."

"Tragic," Angelique said.

With an exasperated tone, her sister said, "Somebody pass me something mind-altering!"

As he handed her the bottle, he asked, "Truth or Dare?" She also went with truth, so he asked, "What attracts your interest in a man?"

"Darkness. A yang to go with the yin you tell me I have. And intelligence. Brains are sexy."

"Good answer," he said then, since it was his turn, he chose Truth.

Josette returned the bottle to him, and he allowed his fingers to overlap hers, the way she handed him the joint. "What is your impression of our family?"

"Must I answer truthfully?" The sisters laughed and insisted that he must. "Alright, your mother is kind, extremely pretty, and very lonely. Your father is intelligent, but disinterested. Distracted. Sometimes a bit of a tool. Your brother is typical of a kid his age, struggling. He has trouble handling puberty, in part because the two most beautiful girls he knows are his sisters and no girl his age can match up to them. What can I say about Angelique?"

"The truth," Josette tossed out.

"In that case, she is funny, smart and much too sexy for her own good. As for you, I see a tortured poet trapped inside the body of a supermodel."

"Wow," she said.

Her sister clasped his shoulder. "This is why you cannot leave!" Her fingers held the doobie to his lips, and he drew deeply. "Truth for me."

"Why are you flirting more aggressively with me than you do with other guys?"

"I figured you'd forgotten about that one."

"I forget nothing."

"When you first came here, I thought, *who knows how long you will stay*? A day? A week? Now we find out you cannot handle more than a few days with our screwed-up family. So, from the beginning, there has never been a long game with you. Another Truth for you?"

When he nodded, her question jumped out. "How soon do you expect sex from a woman? First date? Second? How long do you give them before you cut them loose?"

"You know you can ask your sister a question, right?"

"Where's the fun in that?"

Josette said, "We can ask each other questions anytime."

"Fair enough. But, if that's the rule, I get to ask each of you one per turn. Deal?"

"Only applies for truth, not dares. Not that anyone is risking dares."

Eddie chuckled. "You don't trust me with a dare, and neither of us trusts your sister."

Feigning offense, Angelique objected. "Hey! Who knows, you might like my dares. Now answer the question or you lose."

"What I have learned is there are things more important than sex."

"Told you," Josette shot at her sister.

"Nice way to avoid the question."

"As long as it takes. I am willing to wait... but only when

patience is absolutely necessary."

Josette asked, somewhat indignantly, "Do you expect us to believe you never dumped a girl because she won't sleep with you?"

"Never—although that may be because of my amazing powers of persuasion. Now, by my count, that was one question from each of you. So I have one for each of you, too. Unless you will take a dare." Both decided another Truth was safer, so he asked, "How can two girls be beautiful as you and not have boyfriends? Is something wrong with the guys in Exeter?"

Matter of fact, Angelique answered, "Good timing."

Turning to Josette, his eyes reflecting flames like mirrors, he asked, "And you?"

"Have you met my sister? She's a guy vacuum. Any boy venturing too close gets sucked into her vortex. Or they live in a fantasy world where twins are just waiting around for some guy to volunteer to have a threesome solely because my sister is going out with him. We intimidate those who live in the real world."

"So, is having a twin good, or is it difficult?"

Josette answered, "Depends. You always have someone who is so close to you..."

"Closer than anyone else on earth," Angelique continued for her, and they slipped into that surreal interchange like a few nights ago, two speaking as one.

"Someone who always understands you, no matter what..."

"And willing to die for, knowing she will give her life for you."

Josette said, "But..."

"And there's always a *but*," Angelique continued.

"Sometimes I wonder how nice it must be to be alone."

"If only for a short time."

"No one considers you an individual."

"Yeah, you are a package. A pair of shoes."

"Who wants *one* shoe?"

Eddie said, "I never thought of it that way."

"No one does," Josette said. "Admit it, when you think of us, it's never me or my sister. It's we. Them."

"Even our parents think of us as *the twins*, not as two individual human beings," her sister finished the thought, falling back into the pattern that made their argument discordant.

"Every birthday, at Christmas, it's always the same presents. They give us each the same thing. Never unique gifts chosen for each of us as individuals."

"Is that enough Truth for you?" Angelique put a period to their lengthy answer.

"Wow. I've never been close to twins before, and you're right—but I will try to remember your individuality when I think about you from now on. I guess it's my turn again. Let's keep this Truth going."

Josette asked this time. "What is the favorite place you have visited?"

"Good question–an impossible one to answer. I love Rome and its history. Wyoming and her Grand Tetons are beautiful. Paris is impossible not to love." He paused. "Exeter, where for the first time in a long time, I've felt at home and been with family."

"Aww," Angelique said, "that's so sweet!"

"Then why are you leaving?" Josette's eyes burned into him, violet irises aglow in the flickering light. "We don't want you to leave. We love having you here. Our Dad may not, but don't pay any attention to him."

"He's such a jerk," Angelique added.

"Our mother loves having you around, too. She's really taken to you, and you get along so well together."

"Trust me, you don't want me to stay."

"Why would you say that? We've only known you a few days, and already you are our favorite cousin," said Angelique.

"With the possible exception of Fleur. She's almost as fun

to have around as you are."

"It's too bad I won't have time to meet her. Why wasn't she at the funeral?"

With a scoff, Angelique answered, "They always have a convenient excuse. This time, her mother was sick."

"It's the same every time," Josette explained. "If you ask me, her parents don't do funerals, so then need to invent some reason. The concept of death still screws with this whole family after all this time."

"Stick around a few months until she comes for her annual visit around Labor Day. We'll all go to the beach and you can get to know another long-lost relative."

"Wish I could," he said, "but it's best I leave now, before wearing out my welcome with everyone else. Now, who's turn is it?"

Angelique handed him the tiny roach to finish and blew a plume at him. "Can I ask you another question?"

Their fingers met, and she clung to the roach far longer than necessary. "Oh, why not? Shoot!"

"Of all the places you've visited, which has the most beautiful women?"

"Honestly? It's only been two days, but Exeter is hard to beat. At least, one particular little farm outside of Exeter."

"Josette, we cannot let this guy leave! How are we going to keep him here?"

"I'm sure you'll come up with something," her twin spat with sarcasm more biting than usual. "If we accept that answer is Truth."

"Smart ass," the other shot back. "It's your turn. Ask her something, but make it a hard one."

"How hard?"

"Give it your best shot."

Whether agreeing with the idea or meant as a warning shot, Josette urged him on. "We should all ask tougher questions if we want to know each other intimately."

"Alright, you inspired me. Josette, tell us about your first time."

"Hard questions, not impossible ones," Josette replied. "Tell you what: when it happens, I will let you know."

Feigned surprise at her response rocked his head backward, and narrowed eyes reflected passable skepticism. "Truth?"

"Truth. But you are only the second person to know that particular fact, so keep it to yourself." Her face pensive, the other two waited for her to continue. "I just hope it happens before I die, because I sure don't want to go out an old maid."

"Oh, I'm sure it will," he assured her. "In fact, for someone gorgeous as you, that hardly seems a difficult problem to resolve."

"That's the thing," Josette said. "Of course, I've had opportunities, I won't lie about that. But I don't want to give it up at a party or with some undeserving guy who only cares about my body and doesn't care about *me*! Call me old-fashioned, but what's wrong with a little romance? Some fantasy, something special?"

"She's too picky," her twin offered her critique.

"I disagree." Eddie gave that smile again. "Why shouldn't you want something more meaningful than casual sex? It's your body, your decision, right?"

"Exactly. I just hope I don't have to wait forever."

"Oh, I am sure you won't." He spoke with the confidence of someone able to see the future.

"Please keep it to yourself, though, okay? Having a sister wild as mine affects people's perception. Like we said, they assume we are exactly alike, even when we are very different, and in this instance, that is fine with me."

"Another example of yin and yang," her twin said.

"Point taken," Eddie said, although he made no such mistake. "People visit the iniquity of one sister upon the other sister?"

"Something like that. Don't quote actual scripture to her, though; it will set her off. But don't let her wild nature fool you

—she considers her family sacred. She will take a bullet before she will betray my trust. Or yours."

Angelique added, "One area where we aren't the yin to the other's yang. If you are family, this girl will always have your back—whether or not you deserve it. And like it or not, you are family. Now, before all these stories about how good my sister is gives everyone cavities, whose turn is it to show our new cousin the proper way to ask a hard question?"

Her sister answered, "Seems to me the honor is all yours."

"Good, 'cause I've got a juicy one! You have a choice—and you must choose one or the other. Who do you choose: Josette or me?"

"Damn, Angelique! Why don't you just dare him to insult one of us?"

"It's a brilliant question!"

"It's an impossible question," he objected. "Choose for what?"

"Come on," Angelique said, "you know what I mean."

"One night? Girlfriend? Marriage? Accomplice to rob a bank with?"

Josette burst out laughing. "He's got you there!"

Not willing to give up, she asked a follow-up. "Would your answers be different?"

"Sure."

"Okay: One-night stand?"

"You, of course."

"Girlfriend?"

"Josette."

"Marriage?"

"I have no intention of marrying."

"Doesn't matter, you must choose."

"You want Truth, right?"

Both girls shouted simultaneously, "Yes!"

Lowered in a soft, grave voice, Eddie explained. "Despite the few days since we met, I love you both. I lost my family, but I found you. You are my blood and I am yours, and it is because of my love for you I would never subject either of you to marrying me."

The light wind blowing the smoke away shifted as he said that, surrounding them with the acrid scent of charred maple. Wind that also blew a different mood over their cheerful game. "Alright, Angelique. Truth?"

"Truth."

"Why do you hate people calling you Angel?"

"The simple answer is, because I'm not. The truth is, it is an insult. Do you know what an angel is?" He held up his palms to signal her to explain, so she did. "Originally, they were mythical, spiritual messengers of god who terrified everyone when they showed up. 'And they were sore afraid.' Then people began to believe guardian angels were spirits who protect people from evil, and other than protecting my sister, I don't deal well with that kind of pressure. Eventually, they perverted the concept to be the spirits of the dead. Well, I am flesh and blood and am not dead, and given the choice, evil is a hell of a lot more fun than good. So, no matter what definition you use, it isn't me."

"She's had a lot of time to ponder that," her sister explained.

"That was too easy. Ask another one. A better one."

"What's the worst thing you've ever done?" He passed along the bottle to her with that question, now down to a finger at the bottom after his latest shot.

"Wow, that is hard." Gone was the typical lilt of her voice that made everything she said sound like it was in jest. After a long pause, she answered. "Josette had this boyfriend in high school..."

"Angelique, you don't need to talk about this!"

"Yes, because it's true. He was all frustrated because she refused to let him screw her, so I cheated on her with him." After contemplating in silence for a few seconds, she said, "Isn't it time to ask Josette a question? A different question

—don't waste your time with that one—the yin never does anything bad."

"Well," he turned to the other sister, "how about this one: What's your darkest secret?"

Silence continued to hang over the three until a slight increase in the breeze caused Angelique to choke on the smoke. "Sometimes I—I cut myself."

Her answer angered Angelique. "Why did you tell him about that? It's too intimate."

"It's true. And he seems trustworthy. Like he said, he's our blood."

"Both of you, your secrets are safe with me. That one in particular. Now, anyone want to get revenge with a question for me?"

Josette asked, without a second's hesitation, "What is your greatest regret?"

"Damn. Is it too late to choose dare?"

"Sure is."

"Someone once meant the world to me, but I was not there for her when she needed me most, and once the chance was lost, it was gone forever."

Josette asked, "Who was she?"

"I cannot tell you, and if I did, you would not believe me. I swore never to tell anyone. Just know: I did not hurt her, and I tried to be there for her. And, in the end, she forgave me for it, although I did not deserve her loyalty. Still, given the chance, I would give it freely again. What she did changed me forever, both a curse and a gift."

"Ask Angelique a tough one," her sister suggested. So he did.

"How long have you had DKC?"

Both girls' jaws hung open and firelight danced in their wide eyes. "How in the hell do you know about that?"

"The rash is visible when you take off your makeup. That rash, the cracked toenails you hide inside boots during the day. Your mom has the same rash a little lower, which shows when she forgets to close the top button. It's not that hard to figure out."

"Do you spend all your free time watching *St. Elsewhere* when you aren't dropping in on relatives? Jesus."

"Sorry, but you asked for tough questions. I want to get to know you at a deeper level than people chatting at a kegger."

"It sucks, if you must know. Nobody knows, outside my family and a couple of my closest friends, and I intend to keep it that way. People will look at me differently if they knew I have a death sentence hanging over me. I don't need pity. Is that why you chose my sister as your girlfriend, since I don't have long to live?"

"No, that had nothing to do with it."

"Sure. But you're right. Who wants to be a widower before their twenty-fifth birthday? Anyway, what do the doctors know? Most of the time, I feel fine; I have no intention of dying anytime soon. If I do? Well, at least I'll leave a beautiful corpse. Let some guy working at the funeral home have some fun with me before they box me up and bury me, right?"

"Stop, that is so disgusting," Josette spat out.

"No one's going to molest you in a funeral home basement," Eddie said. "I happen to believe you. DKC doesn't stand a chance against you. You'll see."

"Okay, my idea to ask tough questions turned our fun to shit. So far, no one has had the balls to take a dare. So, I dare anyone to take a dare." To lift the gloom, they all agreed. When Josette pointed out that the only way to avoid the sisters daring each other—and what fun would that be?—is if he dared each sister, and they each dared him. They all agreed with that, too.

"Eddie, you start. Who do you dare?" Eyes flickering in the light turned from one twin to the other. Angelique goaded him. "After your crappy questions, start with something fun, okay?"

"Thanks for volunteering. I dare you to take something off."

"See? Now that's how you dare someone!" A sly grin turned her lips up as she unbuttoned her jeans, pulling down her zipper in a teasing, slow display. "I want you to know, all your crappy questions are forgiven."

Slender, pale legs slid from her jeans, revealing lacy boyshorts, brilliant red as glowing embers in the firelight. If embarrassed by exposing her panties to her cousin, she disguised it well with a relaxed smile. "Okay, cousin, will you take a dare?"

"Can't very well say no after that, can I?"

Leaning close to her sister without taking her eyes off their cousin, Angelique asked her, "Shirt or pants?"

"Oh, shirt—no doubt. Let's take it easy on him for now."

"I bet he looks yummy without a shirt."

"No doubt."

"You know I can hear you, right?"

Wagging all four fingers toward him from an extended arm, she said, "Off with your shirt!"

"Undershirt, too?"

"Why the hell not?" Josette said, forcing a smile.

The flickering, failing light made it impossible to tell whether his chest hair was lighter blond than on his head or his chest was bare as a baby's, although the glistening of skin only a shade less pallid than his cousin's legs suggested the latter.

"Good choice."

"You ladies are enjoying this way too much," he said, making a point of glancing down at his cousin's exposed lingerie. Two sets of curls, turned a darker red by the night, nodded in unison. Seizing the opportunity to deviate from the agreed-upon rules, he asked, "Is it my turn?"

Josette issued a dare of her own in reply. "Hit me with your best shot."

Although expecting something similar, the form of her dare startled him. "Show me where you cut yourself."

Only snapping logs in the bonfire made a sound as

she rolled up her left sleeve and held her forearm up to the firelight. A half-dozen light, pink scars lined the inside of her arm below the elbow, spaced an inch apart. "These scars disappointed me. Too pale. Fading. Even so, I figured someone would see it, even if I can't, so after those, I did this."

"Josette, don't do this," her sister pleaded.

"Look at you!" She turned her head toward her sister's bare legs, then her panties. "Besides, why do it if no one will ever set eyes on it? Because at this rate, the only person who will ever see my handiwork is going to be my sister." Slowly, she unbuttoned her shirt, tugging it from inside her jeans to open it all the way, then turned to allow the fire to illuminate her torso. Two inches below the bottom edge of her bra, at the upper reaches of her abdomen, faint, jagged lines spelled out a faded word. Eddie moved close to read it, and she arched her back.

Carved into her pale flesh were four letters.

HATE

His finger followed the knife's path over the H, and when she did not flinch, the letters after it. "What do you hate?"

"At the time, pretty much everything."

"And now?"

"Not so much. Now is pretty good."

"Wow, I did not expect this," he said, retracing each letter. "Did it hurt as much as I imagine it did?"

"Worse. Recently, though, I tried a place that's easier to hide and easier to bandage. Blood leaking through Band-Aids onto a shirt in the middle of history class is hard to explain."

As she undid her jeans and began wriggling out of them, her sister began crying. "Please don't."

"It's okay," she said, and Eddie comforted Angelique with a hand on her shoulder. Sitting in only her black bra and panties, Josette pointed one knee out to the side and pulled the soft flesh inside the thigh to lift the skin into firelight. There in the pale, tender skin of her thigh, several scars lined the upper third. Some had faded as faint as those on her arm and belly; others appeared fresh. One yet to scab over may well have been slashed into her flesh since he arrived.

"Has anyone seen these other than her?"

"No," she answered. "And I tried to hide it from her—like that might work."

"I never saw your legs," Angelique sobbed and crawled over to hug her twin. The two of them sat side by side on the blanket, staring at their cousin. "Well, you are the only one with goddamn pants on. Take them off."

"Sorry, I went commando yesterday, but I screwed up today and wore boxers," he said, trying to break the grim spell as he pulled off his chinos.

Angelique let loose an exaggerated exhale. "Okay—my mood is improving already."

"Mine, too," her sister agreed.

"Dude, how much time do you spend in the gym?"

He asked, "Having fun?"

The twins looked at each other and again nodded. "Angelique, my non-angel, seems to me you still have a dare left."

"In that case, cousin, I dare you to… kiss one of us."

"One?"

"Do they speak English in California? One!"

Eddie knee-walked toward them, stopping when close enough to touch. In the flames' shaky light, the two were mirror images, the only difference being one wore only lingerie, the other still covered partly by a shirt. The options offered him neither a bad nor good choice. Light pink scars did little to diminish Josette's sex appeal; Angelique was perfect. The word angel came to mind, but the last thing he wanted to do was annoy her in this crucial moment. "You may be the two most beautiful women I have ever seen. That is absolute Truth."

Before either could respond, Eddie made his choice and

sprang at them like a lion.

One arm around each sister, he pulled both onto the blanket under him and turned both faces toward him. Neither one objected as the three shared a kiss together. At first, tongues and lips entangled with abandon, but he soon indulged each twin their own kiss. Passionate. Deep and wet. Lying on top as he was, one of his legs naturally fit between each girl's legs, and their bodies moved together.

Then reality hit.

"When will someone start wondering what is going on down here?"

Angelique asked, "By someone, you mean our father?"

"Or your mother."

"One or the other is probably already thinking about it," Josette said.

"Mama won't bring a shotgun." Sometimes, even a twin cannot tell whether the other is joking or totally serious.

After dressing with phenomenal speed, hastily dousing lingering flames with buckets hauled from the pond, they made their way back under a moonless sky. "I need to explain, after what you said."

"No, you don't," Josette said.

"Shut up and let him explain, will you?"

"That was not some twins fantasy experience. There simply is no way to decide."

Angelique laughed. "It may make you feel better knowing you are the first and only guy we've ever triple-kissed."

"Then I am the luckiest man on earth." He put his arms around their shoulders, and the three walked as one. By the time reached the house, it was dark, save for the light left on for them in the kitchen. The twins ascended the stairs. In a loud whisper, he called up after them.

"Pleasant dreams."

FADE TO BLACK

Steaming water seared Celeste's delicate, pale skin, close enough to scalding to render it pink as sunburn. Steam coated frosted glass doors an opaque white. Some days require extra heat to relax taut muscles. While shampooing, she allowed the water jets to massage her aching back, savoring the decadent sensation.

A sound caught her attention, not quite lost in the shower's white noise. Mist obscured her view past the glass door, she realized after smoothing her hair back over her scalp. There it is again, and the light showing through foggy glass changed. Shadowy movement. A hazy rectangle of light revealed the bathroom door to be open and, as she watched, it shut like a languid closing eye.

Panic sped her heart. Through an arc wiped from the steam coating the window, an indistinct silhouette took shape in the doorway. Instinct brought her protective hand across her chest to cover her from whoever invaded her privacy and she thought of screaming, but the children were not home. Better to take a futile stand than cower naked, pathetic and helpless, so she flung open the door to confront the intruder.

"Oh, it's you! You scared the shit out of me!"

"Sorry." Eddie watched glistening beads of water run down the lines of her body, rivulets curving on her thighs and down her calves. Measured and unhasting, his head panned upward as he followed her body back to her face. One hand cupped loose over her breast in subconscious modesty. He studied her so long and with such intent, her heart resumed its racing.

"George called. Said to tell you not to wait for him at dinner. He's running late. So, I came up right away to tell you because I thought you should know."

"Thanks for telling me." Despite the scalding water, she felt a chill.

"The girls have their chemistry lab this afternoon."

"Bernie has baseball. The twins pick him up on Wednesdays."

Eddie peeled his shirt over his head, muscles rippling in waves, and held it dangling against his leg. "Is there room in there for one more?"

"There always is room for you."

His tossed shirt landed on the counter and he stepped out of his khakis. The water stung like fire, making him flinch. Once inside, he stepped behind Celeste, hands on her hips, pulling her smooth, round bottom to his loins. Water and remnants of soap made her skin slippery all the way up her sides until fingertips reached the soft bulge of the sides of her breasts. One in each hand, they molded to him, yielding yet firm, pulling her back to his chest.

Lips met the nape of her neck and strands of hair, clinging almost brown from the water, which she reached up to pull behind her, out of his way. His lips enveloped her, teeth raking and tongue licking sensitive skin, arousing a sensation midway between pleasure and tickle. Without being aware, her head tilted away, giving him her neck.

Strong fingers kneaded her flesh, one fingertip tracing spirals on her nipple. At any second, her knees might no longer be capable of supporting her, so she leaned forward, braced against the tiles in the corner. Heavy hair fell forward as her chin dropped. Lips, tongue and teeth explored with increasing aggression from the left side around the back of her neck, over her spine to the right. Down her shoulder.

"Oh, my God, you are driving me insane," she gasped.

"I'm already there," he said, squeezing her breasts more lasciviously.

How can a guy so young achieve the effortless, perfect balance between tenderness and wantonness? The experience in those hands, those lips and tongue were well beyond his years. Without even venturing to the aching between her thighs, she felt already primed for a climax and braced her knees for its inevitable jolt. He was hard now, sandwiched between her buttocks, yet making no effort to satisfy himself inside her. Breathing turned to panting. He sucked her neck hard enough to leave a mark, but she had passed the point of caring about anything but the moment by then.

Water diluted a trickle of blood, hidden from her as it ran down her shoulder and upper back. Not much escaped, and by the time it reached where his chest pressed against her back, sufficient water mixed with it to leave only the pink of scalded flesh.

"Oh, Jesus," she gasped, a trickle of water raining off her lower lip. His mouth was back on the left side, so at least he'd leave symmetrical purple proof of what he'd done. One hand reached back behind her head, behind his, holding her up by fingernails dug into his scalp. "Oh, Eddie!"

That climax wracked her body with the power of a punch to the gut, but his powerful hands kept her on her feet. He moved with malicious languor, skillfully milking her rapture so long she began wondering if one had become two. Not that it mattered, nor did time. Still, he had not even tried to have sex. Just his hands roaming her body and his kiss on her neck did this. It was like some sort of dream, although she knew there was nothing imaginary about any of this.

He turned her, pinned her against the tile, penetrating her with those beautiful eyes. Electric blue and dangerous. The eyes of a killer, his face serious until at last, he too climaxed, his facial muscles melting and his eyes rolling back until only azure half-moons remained.

She returned the favor, biting his neck before he finished. Even then, fingers dug deep into the flesh of her behind, driving her, controlling her.

Holy Hell, she thought, as her core tightened up, forming the first wave of another climax as he sucked her neck behind her ear. "Take me, Eddie! Take me there!"

The kid follows instructions as, this time, it was her eyes which rolled back.

†

"Jeepers, Mama—it's eighty degrees! Why are you wearing a turtleneck?"

A frog in her throat needed clearing, which she did while covering her mouth with a clenched fist, then answered, "It's light silk, so it's really quite cool."

"You are so damn weird sometimes." Angelique's eyes drifted down for a second before shaking her head and turning away. For a moment, she questioned her decision to skip wearing a bra—but, then again, her daughter obviously was not wearing one, either, giving her little room to criticize.

"Where is your sister?"

"She's off doing something with Eddie."

"Doing what?" The frog was still there, so she cleared it again, ending with a little cough that did the trick.

"How should I know?" Angelique answered. "Sounds like you are coming down with something."

"Oh, it's my allergies again. They've been giving me a hard time today."

"Uh-huh," she acknowledged, then stepped back from the counter. "There! Did I chop this small enough?"

Diced red and orange pepper covered the cutting board. "Perfect! Now if I can just find the coriander."

"What got into you, trying something fancy as this?"

"I saw it on Julia Child. If she's cooking it, it's going to be delicious."

"Burgers would be easier."

It was Celeste's turn to roll her eyes. "What do you suppose your cousin and your sister are up to? This sauce cooks in only five minutes."

"Then they'll miss it. Like Daddy. No matter how it turns out, we'll tell him it was delicious. That should piss him off for missing dinner again."

"You do that," she answered, looking out the window. Early summer greens and a blue sky dotted with small wisps of clouds created a cheerful sight increasingly out of synch with her mood.

"What are we supposed to do with this garlic? Want me to chop it?"

Celeste narrowed her eyes, looking at her daughter, wondering what got into her? The last time she helped in the kitchen had been to bake cookies; the girls must have been twelve then.

"Slice it. And be careful—it is supposed to be paper thin. Want me to do it?"

Offended, her daughter said, "I've got it!"

Outside, patrolling the farm, one cat stood staring, twitching its tail. Other than it, nothing moved. Why did she feel so nervous about her daughter being off with their handsome cousin? Josette always had been the more fragile of the two, the one who needed someone to look out for her, a protector. Between her mother and sister, she had grown up safely, but as a beautiful young woman still unsure of the power of her sexuality, was she any safer now? Celeste wondered whether Angelique being off with him alone might invoke different feelings?

Different, yes, but no more reassuring.

"Goddamn it!"

Her daughter's cry caused her body to jerk, almost physically jumping. Metal clattered as she spun to see what was wrong. Angelique held one fist in her other hand, just below her chin, close to her body. She saw blood. "Oh, no! What happened?"

"Damn near cut my finger off, that's what!"

"Okay, let me see." A gash opened the tip of her index

finger to the bone. "You're okay. Same thing happened to me last week. Let's wash it out, make sure it's clean, then you need to keep pressure on it."

Angelique pivoted her head, refusing to look. "Does it need stitches?"

"I don't know, honey." She turned on the cold water and held her daughter's finger under the flow as Eddie had done for her, watching the swirl in the metal sink turn pink. Blood rushed twice a second, echoing her rapid heartbeat.

"Oh, shit!" Angelique's voice sounded off, and when she turned to her, her normally pallid skin had taken on a chalky cast. Dilated pupils stared a thousand yards out the window for a second before rolling back and her knees giving way. Somehow, Celeste caught her and lowered her to the floor. This was not the first time Angelique passed out at the sight of her own blood, but years had passed since the last incident. Applying pressure to the wound, with the other hand she straightened out her knees so she lay straight, diagonally across the floor.

Sounds of laughter rang from the front of the house, and the door closed. She called out, "I'm in here—we need help!"

Josette rushed into the kitchen with Eddie close on her heels, and she dropped down on her knees beside her fallen twin, white shirt smeared with blood. "What happened?"

"She cut her finger and passed out when she saw blood."

Eddie asked, "How bad is it?"

Celeste's green eyes rose to meet his. "Worse than mine the other day, but she'll live."

Crouched down with the other two, he asked, "Has this happened before?"

"Only every other time she hurt herself," Josette answered, more annoyed than concerned with the news.

"Let's get her up off the floor," Eddie said, glancing around.

With her mother continuing to apply pressure, he scooped her up and stood. "Careful! Don't hurt yourself!"

"She's barely a hundred pounds. Now, where should we put her?"

"A hundred and nine pounds," Josette corrected, unnecessarily.

"Take her to the couch," Celeste instructed, following along, pinching the sliced finger. There, he laid her with care. "Should we call 911?"

"Let me take a look," Eddie said, fingers pressing against her mother's to take over the pressure himself. A trickle of blood ran onto his thumb. Her unconscious heart now pumped, its beat slow, and it took a second or more until the gash pooled red and dripped again. "It should be okay. Did she hurt herself falling?"

"No, I was right there and eased her to the ground."

"Well, I may not be a doctor, but I think she will be fine with a little TLC. Keep the pressure on until it stops bleeding." He guided her mother's hand and placed her fingers over his before slipping them out. Somehow, in moving her or checking the wound, another drop had spotted her shirt with brilliant red, this one over her left breast. Moments later, her eyes flickered dully and soon she was awake. Her sister fetched alcohol, Neosporin and Band-Aids from upstairs while they filled her in on the story. Before long, only her shirt appeared the worse for wear. Nobody noticed how the blood disappeared from Eddie's hand.

"Need some help in the kitchen to finish up?"

"Oh, no. I forgot all about it. If you don't mind, Eddie..."

"My pleasure," he said. His back to the girls, he gave her a reassuring wink.

†

A storm rolled in during the darkest hours of the night. Everyone woke, at one time or another, roused by thunder, wind or the pounding rain which swept through, leaving a gentle shower and its soothing sounds to lull them back to sleep. All but Angelique, who lay awake until birds chirped in anticipation of sunrise, too excited to sleep. But sleep eventually took her again, too, and when she awoke, she found her sister gone already, out running errands.

So, she kept it bottled up within her all day. The tinny sound of her sister's little Honda hatchback coming down the driveway did not carry far, but when she heard it, she bounced down the stairs two at a time to greet her. There, she found her sister engrossed in deep conversation with Eddie. "Hey, can I talk to you for a second?"

"Sure, is everything okay? How's your finger today?"

"Oh, it's fine. Almost forgot about it. Funny, it doesn't hurt at all."

"It's cool out. Good afternoon for a run; I'll leave you two alone," Eddie politely excused himself.

Not seeing their mother anywhere and desperate for privacy, Angelique took her sister by the hand, dragged her back up to their room, and shut the door behind her. "Have you ever had a sex dream?"

Josette leaned forward; eyes wide. "A what?"

"A sex dream. You know."

"Maybe a few times. Nothing much to remember."

"The one I had last night was one to remember."

"Oh, really?" Josette's eyebrows raised. "Tell me more!"

"It was... amazing! It was like I woke up all tingly and dizzy, but I'm pretty sure I was asleep the whole time. It felt like when you go to bed so drunk the bed starts spinning, only I didn't drink or smoke anything yesterday. Then he was there with me."

"Who was there?"

"That's the thing: I can't be sure, but in my dream, I knew it was him."

"Who?"

"Don't be an idiot. Eddie!"

"Oh, shit!"

"Right?"

"Well, what happened?"

"He watched me. My whole body tingled with anticipation, yet he stood there in the shadows. Suddenly, he was there with me, touching me everywhere. Everywhere! He started kissing my body. He pulled my nightshirt up, like it was over my head, so I could not see, only feel him. His tongue was all over me…"

"Oh, my god!"

"It felt like a snake—how's that for symbolic? And he kissed my body."

"Where on your body?"

"He focused on my stomach and arms and neck, but it was like he was licking and sucking everywhere. When he got to my boobs, I thought I was going to die! I mean, you can't imagine how incredible it felt."

"You're right about that."

"Not just you. I couldn't have imagined it. It was a dream, so it was like all my senses were heightened. He kissed my hands and started sucking on my fingers, and, you know, I can sort of imagine how a guy feels when, you know…"

"You're blowing him?"

"Exactly! I mean, he wasn't sucking my fingers, he was having sex with them. Each time he touched me or his lips found an unknown part of my body, it was a shock, because I couldn't see. But at the same time, I kind of could see—you know how screwed up dreams are."

"So, it was all intense and crazy, and I just lay there because I didn't want to move. Why should I? He knew where to touch me, and where I wanted to be touched."

"Did he go down on you?"

"No! That's the crazy part—he didn't have to. He was playing with my boobies and sucking my fingers at the same time when I had this massive orgasm. I mean, massive! And this part is even crazier: I think it was real! I mean, it felt like a real orgasm, and when I woke up this morning, you know that feeling you have the morning after amazing sex?"

"Not really."

"Oh, right. Well, you feel happy and satisfied. Content. That's how I felt when I woke up. What do you think that was all about?"

"I think you've got it bad for our cousin. Can there be any other meaning behind a dream like that?"

"How should I know? It could be, but somehow it felt like more than that. It was so real, and the way I felt during and after—I don't know how to explain it."

"Will you tell Eddie about it?"

"Are you crazy?"

"Not the whole thing—that would be crazy. I mean, tell him you had a dream about him."

"And when he asks what happened, what am I supposed to say? Should I lie to him and leave out all the good stuff? Or do I tell him I forget, but act like I'm just not telling him the whole thing to see how he reacts?"

"Look, it's that game the other night, and when he was making out with us—while you were half naked! Since then, he's acted like nothing happened, so your mind is just playing out your desires. I mean, that is what you want, isn't it?"

"What kind of question is that?

"We both know you have the hots for him, so your dream took it to its natural conclusion, playing out what you want him to do."

"I'm pretty sure I don't want him to blow my finger."

"That's all allegorical. Don't make me explain that part! It's like he was playing both roles, just as you were on the receiving end of both."

"So what happens if he's into it?"

"Oh, he's into it—he literally told you he wants to sleep with you! If you tell him and he's receptive, will you do it?"

Angelique's left eyebrow raised. "He said he wants you for his girlfriend."

"That's not going to happen. Tomorrow he will leave. We'll probably never see him again; if we do, he'll be with someone by then. So, are you going to take the bull by the horns, or are you going to sit back and wait for him to take the initiative tonight? Or will you just hope he sneaks back up to our room in the dead of night to make your dream come true?"

"If he does that, I apologize in advance, because this time we are going to wake your little ass up!"

"Having a kissing cousin is not enough for you. Don't let him get away without the two of you doing what both of you want to do. You've got to tell him!"

†

The phone rang right about the time George should arrive home. Everyone was hanging around downstairs, Eddie and the twins laughing on the front porch like they'd known each other their whole lives. Dinner was half an hour from being ready. Celeste plucked the receiver from the wall phone next to the refrigerator. "Hello?"

"Mrs. Brown?"

"Speaking."

"This is Captain Felix from the West Wickford Police Department. I'm afraid I have some terrible news for you. Are you sitting down?"

Underneath her, knees wobbled, strangely unsteady, and her heart pounded in her neck. She heard the kids on the porch, and Bernie had gone upstairs right after practice, so she could not imagine what sort of bad news he had for her. "I'm in the kitchen. What can I help you with?"

"Are you the wife of George Brown?"

"I am."

"Well, I am terribly sorry, but there has been an accident. Your husband..."

"What's happened to my husband?"

"I'm sorry to inform you, he suffered injuries which are quite severe. We don't know whether he will make it. He is in the emergency room of..."

The voice on the line faded. The phone clattered to the floor, spinning and dancing on the tile with one end suspended at the end of the stretched, kinked cord as she slumped against the counter. Numbness took her, and her body felt limp, though she remained standing—well, leaning back, propped up against the cabinetry.

Eddie appeared in the doorway. "What's the matter?"

Words refused to form. She raised one hand above her waist almost in a wave. He rushed across the room and took her face in one strong hand.

"Celeste, what is it?"

"He had an accident," she said, motioning to the phone still rocking at her feet.

He grabbed it. "Hello? This is her cousin. She's here, but I don't think she can talk. Yes. Oh, no. Where is that? Okay, she and her daughters will know. We will be there right away."

Strong arms took her, wrapping around her, pulling her in, and she let herself melt into them. It was not sadness she felt. She was falling. The ground opened up beneath her. His cheek pressed against her, cooler than her skin, which had already covered with sweat. Lips against her ear, and she felt breath blow her hair. "I'm here. You are safe with me."

Minutes passed. She pressed her body against his, wanting, hands balled into fists gripping his yellow Izod shirt. When his calm voice broke the silence, with lips against her ear, brushing it with each word. "We should tell the girls. I will drive, but we must go."

†

Eddie found the girls still swinging on the hanging loveseat where he left them. Kneeling down before them and taking one knee, they both regarded him peculiarly, with expressions half smile, half shock, as though expecting a bizarre marriage proposal. "Your mother has had quite a shock. I'm afraid it is bad news: your father is in the hospital in

Wickford, but they are flying him up to Providence. He took a fall."

Both twins gasped, followed by Josette's question: "How bad?"

"Bad. The reason they are flying him to Providence is the Wickford Hospital cannot handle injuries severe as his."

Angelique covered her face with her hands, her sister crossed her arms tight over her breasts. Eddie left a hand on each girl's knee, a familiar touch that might have drawn rebuke earlier in the week. Angelique's hands dropped, and she clutched his with both, her eyes dry. "Is Mama okay?"

"Yeah. She went to tell your brother. Since we are so close, she thought..."

"How did it happen?" Josette glared at him with eyes thin slits.

"They didn't say. I spoke to some police chief, and he did not give much info. From the way he said it, there's something odd about it."

Josette's grip on her torso tightened. "You don't get life-flighted if you fall out of a chair or trip over a curb."

"Go get your mother; I'll drive, so none of you have to."

†

The family marched as a cohesive unit through the sliding glass door of Rhode Island Hospital, the Level 1 trauma center serving much of southeastern New England. Across the entryway, crowded with a random sample of the community working or visiting under extreme duress, heads turned to follow the stunning redheaded twins walking with elbows locked together. Bernie held his mother's hand, Eddie in the lead. At the desk, he asked for George Floyd.

The receptionist flipped through papers on a clipboard, then pointed. "Go through that door. There's a window on the right. They will take you to the surgical waiting room."

Angelique said, "Oh, shit."

The surgical receptionist asked in a voice rough from smoking, "Are you family?"

"I'm his wife, and these are his children and our cousin."

"He's been in surgery for an hour. It looks like multiple systems. A doctor will be out to tell you any news when we have some."

A detective arrived ten minutes later. He was no less tight-lipped. "What was Mr. Brown doing in West Wickford?"

"Who knows?" Celeste threw up her hands. "His business is up there, and he doesn't tell me much about what he does there. I thought he was in Warwick. When will someone explain to me what happened? And why are the police involved with a slip and fall?"

"Do you have any reason to suspect your husband may have intended to harm himself? Perhaps a note or threats?"

The twins gasped, but Celeste remained stoic. "Are you implying this was a suicide attempt?"

"That's what it looks like, Mrs. Brown."

Suicide sounded impossible, a cruel joke or at best a regrettable mistake of a kind impossible to piece together. Until the detective related the facts.

A passerby found him behind a house under renovation on Main Street. The historic Colonial House—one of the tallest buildings in town at three stories—has a balcony on the roof over the second floor. No one saw how he got there. Nor did anyone know when, how, or why he went to this location. A worker delivering wood for the next phase of the renovation found a pile of what he mistook for discarded trash hidden behind a boxwood bush. What he found instead was George, barely clinging to life.

Celeste knew of nothing suspicious, nor did any of the children.

An hour later, a weary surgeon appeared. The doctor, about the same age as Celeste, told the story on her face before she opened her mouth to speak. "I'm sorry. We did all we could, but his injuries were too severe. He's gone."

ENJOY THE SILENCE

Death, they say, is the great leveler. The one thing that lays all men equal. Rich, poor, prominent or unknown—all eventually end up in the same place. Everyone must serve a life sentence. The time and manner may vary, but outside the Bible, no man or woman born has yet escaped the inexorable pull of death. Some may be tragic, others heroic, and while rare instances achieve the level of infamy, most of the billions who have died throughout history have done so unnoticed, private, whether surrounded by family and friends, on a frigid park bench in the depths of winter or alone in a prison cell.

Families may achieve some measure of fame for every reason under the sun. America has few bestowed with fame for the simple act of dying. Lizzie Borden's family. The Kennedys. The Brown family is among of that exclusive group. While its infamy is less well-known than the Bordens or JFK's, thousands still follow the story of Mercy Brown. News of her death in 1892 and the horrors following it reached across the Atlantic, inspiring Bram Stoker as he penned his masterpiece, *Dracula.*

To this day, visitors flock to her grave every St. Patrick's Day to mark the second time Mercy died. The first came privately, in her home; the second occurred two months later in the small crypt constructed from rough rock in the back of Chestnut Hill Cemetery, next to the Baptist Church.

Since that horrific day when death transformed Mercy Brown from a teenager tragically taken too soon into legend, this legend has haunted each generation of the family that followed. Given its history, it is little wonder some members avoid family funerals. Particularly those which are sudden or strike those who die before reaching a ripe old age. Nor is it a surprise that the grim subject of death has obsessed generations.

None of this, however, prepares those left behind when death's inevitable, icy grip reaps another.

Although short, the drive back to the Brown farm lasted an eternity. Celeste reached over to click the stereo off, so only the road rolling under the tires and ceaseless wind broke the silence. Eddie fought road hypnosis by asking questions, most checking in on how his passengers were holding up. Oddly, it was Bernie who engaged him in conversation, once to inquire about the funeral.

Later, he asked, "Did he really kill himself?"

"I don't know, honey," his mother answered. "The police don't have any other explanation."

"I don't think so," he said.

Celeste responded, "We may never know what happened."

Clouds grayed the sunset, and Eddie pulled the car into the driveway well after dark. Once inside, Eddie asked the recent widow, "What can I do?"

"No one ever knows what to do after someone dies."

"I'm here if you need me," he said, placing his hand on the small of her back after checking to make sure no one else was around. She pulled away, the bitter taste of guilt too fresh. He took a glass of Two Buck Chuck Cabernet from the bottle George re-corked and left on the counter two days before, and retired to the porch. Half remained when the screen door swung open and the twins stepped out, one holding the door against a spring intent on slamming it closed. In the dark, he only could tell them apart when they spoke.

"Let's get out of here." That was Angelique, another bottle in her hand. Her sister carried something else. They led him to the barn. "We came out here all the time when we were little. No one ever bothers us here."

The light revealed what Josette carried was his small boom box. "I found this in your room. I grabbed a few cassettes, too."

"You went through my stuff?"

"Pretty much."

"I'll remember that when you go to school tomorrow," he said.

"They will give us time off for bereavement," said her sister as she uncorked another bottle of wine and filled his glass to the rim. "So, we were wondering if you were staying?"

"I haven't given it much thought," he lied.

"You can't leave now. Our dad was the only reason you were leaving."

"This is so fucked up," Josette said before grabbing the bottle from her sister and drinking straight from it.

"How are the two of you doing?"

Angelique plopped down on a square hay bale. "Numb. I mean, he was my father and all, but sometimes I wished him dead. Now he is."

"He was a real asshole sometimes," Josette said, as if her sister's morbid wish needed explanation.

"And I was going to offer a toast to him," Eddie said in an attempt at levity.

"Save it. There are so many better things to drink to."

"What did he do?"

Josette snapped, "This isn't Truth or Dare."

Duly chastened, he veered off in another direction. "This family sucks at death."

The twins exchanged a glance, then giggled. Eager to avoid her last comment being misinterpreted, Josette said, "Play something. We have shitty radio here. I picked some bands I've never heard before. When I hear your music at night, sometimes I wonder what it is, and if you are leaving, might as well expose us while you still can."

"Ever hear of The Cure?" Two heads shook, so he popped in *The Head on the Door*. The tape began on the third song,

The Blood. "Their new albums are drifting a little too close to pop for comfort, but it's great entry-level Goth. Will match the mood."

"It's dark," Angelique said.

"It's perfect," her sister added, eyes closed, listening. When the song finished, her voice weak, she said, "We miss so much here. Tell me there are better places."

Eddie focused his eyes through her. "Doesn't matter where you are, there always are better places."

"Take me with you. I want to experience the world."

Offended, Angelique said, "Hey, and leave me behind?"

"Take us both."

"I'm only going back to Providence."

"And after that?"

He shrugged his shoulders. "Maine? Maybe Boston."

Angelique studied her doppelgänger as if for the first time. "Would you really leave?"

"Don't you get it? He borrowed the money for that fucking business of his. This farm is the collateral. And half the reason he did it was the taxes on the land were killing him. We're all going to leave, so let's leave on our own terms, not because a bank pulls in a loan."

After a slow sip, Eddie said, "There must be some options short of selling the family farm."

"We're nineteen," Angelique said to back her sister up. "Other than taking care of his books, Mama hasn't worked in years, and she dropped out of college when she got pregnant with us, so what's she going to do? Damn it, Josette! I hadn't stopped to process things yet. Our father breaks his neck jumping off a roof and you find a way to fuck that up!"

"Let's stay here all night listening to this fucking amazing music and drink until we can't remember."

"Sounds like a plan to me," Eddie said. Josette came over and sat down on his lap, head on his shoulder, weaving to the driving, hypnotic music echoing through the barn. "What if I stay?"

One arm snaked around his neck, the other hand took the wine from his hand and drank. "Don't tease us."

Angelique brought her feet up on the bale and turned to the side, leaning against a post. "He can't leave before the funeral."

"Everyone leaves," said Eddie. "The art lies in choosing the proper time."

"Then our father was van Gogh," Angelique said, his suicide before achieving fame or wealth coming to mind. "And you have an opportunity to be Michelangelo by staying. Where else are you going to find a girl as beautiful as my sister?"

"I can only think of one place," he answered, "one certain hay bale."

An hour later, he carried the sleeping form of Josette back to the house and up to her bed. Her sister's arms wrapped around his waist, sensuously pressing her body against his as they walked. "You won't be sorry," she breathed into his ear.

"Nor will you." Deep in his darkest depths, he hoped he still spoke Truth.

†

In the dream, the music returned with a dark, haunting beauty.

An unseen hand from the blackness touched her. A slow rhythm guided it toward the top button, opened on the precise beat of a drum. And staying with the beat, the next. Static electricity charged her body. The hand reached inside to her skin, and as it moved across her shoulder, pushed the open blouse aside. Next came the fat belt. The buckle's tongue eased from the ring. A shadow moved somewhere nearby. Once the zipper reached the bottom, she tried to lift her hips, but her muscles refused to respond. Another hand joined the first, one pulling each side. Pale skin glowed from her legs, freed from her jeans, slowly exposing more until the fabric passed over her feet.

"I want you," she thought or said, although she wasn't sure which. Unnecessary words, because he knew, yet still important. Starting at the ankles, those hands caressed her skin all the way up her long, doe-like legs, up her stomach, slowing over breasts still concealed in a bra. As she repeated the words, *I want you*, the blouse tugged violently aside to lie flat on whatever it was she lay upon, again with precision timed to the music's beat. Then the hands retreated, following the exact path. Her body was embers which those hands stoked into all-consuming flames.

Just before those hands reached her knees, they stopped and, with a surprising harshness, pulled her legs open.

I want you.

A voice spoke to her from far, far away, "I need you."

Icy lips touched her flaming skin inside one knee, their kiss extinguishing the flame where it touched. She watched with increasing terror. No one was there, yet her burning soothed upward with kiss after tormenting kiss. No, not terror, desire. Yet, they felt the same. The lips moved to the other thigh, licking away unseen flames. Each kiss, each lick salved yet increased another ember, one deep inside and untouched. Warmer now, those lips—warmed with her heat. Pain flowed from her into those lips, taken away. They stopped so close to that final ember that it remained the last unquenched pain.

I want you, she pleaded in a silent scream. The lips left her, followed by those beautiful, invisible hands, and from much farther away now, she heard the lips answer her.

"I need you."

†

"I know how terrible this will sound, coming after yesterday and..." Josette stopped herself from attempting to distill the previous day into words.

Angelique clenched her eyes to ward off assault by the

morning sun. Her head throbbed with pain. “Say it.”

“I had the best dream ever last night.”

“What happened?”

“About what you told me happened in your sex dream. Only this—I can’t begin to explain! Every nerve in my body felt like pleasure. Remember that time I broke my tooth, and I was screaming and crying all the way to the dentist? He stuck a needle full of Novocaine into my jaw, and then the pain went away. It felt like that times a million, only not with a tooth but with sex.”

“Yes! That is a perfect description. Did you come?”

“No. I mean, it wasn’t like that. More like my entire body had an orgasm, if that makes sense.”

“Now you’re just talking nonsense, although I could use one of those right about now. I think I got run over by a train while I was sleeping. How’s your head? You drank more than me.”

“My head’s fine. Like I didn’t have a sip last night.”

“Damn, I want your dream.”

“Yeah—you sure do!”

“So, was it Eddie?”

“I guess. Has to be, right? What else—who else could it be?” Josette’s hand on her forehead covered her eyes, as well. “Oh, no—please tell me I wasn’t all over him last night like I now remember.”

“That boy is going to be so glad he stayed by the time we get through with him.”

“Stop!” She started laughing almost uncontrollably. “Besides, he could have last night. I don’t think he’s interested in us that way. He loves the flirting and all, but sometimes he’s such a Boy Scout. He probably thinks it’s fun right up until he realizes we’re cousins. Then it weirds him out.”

“He’s like our fifth cousin. Think about it—everyone in Exeter is our fifth cousin, just no one realizes they are.”

“Sometimes he seems so old-fashioned. Like the first night he was here, you know what he called the living room?

The parlor. It's so cute when he does things like that, but maybe that's why he doesn't try to seal the deal."

"What's old-fashioned got to do with it? Everyone used to sleep with their cousins. Look at FDR and Eleanor Roosevelt. That's old-fashioned!"

"I want to go back to sleep. Maybe I'll have another dream."

"You do that. Meanwhile, I'm going to take a handful of Tylenol and drink some coffee downstairs with the real Eddie. Don't worry—I'll let you know if real life is good as a dream."

"Promise me we won't kill each other trying to seduce the same guy!"

"Deal. Just let me enjoy that one-night stand he wants before you become his girlfriend."

"Our father is dead," Josette said.

"Yeah." Angelique opened her eyes. "I fucking hate funerals."

†

In that way of small towns and close-knit communities, neighbors and friends began arriving at ten on the dot to offer their condolences and casseroles. Celeste remained shut in her room behind a closed door, so the young folks allowed her the rest, or whatever it was she needed. Josette checked in on her after breakfast, finding her buried deep under the covers, and sat on the edge of her bed. "How are you feeling?"

"Like crap," her mother answered.

"It was an awful shock."

"More like actual crap. In that hospital yesterday surrounded by sick people, I must have caught something."

A touch on the forehead confirmed it. "Feels like you may have a slight fever. Can I bring you something?"

"Thanks, but no. Just let me get some rest. I'll be fine. How are you guys holding up?"

"Oh, we're fine. Bernie's taking it kind of hard. Believe it or not, he's been talking to Eddie all morning." The image made Celeste laugh, cut off by a cough. "That sounds terrible! Sure you don't need anything?"

"No. Water is all I want. Eddie hasn't left yet? I wanted to say goodbye, but I must look like hell."

"Now that there no longer is any reason for him to leave, we convinced him to stay."

"Good. Let me rest for a bit; I'll come out a little later."

Downstairs, Josette explained the reason for their mother's absence.

"Well, there's one thing we can do, but I'll need a volunteer. Which one of you likes to cook?" Eddie waited for an answer, but the twins turned to each other and laughed. "Let me rephrase that; if one of you does not step up, I will force one of you."

"Ooh, that sounds fun," Angelique answered.

"Thank you for volunteering," he said, grabbing her by the wrist and pulling her off the couch in the kitchen's direction. Josette pointed out they already had three casseroles, only one of which they cracked open for brunch, but he ignored her. Removing an apron from its peg, he draped it over Angelique's head and tied a bow just above her bum. "Imagine your mother trying to gag down potatoes *au gratin* while she feels awful."

By noon, the twins' friends began arriving. A few carried bottles in brown bags, while others, seeing Eddie holding Angelique captive in the kitchen, surreptitiously tried to slip something into their hands without him noticing. Josette announced the tally as the chefs were finishing their cooking. "We've got enough alcohol to keep us drunk for a year and enough pot for a bonfire. And a few of these."

Tiny baggies held up in her palm contained pills of different colors. Eddie snatched them up, walked to the sink and dumped them in the garbage disposal. When Angelique objected, he asked, "Got a problem with that?" When the girls shook their heads, he held out his hand. "Give me the marijuana."

Reluctantly, her face like a child being reprimanded by her parents, Josette pulled several larger baggies from her pockets. Eddie examined each one, then handed all but one back. Taking that one to the stove, he shook into the simmering pot over the burner.

"Ever try pot as a seasoning? This is why you need to study the culinary arts."

Ten minutes later, he ladled the dish into five bowls. Before sitting down with the three kids, he put one on a lap tray and carried it upstairs.

"Come in," a weak voice replied to his knock. Celeste's eyes widened as he entered the room, and she pulled up the covers and tucked stray blonde strands behind her ears. "Eddie, what are you doing?"

"Serving chicken soup—still the best medicine." After setting the tray over her and handing her a spoon, he sat beside her and stroked her hair. Her ashen face drawn and clammy, and the green of her eyes dull. "How are you feeling?"

"Okay," she answered, then smiled. "Like shit, if you want the truth."

"This will make you feel better."

Once she blew on a spoonful to make sure it was not too hot, she sampled it. "Oh, this is delicious! What kind is this? I don't remember buying some new brand of soup."

"Angelique and I made it. From scratch."

"Angelique. My daughter Angelique?"

"*Mea culpa*. I am a bad influence on her," he said, hands held up at his sides. In a low voice like he was sharing a secret, "she enjoyed it, too."

"Does she still have all her digits?"

"No blood was shed in preparing your soup."

After another spoonful, she said, "You are a fantastic chef."

"An old Brown family recipe, with a few tweaks I made to the herbs for my signature version."

"What is that spice? It's vaguely familiar, but I can't place it."

"Medicinal marijuana. I added some specially for you."

"Oh, you are terrible!"

"Took you this long to figure that out?"

With a dip of the head through squinted eyes, she said, "Tell me you didn't give the kids any of this."

"Would I do that?" A triple-glance revealed her skepticism, but she said nothing. "There's more, if you want it." Still chewing, she waved her hand to signify more, so he sprinkled a garnish on top from a baggie in his breast pocket. "Bet you didn't know ancient Native Americans considered pot sacred because of its healing properties."

"I feel better already," she smiled at him, the sparkle returning to her eyes.

Before carrying her tray and empty bowl downstairs, Eddie bent down and gave her neck a long, gentle kiss. "I will check in on you again later. There's an entire pot full of chicken soup for you."

†

Among the steady parade of visitors arriving throughout the day, one stood out. A young Black woman of rare and exceptional beauty arrived, greeted with a long, hard hug from each twin. Angelique made the introduction. "This is our cousin Eddie, visiting us from California; meet Abby Strong. We've been friends since kindergarten."

Familiar as he was with the way beautiful women attract one another to form their particular constellations, what took him aback was the unexpected pleasure of finding another so exquisite in a town with Exeter's minuscule population. Taking an offered hand, which she held more than shook, he had to choke back an urge to lift her fingers to his lips in a kiss. Instead, he locked onto her almond-shaped eyes the color of coffee and held onto them the way she did his hand. "Pleased to meet you, Abby. Are you, by any chance, related to Abdiel Strong?"

"He's my great grandfather. Or great-great. Something like that. How do you know?"

"He was the best friend of Mercy Brown's father, George. They say he was quite a man, the one who discovered Mercy was a vampire. Our families go way back."

"Yeah, well, we're still trying to live down our role in that legacy. It's like your ancestor founding the Flat Earth Society. Where did you hear about him?"

"Eddie is our family historian," Angelique explained. "He knows everything about our family. All the dirty and terrible secrets."

"Ooh, sounds delicious. Do you share?"

A smile on her face that almost resembled innocence, Angelique locked her elbow around his. "We don't share our cousin with anyone. But he can tell you the stories. Most of them, at least."

"When we have a moment alone, I will share a few with you about Angi and Josi."

"Angi and Josi?"

"Both ending with an 'I'," she said. "That's what everyone called them in grade school, probably because they hated those names so much. They typically retaliate by calling me Dear Abby."

"Dear Abby—what do you do with a visitor who threatens to reveal all your secrets to your family?" Josette's expression failed to betray a shred of humor.

"See?"

At some point, they released hands, but Eddie refused to let go of her gaze. Their friend's eyes frozen, unblinking. Angelique let Eddie's arm go and took Abby's, turning her away. "Excuse us for a minute. We need to talk."

He watched the three walk to the top of the stairs. Abby looked as good going as she did coming—a trait she shared with his cousins. A knock on the door beside him diverted his attention, and he greeted another green bean casserole and the kind neighbors who brought it.

†

Hours after the last caller left, after Celeste ate another bowl of soup sprinkled with a liberal dose of herb on top and Bernie retreated to his room, the twins took Eddie back out to the barn. Each carried a bottle, along with the boom box and several tapes Eddie selected for the occasion. Josette's jeans pocket bulged, a large baggie stuffed inside. Shortly before dawn, three dark shadows weaved through the gloomy yard. No one saw them, but Bernie woke at the sound of laughter from coming from outside. Familiar voices, those of his sisters, so he rolled over trying to ignore them, and dropped back to sleep.

DANCING WITH TEARS IN MY EYES

Denial. Anger. Bargaining. Depression and acceptance. The five stages of grief.

Celeste and her children stumbled through the list, although the duration each suffered varied widely. Bernie remained in denial long after the three women hurried on to anger. The day before the funeral, Celeste attacked the house. Every speck of dust, every item left unattended for a minute, every single thing out of place somewhere set her off. Those once belonging to George received particular venom. Too soon to discard things, in order to avoid the appearance of callousness, she stuffed every reminder of him into drawers and closets—anywhere out of her sight.

The others sat downstairs, listening to slamming and feet rushing back and forth, punctuated with occasional brief outbursts of cursing. Bernie sought sanctuary in his room and closed the door, no doubt with large, round headphones covering his ears. Josette stepped out to the porch; her sister and cousin soon followed, and through the window kept watch as they passed a joint among them.

Concerned, Eddie asked, "Should someone go talk to her?"

Angelique plucked the roach from his fingers. "Wait 'til she comes down. I'll say something then." Whether meant literally or figuratively, she did not explain.

"This morning, she still had a fever. Shouldn't she still be resting?"

"Don't worry, she's going to be fine. You'll see." He filled deep his lungs, then motioned for Josette to lean close, and with his lips a tiny fraction of an inch from hers, blew smoke from deep inside into her mouth. Her inspiration halting, a chill coursed through her body. He turned and did the same with her sister, who allowed her lips to brush briefly against his as he finished, then her eyes widened.

"Oh, shit—she's coming! Stay here and get rid of it." A wisp of smoke trailed from her nostrils and she bolted through the door to run interference.

Inside, her mother swept past her, sweat glistening on her brow. "Do you have a rubber band?"

"What for?"

Celeste bunched her hair at the base of her skull with one hand. "For my hair. It's hot as Hades in here."

"There's usually a few spares in the key bowl. Why don't you stop for a while, take a rest? You're going to make yourself sicker."

Flipping through the hair bands she fished from the bowl, she selected a black one to match her conscience. "There's too much to do." Angelique followed her as the other two came in through the front door.

Their mother stood on tip-toes to reach the top shelf of the cabinet where they kept glasses and cups, reaching the Shakey's Pizza beer mug George stashed up there. What Angelique saw made her gasp. "What happened to you?"

"Where?" As Eddie and her sister came in behind her, Angelique pointed to the back of her neck, where her hair pulled into a ponytail exposed some sort of gash behind her ear, above where the shoulder curved upward to meet the slender neck. "Oh, I don't know. Must have scratched it somehow."

"Let me see." Josette used her mother's shoulders to physically turn her. "Jesus, Mama! You cut the heck out of your neck!" A concerned Angelique rushed over to see for herself as her mother blindly groped, trying to find it.

"It doesn't hurt or anything…"

"Christ, looks like someone stabbed you," Angelique said, eyes inches away for a close inspection. "Look how deep it is!"

Josette leaned in to inspect more closely. "Why isn't it bleeding?"

"No idea. It's fresh. See—no scab or anything."

"Let's put something on it before it gets infected."

"Where is the Neosporin?" Angelique started toward the bathroom.

Celeste again asked, "Why I don't feel anything?"

Turning to Eddie, Josette asked, "Have you ever seen anything like this?"

"You wouldn't believe all the injuries I have seen during my lifetime," he cryptically answered.

Returning with a box of antiseptic, its metallic tube inside rolled halfway like toothpaste, Angelique began dabbing at the wound, jerking back her finger in fear the lightest touch might hurt, but her mother never flinched. "Good thing it's not already infected. How is it possible you don't know how this happened? There, that should do it."

"Why don't you sit down, Mama? Daddy's suicide hit us all hard, and it's impossible to handle. Dealing with his things can wait."

"Yeah. Sure—you're right." Her attention went from one to another, then around the room. "Sorry, for a moment there, it was like I was compelled to do something."

Josette hugged her mother. "We can't do anything about it now. Come sit with us and just relax for a while."

"No. No, maybe I should go upstairs and lie down." As they watched her leave, only Eddie knew exactly what she was dealing with.

†

A few hours after Celeste retired upstairs, a high school

classmate dropped by, a handsome devil named Kevin, who Eddie recognized from the impromptu wake the day after George died. After chatting longer than he cared to, Eddie excused himself and left the old friends alone. So engrossed in their own conversation were they, no one noticed him slip up the staircase. After a few light taps, the door at the far end of the hall opened. Seeing him standing there, Celeste opened it wide enough to be an invitation. Neither noticed the door at the other end of the hallway by the stairs, or Bernie's face peeking out.

"Are you okay?"

"Much better now. Still a little tense, though."

"Sounds like a massage might help."

"Mmm, that sounds nice and relaxing."

"If that doesn't work, there may be other methods of relieving tension we can try."

"Which do you recommend?"

His gentle hand cupping her cheek caused her eyes to close and head to tilt toward his touch. "Turn around, beautiful."

"I don't feel beautiful," she protested, but relented to subtle pressure on her face, eyelids closing, which dropped to her neck. Fingertips tickled over and around her throat and the nape on the other side. When he stopped, his thumbs massaged just inside the loose neckline of her robe. Next, strong fingers squeezed tightly knotted trapezius muscles down to where her shoulder curved into arms. Those knots melted, her chin dropping limp.

Thumbs pressed with painful relief down either side of her spine, stopping only where the delightful curve of her bottom started toward him; below which pressed against him. One hand made its way around her hip to the knotted belt at her waist. She offered no resistance as one end slowly pulled until it unraveled and fell loose.

Cool breath pulsed on her neck, sending goosebumps up her arms and around her chest. At a painfully slow pace, he peeled her robe back, running one finger up tingling skin from an inch below her navel to her collarbone. Then he eased it toward the shoulders until it slipped off and fell to the floor. Underneath, she wore a white camisole so tight, he suspected it belonged to one of her daughters. Lips soft as fire kissed her shoulder and moved aside the tiny strap until it, too, fell off her shoulder, and his hand pulled the other ribbon of fabric off the other side. Only pert breasts held it in place.

Hungry lips burned her other shoulder as his index fingers slipped down inside the fabric with enough pressure for it to slide free, stopping where her derriere pressed against his loins. Those breasts filled his hands, squeezed with a firm, patient rhythm, and his lips kissed her neck. His tongue licked the open gash, around it, sending an intense wave of pleasure through her torso.

Her moans came from far away. Lightly tracing the contours of the wound with his tongue, he pressed her breasts, forcing her body tighter against his. Then, when the pleasure blossomed to impossible levels, the firm tip penetrated her, a quarter inch inside the laceration. Pressing, straining the intact flesh at the ends of the tear. Like in the shower, her knees collapsed from under her, but his grip on her breasts holding her to him prevented her from falling.

With his lips open wide against her skin, he sucked deeply from her. Uncontrollable moans welled up inside from the pleasure of giving herself to him.

When Eddie finished, he threw her prone across the bed and pulled off her panties. Now his lips kissed her back, concentrating his attention on the red marks left from the force of his massage, every inch down to her thighs, rolling her over so her knees fell onto his shoulders. And he feasted upon her again.

†

"Remember what he said the night we had the bonfire?"

From the other bed, Angelique chuckled. "He said a lot of things that night."

"Remember when he said he loves us?"

"Yeah, I caught that."

"What do you suppose he meant by it?"

"I took it to mean he loves us as family." Then it clicked, and she rolled over to face Josette. "Oh, no! Don't you dare fall in love with him! He didn't mean it the way you are trying to twist it into."

"Are you sure?"

"Listen, Eddie's great and all, but don't fool yourself into believing it's anything other than a little cousin crush. There's a lot of that going around, but that's all it is. By the way, that sexy little top looks great on you. Now, go to sleep."

"You should paint him."

Angelique cackled unreservedly. "Yeah, right."

"No, seriously! You're good, and you could have something to remember him by."

"I *was* good—for a kid." Angelique corrected her. Several years had passed since she drew or painted anything. She claimed to have outgrown it, but they knew she quit the night of the incident. The night their childhood ended with the trauma that changed them, at the same time bonding them closer than even the closest of twins. "Hey, here's an idea: why don't *you* paint him?"

"My lack of talent proves identical twins are not identical at all," said Josette.

"He doesn't know that."

"After five seconds, it will be obvious."

"Oh!" The mattress let out a groan as Angelique raised up on one elbow. "Tell him you are one of those artists who doesn't reveal their work until it's completed."

"What's the point?"

"Besides hours spent alone with him? Wow, I may wind up talking myself into taking up sketching again."

A thought occurred to Josette that made her laugh. "Ask

him to pose nude."

"Oh, wow! He'd never do it—would he?"

"You'll never know unless you ask."

The problem was, drawing and painting required practice. Hours and hours of practice, and seven years passed since she last picked up paintbrush or charcoal. Back then, when twelve-year-old Angelique still drew, the thought of sketching a nude man never caused serious contemplation. In fact, knowing a career in art required learning to draw nudes—at the very least—filled her with trepidation in her innocence.

She sighed. "Too bad we didn't think of this while we were playing Truth or Dare!"

†

And while the twins held onto their anger, masked behind a blasé façade to hide it from the world, their mother made quick work of bargaining. And she had so much to bargain with.

At the time of his death, she was screwing his cousin. Their cousin, all three tracing their family back to the Browns buried up at Chestnut Hill.

What if he knew? George's initial distrust focused on the girls flirting with Eddie, so blatant and right in front of his face, but one thought proved impossible to get out of her head. A mental image so damaging, she often found herself saying it aloud. "What if he somehow found out about us?"

The truly scary part is, this was the best scenario her mind conjured up. If only the police knew for sure how he died. The only conceivable reason for his suicide was he found out his wife was cheating on him right under his own roof, but was that believable? A man who cheats on his spouse and who stopped loving her years before does not commit suicide when she has an affair. Particularly after the many times he cheated on her.

Nor was it an accident, for George did not go alone

to some historic mansion, climb up onto the roof for some unknown reason, and simply—oops! The coroner dismissed this possibility out of hand, improbable enough to rule it out in favor of suicide.

If the kids find out about this, it will kill them. More so the girls, who had forged such a close bond with her lover.

What about George?

It was the only possibility that made sense. Her brain hurt. Even the slightest chance that she had invited into her home, where her children slept—into her bed—the man who murdered her husband? Her entire body shuddered, started deep down inside. Then she pushed it from her mind. At least as far back from her conscious thoughts as humanly possible.

ONLY IN MY DREAMS

Angelique laughed out loud when she got an eyeful of her sister dressed for bed. "Please tell me you aren't serious."

"What? It's comfortable!"

"I hope my ass looks that good."

With a roll of her eyes, Josette said, "Trust me, we're identical."

The sheer camisole made of pink silk accented with white lace surpassed everything else in her sister's lingerie drawer for pure sexiness—with the possible exception of matching thong exposing virtually her full, tiny moon. "Do you actually believe he will share your dream downstairs in his room?"

"I didn't tell you everything about my dream. Let me ask you something: how was I dressed when you went to sleep?"

"Eddie carried you up here and put you to bed fully dressed in the clothes you wore. He behaved like the perfect gentleman he is and laid a sheet over you."

"Then why did I wake up with my jeans on the floor and my shirt unbuttoned and pulled back? In my dream, he undressed me, and when I woke, that is exactly how I found myself."

"You were drunk and stoned as shit—probably took them off yourself while imagining your mysterious dream man doing it. Or maybe you woke up—those are tight jeans, and I'm sure they feel miserable to sleep in—so you took them off and started on your blouse but passed out again before you could finish. Then when you had your dream, your fantasy took it from there."

"What if..."

"What if—what?"

"I don't know. What if I didn't undress myself?"

"Are you saying Eddie came into our room and molested you while I was lying right there, not five feet away, sleeping through the whole thing?"

"I know. It makes no sense. But where's the harm in feeling sexy when I go to bed?"

"No harm in that, girl. Who knows, it might inspire you to dream a man into bed with you again. If it works, I may start sleeping in the nude."

"Oh, please don't," Josette pleaded. "I spent my whole life feeling like you were the sexier twin, regardless that we look alike. Don't lure the man of my dreams away from me into your bed while we are sleeping, too!"

"Maybe he'll have a dream-threesome. Wouldn't you, if he is real and able to imperialize on our dreams? If he doesn't, he's a damn fool."

Josette chuckled, despite an unsettling sensation in her gut, one too amorphous to grasp.

"That must have been one hell of a dream, though," her sister said after they turned out the lights.

"It sure was."

"In that case, have sexy dreams."

"Sexy dreams," Josette said. And they giggled together in the dark.

†

Angelique awakened in a shimmering pool of moonlight. Somewhere outside the light, a shadow moved toward her until it, too, emerged into the light. A man dressed in strange clothes that looked straight out of another century —dull gray pants, baggy and of rough cloth, and an odd white shirt. He slowly unbuttoned the shirt, the skin underneath glowing white in the flickering gloom.

Trapped, almost as if tied to the bed or held there by some paralyzing force, part of the tingling she experienced came from fear. Her bed rocked like she was sleeping on a raft swept away by rough waves. The man walked around beside her, between her bed and where Josette should be, but she could not turn her head, and everything beyond the light's reach lay in pitch darkness. From the side, a hand came into her view and pulled the sheet from her.

Anticipation shook her body as she waited for that hand to touch her.

†

Warm sunshine glowed in a brilliant sky unblemished by clouds on that perfect early summer's day. As far as funerals go, George Brown's was a remarkably unmemorable affair. So unremarkable, in fact, that perhaps the only thing any of those in attendance at the little white Baptist church remembered was Celeste.

During a short and generic eulogy, the periodic sound of her coughing interrupted the pastor, throwing him off a few times, enough to force a pause in the middle of a sentence to allow her hacking to subside. Josette sat beside her, once slapping between her mother's shoulder blades like a half-chewed chunk of steak lodged itself in her windpipe. Her problem was trying to hold them in, because when the repressed cough finally forced its release, it erupted deep, uncontrolled, and loud.

If not for Grampa Brown's funeral only weeks before, the Brown Twins may well have been memorable as their mother's pulmonary distress, if not more, dressed as they were in the form-fitting black dresses which might have looked almost demure on most other women. But they wore the same dresses to the previous funeral. Although a smaller, more intimate crowd than his father drew, most attending George's ceremony had seen the girls in those dresses weeks before. No one forgets their first time.

"Our deepest condolences," guests repeated to his widow and children in the reception line, some with conviction. Inevitable inquiries about her health followed. More concerning than her visible and audible symptoms, the word sent out—that there would be no gathering at the house that afternoon—made clear the severity of her illness.

Outside, gathered in small groups, a tall young man dressed respectfully in black—suit, shirt and tie—stood unobtrusive, off to the side. Assembled mourners oblivious to who he was, or they might have been more circumspect with their opinions.

"Can you believe how awful Celeste looks?"

"I didn't know she was ill!"

"She must have lost ten pounds since last month."

He missed the murmured comments at graveside when the twins escorted him to stand with the members of the immediate family. A cousin, word spread like wildfire, though the absence of additional details invited imaginative speculation. After the prayers and with George's casket lowered into the rocky soil, the handsome young man escorting the suffering widow to the limo and climbing in with the family turbocharged the rumors.

At the very moment the hired chauffeur closed the limo's door behind the family, a gust of wind kicked up dust from the packed dirt parking lot as an ominous squall line drifted unobserved from the west. As the black, stretch Lincoln Town Car limo turned left onto Ten Rod Road, the cloud's shadow raced across the green landscape, blocking out the sun. A second gust, stronger than the first, scurried the assembled mourners toward their cars to avoid the approaching storm.

†

"Dr. Kane can see Mama in the morning," Josette told her sister as she came down the stairs from checking on her.

"Good. Whatever she has sure is not allergies. Those damn emergency rooms are petri dishes full of every disease known to man. That's where she caught it." Angelique plopped down next to her sister and drank from her glass of Shiraz. Off in the distance, the low, continuous roll of thunder rumbled. "How long 'til this storm passes?"

"Who knows? Where's Eddie?"

"He's staying with her. Said he's going to read to her until she falls asleep. He's so cute, the way he looks after her like that."

"I'm just glad the doctor can see her. I don't want to see another ER again long as I live."

Still dressed in their little black funeral dresses, a casserole from the freezer warming in the oven, at last Angelique had the opportunity she had been waiting for. "I've wanted a chance to tell you this all day: this damn house is haunted."

"What?" Josette half-laughed at the absurd statement, with her sister's earnestness, stating it as concrete fact.

"The man, the one in our dreams? He's a ghost!"

"A ghost is molesting us during the night?"

"Exactly." She described the man in her dreams, his clothing straight out of a costume rack for a period movie set long ago, then asked, "Give me another explanation."

"Um, maybe we're dreaming? Our father just died, our hot cousin is here—the one who made out with you last week while you were almost buck naked—and we were talking about dreams right until we went to sleep."

"Says the girl who wore sexy clothes to bed to entice a ghost."

"You expect me to believe we spent our entire lives here, and suddenly a ghost starts attacking us? Where's he been all this time?"

"What's a male succubus? Incubus?"

"Yeah, I think that's it."

"What if trauma lures an incubus? Or maybe sexual

tension of some sort attracts them?"

Josette scoffed, dismissing the harebrained theory with one of her eye-roll insults. "So, now that you got a good look at him, it wasn't Eddie haunting our dreams, after all?"

"I'm not sure..."

"But you saw him clearly enough to describe his clothes."

"The weird thing is, I can't remember seeing his face. Sure wasn't a prepster like Eddie. Strange—while I was dreaming, I knew he was a ghost, and that scared the hell out of me. Made it even hotter."

†

Eddie stayed behind with Bernie while the sisters drove their mother to the doctor's appointment down in South Kingston. With the women gone, Eddie took the opportunity for some time to bond with his reclusive cousin. He found a pair of old gloves when partying with the twins out in the barn. He rapped and stuck his head in. "Baseball?" A little flick sent the ball in an arc into the glove. Bernie caught the glove Eddie tossed to him and turned off the Nintendo.

The kid's got an arm, he realized. The ball popped in his glove with each catch, hurled with venom and accuracy. No wonder he spends so much time at sports—he's a natural athlete. The soft arc on Eddie's throws anemic by comparison, although the idea of competing with a fourteen-year-old brought an inward chuckle. Still, he tried to match the boy's accurate power, but failed. Eddie never had much time for sports when he was this age.

"Remind me not to try to hit your fastball," Eddie said, walking back to the house after a good half-hour.

One side of the kid's mouth curled up into a smile, much like his cousin's. "Thanks." A kid of few words. A few seconds later, he blurted out, "Are you screwing my mom?"

"What?" The utter brashness of the question caught him off guard. "What are you talking about?"

"I've seen you going into her room when you think everyone is asleep at night, and sneaking out later."

"Look, Bernie, your mother has been going through a rough time. We've grown close. I like to be there for her when she needs me."

"There, meaning in her bed?"

"Christ, dude, you're talking about your mother," he said, trying to laugh it off.

"You haven't denied it."

"You're going to make a fine attorney someday," he answered. "Tell me the truth: would you believe me if I denied it?"

"No."

"Then what's the point? You will believe what you want to believe. I remember being about your age a long time ago. That's about the time when all you can think about is sex, what with all the hormones raging and not knowing what to do with them yet. When you've been around long as me, you will realize not everything in this world is about sex. Might seem like it now, but you'll learn."

"Do my sisters know about you and our mom?"

Eddie stopped in his tracks, his expression turning on a dime in a way Bernie had not witnessed. "Don't threaten me. And don't threaten to say something that will hurt your sisters. They are very important to me, and I will not allow you or anyone else to poison the bond between us. Do you understand me?"

Something about the menace of his words, his expression, the sudden shift of his posture, made Bernie step back, away from him. "I didn't mean anything by it."

"I asked you a question. Do you understand you are to discuss none of this with your sisters?"

"Sure. We're cool."

Eddie's face returned to normal, a trace of a devilish grin even making a brief appearance. "Let's just keep all this between us. Man to man." Then he put his arm around the kid, shaking him by the shoulder in a friendly manner, guiding him toward the house. "It will be a significant benefit for you to remain in my debt. I can show you things your mind has never conceived of; wondrous things that will alter your world. It's up to you if I will."

†

Down in South Kingsport, Dr. Kane's brow furrowed the way doctors do when examining a seriously ill patient. The expression that brings dread to the person whose test results furrowed that brow. For a moment, Celeste wished she'd brought the girls into the examining room with her. But the three, plus the doctor and nurse, would have rendered such a cramped examining room truly claustrophobic.

"I'm going to give you a little injection under the skin," the doctor explained.

"Is it for my allergies?"

"I'm afraid you are not suffering from allergies. This is a TB test."

Perplexed by such an archaic test, Celeste asked, "Is TB still a thing?"

"It is, although these days it's no cause for worry. It responds very well to antibiotics."

"Doesn't TB make you cough up blood?"

"It can. That's usually the advanced stages. You have all the symptoms of tuberculosis, but hopefully we've caught it early." The shot caused a minor prick under her skin, the penetration stopping shy of the muscle in her arm. "Give it two or three days. We'll have you back on Thursday. If there is any reaction, we'll send you for an X-ray and get you started on antibiotics. You will see it before me. If you don't see a bump or area of swelling, then you are negative for TB."

"That's good, right?"

"It means you don't have TB, but if you're negative, we will need to look further for the cause of that nasty cough."

†

The strangest thing about their dreams was the twins never both experienced a dream on the same night.

Each morning they awoke and the one who had the dream confessed every delicious detail about it, no matter how dirty. In fact, the dirtier, the better. The dream alternated between them: one experiencing hers one night, the other having hers the next. Ridiculous as it seemed, Angelique followed her sister's lead and stopped wearing a boring old tee shirt to bed. Instead, she, too, slept in her sexiest lingerie. Neither admitted it was a competition, and Josette refused to accept an incubus or some other form of ghost ravaged one of them each night, but for the first time in her life, she received the same attention as her more approachable twin.

And if a ghost was visiting them in such a bizarre and stimulating way, what harm could come of this particularly pleasant form of a haunting?

†

An hour passed in which the only sounds came from outside. Another half hour, and still it remained quiet. Stealthy movements in bare feet added nothing louder than controlled breath. The unlocked door let out its usual squeal, prolonged by the slow pace, which also dampened its volume to a whisper. Another pause with absolute stillness. The door closed. A click produced the loudest sound, one lost in the night.

She awoke from a light sleep when he climbed into bed beside her. Her hand, reaching behind her, ran from his upper thigh to his waist. He was naked. "What are you doing?" Her body shook with a laugh that morphed into a cough.

Eddie wrapped his arm around her as he nestled against her, patting her upper chest to calm the cough. "I needed to be with you."

Once she stifled the cough, he took a breast with one hand. Snapped awake from the edge of sleep, her voice strengthened to her normal speaking tones. "I'm afraid I'm not up to that tonight."

"Up to what?"

Tenderly wrapping her hand over his, she squeezed ever so slightly. "What you came for."

Pressing her breast against her and rubbing firm, delightful slow circles, Eddie whispered, "Why do you believe I come to you?"

"For the same reason, I want you to come. You come for sex. Tonight, I am tired and sick and not in the mood —even though that feels damn good." Her hand pressed his, increasing the pressure on her breast.

"That's all you believe it is for me? Sex?"

Stiffening, she half turned over her shoulder to see his face. "Isn't it?"

His rubbing, so unhurried and tender, had an hypnotic effect. "Making love with you is pretty darn amazing, but I want more."

This time, her voice sounded nervous. "Eddie, please don't fall in love with me. You are a wonderful young man, but I am old enough to be your…"

"You are old enough to understand I am already in love with you, and have been since the moment we met. And you are smart enough to know I want more than that. Much more."

He kissed the back of her neck where her daughters discovered that cut, the delicate spot he always kissed. Although he was only massaging her breast, the first, familiar wave of pleasure welled up inside her. A gasp escaped her lips, more from the shock of his seductive powers than even the pleasure, but soon, her soft, intimate sounds were from pure pleasure. Then she fell into a dark sleep.

In her dream, Eddie still was there, although he sat on the edge of her bed, still naked. He undressed her and gazed at her body. His hand reached for her, feather-touching her abdomen. "You're dying."

"I know," she answered without sadness.

"Do you want to die? Or do you want to stay with me?"

"I don't want to die."

"Allow me to help you." His palm moved across the skin of her body, wherever he pleased, and she knew she was powerless to stop him.

"I have taken from you, but also I wish to give to you."

"What have you taken?"

"Your life. In exchange, I can give you mine. Do you want it?"

"Yes."

He lifted her hand to his chest, guiding her fingers to his left nipple. She circled it, the way he did hers—the way which drove her mad. A long, pink scar on his otherwise perfect chest, more than an inch long, which continued most of the way through, marred the perfection of the dark ring. He pushed aside her hand and ran his thumb along the scar. The glistening sapphire of his eyes somehow penetrated the shadows, focused on her with an unrecognizable intensity. Thumb turned on its edge, his thumbnail pressed into his skin. The nail dug into the scar, ripping through fragile skin. Blood slowly oozed from the gash as his nail followed the scar, tearing it open to the edge of the nipple. Into it.

In her dream, the sight of Eddie mutilating himself so painfully made her cringe, yet she could not turn away as he rent his breast open, only stopping at the far end of the scar two-thirds of the way straight through the center of his tender nipple. Two trails of blood ran down his chest, followed by a third. The red spread from the flow's intensity. His hand hooked behind her head, thumb smearing her cheek with his blood, and pulled her to his chest. Disgusted and terrified, she fought against him, against his straining muscles, yet the power in his hand proved too much to fight.

He forced her lips—pressed closed tight—against the

bloody slit, mashing her nose against flexing pectoral muscle and skin. Then, to her surprise, his hand relaxed, and she lifted her face to look at him, smearing blood down her chin.

"Drink. It's okay."

The blood on her upper lip tasted oddly sweet as she ran her tongue across it, so she licked more from his chest. It had the taste of something lost, satisfying. A memory came to her, of her strange hunger while pregnant with her children and her insatiable craving for rare steak. The mere sight of bloody steak triggered her gag reflex, but not then. Not his blood.

Now her tongue licked the blood flowing down his chest, starting at the lowest point of each trail up to where he tore himself open for her. Each time she finished cleaning one, it flowed again. Frustrated, she looked to him, and he gave one of his reassuring grins.

"It's okay."

Instinctively, she knew. She closed her lips over the whole of the gash and began suckling from him. His back arched, pressing into her, and he let out a long, mournful sigh. In her mouth, his blood felt viscous, coating the inside, an odd hint of wine. His fingers glided through her hair, no longer pushing her against him, but holding her in place. In a moment, she knew why.

His body collapsed back across her bed, bringing her forward onto him, her lips locked onto his breast as he writhed beneath her. Along her back, down to her bottom, one hand followed her curves. By then, he was gasping for breath, much the way he did when he reached climax inside of her. With her hand caressing one side of his face, her fingertips traced the soft, moist oval of his open lips. Inside his mouth. Over his teeth. His tongue flicked them. Then his lips closed, the undulations of his body intensified, and he held her close as she sucked blood from his nipple.

When she awoke, he was gone, but fragments of her dream remained. Not much, more like photographs frozen in time than a film. Body aching to her core and parched as if she drank like a sailor the night before, she staggered to the bathroom. Cupped hands filled from the faucet splashed her face, then she drank from those hands. When she had enough, she stared at her face in the mirror.

Those tiny, fine lines at the corners of her eyes and frown lines near her lips first began marring her beautiful skin a decade ago, but she had yet to accept the inevitability of her own decline. Must be the light, she thought, turning her face from side to side, raising and lowering her chin for a better view. Either the light or her eyesight. Crappy and weak as she felt, those lines were almost invisible.

Celeste smiled. "Huh. How about that?"

LET'S GO CRAZY

Dressed only in a powder blue gown made of paper, they lay Celeste on the cold, narrow slab. Nothing more than a hard shelf. Under that flimsy gown, she was naked, save for gray cotton panties she bought for yoga class, before she discovered the ugly lines it cast on her favorite, skin-tight Spandex exercise pants. The shelf, indeed everything in the room, was uncomfortably chilly. Hospitals stay this same temperature year 'round. Down here, two stories below the main entrance, must be the coldest part of the building.

Well, except for the morgue, she thought.

"There, now hold still," the radiology technician announced before fleeing the room. The little slab she lay on protruded from a hole in a machine shaped like a donut, but as the long, narrow slab carried her to penetrate the circle, she started laughing. It reminded her of something else, a wicked thought. The more she tried to stifle the laughter, the funnier it became as she slipped inside the circle. The technician called out, annoyance palpable in his voice, "Please hold still. If you keep moving, we will need to do this all over again."

Celeste had heard of MRI machines, but never had seen one, let alone been shoved inside. After her test for TB caused no reaction, Dr. Kane sent her for a chest X-ray. When that also turned out negative, the next step was an MRI. During that visit, she mentioned the word cancer for the first time. Unlikely, she assured her, but with all the other tests coming back completely normal, they must rule out every possibility. All the tests showed so far was an acute anemia, which might explain her fatigue and pallor, but not the other symptoms.

The cough, the achiness, the cold chills that awakened her during the night.

The disturbing dreams that left her so aroused afterward, those she decided not to mention to the doctor.

They told her to remove her bra because of the metal it contained, something to do with the giant magnets that put the M in the MRI. Not exactly what she needed wearing flimsy paper in a room with the A/C set to Arctic, taking away that last bit of security. The lab tech tried to hide it, but his eyes, his smile, betrayed how much she entertained him. He might have been Eddie's age.

He was waiting outside with the kids, and when she came out after the test, they greeted her like she came through major surgery. "It was only a test, and painless. Just a little cold, is all," she explained, fielding their questions, giving assurance they needed so soon after the death of their father. He also hugged her warmly.

"Let's get out of here," he said, and with his chest pressed to hers, his voice resonated through hers as a pleasing vibration.

†

On Saturday evening, Bernie had a baseball game over in Narragansett. Eddie volunteered to go, to keep Celeste company, but the twins had other ideas. "You'll have so much more fun around people your own age," she rationalized. So, in the afternoon, Josette got behind the wheel and headed toward the mountains just outside of town. In the state park, she parked the car under a sign reading Picnic Area.

"The last place I expected you two to take me is a park."

Angelique explained, "We used to come up here to party in high school. The cops never bother us here."

"Are we going to party?" The twins found something funny about that question. From the trunk, they produced a wicker picnic basket and led the way down a path. Down the trail a half mile, ancient maples and towering hemlocks opened up to a small field with a marvelous view of the valley below. The girls spread a plaid blanket over the grass—just large enough for three—and while Josette screwed the cork remover in, Angelique set the family's fine crystal wine glasses out, searching for flat spots where they might stay upright. Kneeling on the blanket, she smoothed the surface, leaning over to reach the corners, drawing his attention to how low-cut her shirt was—and the fact that she wore nothing at all underneath. "Come, sit down."

Josette forced the cork out of the bottle with a giggle and poured Pinot Noir into each glass. Fine movements under her more conservative shirt suggested she, too, went without a bra, the first time he could remember her doing so.

"This is where you used to party?"

"This is where we still party," Angelique corrected him, holding up a fattie, which she extended toward him. "Will you do the honors?"

"Ladies first," he said, raising his glass. "It is beautiful here," he said, allowing his eyes to remain on her as she lit the joint, following down to her breasts before turning to the valley below.

Josette said, "We hoped you'd like it here. All those places you talk about, where you visited, the mountains and deserts, and we realized we have mountains right here for you to see."

"Where I come from, the Sierras, these aren't called mountains. These would be considered hills. Beautiful hills, but not mountains."

Josette frowned. "Are you disappointed?"

"Not in the slightest." A quick glance down toward her chest, and he said, "Hills are usually more beautiful than mountains." Her eyes acknowledged the compliment, but Angelique missed it from where she was sitting.

"Are the California mountains the most beautiful you have seen?"

"Oh, no. Switzerland. There, the mountains are covered

with snow and ice all year, rising from valleys filled with the most picturesque Alpine villages, surrounded by massive fields of flowers. Waterfalls drop from cliffs a thousand feet high. Maybe someday I can show them to you."

"I'd—we'd like that," Angelique said.

Josette said, "Sounds like a dream," and the girls giggled again, this time nervously. They chatted and sipped wine, the twins asking him questions about the places he visited, the women he took there. Rarely had they traveled far from New England, and wholly disinterested in the boys they knew, he asked about their goals, their dreams. Angelique wanted to see the world, to experience everything it had to offer. To dive with sharks, skiing the Alps, to sunbathe naked on the French Riviera.

Not surprisingly, Josette's fantasies were much more grounded. "I want to love someone who loves me, to have a family who is my everything, who I can always rely upon."

"Yin and yang," Eddie said when they finished. "Two equally beautiful visions for your lives, yet both alluring in their own, opposite ways."

"Let me ask you a question about your dreams," Josette said. She looked about, hesitating. "Do you ever have dreams? Intense dreams, but not the ordinary ones."

"Not ordinary?"

"No," she explained, her pallid skin glowing ruby red. "Dreams you cannot talk about, because they are too..."

"Intimate," Angelique jumped in to help her out.

"Sure, doesn't everyone? Dreams of what you've done, dreams of what you hope to do, and who you hope to do it with?"

"Yes, those dreams."

"Some nights, I've dreamed those dreams." His eyes did not blink, did not turn away from hers, and Josette felt gloriously naked in those eyes. "Who do you dream about, Josette?"

"Well, I..."

"The Truth."

Rather than answering, she asked, "Do you ever dream about me?"

"Yes," he answered.

"How do you know you it isn't my sister in your dreams?"

"Who said she is not there, too?" Finally, his attention turned to Angelique. "Do you also dream of me in that way?"

"I do," she admitted, and the way it came out like a wedding vow brought a wide grin that brightened her face like the sun.

"So, that is what this was about. It feels so deliciously romantic, in a place where the beauty is surpassed only by the lovely women by my side?"

"Since that night, when we bared our souls to each other, and we kissed—when you didn't do anything or speak about it —we worried maybe we scared you off."

"Do I look like a guy who scares easily?"

Angelique smirked. "Well, you wore a pink Izod the other day, collar popped under an Oxford button-down."

"It looked great on you," Josette added.

"A little too preppy for me," her sister said, although her expression suggested otherwise.

"How is any man supposed to choose between the two most beautiful women he's ever seen? Women as different as day and night, yet each so utterly perfect in their own peculiar ways?"

This stunned even Angelique, who had been holding the smoldering joint on one knee, surveying the view of the valley after drawing a deep hit. Rather than answering, she coughed. A little one, at first, but then one from deep down, expelling smoke with the force of a cannon. Her arm jutted toward him, holding out the joint, which he took and dropped onto a small plate waiting for food. Vigorous pats on her back, curved forward in distress, did nothing.

"Angelique?" Her sister scampered across the blanket

on hands and knees over Eddie like he wasn't there. "What's wrong? Are you okay?" Eddie rubbed her back while her sister held onto one arm with eyes wide and mouth agape. "What's happening to her?"

"Let it out," he said, his voice soothing. His palm slapped her—hard—three times, four. She gasped, inhaling, then after a few more hits over her lungs, she drew in a deep breath, face a deep, mottled shade of purple.

In a panic, Josette asked, "Are you alright?" In reply, she held out a hand toward Eddie, fingers opening and closing. The only thing they had was wine, so he handed her his glass; hers lay spilt on the grass. She downed it like water.

It took a few minutes, but finally she could speak, albeit with a raspy voice. "What in the holy fuck?"

He could not help but chuckle, earning him a rebuke from her sister's red-rimmed eyes.

"I'm serious! What the fuck? I felt like Mama sounds. I was sitting here, gasping for air, and you know what I thought?" Eager for details, Josette asked what? "What if whatever she has is contagious? Have you ever heard me cough like that? I don't cough like that," she said to Eddie, as if an explanation was necessary.

"Well, you seem okay now," he refilled his glass and handing it to her. While she gulped it, he took a long drag of reefer and let it sit in his lungs. When she handed his glass back, he drank from the little drop left where her lips had been.

Josette helped him finish the joint, but her sister waved it off, having had enough for the day. She coughed a few more times, though none so vicious, and the sun sank behind them, casting the mountain's shadow over the valley.

"The park closes at sundown," Josette said as the fluffy little clouds above pinkened. No one moved a muscle, lying side by side, Eddie flanked by the two loveliest women he knew, their heads resting on his shoulder spilling orange curls across his neck and chest. All three wishing it could stay like this forever.

†

"Excellent news," Celeste announced as she hung up the phone. "My lungs are healthy. The doctor says there is no sign of cancer!"

The twins squealed with joy and rushed to give her a massive hug even Bernie came over to join. Eddie stood to join them, and as he did, he stumbled, as if his legs gave out. Only Celeste was looking in that direction.

"Are you okay?" A little wave assured her he was.

"Then, what is it?" Josette asked the question hanging over them. "After all these tests and they can't find anything wrong with you!"

"They don't know," she answered. "Only thing I can think of must be the old Brown family curse. It's not my lungs, there's no infection. Anemia isn't causing these other symptoms, although that isn't helping any—and they can't figure out what is causing that, either."

That question weighed so heavily on the kids that each, in their own unspoken mind, accepted that the MRI would show a tumor the size of a grapefruit in her lungs. What else could it be?

"You know what I'm going to do tomorrow? I'm driving up to Brown University to visit the medical school library. If the doctors can't figure it out, maybe I can do it myself, find some answers in the medical books. Anyone want to join me?"

Angelique stuck out her tongue, miming gagging in a juvenile way, and Josette shook her head vigorously enough to send her curls flying.

"It's not a good idea for you to drive that far alone—not as weak as you've been," Eddie said. "If no one else is interested, I know my way around a library."

It was near ten the following morning when they set out. Celeste intended to leave before then, but getting out of bed in the morning verged on the impossible those days. Eddie drove, and much of the way they listened to a classic rock station, singing along to every song. About halfway there, U.F.O.'s *Too Hot to Handle* came on, and Eddie cranked the volume up to 11.

Sha-na-na-na, roll me over
Turn off the lights and do it again
'Cause I'm too, too hot,

"Baby," Celeste sang the word solo, then joined in continued in duet,

Too hot to handle.

"Okay, that's weird," she said when Eddie turned the volume down on an ad.

"What's weird?"

"How do you know that song? It's like fifteen years old or something."

"So?"

"Well, you would have been eight or nine when it came out. It was popular then, but it must've been ten years since I've heard it played on the air."

"I just drove across the country, from the Pacific to the Atlantic. That's a lot of time listening to the radio."

"I've driven coast to coast, too. And except for Chicago and parts of Ohio, the only music you can find is country music. Drove me crazy."

"What can I say? I've heard it for years."

"The twins tell me about all that new wave Gothic music you've turned them on to."

"Alright, you got me. I confess: I listen to rock music whenever I can. Goth, metal, new wave, classic rock—I love 'em all."

"It's just odd. Sometimes I look at you, hear something you say, and I swear you are older than twenty-three. A lot older than twenty-three."

"I have another confession: sometimes I look at you and think you cannot be over two or three years older than the twins. Max!"

†

Brown University's Alpert Medical School stands a hundred yards from the Providence River within sight of where the Seekonk River flows in to triple its width. Housed in a modern building with a design most generously described as functional, in downtown Providence, separated from the main University campus by the river, they felt much farther from Exeter than the forty-five minutes it took to drive there. An hour, if you count time spent finding a parking spot without a meter that required regular two-hour feedings.

Although she completed a year and a half of college before the twins began to show, Celeste had never set foot in a medical library. The contrast with a bustling college library and its system of book organization, separating fiction from various non-fiction topics, the medical library was stark, quiet, utilitarian. A significant quantity of its collection made up of medical journals, the rest shelves of books bearing dizzying academic titles which often left her guessing. A cute, if somewhat serious female undergrad assistant there on work-study, noticing Eddie wandering aimlessly, helped start them in the right direction. Celeste took a carrel along the back wall, tasking Eddie with scouting books for her to read.

To their chagrin, medical books are neither organized by nor named for symptoms.

A half-hour in, Eddie struck gold with a book entitled *Taylor's Differential Diagnosis Manuel.* Not long after, he discovered *Current Medical Diagnosis & Treatment.* Between them, the two volumes allowed Celeste to find various illnesses and syndromes matching her symptoms.

"Well, far as I can tell, pretty much every illness in these books causes some combination of coughing, fatigue and muscle aches, let alone anemia. Do you suppose they are related, or is fatigue from the anemia, and the coughing its own, separate illness?"

Eddie shrugged his shoulders. "Beats me. Today, you are

the doctor."

"And you are smart as hell. Help me make some sense of these." After breaking for lunch in the medical school cafeteria, they continued their work. Maintaining their voices at a low volume in the crypt-like silence required immense effort. Mid-afternoon, struck by something she stumbled across in one book, she went off in search of a book further explaining the brief listing in the diagnostic manual. Five minutes later, Eddie spotted her trotting toward the front exit. He caught up with her on the sidewalk outside.

"Where are you going? Stop, will you?" Celeste stopped and turned around, allowing him to catch up. Dark streaks of tears and mascara ran across her cheeks from eyes turned red. "What happened? What's wrong? Oh, don't cry—talk to me."

"Well, I found it."

"What did you find?"

"I may be insane," she said. "In fact, I'm pretty sure about it."

"What?" The absurdity of her self-diagnosis, coupled with her earnestness, almost made him smile, an unhelpful urge he successfully fought off.

"Have you ever heard of Pica?"

"Sure. They live in the Sierra Nevada. You see 'em all the time up above the tree line."

"What are you talking about?"

"What are *you* talking about? Pika are little animals. A rodent; they look like tiny jackrabbits with less extravagant ears, about yay big," demonstrating with hands held about eight inches apart.

"Well, it must be a crazy rodent, because they named a mental illness after it."

"Come here," he held open his arms as an invitation; she accepted. "You aren't crazy, I promise you. Nor will I believe it, no matter what any book says."

"I've been having some dreams, and over about the past week, they've changed. They started off sexy, but now they're different. They're still sexy, but now they're frickin' weird and dark and creepy as hell, and even before I read that book, I wondered if what is wrong with me is my mind."

"What sort of dreams?"

"I cannot tell you. You will think I'm insane, which apparently I am."

"Am I in those dreams? The sexy ones?" Her head bobbed up and down against his chest. "Well, sounds completely sane to me."

"We do the most fucked-up shit in those dreams," she protested.

"We've done some fucked-up things. Remember what you and I did the night we buried your husband? That's fucked up." The way he said it, the guilty innocence and his arms holding her tight reassured her enough that she laughed. "Tell me."

"I can't," she said. "Let's go home."

"Did you learn anything else about what you might have?"

"Other than mental illness that can explain everything from the fatigue to the headaches, no. Even a cough can be psychosomatic."

"Let's go gather up our notes, and then I know something we can do before going home."

NEED YOU TONIGHT

It only took a few minutes to figure out what he had in mind.

Eddie insisted on treating her to dinner at a fancy restaurant. Celeste put up a good show of objecting, caving to an irrational fear over the possibility of running into someone she knew, fuel for more well-founded rumors, but deep down the idea of such a handsome young stud taking her on a date sent chills down her spine.

How he discovered this fine French restaurant remained a mystery, and with exorbitant prices starting at ten dollars and shooting up from there, one glance at the menu made her blurt out, "You cannot afford this!"

"How do you know what I can afford? What if I've been saving up for years?" The twinkle in his eye forced her to relent, even when she saw the price of the vintage bottle of Bordeaux he ordered.

"They say red wine is good for the blood," he said after a stiff waiter wearing a black tie and vest filled their glasses, and he raised his to her. "To a long, happy life!"

"This is wonderful," she said, leaving unstated whether she meant the wine or the evening. Their conversation began with the day's research, a topic abandoned before their meals arrived. Casual, at first, drifting to more intimate topics.

"Do you miss George?"

His question startled her, blunt and potentially accusatory. "Yes, it came as such a shock, with no hint that I… Do you want to know the truth?"

"Always," he answered, peering over the deep red wine,

elbow propped on the table.

"No, I don't. He was... we had grown apart. Sure, his death shocked me. More shocking, though? The relief. There was so much tension between him and the twins. They didn't like him much, and although I truly believe he loved them, it had been dysfunctional between them for a long time. And I'm no fool. He'd been banging waitresses his daughters' age for several years. Girls half my age."

"Don't get me wrong—he was a good man. Started off that way, at least. Or so I thought—sometimes I am not sure which. Along the way, something happened. He changed. These last few years, I didn't even recognize him anymore."

"Must be another family curse."

Head tilted, she asked, "In what way?"

"Sounds like the original George Brown."

"Funny, I know so little about him. Everybody talks about Mercy Brown, but other than being her father, I don't know much of anything. How is he like ours?"

"Seems to me like both lost their moorings along the way. By all accounts, everyone in Exeter respected George the elder, got along well with him. Religious, hard-working. Then the deaths of his wife and children changed him. Those close to him hardly recognized him. Only one of his four children survived. They say she never married. Back then, they called unmarried women like her spinsters. Then there was her scandal."

She asked, eyes narrowed and with a curious grin, "What scandal?"

"Well, she had two children. Since she never married—well, you can imagine how people reacted back at the turn of the century. Those two girls formed your branch of the family, so in the end, it turned out well. No one ever knew the father, and she gave her daughters the Brown name, so you can imagine every man in town came under suspicion. Nothing new for the Browns, though. The family had scandals going way back. So far back, no one remembers what they were, only rumors of their existence. Hence, the prevalent belief in a family curse."

"Where does the kids' father's branch come from?" They say a person suffers the second death the last time their name is spoken, a death she hastened by her refusal to speak the name of her dearly departed husband.

"Little did anyone know, but when Lena's brother died, his wife Lydia was pregnant. Gave birth to a son right after New Year's. The year before, she had lost a baby, so she kept it secret in case the same thing happened again."

"So, the original Eddie never knew he had a child on the way?"

His expression clouded. "No, he went to the grave knowing nothing about it." Years passed before he learned of Edwin Brown, Jr., but she was not ready to hear this part of the story.

"Your knowledge about this family is so impressive, and I love the way you talk about them, like they are real people."

"They were very real. Wonderful, deeply flawed like all of us, I suppose. But made of flesh and blood and dreams and desire. All people remember today is the best of them was the last vampire, and the horrible way George killed her." His face darkened; so much, Celeste involuntarily glanced up at the lights overhead, wondering if a bulb had flickered out. "What I always wondered is, how could he do that to his child? You know that part of the story, don't you?"

"How they exhumed Mercy? Cut out her heart and burned it on a rock behind the church? The kids all teased us with that when I was growing up, and told the story in hushed voices around campfires at Halloween and around St. Patrick's Day, when they dug her up. Bernie says they still talk about it at school."

"As a parent, can you imagine deciding to do that to one of your daughters? And then to literally feed her body to your other two kids?"

Again, a chill washed over her, but this one was not the

same as the pleasant feeling he gave her earlier. "Not put that way. But you make it sound so sinister. Surely he must have meant well, believing his one daughter was a vampire, killing her to save the other kids. It sounds so harsh to us, so primitive, but he must have been totally desperate. Imagine finding out someone you love so dearly is some kind of monster, praying on members of your family!" The chill climaxed, sending a visible shake up her body.

From across the table, face half in shadow, eyes like two torches penetrated deep into her. "Tell me, do you believe in vampires?"

"Me? No... well no." She chuckled. "It's romantic to believe those old stories may be true and that they exist, but no one really believes they do."

Leaned forward for emphasis, he said, "Does not matter whether you believe in vampires, no more than whether Mercy Brown was a vampire or a normal teenage girl who died much too young. Think about this: If she was not a vampire, then her father desecrated his daughter's body and turned his children into cannibals by forcing them to consume her flesh. But, let your mind imagine for a minute she was a vampire. How did he not realize he was killing his own child a second time?"

"But she killed her mother and sister, right?"

"How can we know?" His voice so quiet, if they were eating in a restaurant only a few decibels louder, the clutter would have eaten his words like a plate of *Coq au vin*. "If she was undead, then someone made her a vampire. She may have been the last vampire, but certainly was not the first. What if the same vampire who gave it to her also killed her mother and sister?"

"But the legend says she attacked her brother! Didn't he die soon after her?"

"Two months after his father forced him to drink tea brewed from the ashes of his sister's heart and liver. Has it ever occurred to you she might not have been trying to harm her brother? Lena did not attack anyone else in the family.

Only her brother died, while her father and little sister were fine. Have you ever wondered why? If she was an evil killer, wouldn't she have murdered her entire family?"

"How do you figure? Vampires prey upon people, drink their blood. Those people die. At least, that's how the stories go." As she spoke, a vision flashed through her mind. A kind of memory, like a partially remembered dream, almost recovered, only to slip out of reach again.

"What if she intended to make him immortal? What if she considered it a gift? Trying to do good?"

"How can killing be good?"

"Suppose someone offers you immortality and eternal youth. Freedom from the fear of death, and forever you will remain as beautiful as you are today. Isn't it possible someone given this may consider it a precious gift, one they wish to share with those they love? If someone gave you eternal life, how would you like to go through eternity while everyone you love grows old and dies, leaving you to remain forever exactly as you are? Can you imagine the torture of watching those you love wither and die—over and over again, an infinite number of times?"

"Wow, I never considered it in that light."

"In that case, who would you choose to accompany you on your journey? Who do you trust enough to confer such power, to hold a secret so dangerous?"

"My family, of course."

"Exactly! No one will ever know for sure, but I prefer to think of Mercy Lena Brown as not a tragic character, but an heroic one. A young woman burdened with a curse that can also be a blessing, which she accepted as a blessing to be shared with someone she trusted with it."

The waiter appeared, hovering over them. Eddie nodded for him to take their empty plates. "That was delicious," Celeste said to both.

"Can I interest you in a dessert? Perhaps some coffee?"

"What is the most decadent chocolate dessert on your

menu?"

"Ahh, that would be our chocolate-raspberry souffle. Made with 72% dark chocolate, fresh local raspberries and topped with a raspberry crème fresh. I believe you will find it delightfully decadent."

"We'll take two."

"Eddie, are you sure? This has been quite a special evening..."

"How do you feel? Today? Right now?"

"I feel better today. Stronger than I have in a week."

"Then let's celebrate that."

She flashed her emerald eyes to the waiter. "Two," she confirmed. After he got out of hearing range, she said, "This meal will put ten pounds on me."

"I can think of a few exercises we can do to work it off."

"Oh my god, you are terrible! Of course, the exact same thing was going through my mind." She turned those remarkable eyes to him with some of the intensity he focused on her a few minutes before while her index finger circled the rim of her nearly empty wineglass. "This is what I love about you. Not this," she indicated the restaurant with a wave of an open hand, "but tonight. Your passion, your heart, your intellect."

"And to think, I had myself convinced it was the way I make your body quiver during the dark of night."

"Well, that too. But if not for your heart, I would never have known about... your other organs. Still, I am surprised how romantic you can be. The last time I went on a date like this was before I had the girls."

"A date? Are we dating now?"

With an expression of slight concern and confusion, she said, "What do you call it? Romance? Pure animal attraction? Mutual need? Does it matter what category we put it in?"

"I like all of those categories." He reached across the table to take her hand, letting go only when the waiter brought two delightfully decadent desserts.

†

A fit of coughing woke her up late, the night dark and still. Eddie was gone. Air refused to fill her lungs, and when she managed to draw a little in, another cough drove it from her body. She was dying, and the sudden reality hit her as she gasped for air in utter futility. Arms flailed in front of her, sending her sheet flying off to one side, and she doubled over. One of her daughters ran into the room.

"Mama? Okay, breathe. Come on, Mama, try to relax. I'm here with you." Remembering the way Eddie pounded the cough out of her sister two days before, she copied what she saw him do. Her hand slapped on her mother's bare skin. After eight or ten slaps, increasing in magnitude, like Angelique, her mother began regaining her breath, and the color of her face and chest began returning to normal. "Let me get you some water."

Her mother gulped down the glass she returned with. "Thank you. Oh, I think I am better now."

"Jesus, Mama—when did you start sleeping nude?"

"Shit!" Celeste tugged the sheet back and held it over her.

"Just be glad I heard you, instead of Bernie or Eddie. That would have been a shock!"

Partially right, Celeste thought, but instead asked, "Where is your sister?"

"Sleeping. Don't know how she slept through this. Are you okay?"

The glass was empty. She wriggled and pulled at the covers to get up. "I could use more water."

"Stay there! I've seen enough skin for one night. Do you have any idea how scarring it is to see your naked mother coughing like that? Shaking and... ugh!" She gave a theatrical shudder.

"Oh, stop! I get the point. What about you? Looks like you're dressed for your wedding night!" While Eddie and her mom were researching, the twins' order from the Victoria's Secret catalog had arrived. This was the first night she wore the gorgeous white silk nightgown with strategic lace inserts. Suddenly self-conscious, her hand rose to hover over her chest.

"You're in no position to talk," she said to avoid answering. "If you are better, I'll let you get back to sleep."

"Would you mind staying, just for a bit? To be honest, that scared the hell out of me, and I don't want to be alone right now."

"Sure, Mama" the two leaned back, propped up on pillows against the headboard, Josette's arm around her mother.

Across the hall, ten steps down through the offset door, her sister was in the throes of a strange and haunting dream.

This one began as the others, a man coming to her as she slept. Touching her. Inciting her. His touch drove her to the highest levels of pleasure her mind could imagine. And, as usual, he blew her finger. It made no sense, but his sucking on her pointer drove her crazy! Must be some male phallic fantasy, she figured during the day when she remembered it. While he sucked on her finger, his hands wandered about her flesh, burning everywhere he touched, branding his fingerprints into her skin.

The strange part came next. He appeared above her as a shadow, leaning over her, and she kissed his body, his chest, the way he kissed hers. But she felt drawn to his nipple, and when she kissed it, a strange taste filled her mouth. She sucked on his nipple like he sucked her finger, lifting the intensity of her pleasure. Arms around his back, holding him there, she nursed from his strong, muscled chest.

He left her gasping, wanting more, desperate. But he just vanished, and when he did, she descended back into her deep sleep.

†

Deterioration worsened around her every day, as did the

terror.

Every person around her. In less than a month, her father inexplicably threw himself from a rooftop and her mother came down with an illness that, since she returned from a trip to Providence to research for herself what no doctor could diagnose, left her basically bedridden. Then her sister got sick and was on course to follow the descent her mother was in.

Over the last couple of days, Eddie started showing signs of being ill, too. Sure, he denied it, but he had taken on the same pale, washed-out complexion Mama has, and now her twin, and she saw his legs give out twice like he simply lacked the strength to stand up. Just that morning, he stood up from the breakfast table, took one step and face-planted on the kitchen floor.

Not an hour later, she coughed. Nothing like her mother or sister's horrible fits of uncontrollable hacking that left them gasping for air, but theirs both started off as little coughs, too. Mama blamed it on Mimosa trees blooming, for chrissakes.

She had to get out of there.

At first, driving aimlessly, just to listen to a cassette she expropriated from Eddie's room during his trip to the medical school, eventually she decided on a destination. Thank god Abby's car was parked in her driveway!

"Damn," her friend said after she spilled everything. "So, no one knows what this is, but everyone has it but you and Bernie?"

"Pretty much. Except I'm worried I may have it. Do you mind?" Josette held up a joint.

"Not in the house! My parents will smell it the moment they come home from work. Besides, that shit's why you're coughing."

"It's some pretty good shit."

"Okay, but let's go out back."

They sat on the old swing set that had been there since she came over to play with Abby when they were in grade school, now outgrown by her younger siblings, passing the joint. "Will you go to the doctor?"

"What's the point? They've done every test imaginable on Mama with nothing to show for it. Angelique refuses to go; says it's a waste of time. Can't really blame her, but wonder if they might find something they missed with Mama. Some false negative test, for example."

"Whatever it is, it must be contagious as hell. Maybe I shouldn't be this close to you," she said as she took the offered spliff from Josette. "Eddie has it, too?"

"Looks that way. The last few days he's been exhausted, weak, pale as a ghost. Everyone around me is dying!"

"Don't say that. I don't want anything to happen to you or your sister or mom. It will be a shame if your cousin is sick. He's so hot, and came across as charming, slightly old-fashioned in a cool way."

"Tell me about it."

"What's his deal with your mom?"

"What are you talking about?"

"You know. I'm not blind." Josette stopped rocking by digging her heels into the dirt and stared at her friend. "Seriously, you haven't noticed?"

"They're close. They get along great. He's just that kind of guy."

"Honey, they're more than close. They were checking each other out at the wake and they kept touching each other when they passed or were talking, like they thought nobody else was there. It might have been cute if your father hadn't just committed suicide."

Josette shook her head, slowly at first. "No. You're imagining things. He's like four years older than us, and..."

"Don't leave me hanging!"

"Well, we sort of made out with him."

"You and Angelique?"

She nodded. "The night that Angelique got sick, the three of us were together. We didn't do anything then, but that was because she almost died coughing. I think he's trying to decide which one of us he wants."

"He hasn't tried to sleep with either of you?"

"No."

"Are you sure? What if he and your sister...?"

"Not possible. She's as frustrated as I am."

"Isn't that strange? There he is in a house with two gorgeous women who want him, and he hasn't sealed the deal with either of you?"

"Like you said, he's a little old-fashioned."

"Or he's already sleeping with your mom."

"Okay, I'm going to puke now."

"I'm sorry. I assumed you saw it more clearly than me, or they let you in on it. Shoot me if I'm wrong."

†

Those who have suffered through serious illness, their families and caregivers are well-acquainted with the fact that some days are good, some are bad. Often occurring without rhyme or reason, but sometimes they follow cycles. The ill and those around them dread those bad days and learn to savor the good days when they come.

This was one of the bad days.

Arriving home in a putrid mood, Josette found her mother and sister both suffering horribly. Confined to her bed by her overwhelming fatigue, Celeste scarcely had the strength to open her eyes, while Angelique's nagging, dry cough cut short virtually everything she said—or tried to say. Despite the absence of any semblance of an appetite, Josette ordered Domino's, half left sitting uneaten in the box.

No one had a clue where Eddie went; he left hours ago without explanation.

†

When he arrived home in the wee hours of the night, Eddie expected to find the house dark. The fact that someone had locked the doors came as a surprise.

Like everyone else in town, the Browns rarely locked their doors. Fortunately for him, Celeste gave him a key soon after George died. “Family should have a key,” she explained. Regular nighttime visits from the guest room up the stairs and down to Celeste’s room at the far end of the hall burned into his memory each squeaky floorboard, which stairs groaned under his weight and every obstacle to avoid. That night, he used all his learned stealth to enter her room without making a sound. Once inside, a tiny beam of moonlight penetrated the room, sufficient illumination to make his way to her bed without awakening her. Her hair glowed in the moonlight. She lay curled on her side into the fetal position, sheet pulled up almost covering her a bare shoulder. This exposed skin glowed alabaster in the feeble light, so fine, pale and elegant. Cold, too, he discovered with a light touch.

She stirred. “I’m here,” he said, quiet as the night.

Her hair splayed across her face; he pulled it back to take in her breathtaking beauty. Pulled it back behind her ear, off her neck. Lips upon her ear brought a smile to her face. Next, he tasted her neck an inch below her ear, moving down with each kiss. Down to the unhealed gash in the back where her slender shoulder muscle turned upward into her neck. The tip of his tongue, held rigid, slipped into the wound, immediately followed by the sweet, coppery taste he sought as the blood flowed.

Her breast fit smaller in his hand than he remembered, the way they always do once the weight falls away. In his experience, smaller breasts are more sensitive, and by her response, coupled with his hungry sucking on her neck, drove her wild. Much the way her beauty and the sweetness of her essence gave him pleasure beyond his capacity to control.

It didn’t matter whether she slept or if he woke her. Once they reached this final stage, reality and dream merged as did sleep and waking. For him, these ultimate acts brought either joy or regret, depending how detached he remained or whether he carelessly allowed himself to become fond of his prey. Celeste gave him joy, the kind he had missed for so long.

He could take her tonight. Her body weakened and her spirit ready, and this one would do so willingly, even without the necessity of deceiving her. The sound of her moans changed, and halting breaths when she inhaled were all she had left to convey when her pleasure reached its crescendo. Desperate as he was for more, he stopped sucking so her bleeding slowed and stopped.

"How do you do that? I can't lift my head, but you did that to me."

"I need you to lift your head."

"I can't. Let me sleep; I'm so tired."

"You must. I won't leave you like this." Her body was limp as washed linen, so he rolled her onto her other side, her face falling into his lap in a position she would have found too irresistible to pass up only a week before. Once he opened his shirt, his thumbnail drove into his chest hard enough to tear his flesh. This is where he always started, the side where he felt no pain. Still unimaginable torture when he tore through the flesh of his nipple, but that is where blood flowed unrestrained.

"Here, you need to drink," he said, and pressed her lips against his bloody nipple. Her tongue licked a few times before she began weakly suckling his life blood. Within seconds, the power returned to her lips and tongue and she sucked ravenously from him. Pleasure grew in him, the way he stoked her passion, and he, too, grew limp, falling back upon the bed, holding the back of her head in place so she came with him. They ended up with her lying across his stomach, and he reached up inside her nightgown to grab hold of the tiny behind he adored so fiercely.

And he let her suckle long as she wanted, to delay the inevitable for as long as possible.

†

There are times when things fall beautifully into place; other times you need to create your own luck.

Eddie awoke late, still exhausted, half expecting to face Josette's barrage of question, if not her wrath. Instead, he found Celeste downstairs and brewing coffee. "How do you feel this morning?"

"Better today. Wish I could say the same of the girls."

"Oh? What's wrong?"

"They both took a turn for the worse last night. I'm worried about them."

Given her condition, such concern for the twins was commendable, although certainly predictable, from a mother. "And I'm worried about you," he said as he took a hot sip from the mug she set before him.

"What about you? You look puny, all pale and drawn."

"I'm fine. Really."

"That's what I said, and look at me? I couldn't drag myself out of bed yesterday."

"Well, you are better today." He blew across the top of the coffee before taking another sip. "Can we talk? I need to tell you something."

"Will it wait? The girls are waiting for me to bring them coffee and sit with them for a while. They're both freaking out a bit, which is totally understandable."

"Will you take them to the doctor?"

"They're both refusing to go. You know how they are when they get something in their heads. The doctor wasted a lot of my time and a few thousand dollars and we aren't any closer to understanding what's wrong with me."

"I'm sure they'll be fine," he said in support. "Don't forget to save some time for me today. It's important."

"Sure. If they're anything like me, they'll be asleep again soon," she answered. "It's strange how one day I'm feeling great, the next I'm wiped out."

"You'll be feeling better than ever soon enough," he predicted.

RAINING BLOOD

Exeter's second suicide in less than a month created a tremendous uproar.

With only five thousand residents of the town, both its limited size and close-knit community made the option of taking one's own life a rarity. A neighbor found her nude body in her tub filled with bloody, lukewarm water, one outstretched arm dangling over the side of the tub over a bloody knife on the floor.

Kelly Quinn was once considered the town beauty, but that was years ago. Forty-three years of poor choices take a mighty toll. Most of those poor choices involved her taste in men. One husband left her with a crooked nose, another with three kids and a mortgage no single mother of three toddlers could afford. One of her many boyfriends left a tattoo on her ass bearing his name she never could scrape together enough money to remove; the last one cost her the kids and seven years in state prison because he was her eleventh-grade student. The kid even admitted he initiated their affair, and that he made the videotape documenting one particularly felonious aspect of their relationship, but the law is the law, and considers statutory rape a big deal.

Male judges can be hard on female teachers who fulfill their students' wildest dreams, the same dreams those same judges relished back in high school.

The ruling of suicide was far from open and shut. Two witnesses saw her walking home with a guy who one described as drunk, the other as young enough to be her student. Death may well have saved her from a violation of the sex offender registry, if that second witness was to be believed.

There were other oddities, too. She slit her throat, a quite unusual method of suicide. And the tub contained an insufficient quantity of blood. The coroner explained that could have occurred if she drained bloody water from the tub then refilled it with clean water, a scenario so bizarre it left most people scratching their heads. Weird, but not impossible. The slash on the side of her neck wasn't severe, and easily survivable had she picked up her phone and dialed 911 rather than draw a fresh bath of clean water.

They checked the knife lying on the tile beneath her limp hand for fingerprints, but even though they did not find a single print on the knife, the detectives did not dust the rest of the apartment.

Sexual predator Kelly Quinn finally taking an early exit wasn't worth the time.

†

Celeste found him drinking a second cup of coffee on the porch, reading the paper. "Okay, let's talk."

"What is pica?" His question made her eyes bulge. After calming her that day, assuring her she was not mad, he never mentioned it again. Instead, he distracted her with a rather traditional—if extravagant—date. "If I'm with a crazy woman, don't I deserve a heads-up?"

"It's a mental illness that makes people eat things—things they aren't supposed to eat. Some people eat shit. Literally. Other things, too: hair, dirt, nails, ice. They feel some sort of compulsion. Some focus on one specific inedible thing to eat, while others are more omnivores. They can't help themselves."

"What's that got to do with you?"

"I've been having these dreams. They are so screwed up."

"How screwed up?"

"Jesus, Eddie—they are insane, okay?"

"Have you been eating shit?"

"In my dreams." She turned toward the house, looked around, then leaned toward him. "I have no idea where Bernie is and don't want him to overhear. In my dreams, I drink... blood."

"Okay..."

"Your blood. It's like we're having sex—then suddenly I am licking blood off your chest and sucking it from your tit."

"Celeste, there is an explanation for that."

"That's not even the half of it." Now whispering, she said, "I can't stop thinking about it. I enjoy it. I want it—all the time!"

"Come with me; I need to show you something. My room should give us some privacy."

†

Whether because, as twins, they were born with some psychic bond, or if pure coincidence, when one started coughing, the other immediately felt a cough come on. Each spell drained their bodies, their energy, and their spirits. And hurt, like a vicious sucker-punch to the gut, although only Josette had experienced a beating so severe, so only she remembered the sensation when her body ached afterward.

Rather than making that comparison, she turned to her sister's bed near the window. "And another bizarre thing about it, I had another of those dreams last night."

"That is strange; so did I. We've never both had one the same night, have we?"

"No, I'd remember that," Josette agreed.

"It's like we alternate nights when we have our sex dreams. That's freaking nuts, if you think about it. Why wouldn't we both have a dream on the same nights?"

"Damn it, now your ghost theory is starting to make sense. What if our ghost friend can only get his haunt on once a night?"

Angelique smirked. "Can you imagine how frustrating that would be to some ghost, only able to get it up once, then having to fade into wherever the hell it is ghosts go during the day?"

"Do ghosts even have dicks? I mean, what the hell? What purpose..." Josette could not finish before the twins fell out laughing, morphing in seconds into two more deep, soul-punching bouts of coughing. So painful and draining it took a few minutes to recover. They lay side by side in silence until Josette voiced another observation.

"Funny how we felt fine before we started having those dreams."

"Oh, wow! You're right! They started at the same time."

"Some diseases cause hallucinations. I think Malaria does. Fever—yellow, red or spotted or something."

"How can we both have the exact same hallucinations?"

"I'm not saying they're hallucinations. I'm just thinking out loud."

"I mean, it's real? Isn't it? How can it feel so real if it's only in our minds?"

"It can't be real. I'd wake your ass up with all the stuff we're doing over here."

Angelique asked, "Was your dream last night a threesome?"

"No! Lord. The closest we're ever coming to a threesome is that night we made out with Eddie. That son of a bitch!"

"Get that out of your head! He's not with our mom, okay? We'd know if they were. Mama can't keep something like that secret. And if it was going on the night of the wake, then they had to be together before that. Can you imagine Mama having an affair? No way. No way!"

"Well, I'm going to confront him. Look into his eyes when he denies it. If he's lying, his eyes will give him away."

They lay in contemplative silence for a few moments before Angelique asked, "Did you really have a dream last night?"

"So freaking weird!

†

He must be insane or she is, and if the latter, then for reasons her brain struggled to comprehend, he seized the opportunity to become her pica enabler. Either way, it was the craziest thing she very heard. Despite the spinning of her head, she paced angrily around the room. How can someone sit after hearing such lunacy?

"Do you expect me to believe I have been drinking your blood?"

"It's the truth."

"Why? Why would I drink blood? Why let me? And if it's true—and that I seriously doubt—why don't I remember it?"

"But you do remember it. What you thought were memories of dreams are, instead, actual memories. People often repress memories of events they find too disturbing to remember."

"Why didn't you say something about it until now?"

"How was I supposed to know what you remember and what you don't?"

Head thrown back to face the ceiling with hands clenched in front of her, she growled, "Argh!" Implications of what this meant raced through her brain, clouded by confusion, denial and anger. Eddie sitting there, so calm, didn't help. "How can you act so nonchalant while accusing me of being a goddamn vampire?"

"Keep your voice down." Eddie stood and gripped her upper arms firmly, yet with odd gentleness. "I never called you a vampire."

"Who drinks blood other than vampires? I notice you ignored answering why you let me drink your blood."

"Because you desire it—you need it. I'll give you anything, and if it means your life, my blood is a small sacrifice for you. You would do the same for me."

She shook herself loose and took a step back. "My god, you are insane! Here I am worried about my mental state when it turns out you are the one who is stark-raving mad!"

"I assure you, I am in full possession of my faculties."

The way her hair flew around as her head shook side to side resembled an adamant dog's ears shaking off when coming in from the rain, but he had no intention of making any such comparison out loud.

"No. No, no, no! Those are not sane words. No sane person has ever uttered those words, at least not in the order you arranged them."

To calm her, he reached for her, but she backed away to escape. "Will you believe me if I can prove it to you, in a way you cannot deny?"

"Is that what you think of me? That I'll believe that nonsense?"

All that exertion yelling, along with the stress and excitement, set off a round of coughing. Eddie tugged his polo shirt over his head, the undershirt coming with it, and jammed his thumb into his chest. To her utter horror, a stream of blood began flowing down his chest, tracing its way along the etched muscles of his stomach, the course altering to follow these contours until gravity pulled it downward again.

Her reaction to his unexpected self-mutilation confounded by its sheer irresistible, primal power. Much like falling, for the knowledge that she lacked the ability to arrest it terrified her even more. She lunged for him, her mouth encircling his wound, sucking his essence from him, aware as she did so that her actions condemned her as evil. The delicious sweetness of his blood clung to her feral tongue as it licked his beautiful gash, thrusting into it.

As she drank him, another sensation soon overwhelmed even her hunger and desire. The most profound pleasure. First as a spreading tingling, it grew exponentially, beyond her capacity to understand, the way the pleasure of sex or the despair of guilt defy rational description.

Fingernails dug into her scalp with increasing pressure as Eddie held her lips to his nipple. Wholly unnecessary, for she lacked the ability to stop, this primitive hunger having taken control of her being. Her will no longer mattered. Her tongue wildly lashed around the chest at spilled blood now smeared everywhere by her face.

Too soon, he pulled away, leaving her desire unfulfilled. She reached for him, fingertips touching around the wound, curiously no longer bleeding. A smear remained off to one side, which she wiped away and sucked from her finger. As he waited calmly, the feverish sensation of moments before faded with the pleasure in her core. One corner of his mouth lifted in that endearing way of his.

Eyes glowing an unnatural green, she whispered, "Oh, shit."

†

She took him on his bed, christening the guest room bed for the first time since his arrival a month before. His blood inside her stoked passions well beyond her usual lasciviousness. After so literally consuming him, she straddled the body she fed from and rode him hard, bracing herself with one hand on his chest, over a wound from which even her weight leaning upon, rocking desperately, drew no more blood now. Besides, he deserved a reward for awakening her in such a way, right?

His skin—always pale—had taken on an extreme, ashen tone. The color of George's face when she identified him in the medical examiner's office that night.

"Oh, my god," she said as she flopped down beside him once satiated, "that was pure animal!"

"Was pretty amazing, wasn't it?"

"I have some questions."

"And I will answer them."

"I'm a vampire?"

"Not yet. It's hard enough for me to understand, let alone explain. The way I figure it, you are becoming. It takes death for you to turn into a vampire—does that make sense?"

"No, but nothing has made sense for the last hour." Her eyes bore into his. "The girls?"

"Yes."

She took this bit of news much more sanguine than he expected. "Why?"

"Not bringing them along with you seemed too great a risk. I didn't plan it, but when I started imagining the two of us living in the house with them without their catching on? They are smart girls, so it seemed the only thing to do."

"You should have told me."

"I know. And you would have said no, leaving me with no choice but to deceive you. This was the only way."

"Bernie?"

"No, I haven't touched him."

"Thank goodness!" After a long exhale, her expression changed from relief to near panic. "Please tell me you haven't been screwing my girls, too."

"No, I give you my word."

"I'm supposed to take the word of a guy who fifteen seconds ago confessed he plans to kill me?"

"It's not about sex. This is so far beyond sex. Not that morality makes any sense anymore—which you'll soon understand. Now that you know, your mind will start asking questions that are unanswerable within the framework you have constructed over a lifetime. Your needs will overwhelm your sense of morality."

"How many?"

"How many what?"

"Women. How many have you turned into vampires?"

"None. You are my first."

Shock showed on her face. "But..."

"Believe me, I have tried. Every time it failed. So many times, until it dawned on me one day that the reason must lie in our genes. The Brown family curse they speak of."

"How do you know it will work?"

"It is working already. Tonight you saw it with your own eyes. You have the hunger. The bloodlust. No one else has ever had it like you do."

And Eddie hoped it was true. Before, when he sought to bestow this precious gift on other women he dared to love, each time ended in failure.

Every one of those women died. Eddie killed them.

†

They awoke as in a dream.

The twins saw each other first, having heard a noise, a voice in the dark calling out to them, only to see their doppelgänger as a shadow in their own bed. Angelique asked, "did you say something?"

"No..."

"I did."

At the end of their beds stood a form in the dark, moonlight passing through the window upon his torso, leaving the head and legs but shadows. Even so, they knew it was him.

Josette rubbed her face. "What are you doing here? Is everything okay?"

"I have what you need." Eddie unbuttoned his crisp, Oxford-cloth shirt, yanking the tucked tail from his jeans to reach the last button. As they watched, he dug his thumb into the left side of his chest, over his heart. Although the dim light took all traces of color, the trickle running down his chest left no doubt it was blood. Had he waited long enough? "This is for you."

Their faces, in deep shadow, pale circles under hair also colorless and dark, any expression hidden in their hesitation. Angelique moved first, leaning forward from where she sat, then crawling across her mattress. Toward him. Seconds later, with a shake of her long curls, Josette mirrored her sister. They resembled two cats stalking prey by moonlight. And Eddie was their prey.

Dressed in a black silk camisole and matching lacy boy-shorts, Angelique created a more dangerous appearance, albeit a distinct form of danger. Copper curls draped across black fabric as she crawled through a moonbeam formed a mane. The image of a big cat, part tiger, part lion. Next to her sister, wearing pink turned white by the moonlight, Josette more closely resembled a domesticated cat—adorable, but no less deadly to a mouse.

The tiger struck first. One hand reached out, grasping his belt, fingers curling inside the waistband of his jeans to pull him toward her. Had he resisted, her slight form and featherlight weight stood no chance, but Eddie came as an offering, seeking no escape.

The heaviest flow reaching almost to his waist and descending rapidly, her tongue lapped up the lead drop the entire distance to his ribs in one long, salacious lick. Taking advantage of the opportunity, Josette came from the side straight at his bloody nipple, sucking while her tongue massaged it. Her sister's tongue continued toward the source, in shorter, more careful licks while her hand felt the front of his pants. Her eyes met his through her sister's mop of hair falling across her face, pupils so distended her eyes appeared black.

Angelique's tongue licked along the edge of her sister's face where it pressed against Eddie's chest. Then he felt Josette's head being nudged aside. He ran his fingers through the locks of the tiger and caressed her face. "Let her finish." Knowing the madness had taken hold, though, he took the hand from his chest and placed her index finger into his mouth and began sucking. Instantaneously, Angelique pulled back and moaned, her body falling limp across her bed.

With one hand holding the back of Josette's head, the other holding her tiny round bum almost covered by a G-string and her sister's finger deep in his mouth, he sucked in blood while it flowed from his breast. Pleasure too intense to bear overtook his entire being, and the only reason he remained upright on shaky legs was Josette steadying him, his hand gripping her ass to hold them both up. Even the strongest oak will fall when the wind blows hard enough, and Eddie had never experienced pleasure comparable to this.

Together, they collapsed to the floor. Incredibly, despite the jarring impact, he somehow did not bite off the finger in his mouth. In all his many years, Eddie never had experienced two women at the same time. Not in this way. One twin fed from him while he fed upon her double. Although he had never indulged in either, he imagined it must be like a simultaneous trip on acid and heroin, two distinctly novel sensations, each overwhelming in its own way. Josette landed atop him with his head cranked against the side of the bed. A thumb and three fingers moved across his cheeks.

"Let your sister take a turn."

Josette complied with the obedience of a well-trained soldier taking orders from a general. Over him as he swept a handful of curls back, Eddie shoved her back toward the bed, rolling her while her sister slunk like the predator she had become, off the mattress onto him. Quickly spreading Josette's knees around him, her sister hit with sufficient force to drive him against the edge of the bed. Blood spurted down his chest the moment Josette's lips let go, and now her sister licked the flow much as she did before.

As her tongue penetrated inside the wound, his head lay upon Josette's thigh as a warm pillow. Her other knee he pushed farther away, then allowed himself to sigh as his blood flowed from him into Angelique's warm and hungry mouth.

In the dark, the skin of her inner thigh so pale he could not see any blemishes, but he smelled her. In a motion every bit as aggressive as when her sister hit his chest seconds before, he latched ravenous lips onto that luscious thigh two inches below panties colorless as her skin.

Warm, fragrant blood oozed from the slice in her thigh into his mouth, coating his tongue and teeth. A few quick, deep flicks of his tongue got it flowing well, his fingers squeezing her flesh like a baby at his mother's breast. As he did, fingers reached inside his pants and gripped him most pleasantly. Head spinning from ecstasy and loss of blood increased the rapture to its breaking point. Moans mixed into an erotic symphony. It was as if every nerve in his body simultaneously received stimulation beyond the capacity of any man or beast to withstand. It wasn't his orgasm to the willful fingers inside his jeans; indeed, perhaps two more minutes of insufferable bliss passed until he climaxed.

His lips let go of Josette's skin and his head fell into her lap, his ear upon warm silk, her body pulsating from rapid, deep hyperventilation. Angelique resisted at first, but he pushed her face more forcefully. "Enough," he pleaded, and she relented to his command. She also limply melted, her breath warm on his chest.

When the first light of dawn lit the room, the three were still in the same positions.

†

"Your mother is asking for you. She is very weak."

Three faces turned to him as he walked into the living room to deliver the news. A mournful chirping from Bernie's handheld video game held his full attention.

"Is she okay?" asked Josette.

"She will be fine. This next part, though, it will be the most difficult," Eddie explained.

"We need to talk about last night," Angelique purred.

"And we will, after you go see your mother."

Bernie stomped by, the twins dawdled, waiting for their chance to have a moment alone with him. Josette drew her arms tightly across her chest, while Angelique passed close, her hand on his leg. Close enough to feel the breath of her words on his face. "You will tell us, though, won't you, cousin?"

"In due time."

"You owe us an explanation; that was the most fucked-up dream I've—we've ever had," Josette said, her voice sad and disbelieving, knowing full well one does not wake up from a dream piled up with the people from the dream. Not to mention, her sister awakening with the precise details burned into her memory.

Of the family crowded around Celeste's bed, Bernie's emotions burst forth most unrestrained. If he noticed the others, he did not let on. A tear ran down his cheek, which he smeared on his sleeve before anyone noticed. "How are you feeling, Mama?"

"Tired," she said, forcing a pleasant smile.

"You look so—amazing! It's hard to believe you are sick at all," said Angelique.

"Oh, stop. I must look like hell."

"No, she's totally right," Josette agreed. "You look ten years younger. No lie."

Indeed, it was no lie. Her skin glowed a lovely color, if pale. Those wrinkles, her constant source of annoyance she fought against armed with expensive creams, simply had vanished. The rash disappeared from her chest days before.

Eddie agreed, rubbing her shoulder in a friendly, if overly familiar, way. "They're telling the truth. Soon as you're back on your feet, people will assume there are three Brown sisters."

Any changes in her skin tone failed to impress Bernie. "Don't you think you should go to the doctor? The ER?"

"Oh, no." She gripped his hand. "I'll be fine. Anemia causes fatigue. Eddie promised to go shopping for some iron-rich food, didn't you, honey?"

Before anyone commented on the term of endearment, he answered, "Spinach, beef, sweet potatoes—I made up a list."

"Isn't he a sweetie?" The twins' eyes narrowed in response.

"Maybe I'll go now and let you all have some time together."

He almost made it to the car when the screen door

slammed shut, Josette close behind. "What the hell was that? Honey? Sweetie? Are you screwing my mother? And what happened last night? Did you slip Ecstasy into our drinks or what?"

"I didn't give you drugs."

"Then how do you explain what...? It wasn't a dream. I woke up with your head lying on my lap! Your drool all over my panties, and my sister holding you like a pillow! What the hell happened?"

"I will explain everything. Now, go inside and be with your mother. She is going to be fine, but she is very, very sick."

"Don't push me away like that! I cannot get those images out of my head. If it wasn't drugs, how do you explain it?"

His eyes penetrated her like a knife, glowing like the sun lit them, even though it was behind him. For an instant, she swayed on flimsy knees. Eddie reached one finger to her, touching her lips firmly yet with a gentleness.

"Shhh. There is nothing to remember. It was only a dream. Remember waking up in your bed, alone?" A slow nod of his head, which she mirrored, he kept his finger on her lips, pulling the full, pale lower one down. "Stay with your mother. She needs your support until she gets better. It will get worse before it gets better; it always does. Go, now. I'll buy some red wine and tonight, you, your sister and I will talk."

"Okay."

His finger lifted, and he smiled. "Don't worry. Everything will be fine."

She was still watching as he set off down the bumpy drive toward the road.

†

The concerned expression of other shoppers passing by as he wheeled his cart through the aisles of A&P made him worry Celeste's blood must be splattered all over his shirt. He glanced down to make sure.

That is the reason he preferred to feed in the nude. Well, one reason. Not the tiniest speck, far as he could see. Both forearms bracing to lean heavily on the handle forced him to bend over like an elderly man—that must explain it. Of course, he had no way of knowing the harsh, florescent light cast his ashen skin tone a light blue tint, nor how his limp facial muscles drooped.

First making his way to the meat cooler, where he stocked up with ground beef, a pot roast and a package of bloody stew meat before filling the basket with half the spinach in the vegetable section. Up and down each aisle, he read the nutritional information on cans and boxes. Each time he stopped, blood pooled at the bottom of the white plastic tray holding two pounds of cubed stew beef caught his eye through clear cellophane, and he had to force himself to concentrate on something else. While reading the label of a can of soup, the letters faded, indistinct and dancing around. The surrounding shelves closed in, his vision narrowed to a tunnel. His head felt light as the first time he drank alcohol and the floor pitched wildly.

The next thing he remembered was waking up in an unfamiliar place, closed-in and claustrophobic. A mask over his nose and mouth obscured part of his field of vision. A dark, youthful face appeared over him as he tried to pull the mask off his face. "Hold tight, buddy—you're okay. I'm Kelvin and you are in my ambulance. We've got you."

"No, I've got to go."

"Hang on now, just stay there. It's oxygen. You passed out in the A&P, so we're taking you to the ER to be checked out."

"You don't understand. Where is my food? I need those things in my cart."

"Shopping will wait until later," Kelvin said, by this point physically pinning Eddie to the gurney. Not yet strapped in, Eddie grabbed one of his wrists with a powerful grip. "Alright, let go. I'm here to take care of you. Just relax and let me do my job.

Despite his best efforts, the EMT lacked the strength to hold Eddie down. In a flash, he was on his feet, tossing the mask onto the empty gurney. “It’s low blood pressure. Sometimes it happens to me. I will be fine.”

“I’m afraid I must insist on taking you to the hospital so they can check you out to be sure. You’re a young dude—young dudes don’t pass out like that.”

“Here, I am checking myself out. Refusing medical assistance—write it up any way you want.” He shoved two hundred-dollar bills into Kelvin’s hand. “That should cover my bill. Keep the change.”

Inside the store, the assistant manager had pushed the buggy aside, but had yet to restock the items on the shelves. Eager to avoid any further problems disrupting the other shoppers, the assistant manager waved him to an idle cash register and checked Eddie’s items out himself. The sooner this guy is out of the store, the sooner things will get back to normal.

Outside, Eddie stuffed handfuls of spinach and half a package of raw hamburger into his mouth before starting the car for the drive home.

TAINTED LOVE

Neither possessed their usual energy. Nonetheless, making love to her retained the same intensity and power as ever. Perhaps more poignant now, since this likely was the last time they would. Her face pressed into the pillow and obscured by long strands of hair sticking to the sweat on her cheeks and forehead, a compulsion to see her face drove him to pull the unruly, damp locks back behind her ear. Eyes closed and mouth opened, she gasped with each thrust. He did, too.

Every inch of her was beautiful. Muscles rippled in her back and shoulders, muscles which, like the regular, undulating humps of her spine, were barely visible a month ago. Now she had the back of a teenager—the tight skin, smooth, pale and aglow, the narrow waist she had two decades before. Same with her tight ass, but he could not see it wedged against his hips as it was, driving with his rhythm. Hair in need of adjusting, again covering the slit through the otherwise perfect, unblemished skin if her neck. Once the blood resumed its flow, he again drank. Their moans rose in volume and meaning from the burgeoning pleasure.

When came her time to feed from him, he wished his wound lay in a spot higher on his body—shoulder or neck—somewhere her mouth could reach with her mounted upon him while their bodies united. Her slow, laconic movements lacked her usual exuberance, and although now skinny as her daughters, she carried that weight on the arms braced against his chest. One finger traced across his scar, hair falling around her face while staring at his nipple intently as he watched the alluring swaying of hers.

The moment he came, those absinthe eyes pleaded with him, her tongue sweeping across her upper lip, so he pulled open his wound. With surprising speed, she struck, her lips enveloping his chest, cheeks pulling inward as she sucked deeply from him, drawing blood from him even before her own blood replenished it. Louder than when he climaxed seconds before, he moaned so emphatically she covered his mouth with one palm to stifle it. An encouraging sign of emerging awareness in the throes of bloodlust.

His hand caressed the delightful curves of her body, possessing her as she possessed him, sharing far greater intimacy than the mortal love they shared moments before. Never again would a man see her this way or enjoy this woman's body as he had. She turned to him, pale pink lips stained red, more smeared on one cheek. "Where is it?"

"Where is what?"

"Blood. It's not coming out like it always does."

He pulled her off, rolling her onto her back beside him. "That's all for tonight."

Before they fell asleep, he kissed his blood from her lips.

†

It didn't take long to corner Eddie alone and out of earshot of the rest of the family the following morning. With a ferocious scowl and eyes narrowed to mere slits, Angelique charged at him in the kitchen. "You owe us an explanation about two nights ago. When we got back from school, the fridge was full and you were gone. What did you do, sneak back in during the middle of the night?"

"I had things to do. At least I left enough beef stew going in the Crock Pot to feed everyone."

Relentless, she continued. "What the hell happened the night before?"

"What do you remember?"

"What we both remember is sucking..." Angelique

stopped, aware her voice had risen precipitously both in pitch and volume, lowering it to a harsh whisper, "sucking blood from your tit."

"I don't really have tits," he answered with a smirk.

"You know exactly what she means," said Josette. "By the way, you look like shit."

"Thanks."

"That's it? Aren't you going to answer our questions?"

"You owe us an explanation," snarled Angelique.

"I owe you an explanation about what you did?"

Jaw falling agape, Josette said, "You asshole!"

With menacing slowness, he stopped inches from her, glaring down. "What are you accusing me of doing? Have I forced you to do anything? Did I even ask you? The way I recall it, I was standing there with an open wound when both of you started lapping up my blood before I could say a word." Neither twin spoke, and Josette backed off when he took another step toward her. "Well? What do you want me to explain?"

"You can tell us what was going on, because that shit isn't normal. Maybe to you it is, but we aren't some mysterious 'cousin' who shows up at our doorstep before all sorts of weird shit starts happening."

"Damn it, Eddie," Angelique chimed in, "need we point out that we come from the most famous family of vampires in this state's history? There you are, creeping around our room in the dark of night, bleeding everywhere, then just let us suck it out of you?"

"It felt like we had no control, like..."

"Like you knew what we were going to do when we saw your blood."

"What if I did know? How can some guy you just met understand things about you that you did not know about each other? Or yourselves?"

The twins were the image of one girl gazing at a reflection of herself in a mirror. Angelique's lips moved in an unspoken question her sister appeared to understand. Then she turned her attention to him. "What do you know about us?"

"Your true nature."

She answered, "Are you saying we are..."

Unable to say the word, Josette completed her question. "Vampires?"

"No, you are not vampires. But it is in your nature—in your blood, so to speak."

Exasperation on her face, Josette asked, "What does that even mean? We're not vampires, but it is our nature to be vampires?"

"Stop speaking in damn riddles and tell us what is happening to us!"

"Walk with me." Without another word, Eddie strode out the kitchen door.

†

Clouds filled the daytime sky, trapping beneath them air dank and oppressively hot. It bore all the earmarks of one of those days which blow in strong winds, yet the air hangs still until the front arrives. The girls followed him across the farm, not quite hurrying yet with a purposeful, long stride that left them struggling to keep up. Not once did he turn or check to confirm they were following, but bore a direct path through rows of Christmas trees a year or more shy of harvesting. Remnants of an orchard more than a hundred years old, the last apples, pears and cherries surviving from the old farm. Ahead lay the edge of the property and the pond where the three drank and shared truth. Where they first kissed.

"Sit." Eddie motioned to a high patch of grass interspersed with scattered wildflowers and waited for the twins to sit before he did. "No one must know what I am about to tell you. Should anyone get wind of this, all of us will be in great danger. You and your mother, as well as me."

"Okay." The girls nodded in unison.

"What some call curse may be a blessing to others. In our blood, we Browns carry this curse. We cannot deny it any more than we can escape it. Long ago, I discovered how to turn this into something wonderful. With no guiding hand, I have made my share of mistakes—too many to count, I'm afraid. Then a theory occurred to me. That night two nights ago, you proved my theory true—far as it is possible to tell."

Nonplussed, Angelique gawked at him. "What the hell are you talking about?"

"The blood. Ours. Yours—the Brown blood. It carries a corruption. Think of your family, your ancestors, those you've known or been told about. What do these people have in common?"

With a roll of her eyes, Josette quipped, "What, besides being really screwed up?"

"Not 'besides'. Untimely death, suicide, strange disappearances. The drinking, the drugs. How many ended up institutionalized for mental illness? Two of your grandparents, your Uncle William. Not to mention the DKC flowing through your veins," he turned to Josette, "and how long do you think it will take before it shows up in your sister, too?"

That had the desired effect on the girls. "What is this curse, and how did you change it?"

"What it is I cannot say; what it *does*, however, is to drive those who fight against it into madness. Our blood needs blood. The inability to harness it drives some to take their own lives or murder or drives them mad trying to suppress it." Directly addressing Josette, he said, "Why do you cut yourself?"

"It seems like the thing to do."

"A compulsion? An urge you cannot control?" A slow nod confirmed it. "A desire for blood, one you were unable to comprehend, so you acted upon it the only way you know how. Rather than drawing the blood of others, you draw your own."

Josette averted her lovely violet eyes. Both deep in

thought, he allowed them to contemplate before continuing. "How did it feel to feed upon my blood?"

"Better than sex," answered Angelique.

"Do you want more?"

First giving her sister a questioning glance, she said, "Are you offering us your blood?"

"Yes."

Josette remained more skeptical. "Have you done this with Mama?"

"Yes. She was the first. Then I came to the two of you."

Angelique cracked a wicked grin. "So we are vampires?"

"In a way. Don't ask how it works, because I cannot be certain. Far as I can tell, it lies latent inside of us until triggered when your blood is taken by another. Then you must pass through stages. You are in what seems to be the second stage, where you have consumed blood." While he spoke, he unbuttoned his polo shirt and peeled it over his head.

After listening to this with brow furrowed, Josette asked, "So it was true?"

Not following, her sister asked, "What is true?"

"Mercy Brown—she truly was a vampire, wasn't she?"

In a deep, reverent voice, Eddie answered, "Yes she was."

To no one's surprise, this intrigued Angelique. "Does this mean we will become immortal?" Eddie answered with a nod, so she continued, "Is the way they killed her the only way you can die?"

"As far as I know. If the entire body is destroyed—by fire, for example—I suppose that might work, too."

Looking down at her finger, Angelique poked around the still-unhealed slice. "So you weren't blowing my finger?"

"That is the wound you feed me from." Fingers pried open the wound on his chest, sending a small trickle running toward his stomach. "Feed from me; then I will feed from you."

Already crawling across his lap, Josette began licking the trickle of blood from his skin. Her sister hurried to join her, and with their cheeks pressed together, they both sucked from the long gash in his flesh.

†

The withering took place before their eyes. Only hours passed since they made love, and in that time Celeste's flame dimmed so severely, lifting her head an inch off the pillow became too much for her.

Regardless how well you prepare, death's toll is excruciating. No matter how many times Eddie had seen death —had caused it—this tore at his gut more painfully than the others. Over these weeks, the fondness he developed for her was deep and true. A bond. Never before had he killed a member of his family, a fact that gnawed more deeply than expected. Celeste was a decent woman. Another departure. How much easier to kill a stranger, or one deserving of death.

For this reason, what her remaining days and hours held were unknown, a terrible mystery. An exquisitely painful one.

The twins tried to put on a brave face, but the tears flowed as they watched the light in their mother dim. However, Bernie took it by far the worst, though he bore it bravely, sitting on the edge of the bed holding her hand for hours on end. More shocking, he chatted with her constantly, comforting and assuring, even retelling favorite family stories. This kid had pro potential.

"Remember that time you took us shopping at Apex over in Pawtucket and you lost the car in the parking lot? You had us searching up and down every aisle, the girls in one, while you dragged me along by the hand down the row next to it."

"Oh, how can I forget that?"

"And the whole time, the car was on the far side of the building! Not one of us remembered what entrance we went in."

"You are the one who wanted to go shopping there," his mother gasped through the laughter. "You wanted me to take you shopping at the pyramid, as you called it."

“Well, I sure got a good look at it, wandering around and around that pyramid for an hour.” He had all four in stitches, and in one hour spoke more than the total of what Eddie heard the kid say in a month.

Their occupied attention afforded Eddie a chance to slip out. Better let the closest family comfort her. All those years of killing have a way of dulling the senses, but another woman dying in this house which had seen so much death touched raw, long-buried nerves. Besides, although there may be nothing worse than a grieving mother, grieving children are too close for any sense of comfort.

The Brown kids barely noticed he’d gone.

Although intending to walk to the pond at the far edge of the farm, Eddie never made it that far. About halfway there, as he passed through the remnants of the old fruit grove, his head began to swim. Again, like in A&P, his vision of what lay directly ahead narrowed to a tunnel, everything in the periphery disappearing from sight. What little he saw drifted away, fading into the void. Remembering his episode of syncope in the store and desperate to avoid a repeat, he staggered to the century-old apple tree to his right and collapsed against the trunk.

“Maybe if I rest here for a minute.” He sank to the mossy ground around the roots, where he drifted off to sleep.

Back at the house, the telephone rang several times during the day. No one answered it.

†

A deep dusk had fallen by the time Eddie awoke under the tree. Still light enough to make out where he was, albeit only for a few more minutes, until night’s full embrace left the farm in darkness, moonrise still several hours away. He never made it to the pond, returning, instead, to the farmhouse. The front of the house was dark, the kitchen unlit, the only lights burning came from the bedrooms upstairs.

The moment he entered the kitchen, he knew. In the living room, the room pitch black with all lights out, a low, harsh voice spoke. "There he is. Had to wait until dark to show your face?"

He flicked the wall switch to see the twins sitting in the dark. One stood and approached him, slowly at first, but lunging the last few steps to pound his chest with hammer fists.

"This is your fault, isn't it? You killed her!"

He did nothing to stop her blows, allowing her frustration to rain down through her fists. Only then did he take her in his arms and pull her to him, where she sobbed against his chest, hands still balled into fists against him.

"She's gone, then?"

"You promised us she wouldn't die," said Josette, standing behind her sister.

"She was supposed to live forever," Angelique snarled, struggling against his arms. "That's what you told us, and we believed you. We must be idiots to believe anything so foolish!"

"Take me to her."

Josette took a step back. "We haven't called anyone, like you told us."

"What about Bernie? Did you do what we discussed?"

"Yes, we gave him one of Mama's Xanax like we were supposed to. Turned him out like a light."

Angelique pulled away to follow her twin up the stairs. Eddie came last. Celeste lay on her bed, peaceful, hands crossed over her stomach, eyes closed. A vision of pure beauty. Other than the waxy gray tone of her skin, she might have been asleep.

The twins stood with elbows hooked together, two lost little girls. Angelique said, "What are we supposed to do now?"

He answered, "Let me think."

Had he taken too much blood? This is not how she was supposed to go. Progress of her illness far too rapid, as if she willed herself to go, refusing to fight. Surrendered. Attempting to prepare all three Brown women simultaneously may have been a fatal error, leaving insufficient blood to fulfill her needs as well as his own. Under the sheet, her body appeared so shrunken, so delicate and frail; her face was so taciturn and lovely.

"What are we supposed to do now?"

"We can't just leave her lying there."

"*Live forever*, you said. *Beautiful forever. Never to grow old.* And we believed that crap!"

"Give me a minute," the bed groaning under his weight as he sat on the corner beside the twin bulges of her feet, head in hands. "Let me think, just let me think."

Drained and fatigued, his brain struggled to conjure up a coherent thought. Images cut through the fog, only to fade beyond his reach back into it. Exhaustion sapped his body and his mind. Josette paced the room like a caged predator, from one side of the bed around the foot to the other side, wearing a horseshoe pattern, while her sister stared through the window into the grim black outside. If only he could think!

"Angelique, please put that Crock Pot of stew on to warm up. And bring a bottle of Cabernet up. Three glasses."

"Get it yourself!"

"That's the thing—I can't." She turned with a scowl, so he added, "Please?"

Her sister stood to leave with her, but he stopped her. "Josette, will you stay? I need you for a minute." While footsteps faded down the hall, she stood in front of him with arms clenched as a shield in front of her. He reached for her, pulling her a reluctant step toward him with a hand behind her waist, which he lowered to caress the curve of her bottom. "Take off your pants."

Face blank with terror yet helpless to resist, she complied, and he lay on the floor with her, again taking her bum in his hand and pulled her forward, lifting one leg and planting her foot beside him. He kissed the soft inside of her thigh, his tongue locating the gash, opening it, allowing the blood to flow into his mouth as he sucked life from her body.

PART II

This Mortal Coil

"Dear beauteous death! The jewel of the just
Shining nowhere but in the dark;
What mysteries do lie beyond the dust,
Could man outlast that mark!"
Henry Vaughan

HUNGRY LIKE THE WOLF

Under an early morning fog, Eddie dug deep into the rocky soil. Every time his foot drove the spade into the earth produced a familiar, telltale scraping sound of steel upon granite. Every second or third shovelful, he stopped to rest on the handle, laboring for breath, steadying his spinning head. Sweat stung his eyes, so he smeared his sleeve across his forehead to wipe it away, leaving behind a smear of brown.

Josette's long curls drifted in the breeze as she approached the pleasant spot next to a stump in the old orchard where he dug. "Need some help?"

"No, I've got it."

"Bernie should be doing this."

"If he misses baseball practice, his coach will start asking questions. He must maintain his usual routine. What if one of his teammate's parents shows up here checking to see if he is okay?"

As he leaned against the shovel, its tip stuck into the soil, Josette looked him over, shaking her head in disapproval. "You look like hell."

"I'll live." Once again, he stepped on the shovel to drive it in.

She sneered at him. "You sure about that?"

"I'm not sure about much of anything anymore."

"Are you sure this is necessary?"

"Honestly?" he leaned against the handle again. "I have

no bloody clue. It's been forty-eight hours. Soon, Bernie is going to start asking questions we cannot answer. You sure we can trust him to keep quiet?"

The look of disbelief she gave him in response needed no explanation, but she put it into words. "Have you met my brother?"

"Yeah, but his mother died. How long can we keep him in the dark about that?"

She shrugged, glancing back at the house. "How much longer?"

She was no longer speaking about her brother. "Your guess is as good as mine. Literally."

With a pitiful expression and shaking her head again, she said, "Maybe you should have some more?" She turned out her leg to offer her inner thigh. The shorts she wore hung low enough to conceal her cuts, but loose enough for easy access to feed.

Now was his turn to shake his head. "I've already fed. Look at you—bet you weigh under a hundred pounds. We need to be careful."

"Isn't that sweet? You really care, don't you?" Voice dripping with vicious sarcasm, she gave him a smirk. "I guess accidentally killing my mom is the sort of lesson to make a guy more careful in the future."

"This isn't a science. You know how awful I feel about this. I was sure she would come back." Josette gave the shallow hole meant to be her mother's grave a look, then her eyes burned into his soul—assuming he had one.

"Kill my sister and I swear, I will find a way to kill you."

As she trudged back to the house, he noticed how great she still looked, even if those shorts fit baggy now. Then he shoveled more earth and rock from her mother's grave.

†

"Holy shit! Come here—hurry!"

One twin called from the porch urging him on, but after hours excavating a trench four feet deep through soil and rock, he maintained his own pace, the best he could manage. From this distance the girls were impossible to tell apart, their voices similar as their appearance, but he had the distinct impression Angelique summoned him. A wave, then quickening his step. Memory of what Josette wore hours earlier when she came outside had disappeared in the fog, other than they both had donned black tops since their mother's death. Luckily, their wardrobes contained plenty of black clothes, since it emphasized the brilliant orange of their curls against the dark fabric.

"Get your ass in gear—you've got to see this!"

Heavy feet thudded up the stairs. Pleased to find his guess was accurate, Angelique yanked him by the wrist. "She moved!"

Upstairs, her sister stood vigil over the bed where their mother's body lay. When they came in, she shook her head. "Nothing."

"I swear she moved."

Porcelain hands still crossed over her stomach where the girls placed them, her face the same color as her placid hands. Still, Eddie's heart raced. "What exactly did she do?"

"She jerked. Like her whole body convulsed. If not for the fact that she didn't make a sound, you'd swears she sneezed."

After hearing the excitement in her voice, this description came as a blow to the gut. Not a hand reaching out or eyes opening or lips moving, trying to speak. Profound disappointment showed on his face. "They say bodies can move after death. Decomposition, gas building up—could be anything."

"That isn't what she did."

A far different argument Josette raised had merit. "Then explain why she isn't decomposing? Look at her! She hasn't looked this good in years. Perfect skin if—you know—pale."

Angelique made another observation. "Does she look

bloated by disgusting gasses to you? See how skinny she is? Josette's right: she looks incredible." To prove her point, she jerked down the sheet that covered her body to her hands. At first, it had covered her face, too, but everyone decided she looked much creepier shrouded like a corpse than lying there dead and uncovered. Involuntarily, the motion of tearing the sheet off her drew all eyes to her cold, lifeless form.

Celeste's eyes opened. First blinking in an effort to focus as all three gasped, then massively expanded pupils surrounded by a thin ring of brilliant emerald went around the room, pausing on each person there. Strange eyes like this he had seen only once. Eddie and the girls stood frozen, Angelique with a hand-tent over her mouth. Tentative and low, she asked, "Mama?"

†

Penrod's is a nondescript dive two blocks from the nearest frat houses on Brown's campus in Providence. Nothing more than a brick front wedged between a bookstore and a head shop. Chipped black paint on the front door allowed green and red to poke through, vestiges of prior incarnations. Windows also painted black, creating an impression ominous enough to discourage the timid from venturing inside.

Few heads turned to the front door when it opened, but those that did followed the couple who entered. Swiveling heads following them, attention redirected from beer pints or conversations. Most ignored the guy, other than to notice he looked out of place as an undertaker at a wedding reception, dressed all in black—suit, shirt and tie, although the scattered female patrons approved. All attention focused on the woman —including most of the female patrons.

Teased blonde hair flowed past her shoulders. Dressed in black tights under an over-sized sweater of antique gold with a massive neck hole dangling off one bare shoulder and just long enough to come tantalizingly close to flashing a butt-cheek with each step, perhaps a few years older than the Brown University coeds who sometimes drank here in groups with their frat buddies. Unlike most women who wore such stylishly gigantic sweaters, this woman did not choose her wardrobe to hide a few extra pounds.

Roger Box said to his buddy John, "She could use a tan, but otherwise, can you find anything wrong with her?"

"Fuckin' A," John replied.

"Let's go with an A+," Roger said as the couple sat at a table in the back. "Do you suppose they are together? She looks a little older than him."

"Who cares? He's not big enough to hold on to a fox that hot." John downed his backwash and slapped the pint glass on the table.

How neck hole flopped when she moved, slid down to a few inches above one elbow as she sat, Roger imagined the best angle to catch a good view of the show. From the looks of it, either close beside that bare shoulder or standing above her would do nicely. With his longneck bottle of Narragansett beer in one hand and John tailing close behind, Roger made his way across the bar.

"Don't believe we've met. I'm Roger and this is John." He extended his hand toward the woman.

Just enough sexy muscle flexed under her pale shoulder and upper arm, which she raised to take his hand, like a woman who religiously Jazzercized. "Don't believe we have. Celeste, and this is my cousin, Eddie."

Her emphasis on the word cousin relaxed Roger a bit. Up close, the kid appeared more formidable, but with a baby face unscarred by fighting. Still, while he knew he could take him, now there was no need for that form of exercise. "Not kissing-cousins, I hope?"

"Eddie, don't say a word," Celeste answered, laughing even harder than Roger did at his own joke.

Dragging a chair from the empty table alongside, he asked, "Mind if we join you?"

"Be my guest."

"Are you two from around here?"

"Eddie's from out west, so I'm showing him around town. All the fun things to do, where we can get into a little trouble, you know."

"Well, if you want trouble, this is the place to go," Roger quipped. John sat observing, the way he always did in his role as wing-man. "What sort of trouble did you have in mind?"

The woman had the most remarkable eyes. The color of Heineken bottles. So gorgeous they momentarily distracted him from his goal of looking down her sweater. Remembering the blonde kid across the table, he asked, "What kind of work do you do, Ed?"

"Oh, you know, nothing much. Taking time off from school. What about you, Rog?" Was that an innocent smile or a smirk? Hard to tell, so Roger ignored it and answered to Celeste as if she'd asked.

"We are steelworkers. Did you see that building under construction a couple of blocks down? We're working up on the girders on the fourteenth floor."

"Okay, I have a question about that," Celeste said. "When you are building a skyscraper that tall, do they have a thirteenth floor? Because whenever you get on an elevator, once the building is finished, there never is a thirteenth floor."

"No, when we're building them, it's just the actual numbers. We don't worry about bad luck and all."

"They don't want to confuse them. Right, Roger? Trying to keep that all straight would be awfully hard."

Roger glared at him. "What are you implying?"

Eddie scooped up a handful of peanuts from the bowl on the table and smirked. "Oh, nothing."

After that, Roger pretended Eddie was furniture. After allowing Roger to go on for a few minutes, soon he'd seen enough. "It's probably time we should think about going, Celeste."

"Are you sure? Can't we stay a little longer?"

“I’m sure,” he slid back his chair in emphasis.

“Ed, feel free to run along. If Celeste wants to stay, we’ll take good care of her. Won’t we, John?”

“Sure will,” he helpfully agreed.

Now on his feet, Eddie extended his hand across the table, which Celeste took and stood. Roger drew himself up to his full height, a couple of inches taller than Eddie, his girth outweighing him by a good fifty pounds.

Roger took firm grip around her other wrist. “She wants to stay, she stays.”

Her grip in turn tightened on Eddie’s fingertips, and she looked back and forth between them. “Take your filthy, stinking hand off her.”

“Or what?” Roger’s turn to smirk now. “What are *you* going to do about it?”

Perhaps it was the paucity of the blood flowing through his veins; hunger always lowered his tolerance. It may also have been protecting Celeste from being defiled by this brute’s touch. More likely, though, Roger’s insulting emphasis on the word *you* is what set him off. Arrogance is annoying, but when displayed by a fool requires a comeuppance. He acted without thinking, not consciously showing off for her.

While still holding hers in his right hand, his left moved with the speed of a viper’s strike, far too fast to see, let alone react to. Extended index and middle fingers drove deep into Roger’s eye sockets. Thick, sticky custard sprayed the back of Eddie’s hand. Eddie pulled downward with enormous force, fingertips curled down to hook onto orbital bones. Not that it was needed, for in the flash it took, Roger’s knees had already given way, so he needed only guidance. His hand missed the table by an inch, and Roger’s jaw slamming to a halt against it freed his fingers to slip from the gory eye sockets.

The only sound Roger made in the fraction of a second it took was the crack of his face smashing against thick wood. Eddie doubted the blow killed him, because the lower face can absorb tremendous damage without severely injuring the brain, for which Roger undoubtedly would curse him the remaining sightless years of his life. He wiped his knuckles on the back of Roger's plaid flannel shirt and scoffed. "If you're going to wear plaid, make sure it's a legitimate tartan."

Around the bar, chairs clattered to the floor, the sound heard around the world when a fight is about to break out. John started toward him, but after what he had seen Eddie capable of doing, thought better of it. Everyone froze, faces in shocked disbelief. Only a few saw the action, the rest murmuring questions and admiration. "Must be some Kung Fu move," a woman in her thirties said as Eddie and Celeste sauntered casually past.

A block away, still holding her hand, Eddie ducked down an alleyway. Sure no one followed, she asked, "What the hell was that?"

"Sorry, that was all my fault."

"No kidding." She quickened her pace to keep up, still not accustomed to wearing high heels after twenty years on a farm.

"Who knew so close to the campus we'd wander into a bar without a single student inside?"

"Really? After what you did back there, the one thing you're upset about is your inability to pick a student hangout?"

For the first time, he let go of her hand, turned and used vice-like fingers to grab both upper arms. "We came here to feed, not to flirt with guys in their mid-forties."

"See? I knew it—you're jealous!"

"Jealousy has nothing to do with this."

"It's not like I was going to date him; we were planning to kill him!"

He pulled her so close to his face that she felt his words as bursts of wind blowing against her lips. "We came here for a purpose! Remember what I told you?"

"Young blood, innocent blood—that is what you want," she recited from memory.

"What *we need*! Again, that was my fault. I should have

turned around and left the moment we saw the patrons, instead of wasting our time with someone who served no purpose to us." Her head nodded, so he let go of her.

"That was pretty damn amazing how you did that. Might be useful for a woman my size to learn some of those tricks."

"Tonight you will learn something far more important."

"You are adorable when you're jealous. Do you know that?" She swatted his bottom playfully.

Half an hour later, in an alley behind another bar several blocks away, Def Leppard reverberating through the rear door, Celeste knelt over a boy propped up against a wall of century old brick. From the look of his handsome face, he must have used a fake ID to get into the bar. She pressed the inside of his wrist against her mouth as she drank lustily. The boy's eyes were open. From time to time, he glanced up at Eddie, standing guard, but always returned to the woman sucking from his open vein.

"Do you want some?"

"No," Eddie answered. "He's all yours."

"How much..." She resumed sucking the boy's life from him without finishing the question, eyes rolling back in ecstasy.

"We should go." With reluctance, she stood. Eddie handed her a small towel from his inside coat pocket and pointed to her face. First, Celeste ran her tongue around lips rubbed free of lipstick but still a bright vermilion in the neon light, then wiped her cheek.

They walked leisurely, once again hand in hand. Anyone passing by saw two lovers strolling back to their car from a night of drinking. And they would be right. "What will happen to him?"

He shrugged his shoulders. "Depends on how soon they find him."

"Will they assume it was suicide?"

"That's why I bring a fresh knife." Before giving her the towel to wipe her face, he wiped the cheap knife from a 7-11 clean of fingerprints with it and placed it in the kid's limp fingers curled on the pavement.

"Why didn't you feed?" Again shrugging his shoulders, she said, "You prefer women, don't you?"

"Yes. Having those emotions when feeding upon men makes me uncomfortable—unless absolutely necessary."

"Too gay for you?"

"Maybe so. Those intense sensations are more enjoyable with women."

Still looking back over her shoulder, she asked, "How sure are you he won't turn into a vampire?"

"He won't turn."

Deep in thought as they made their way to their car, eventually she said, "Well, maybe I need to try a woman to find out for myself."

"Choose whoever you want. Remember, though: the younger, the more innocent, the better. Take from them what you wish for yourself. It's no different than what happens when people who subsist on a diet of fried foods end up fat themselves." Advice learned over time but seldom followed. He opened her door for her and, as she backed into the passenger seat, held her hand up like the perfect gentleman he was.

ELECTRIC BLUE

Out on the porch enjoying a fiery sunset on a spectacular summer's evening, Eddie sat between the twins on the bench seat, Celeste in her usual wicker chair, each holding a glass of red wine. This was one of those picture-perfect nights when families take photos to remember.

The girls paid rapt attention to their mother, and when she finished, Angelique asked, "It was that easy?"

"Easy as pie," Celeste said, and sipped her wine.

"He just went outside with you?"

Eddie said, "Remember how incredible your mother looked in that outfit?"

"See? Told you that sweater looked great on you," said Josette.

"Oh, thanks," she answered.

"You'll find people are remarkably malleable. Usually, all you need to do is suggest they go with you and they will. Some form of hypnosis, I guess, although without the *you are getting very sleepy* crap."

Josette asked, "Did you use that on us?"

"If memory serves, that's what you two tried on me." Eddie winked at her. "The only times I have used it with you is when you were asleep and I awakened you. Then it feels like a dream and you are powerless to fight it. In fact, you welcome it."

Celeste asked, "Is that how it happened to you?"

The low sunlight striking Angelique's face lit her eyes a brilliant amethyst with tiny, black pinprick pupils. "Who was it? For you, I mean?"

“Someone very close. She’s gone now, if that’s what you are thinking.”

“What happened to her?” Josette’s eyes caught the low sun identically. In fact, if anything, the twins had become even more difficult to tell apart since they began the turn.

“Long story—one that gives me no pleasure remembering.”

Whether picking up on his cues or lost in her own thoughts, Angelique asked, “When will you take us? We’re ready, aren’t we?”

“Not yet. Not until your transformation is complete, the same as it went with your mother.”

“It sounds so exciting; I can hardly wait!”

Josette leaned forward to see her mother around the others. “Did it make you feel bad? I mean, you don’t even know if he survived or not.”

“No worse than I feel eating a steak or a chicken breast. I realize how strange that sounds, but that’s how it feels. Well, except the cow is dead, and this boy at least has a fighting chance. Right, Eddie?”

“He’s probably fine. Sometimes it’s best not to know. That’s why I never watch local news coverage. It’s not guilt, but more like after a nice dinner, you don’t need anyone to remind you the red chicken is missing from the yard.”

Not that George and Celeste raised chickens on the farm when their kids were growing up, and for a minute he wondered if the analogy was lost on them.

“So, until we die, we need to keep feeding on you?” The otherworldly glow of Josette’s eyes gave Eddie pause; perhaps they already possessed the power to lure men willingly to their death.

“Yes—if you still want to become like me and your Mama.”

“And after, will we still feed on you?”

“He fed off me, after,” her mother answered. “He thinks it’s gay to feed off other guys.”

"It's not that simple," he objected.

"It's exactly that simple. Don't worry, nobody's complaining." Celeste flashed a side-glance, then added, "When will you teach me some of those self-defense techniques you demonstrated at the bar?"

Eagerly nodding, Josette said, "That doesn't need to wait until we transform, does it?"

"Good question. Perhaps tomorrow?"

"It won't hurt to teach the twins a little self-defense before it is over. Better safe than sorry," Celeste said, without a hint of sarcasm. "It truly was amazing. After seeing what he's capable of doing, everyone in the tavern stopped and let us walk by without a single one trying to stop him."

Impressed, Angelique asked, "But it will come naturally?"

"To a certain extent, once your transformation is complete."

Angelique rolled her eyes. "Why is the answer to everything *only when our transformation is complete*?"

"Because, my dear, that is the way it is. We do not choose how this process works. If someone had instructed me the way I am teaching you what I know, my answers might be more satisfying. All I can do is share my experiences with you."

"When will you and Mama go out again?"

The two exchanged glances before he answered. "I must hunt tonight. Care to join me?"

Celeste beamed ear to ear. "What shall we wear?"

†

Few paid attention to the couple in the far corner of the parking lot. Those who did observed nothing more than young lovers amidst a seduction, deep in conversation and sometimes embracing in a kiss. Adjacent to the Narragansett Bay Campus of the University of Rhode Island, the sight of couples making out struck no one as out of the ordinary.

The door at Hannigan's Pub across the street opened and two young women strolled out, giggling and chatting. After stopping several times, the sound of laughter carrying across the parking lot, the dark-haired one escorted the blonde to her car. Headlights lit up the night as the engine turned over.

The woman's eyes momentarily reflected green in the car's headlight as it flashed on the couple leaning against their car. "You're on." Two pats on his shoulder emphasized it.

As the dark-haired girl passed by on her way to her car, parked on the far side of the one the lovers lay against, the woman's eyes widened in recognition. "Oh, hi."

"Oh, you startled me! I didn't recognize you there. The trivia champions."

"We thought you and your friend had us there at the end," Eddie said.

"Are you kidding? You aced every history question. We figured you two are history majors."

"That obvious?" Years had passed since Celeste was last confused for a college student, let alone an actual undergrad, bringing a smirk off her face impossible to wipe away.

The student's pace slowed when Celeste spoke to her, but resumed until Eddie slowed her again. "May I ask you a question?"

"Well, I was just going...," her hand waved toward the car parked alongside, making keys jingle and exposing the pepper spray canister attached to her key ring. But the question caught her off-guard, enough to lock eyes with Eddie. Beautiful eyes, electric blue—odd, for this dim corner of the lot should not have been bright enough to see color so vividly. She stopped dead in her tracks. "Sure."

Eddie stepped close. Too close. Ordinarily, a strange man might cause her to step back, if not turn and sprint the short distance to her car. He encroached well inside her personal space, but she did not move. "We were hoping you might allow us to take you home. Only, since we don't know where you live, well, we need for you to invite us."

"Why..." she stumbled over her words, "what do you want from me?"

"Life. And for it, we will give you an experience beyond anything your mind has ever imagined possible."

Fingers fumbled around the pepper spray, still held about shoulder level, elbow pulled tight against her side. Confusion visible on her face, the girl hesitated, eyes pulling away several times, but always quickly returning to Eddie's. "I don't know... I don't do that sort of..."

If it is possible for a person's face to visibly display the thought process going on inside, hers did. Questioning why she did not simply leave. Why not dismiss this stranger's bizarre request? Isn't this why she carries the pepper spray? Terror showed in her eyes, but her lips twitched into an unwilling smile.

"We know you don't normally do this sort of thing, but there's nothing to worry about."

Frozen in place, she chuckled dully. "You aren't going to hurt me, are you?"

"Do you want us to hurt you?"

"No."

"Neither do we. What I want to give you is a type of pleasure so far beyond your wildest dreams, you will believe it must have only been a dream. Something no one else can give you. How does that sound to you?"

Despite the terror in her almond-shaped brown eyes, she answered, "Very nice."

Still holding up her trembling hand, Eddie lifted the keys and gas canister from it, which he handed to Celeste. "She will follow in your car, so you can drive to class in the morning as usual."

After Eddie held the passenger door for the girl, leaning close, Celeste asked, "So that's how you do it?"

"That's it."

The little blue Datsun followed their car out of the parking lot and into the night.

†

The clock read ten minutes 'til five as the four sat in the living room drinking glasses of Pinot Noir. Still more than an hour until dawn. Bernie slept upstairs, so they spoke in muted tones. The twins listened in awed silence as their mother related the story. Leaned forward with elbows on her knees, Angelique asked, "As simple as that?"

"As simple as that," her mother confirmed. "She just said yes and got into our car with Eddie and we drove to her apartment. She even gave him directions on the way!"

Josette's eyes bulged. "How do you do that?"

"It's hard to explain—I barely understand it myself, let alone can put it into words. One of those things I had to figure out for myself. All I do is concentrate, focus my attention, almost willing her to say what I want her to say. Something about the eyes, because if they avoid eye contact, it doesn't seem to work."

"The Jedi mind trick," she answered.

"Does it work every time?" asked Angelique.

"Most of the time. You can tell right away, and if they aren't receptive, immediately quit before they have a clue anything is going on."

Slyly smiling, Josette asked, "Tell us the truth, did you use your powers on Angelique?"

Offended at her sister's suggestion, Angelique gasped while he chuckled, "Only when waking you up during the night to feed. We share a bond that made it unnecessary. All three of you. Before we ever met, blood bound us together. That is one reason I grasped your potential right away."

Eager to get the rest of the story, Angelique asked, "Alright, what happened next? When you got back to her flat?"

"She led us to her apartment, and since I had her keys, I opened the door. Eddie walked beside her, so it looked like they were on a date or something."

Josette cut in with another question. "What was her name?"

"It's better not to ask names, if you don't already know," Eddie said, his face serious.

"So we get inside," Celeste continued, "and she's very cute in a librarian kind of way. Lovely eyes she never took off him. We went into her bedroom and he asked her to take off her shirt. She did like it was nothing, although from the looks of her, she doesn't take off her shirt for men she just met. Then she says, *Please don't hurt me,* and Eddie promised not to. He touched her, and I've got to tell you, it was so sexy! Her face, stroking her arms, her body. By this time, she was getting into it as much as Eddie and I were, already acting like she was having one of those climax things he causes."

"She was sitting on her bed and he turned her and lifted her hair—she has really beautiful raven hair—and began kissing the back of her neck and shoulder. Then he opened up his ring and poked her about the place he poked me with it. And then he fed."

With a wink, he gave the masculine sapphire and gold around his left middle finger a twist. The gemstone opened, exposing a tiny silver point concealed underneath. Neither twin had experienced his ring, each having their own wounds ready for him. No one thought to question why he used it on Celeste, when she also had helped by nearly severing a digit, which should have been quite satisfactory for feeding.

Josette smiled. "Did you get enough?"

He turned away. "No. She's tiny—smaller than either of you."

Brow wrinkled and head cocking back, Angelique asked, "What does that matter? Why not take your fill from her?"

When Eddie hesitated, Celeste explained for him. "Eddie liked her. It showed plain as day on his face. And she seemed like a really sweet girl. Draining too much might have killed her. Am I right?"

Pale as his face was, slight color reddened his cheeks.

"Careful is the way to go. Too many people bleeding out over a short period raises too many questions."

Filled with excitement and curiosity by the account, Angelique wanted every detail. "What about you, Mama—did you feed from her, too?"

"Not much—he let me try but stopped me before I had much."

As was their custom, her sister followed up. "Well, how was it? Feeding on a woman, I mean."

With a wistful smile, she answered, "While I can understand why our cousin prefers not to feed on men, to me, there was no difference. Tasted the same and felt… the same."

"Did you get off on her?" asked Angelique. "Oh, my god, you did! You got off on a woman! I knew it!"

"Oh, stop! It was nice, but I didn't do it for pleasure—it was feeding."

The twins' enthusiasm, as well as their mother's, pleased their cousin, and although the lessons he taught them from his years of experience were deadly serious, he sat back enjoying their fun. "We each will find our own preferences and limits. Only when it interferes with your ability to feed does it become a problem. Once you learn how, then you will decide the ways most pleasing to you."

†

The desk clerk watched the young woman approach the window. By a long shot, the cutest girl to show up during the shift, so he eagerly offered his help.

"I need to see a detective."

"A specific detective? Is this about an open case?"

"No," the petite brunette answered. Shaking and looking about like someone was following her, in a quiet voice, she said, "A female detective, if one is available. I believe… a man may have raped me last night."

In a private interview room, Det. Brenda Russo met with

Sabrina Malinkal. "If you don't recall being sexually assaulted, what makes you believe you might have been?"

"Those two started speaking to me, and the next thing I knew, I was home and it was morning. There are some vague memories, almost like a dream, yet not a dream. Not exactly. All I can think of is they gave me a Roofie which must have taken effect just as I was leaving."

"You don't know who these people were, but they played against you in the trivia competition, then you ran into them again in the parking lot. After that, you lost time?"

"The rest of the night."

"Did they give you a drink? Come near your table where they could have slipped something into your wine glass?"

"No."

"Then it likely wasn't them. But your story is similar to what other women have reported, and just because that couple didn't tamper with your drink does not mean someone else did not drug you, which they took advantage of to assault you. I would like to have you tested down at the ER. Blood test for drugs, a rape swab. It is invasive—I won't lie to you—but it will determine if you were raped and whether you have traces of any drugs in your system. If a man left any evidence, we can get his blood type."

A single tear ran down her left cheek as she nodded her head. "I need to know."

†

Before sunrise, Eddie escorted the twins into their room to feed. Barely had the door shut when four hands flicked open his buttons and yanked at his shirt. The way Angelique moved toward his chest, so ravenous—lips open, pushing her curls pulled back over one shoulder—she relished the teasing. He dodged her advance with graceful, seductive motion, joining in the fun by keeping himself slightly out of reach. Fingernails raked his chest as he flopped on the bed.

It would not be long now.

"Hey, gorgeous, isn't it your sister's turn to feed first?"

"But I need you!"

Her face cradled in his palms, he lifted her up. At first she fought, but then submitted to him and allowed him a passionate kiss. Josette pushed her sister to one side and took his wound in her full, pale pink lips. An involuntary moan escaped into her sister's mouth, only increasing the desperation in her kisses.

"Breathe into me."

This made Angelique pause, pushing her long fountain of curls back behind the shoulder from where they had fallen while kissing. "What do you mean?"

"I want you to breathe into me; then let me breathe back into you."

"That sounds hot!" Mouth open wide, she sealed her lips around his and exhaled, deep but slow, into his mouth. A few heartbeats later, he breathed into her, and she inhaled his air into her lungs. Back and forth they shared the same sweet breath, lips sealed together. While Josette drained his lifeblood from his chest, he gave his breath to her twin.

Sharing their air grew too intense. She had to pull away, fanning her face as she inhaled and exhaled several times, exaggerating for effect. Then she kissed his cheek, his neck, down the other side of his chest from where her sister still fed. "I wish you had two cuts so we both could feed together."

"Make one, if you wish."

"Are you serious?" She backed away, fingernails running now across his chest and stomach, one side of her lips curled up in a way slightly less sinister than sexy.

"My knife is in my pocket." Her hand shot into his front pocket, groping around even after she located the knife. Light reflected off a stainless-steel blade when she opened it. Josette continued feeding, and his head slumped back before catching himself. "If you want to cut me, it will cost you."

The way the light flickered off her lilac irises with her

head at a jaunty tilt, his challenge had its desired effect. "Deal! What will it cost me?"

He waved an open hand over her body. "Your clothes."

"Ooh, aren't you naughty tonight?" She began unbuttoning.

"To avoid stains. It's a pretty shirt."

"Always thinking of others, aren't you?" Her blouse brushed his shoulder sailing toward the bed behind him. "What about my jeans?"

"Better safe than sorry."

This time, one denim leg slapped his face as her jeans flew past. Her hand ran down his arm, over his chest, across his neck. "Where do you want me to cut you?"

"You are the one who wants to cut me—you chose." His eyes closed, and he moaned again.

"You trust me to stab you?"

"Why? Aren't you trustworthy?"

Josette stopped long enough to say, "Need I remind you who is holding that knife?" Then she licked around the wound, savoring the trickle that already began flowing across his skin.

"Both of you entrust your lives to me. Why should I not do the same?" Whether buoyed by arrogance borne of immortality or from genuine trust was impossible to tell. Or did the pleasure Josette aroused by feeding cloud his judgment? Not that his reason mattered to his protégé as she ran the knife down his pectoral muscle for the third time, along the center line cut by visible abdominal muscles, across his boxers. Its needle-like tip serving as a finger, she opened the fly and cautiously probed inside. Cold steel on his genitals made him jerk, eyes locking on her.

"Someday, you might regret that choice."

"Just think how much fun feeding us will be."

"Let's revisit that once you have a surgical degree and know where to cut—and how deep."

"You're so funny! That's my problem—I don't want to hurt you, but I want it somewhere fun. Like the other one."

"Keep lollygagging and Josette will finish, and there won't be a reason to slash me at all."

"If I cut you, then I want you to cut me, too," she said in the coquettish voice of a girl, holding up a finger. "This sucks. There must be a better way than you giving my finger oral sex."

"Deal. Why not cut my other side so you two can feed side by side?"

"Won't that hurt?"

"Probably less than slicing my balls open."

Annoyance boiling by their indecision, Josette interrupted her feeding long enough to mock them. "If you don't stab him right now, swear to god, I'm going to stick that knife in his pinkie so you will have to blow *his* finger!"

With uncharacteristic care, Angelique sliced a mirror image to the wound she knew so well. His muscles tightened, but only when she slit halfway through his nipple did he flinch and let out a groan through his teeth. "Sorry. Does that hurt?"

"The pain will go away soon as you feed." No need to rush her, as irresistible bloodlust drew her lips to the new, steady flow draining down his pectoral muscle toward the sternum. One mop of red at each nipple, mingling together across his chest and stomach, looked unreal, a sordid work of art. To keep from screaming loud enough to wake Bernie, Eddie gave himself a taste of his own blood biting his tongue. Soon sated, Josette lay in his arms, watching her sister feed.

Eddie's face had a ghostly pallor.

"Oh, shit. Don't pass out again! This isn't A&P!" Josette knelt next to him and extended her thigh across his face almost in a half-split so he could take from her. At the same time, he wearily pushed the top of Angelique's head away, meeting stiff resistance until his strength eased her away. "Enough."

"But you taste so good," she protested.

"So do you," he said, lifting her sister's thigh back away from his face. On the bed, the knife lay open where she left it, and she shrank back when he picked it up. "We had a deal."

Wide eyes a deep amethyst followed the blade. "It seemed like a good idea at the time."

"It's a fantastic idea," her sister smirked.

His face panned from her shoulders to knees. "Where should I start?"

"When she cuts herself, it leaves those light pink scars; my skin will do the same. How much do you think it will hurt if you scar me in the shape of a heart?"

Simultaneously, both her sister and Eddie answered, "A lot!"

"A small heart. Like a tiny tattoo."

"Where?"

"Which part of my body do you want to suck on?"

"Do you want a visible heart cut into your flesh?"

"Maybe somewhere private—where a bikini will hide it."

He caressed one breast in his free hand. "Like where you cut me?" Although her head nodded, she bit one side of her full lower lip, which Eddie surmised she did not intend to be as alluring as he found it. His fingertips brushed across her breast, then he said, "There is no way I can mar such beauty. Nor can we have you screaming the way I suspect carving a heart into your breast will evoke."

"What about this?" Her panties already low on her hips, she rolled the narrow elastic band to reveal the lowest section of her abdomen, allowing the flame of a few unruly hairs to escape.

"You are a naughty girl, aren't you, my Angelique? Much better than blowing your finger—likely for both of us. If you're sure, lay back… and you may want to bite something."

"Now who's the naughty one?" She bravely winked.

Amazingly, only a slight squeal came from deep in her chest as he gouged out a crescent an inch long into her white flesh. Blood flowed in a rush. A quick wipe of his thumb saved her panties from ruin, although he suspected she didn't care. He sucked her blood from his thumb.

His steady hand cut a matching crescent in only seconds,

and soon as the twain met, he lapped up every drop spilling over her tender body before feeding from the fresh wound. Soon as his lips touched her bloody heart, she sighed with relief as he took her pain with her blood.

"Will you kiss me the way you kissed her?" Josette's dilated pupils and blazing cheeks lying on his chest afterward were impossible to resist.

"It's amazing," her sister, lying as a mirror, said then, although the blood had stopped flowing, licked the fresh wound she'd gouged into him a half-inch in front of her face.

"My blood is your blood," his eyes went from one twin to the other, "my breath is your breath."

His voice, solemn as an oath, bestowed upon his words the gravity of a sacred ritual. Still wearing a shirt—the only one of the three to have one on—she crawled until her face was over his. Both hands pulled her hair back out of the way, tucking curls behind one ear. Her breath on his face carried the sweet scent of blood and wine. "How do I…?"

"Just breathe into me, then take your breath from me."

Like her sister had, with mouth open wide, soft, sumptuous lips sealing against his, she exhaled into him, and he drew a deep inspiration. When he exhaled, her lungs filled with his breath. Her twin's hand caressed his stomach as they shared this new, strangely moving form of intimacy.

Neither knew how long a breath can be shared until depleting its oxygen to the point it no longer can sustain life any more than they could determine the precise moment when too much blood drained from a body. For the longest time, neither cared.

Afterward, laying her face back on his chest alongside her sister's, who asked, "Did you kiss our mother like that?"

"No, should I?"

"Don't!" they replied in unison, and Josette continued, "Oh, please make it something special just between us!"

PRETTY IN PINK

Sparks flew high into the black sky to mingle with the indistinct Milky Way haze bisecting the thousands of other stars. Dancing, spinning in the light breeze until eventually burning themselves out.

Around the fire bunched in a half-circle to avoid the northeast-blowing smoke, the four paused for a momentary lull in the conversation. Eddie offered the bottle to Celeste on his left, filling an antique cordial glass she found at the back of an upper shelf which she held out, then turned to fill the twins' glasses to his right.

After a sip, Josette asked, "What exactly is Madeira?"

"Fortified wine," he answered. "Back when Portuguese Man o' Wars ruled the high seas, the sailors discovered adding brandy to wine stopped it from spoiling on long sea voyages."

Angelique smirked. "Is that the excuse they used for making wine stronger?"

"It is delicious," their mother said. "Do you drink red wine because it looks so much like...?"

"Probably so. Or maybe it's because red, red wine makes me feel so fine."

"Why aren't there fangs?" Angelique flashed a well-practiced pout. "Fangs would be so cool."

"They sure would," her cousin agreed. "Sure would make things a lot easier."

After another sip of hers, Josette said, "It's hard to imagine you had to figure all this out on your own. At least we have the benefit of your knowledge. How did you learn all this?"

"Lots of trial and error. More errors than I care to admit."

"Speaking of errors, how should we handle Bernie? He never quite bought your story about my supposed coma when I was dead. Ever since, he knows something is up."

"Yeah, well, we need to come up with a plan for him."

"Now that there are two of you," said Angelique, addressing her mother, "since Eddie thinks it's too gay, can't you do it?"

"She's not ready. For now, she needs to build up her strength. It takes quite a while to become strong enough. And it's not that I don't want to. I totally underestimated how much it takes out of me to turn more than one person at a time. I should have completed your mother's transformation before starting on you two."

Celeste shut that down. "Let's not talk about Bernie right now. It is too soon to even consider him joining us."

"Well, we need to do something soon. We cannot hide from him forever. Not all of us, leaving him the only person in a house full of vampires." Angelique emptied her glass and held it out for another refill. These days, it took a tremendous amount of alcohol to launch a buzz. "When will we be ready? For a while we were sicker every day, but now we've plateaued."

"I'm feeling stronger," said her sister.

"Your guess is as good as mine. They don't write this up in medical books. For me, it took nearly a year, but I've seen people go much quicker. Your mother, for example."

"They've always been strong, even when they were babies." Some things even death cannot change—Mothers still love boasting about their children.

For a few moments, they watched sparks fly up to the heavens, until Josette broke the silence. "What was your plan? I mean, why us?"

They were not ready to know all of it. Not yet. "It has something to do with the blood. The Brown family blood. Every time I tried to convert someone, it failed, so I decided some inherited trait must already be in our blood. All it needs is to be triggered. Hopefully, you will never know how lonely being immortal and undead can be."

Celeste shook her head. "It's so hard to accept that Mercy Brown really was a vampire."

"And since her blood runs through you as well as me, I hoped it would work. Turns out my theory was right—it is the Brown blood. It may come from her mother. Supposedly, her father hid some dark, mysterious scandals back in Ireland and again when he came to America. The truth is, we will never know the complete story." Eddie sighed. "All we know with certainty is, if it worked with you, then it must be because of our blood."

Intrigued, Josette again asked him, "How many times have you tried?"

With a rueful chuckle absent any trace of humor, Eddie answered, "More times than I care to talk about."

That unsuitable answer dodged her question, so she dug deeper. "Then how can you be sure it will not fail with us?"

"Oh, trust me—I know. The bloodlust. The first time I saw that in another person was your mother. The second time was with you two. It was there all along, waiting to be awakened. It's stronger with you two than with your mother. There's no doubt about it."

"Okay, this might be nothing, only my imagination, but my vision seems to be improving." Celeste leaned forward. "Right now, dark as it is out here, I see fine, but for the last few years, my night vision has sucked. And I hear things I never heard before. Even my sense of smell—I can literally smell blood, but even raising three kids, despite how many times the three of you cut yourselves open growing up, I never knew blood even had a smell." Her voice rose, excited.

Despite the dim light of the fire, Angelique's eyes lit up. "I noticed that smell, too! I wondered what was up with that!"

This time, Eddie's chuckle rang with humor, mixed with pride. "Oh yes, that is true. What we lose with our childlike view of the world and our antiquated concept of morality is more than made up by much more acute senses. A welcome trade, if you ask me—heightened perception along with true freedom."

"All of our senses?" asked Josette.

"Far as I can tell," her mother answered. "Smell, hearing, sight, taste. Touch."

"Every sensation except pain." Starting at her wrist, Eddie ran one finger up Josette's arm, feather-like in its lightness, producing a sensation just shy of a tickle. Her skin tightened into goosebumps. "Which is strange since our sensitivity to pleasure is now so intense. Don't ask me why—I haven't figured that one out myself."

"More than now?" Josette pulled her eyes away from his finger which, by then, was up to her bare shoulder. "After we—after death? Already touch is so intense."

"Sure does," her mother confirmed.

"This should be interesting," said her sister.

Eddie smiled, hearing Celeste speak so much more freely to her daughters than when he arrived only a couple of months before. "Oh, let me assure you—it is. You will love it!"

"I sure do," their mother said, setting her girls off giggling. At that, she rose. "Well, I should get back. If Bernie wakes up, he will wonder where everyone went. If he walks up on us—well, that's the last thing we need."

"Let me walk back with you," offered Eddie.

With a grin, she waved him off. "For twenty years I have walked this farm without an escort, and back then I was a mere mortal. I sure don't need one now."

The conversation fell into a lull when their mother left. Something remained unspoken, yet no one wished to be the one to raise it. On such a nice evening, though, it was easy enough to enjoy just being together while ignoring what needed saying. The person to rise to the challenge was Angelique.

"What's wrong with us?"

His raised eyebrow was not a ruse—he did not

understand what she meant. “Nothing. Nothing at all.”

“Then why haven’t you tried to seduce either of us? A blind girl can see you like us, and we like you, but you don’t seem interested in us in that way.”

“Wow! I’m sorry, I did not realize…”

“Then you aren’t as bright as you look.”

“Sorry, how was I supposed to know you were interested in me romantically? Why haven’t you just said something?”

Angelique’s eyes narrowed as if she confronted a crazy person. “What do you think we’ve been saying for the last month?”

“Six weeks,” her sister corrected her.

“All you are interested in is our blood, not our bodies.”

He gave each a hug, wishing these women asked simple questions.

†

When no one answered her knock, Celeste tried the door and discovered it unlocked. Crowded on Angelique’s bed, the three lay in a pile, a sheet draped only over their legs. Among the three, Celeste saw only two articles of clothing: Eddie’s boxers and Josette’s black thong. Angelique wasn’t wearing a stitch. “Alright, everyone—time to wake up. It’s after 9:30.”

A light swat across Angelique’s bare bottom brought a flutter to her eyelids as her mother pulled the sheet up to her waist, covering her naked body.

“Morning,” Eddie said, half-buried under twins. Josette’s head lay on his shoulder, her twin’s on his sternum, and he squinted to ward off the morning sunlight. “Morning comes early after feeding.”

Celeste scowled. “You should consider locking this door. What if your brother came in and found you like this?”

“He knows better than to come into our room,” Josette mumbled without raising her head, one hand sweeping a shock of curls from her face. Beneath her, Eddie’s shoulder and upper chest glistened with a drizzle of saliva.

"Even so, lock it next time."

Still as her sister, a palm spread over Eddie's stomach, Angelique asked, "Then how would you wake us up?"

"Oh, believe me, I can knock loud enough to wake the dead."

Only her hand stirred, caressing his stomach, and Angelique pleaded with her mother, "Can't we sleep a little longer?"

"Sure. What shall I tell Abby? She's drinking coffee downstairs. Came by to see how you two are."

Josette jumped. "Oh, shit! Tell her we will be a few minutes. Go on, you get out of here," she swatted and nudged Eddie, who dragged his carcass out of bed soon as Angelique rolled off him.

Celeste asked, "How do you feel, by the way?"

"Still alive, thanks to Eddie," Angelique answered. "We may have fed too much from him."

Downstairs, Abby gasped when the twins descended the stairs a few minutes later, robes tied over hastily donned PJs. "Wow! You two look like crap!"

"Nice to see you, too," Angelique responded.

"After missing a week of school, I got worried about you. Is this the same thing your mother had?"

This time, Josette answered. "Who knows? The doctors never could find anything wrong with her, so why waste our time on tests? Same symptoms, so we are doing the usual: chicken soup, OJ, plenty of rest."

"You look pale as ghosts."

"When haven't we been pasty? Especially compared to your delicious cappuccino complexion."

"We can't wear pink—not like you're rocking that tee-shirt. I'd kill for your complexion," Josette said as she took a seat next to her sister on the couch.

"Well, I'd give you a month of being Black before you were begging to have your pasty Irish complexions back. Less than that if you get pulled over a few times for driving while Black."

Angelique agreed with her twin. "People are stupid. You've got the prettiest skin."

"We need to get you out in the sun or something. You look like redheaded chalk sticks. Seriously, how do you feel?"

"Some days are better than others. Today's not great," Josette confessed as their mother brought two steaming mugs of coffee for the twins.

"Need more, Abby?"

"Not yet, but thanks!"

"We just woke up," explained Angelique.

"Well," their friend said, blowing her cup before taking a sip, "in that case, you may look like crap, but most women I know would love to wake up looking that bad. I brought some assignments from Brit Lit if you are up to a little light reading. We start in on the romantic poets Monday, so you may want to get well before you miss out. They didn't tell us in high school those poems were all about sex."

"Take good notes for us for when we are better."

"Should I be here? Is whatever you have contagious?"

"Probably not, although you never know for sure," Angelique said with a curious grin. "Other than poetry, have we missed out on anything? You know: parties? Breakups? DUIs?"

"Oh, of course. The usual. Christie caught Scott sleeping with Beth, but we already knew about that, so it's not news to you. Otherwise, if anything, less drama than usual. So, has your brother caught it? And how's your adorable cousin?"

"Bernie's fine, but Eddie's sick, too," answered Josette. "Same thing we're all sharing. Nothing the stupid doctors can do anything about. Why are you here so early in the morning?"

"My ten a.m. class was canceled. Teacher is sick—whatever you have is going around—so I don't have class until 1:00 today."

"Glad you came to see us when you have no class." Josette

winked over her coffee mug.

"Okay, Rodney Dangerfield. Figured it's easier to come by in the morning. What's up with your cousin? He's still here?"

Angelique twirled a curl just above her breast. "Can't just kick him out while he's sick, can we?"

"I didn't mean it that way. He's hot. You two haven't decided to keep him for yourselves, have you?"

"Oh, I get it—you stopped by to hit on our cousin, not to visit with us?" With her creased brow and deadpan expression, it was impossible to tell if Angelique meant it as a joke.

"No, that's, uh, I mean..."

"Hi, Abby. Nice to see you again." Mug of coffee in hand, Eddie walked in and squeezed in beside her feet on the Ottoman.

"Oh, hi. How are you feeling? They were just telling me you are sick, too."

"I'm fine. Much better today, thanks. How are you?"

"Good. It's just—how long were you listening before you came in?"

"Not too long," he said with a knowing smile.

Face blushing, Abby tried to hide behind her coffee mug. "I'm going to die now."

"Will it help if I say you are hot, too? Or will that just make it worse?"

Suddenly, Abby found intense interest in her feet. "Just shoot me now. Lique, don't you have a shotgun in this house?"

"And miss all this fun? No chance. Should we leave you two alone?"

Eyes wide with an expression of horror, Josette blurted sternly, "Don't you dare!"

Everyone looked at her, then Abby asked, "What just happened?"

"Nothing." Eddie stood. "Well, carry on. I will leave you. Sorry to barge in."

"Stay," Angelique said, her voice pleading, but began coughing before she could say anything else.

"Abby came to see you, not me. Come back, though. Fingers crossed, we'll be feeling great soon, and I am sure you have some stories you can tell me about my cousins."

"Oh, I've got some stories." With another smile, Eddie tapped the back of the chair next to Abby's head and went into the kitchen with barely repressed, nervous giggles and a few coughs behind him.

†

Jimmy Miller hurried to catch up to his friends, but his legs had stopped working. Unsteady, weaving, he willed one to step in front of the other in something resembling a straight line, but when they didn't respond, he leaned against a maple growing through a hole cut in the sidewalk. They were heading to the Phi Rho house, or maybe Thai Pho house, he thought, and that made him laugh.

"Hey, wait up!" One friend turned and waved him on while walking backward a few steps, then spun around to rejoin the herd onward to the next party. Jimmy took another sip of Purple Jesus from his red plastic cup before trying again. With a shove off the tree trunk in the general direction he was heading, he set off with an audible, "Shit!"

"Need some help?"

She looked like an angel. No, better than that, because angels don't dress as sexy as this woman, nor do they wear black. From the looks of her, she must be a senior, if not a grad student. Not that it mattered—he didn't stand a chance with a woman as beautiful in either event, but alcohol has a way of suspending logical disbelief.

"Nah, I'm good. Want to go to a party?"

"A party? Sounds fun—where?"

"Thai pho," he said.

Nodding as if that made sense, she repeated it. "Don't know where that is. Can you lead the way?"

"No problem!" He offered his elbow in an oddly archaic

manner, which she hooked her arm through.

"Lead on!" Celeste held him up as legs of overcooked spaghetti failed, but he gamely continued on. Until Eddie stepped out of nowhere into his path.

"This one?"

Celeste nodded. "Will he do?"

"Thai Pho," Jimmy slurred through purple-stained lips only a bit more functional than his legs. Grain alcohol can disrupt the nerves between brain and muscles with lethal effectiveness. "I don't want no trouble."

"We don't want any trouble, either," Celeste assured him as she led him into a narrow, hedge-lined gap between two dark, brick houses. "Who needs that party when we can have our own? You do like to party, don't you?"

"Hell, yeah," Jimmy answered, and willingly followed the angel in black.

†

Women are much more cautious than men.

After Celeste cleaned the last traces of blood from her face and reapplied makeup in the car, it was Eddie's turn to feed, but he needed a different strategy. The women he preyed upon were not the type to stumble home shitfaced. In fact, he avoided most women he encountered in such condition for their blood was often tainted, not the innocent blood of a freshman kid experimenting with alcohol. And friends care for female freshmen in such a state of intoxication, not left to their own devices by their buddies.

"Will you demonstrate your abilities again?"

"We'll see. Tonight may be an opportunity to demonstrate yours."

"I don't feel any powers."

"Well, in that case, this may get embarrassing."

Frat parties may work well for her, but he avoids them, he explained as they walked. Any female visitor there is certain to be stalked by rival predators while keeping their eye on him as uninvited competition. Sorority parties had a similar, if opposite, dynamic. "The key is either a party too packed for anyone to notice what others are doing or low-key gatherings. Oddly, chorus groups make great hunting grounds. Usually more gals than guys, and the women there tend toward innocent there."

This Friday night, though, they found nothing like that. But the sound of Prince drew them in from two blocks away. "Sounds like a party; let's check it out."

Their ears did not deceive. Students spilled from a two-story wooden house out onto the front lawn and, by the time they arrived, the Gap Band blared from giant speakers inside. A crowd formed around a tapped keg on the front porch. Inside, the living room served as a packed dance floor scented with the fragrance of clove cigarettes. Men watched the petite blonde in the little black dress, while women paid attention to the tall blonde man she danced with.

Hands on his shoulders pulled him down enough to shout in his ear, "Your dancing could use some work!"

"Well," his lips brushed against her ear, "now is your chance."

"Relax. Loosen up. I'm afraid you may break into a waltz."

After taking a moment to survey the dancing throng, he began mimicking a guy on his right, loose fists at his shoulders bobbing up and down like pistons. "Like this?"

Head back, hair falling long behind her, she let out a loud laugh. "Please go back to how you were doing it before!"

As they danced, Eddie revolved counterclockwise, spinning her into a planet revolving around him. Although no student there rivaled her pure animal sexiness, Eddie scanned the room as they rotated, only giving her his occasional undivided attention. Finally pulling her close, he motioned with a flick of his head toward a corner. "Brunette in the pink sweater trying to extricate herself from a conversation with that preppy guy sporting the popped collar."

If up to her, Celeste never would have noticed her. Petite, perhaps a few pounds overweight, although her pressed oxford shirt and below-knee plaid skirt in the pink and green colors prepsters loved hid it well. If the university catalog features a photo of a student in the library sciences department, she must be that student. Judging by the uncomfortable way she stood apart from the surrounding dancers, she felt as out of place as she looked. "Isn't she a little boring for you?"

"But a pretty little thing." He had a good eye. At that moment, she smiled, a beautiful smile that lit up her face and a pair of lovely hazel brown eyes. Get rid of that awful preppy uniform, a little makeup and just pull her boring hair into a ponytail and she might attract attention.

"You or me?"

"Break the ice," he said.

Dancers packed tight as a twelve-pack, Celeste had to wedge her body sideways to make her way off the dance floor, taking up a spot next to the girl. "Whew! I needed a break—it's hot on the floor!"

"I guess so." The girl passively watched those having fun.

"Why aren't you out there dancing?"

"Me? Oh, I'm not much of a dancer."

"Why not?" Proximity confirmed her impression of the librarian's eyes. If anything, more spectacular, with a golden ring around the irises surrounded by bright, light tan. Once the girl turned to lock eyes with Celeste, her face changed almost imperceptibly. Was that it?

"Well, I can't say. Not my thing."

"You should meet my cousin. He'd like you. He's a sucker for beautiful eyes."

"I don't know..."

Pointing to the popped collar guy standing on her other side, she asked, "Sorry, is that your boyfriend?"

"No. Not at all."

"Good! My cousin is around here somewhere. Oh, there he is." She waved him over from where he waited on the far side of the dance floor. "Here he comes."

"That's your cousin?"

"Hot, isn't he?"

"He's not exactly my type."

"What's your type?" They watched him move through the dancers with ease, turning women with a smile and gentle hands on their shoulders; men took one look and gave him room. Dressed in black like her—his a tee-shirt and black jeans—he certainly did not look the type to date a preppy librarian sciences co-ed.

"Not him."

"Too...?"

"Too hot. Guys like him aren't interested in me."

"Trust me—he'll eat you up."

"Don't tease me like that." The last of the dancers parted and Eddie handed Celeste a beer.

"Who's your friend?"

"Eddie, this is... sorry, I didn't get your name."

"Anne," she said, repeating it louder to be heard above the music.

"Don't be an idiot—ask Anne to dance!"

She accepted his offered hand and followed him onto the dance floor as the stereo began blaring *You Spin Me Round*. Anne made Eddie look like a Soul Train dancer by comparison, but her expression changed to a smile, and she gave him her full attention. After the song, Eddie put one arm around her and turned her toward a door, looking back over his shoulder and motioning with his head for Celeste to follow. They made it to the kitchen door around back by the time she caught up, in time to hear Eddie asking, "Who are you here with?"

"My roommate and some of her friends."

He leaned down to whisper in Celeste's ear. "You are on. Ask her to tell her roommate she's going outside to talk to us. Tell her something specific, like she's claustrophobic or something. If she says it, you made her do it."

Quiet enough here to communicate at lower than a shout, Celeste said, "Don't you need some air?"

"I do," Anne dutifully answered.

"Go tell your roommie; we'll be right out back."

"I'll be right back," Anne answered and went out of the room.

"That's it?"

"That's it. We'll know for sure in a minute."

The answer was obvious when she returned a couple of minutes later. Without saying a word, Eddie held open the door, and the three walked outside. Celeste asked, "What did you tell your roommate?"

"I told I need some air."

Excitement lit her face, followed by a moment of understanding. "Do you want to leave with us?"

"Sure." Other than a slight flatness in her voice and an expressionless face, Anne appeared quite normal. They left thorough a gate on the side, Eddie leading down a series of quiet, residential streets. No one saw them, and if their route far off the beaten path worried Anne, she raised no concerns.

Sidled up beside Eddie, Celeste quietly asked, "How do we know it worked and she's just not... you know?"

"When we get there, ask her to do something she won't normally do. Then we'll know for sure." Their stroll led to a wooded neighborhood park. The three followed the sidewalk inside, where they stopped at a grassy opening among the trees. "Let's stop here." Celeste just stared at him. "Go ahead."

Turning to their prey, she said, "Anne, why don't you lie down here in the soft grass and take off your clothes?"

Without a word of objection or questioning why, she dropped onto the grass and lay back. She began unbuttoning her blouse.

Eddie stopped her. "That's good, Anne. Leave those on for now. Why don't you get comfortable?" She lay back, wriggling, the way someone does in a comfy bed.

"That's amazing!" Celeste's eyes caught the soft light of a quarter moon as Eddie lay down beside the girl and kissed her shoulder, her neck. Anne's eyes closed and soon she began softly moaning. A quick slice of her wrist and Eddie lay on her shoulder and held her wrist to his mouth. Anne's moans increased in frequency and volume, soon much more ferocious than her bland appearance suggested lay inside her.

"Do you want to try her?" Eddie's finger staunched the flow from the small tear in her skin.

"Can I?"

"Of course."

Knelt down beside the girl's body, she whispered, "I don't know. Maybe I'm like you, or maybe I got enough from that guy. I got a little buzz from his grain punch. I drank so much."

"Suit yourself." He stood and turned to the still figure on the grass. "Anne, it's time we leave. We'll take you out of the park."

A small amount of blood smeared one sleeve and along the front near the placket, and they supported her arms and led her back down the empty path. At the road, they sat her against a tree with her feet out onto the sidewalk, where she lay until a couple coming home found her there and called 911. With the cut to the vein on her wrist and her insistence that she did not remember how it happened, the fire department reported this as another attempted suicide and sent her to the ER. Let the doctors decide if she needed to be committed.

"A typical Friday," the paramedic informed the responding police officer. "Drunk, stoned maybe—blood work will tell what. All she keeps talking about is some craziness about a woman making her take her clothes off. We get one or two just like her most weekends."

No one gave Anne another thought.

POUR SOME SUGAR ON ME

The doorbell rang for a second time.

The clock read 9:20. Bernie's bus left two hours before, only an hour after they returned from their road trip. After ignoring the first ring, Celeste rolled over when its insistent ringing continued several times in a row. "I guess the girls aren't going to get that."

"Should I answer it?"

"Would you mind?" Eddie's offer sounded perfunctory, merely to score points knowing she had to get it. To sweeten the deal, she administered a lascivious kiss on his jugular vein. He swung his legs off the bed.

Jeans—donned commando style and recycling the black tee-shirt from last night left hanging over the back of the bedside chair—he hurried downstairs. On his way down, he used his fingers to give his bed-head some semblance of grooming. Groggy not only from the brevity of their sleep; hearty feasting left him drained for hours. The bell rang again as he reached for the doorknob.

Abby Strong jumped back. "Oh! You startled me!"

"Sorry, I assumed when you ring a doorbell, you expect someone to answer it."

Relieved and embarrassed by her reaction, she made a joke out of it. "When no one answered, I got worried, what with everyone's cars here."

"We're all a little under the weather today, and I think

Celeste was up all hours and the twins were feeling quite puny last night."

"Are they still asleep?"

Again making use of his finger-comb, he answered, "I didn't check. Sorry, come in. I'll brew some coffee and we'll check in on them."

For a second, she hesitated to accept his offer; the door held wide inviting her in, but their illness worried her. "Coffee will be nice. They had a rough night?"

"Is the term *sick as a dog* insulting when referring to women?"

"I wouldn't recommend it."

"Well, in that case, they are drained. Weak, tired, coughing. After spooking you so bad at the door, I think it's necessary to prepare you. Hang on." The coffee grinder screamed for ten seconds, rendering conversation impossible. "This should wake them up."

As he put Mr. Coffee to work, Abby asked, "How are you feeling?"

"Me? I'm fine."

"But you just said you were sick."

"Yesterday, but now that I'm awake, not so bad today."

"You guys should see a doctor."

"Tell that to your friends. You don't need me to explain how stubborn they are."

"Do you have health insurance?"

"Me? Nah, I haven't seen a doctor in ages."

"What if you need it? A car wreck or AIDS or something?"

Eddie scoffed. "AIDS?"

"Well, I don't know! If it can happen to Ryan White, anyone can get it."

"I'm pretty sure it's not AIDS."

"I'm not judging."

"Celeste had the exact same thing the rest of us had; the doctors tested her for every known malady and came up empty."

"I didn't mean this... this, whatever you guys have. Okay, forget I mentioned AIDS." A deep red flushed the caramel complexion of her face. "Maybe I should go check on the patients..."

"How 'bout I bring your coffee up when it's ready? The girls will need some too. They can't function without it."

"Wait," he called after her, "how to you like it?"

"Sugar, and extra extra cream," she said, spinning around and taking one step backward. "Half and half will do if they don't have cream." She completed her full spin, then turned again after one step. "How do you like it?"

"Black."

Abby nodded, cheeks and ears glowing again, then turned to hurry up the stairs.

Ten minutes later, Eddie brought a tray to the twins' bedroom, their voices carrying through the open door. "... nothing to worry about," one twin was saying, but their voices were so similar, at distance, the sound of one impossible to differentiate from the other.

"*Nothing to worry about*?" answered Abby, incredulous, then in a hushed voice unlikely to be audible to a mere human, "Then why do I hear through the grapevine Bernie told his team your mother was in a coma for two days? Why didn't you tell me? Hell, why wasn't she in the ER?"

An unidentifiable voice answered, "Coma might be a slight exaggeration. More like a deep sleep."

The other twin said, "This virus saps it out of you. Makes you tired 24/7."

"What? *What* makes you tired? What is *this*? You should be in University Hospital before one of you ends up in a coma, too." One twin coughed, a deep, painful, dry cough. "Listen to that! You're hacking up a lung. You are literally whiter than your sheets and you," she said, presumably to the other twin, "there is something going on with your eyes. Your pupils look hollow. They are holes! I could stick a pencil in your eye and not touch anything."

"Did you wake and bake this morning? Her eyes are a little dilated, that's all."

"Here you go!" Eddie entered the room as if oblivious to their conversation. Head nodding toward one cup, he held the tray toward Abby. "Sugar and extra extra cream. Sugar for Josette and extra extra sugar for Angelique."

"Listen to you," said Angelique as she took hers, "already talking like a true Rhode Islander." Abby wasn't lying—her eyes really were messed up. Each twin hefted their cups as though served in gallon jugs.

"How do you feel this morning?"

"Not so bad," answered Josette.

Angelique peered over her mug. "Hungry."

"What do you want? I can whip up some oatmeal or cereal; if you can wait a few minutes, I can cook eggs and toast."

Those eyes, thin rings of violet around gaping black holes, bore into him. "You know what we want."

Face burning as he tried to answer calmly, stifling any trace of anger in his voice, he hoped Abby assumed he blushed with embarrassment, instead. "And you will get it. But for now, let me make you breakfast."

In a transparent effort to divert the conversation, Josette said, "Coffee's delicious." From her appearance and movements, Josette was not as far along as her sister.

Informative as sticking around to hear what they had to say might prove to be, leaving the girlfriends to talk alone was a far smarter move.

"Let me see what I can whip up for breakfast. Abby, do you want any?"

From where Abby sat on the edge of Josette's bed, she answered, "No, thanks—I already ate."

Too close. From there, what could she see in her friends?

†

Torrential rain fell in waves that unseasonably chilly

summer afternoon. After intensifying again, while thunder rolled closer with each rumble, knocking on her front door roused her. Usually people drop in for unexpected visits on bright, warm summer days while out enjoying the sunshine, hoping to drag her to join them on some fun adventure. Never on stormy days like this.

As she reached for the deadbolt knob, visions from horror movies flashed through her mind. That is how the day felt. But someone's car may have slid off a slick road into a ditch and was desperate to find a phone. A quick peek out the window beside the front door eased her fear, although the sight was even more unexpected than Jason standing there in a hockey mask.

"Eddie? What brings you here?"

Huge circles on his shoulders marked where raindrops landed. He must have sprinted from his car. Despite the drenching, he greeted her with a warm smile. "Hi, Abby."

"Don't just stand there in the rain, get in here! What are you doing way out here? Is everything okay?"

"Oh, everything is fine." He scurried through the door, in from the gusts of wind driving rain under the supposed shelter of the small rooflet over the landing.

"Whoa, you're soaked! What brings you out on a heinous day like this?"

"A little less heinous now, don't you think?"

She couldn't help but smile along with him. Weird as his visit may be, his infectious boy-like charm ensnared her. For a second, she regretted dressing so casually, in comfy old sweats that still fit, if too tight to be exposed to public scrutiny. "Okay, explain yourself. You are about the last person I expected to discover at my door."

"I hope you aren't disappointed?"

"At least it's not some serial killer. It's a perfect day for that."

"It is."

"Well, come sit down and dry off. Can I offer you

something to drink?"

"Do you have tea?"

"It just so happens I love tea."

While the teakettle warmed, they leaned against the counter, Abby still waiting for an explanation for his unexpected visit. Instead, Eddie looked around the room, inspecting the cabinets, ceiling beams, the counter behind her which she leaned upon. "This was Abdiel Strong's house, wasn't it?"

"He built it in the 1870s and it's remained in the family for over a century. How much do you know about him?"

"As much as I can dig up, in my role as the unofficial Brown family historian. Since Abdiel was the original George Brown's closest friend, I've heard many stories about him. A great guy, they say. Intelligent and with an iron will. Everyone respected the hell out of the man."

"Impressive. The way you tell it, someone might almost believe you knew him."

"What was he, your great-great-grandfather?"

"Three greats, I think. It's all in the family Bible. Can't claim to know all the details."

"Will you give me a tour? I love nineteenth-century homes."

"This isn't some ploy to get me into my bedroom, is it?"

With an expression in the gray zone between shock and offended, Eddie replied, "Wow! Do you always suspect such ulterior motives?"

"Chalk it up to experience."

"Let me assure you, when I want to get a woman into bed, my methods are much more direct."

"In that case, come—I'll give you a guided tour."

Although constructed by hand—the craftsmanship obvious—the ornate carpentry well made, with a charm no longer having any place in modern homes. Oak beams support the ceilings in each room. A massive fieldstone fireplace fills much of the living room. Like the Brown house, with additions tacked on over the years, but this home retained more of an historic air, carefully preserved over the generations. Judging by the fixtures and construction, Abby's room must have been added on to the rear in the forties, likely by a returning veteran to make room for his expanding family.

"It's a lovely home," Eddie said once seated in front of the fireplace, sipping cups of Earl Grey. "Chilly enough today to light a fire."

"Do you want me to find you a dry shirt? My brother left some old tees here that should fit. He's in college down in New York."

"No, it's drying off well."

"What's going on with 'Lique and Josette? How are they today?"

"They are having a rough time right about now. Just like their mother, it gets worse right before it gets better."

"What about you? Are you back to normal?"

"Me? Oh yeah, I'm fine now." He took a sip without further explanation.

"Maybe I should to visit them again, see how they are doing."

"Now is not a good time. They are both feeling like crap. Most of the time, they just sleep."

"Why do you suppose they all got so much sicker than you? Mrs. Brown went into a coma, didn't she?"

"I'm not a doctor, so I may not be the best person to ask, but that coma might have been exaggerated just a wee bit."

"Aren't you worried now that the twins have it, too?"

"A little. But since I had it, and look at Celeste—after terrible a case, now she is fine. Better than ever, if you ask me. And you don't need me to remind you how ornery they are. That gives me confidence Josette and Lique, as you call her, will do even better. By the way, I enjoy calling her Lique, but you seem to be the only one she lets get away with it."

For several more minutes, Abby pitched questions at him, each of which he batted away until she paused long enough for him to change the subject. "Do you know what most surprised me about Exeter?"

Her face betrayed how effectively this sudden turn threw her off. "No. What's here to surprise anyone?"

"See? That was my expectation level. All I knew were the dusty old family stories, memories passed down through generations."

"Nothing much has changed, far as I can tell," she smirked.

"Maybe not. Imagine my pleasant surprise with the incredible women I have met here. Intelligent, independent women. Women with actual substance. They're even more beautiful than a guy can imagine, to boot."

"Well, everyone agrees the twins are the two finest women in town."

"I'm not sure I can agree with that."

A tilt of her head and narrowed eyes told she was not buying it. "You're blind, baby, you can't see; you better wear some glasses like DMC."

"Run-DMC! Love those guys."

"They told me you were into all kinds of esoteric, alternative Gothic music."

"Let's just say my taste is eclectic. Perhaps that helps explain my resistance about the twins. No doubt they are stunning. You can travel the world and you won't find their equal. Take it from me—I have. But you need go no farther than their mother. She's a knockout."

"For sure. And since her illness, doesn't she look stellar? You'd think she was their sister, not their mother." She gave him a look.

"What?"

"This is a small town; I hear the rumors about the two of you."

"Did Angelique tell you that?"

"Nope—neither did Josette. Remember, this is a small town, and I have eyes."

"Yes, you certainly do. Remarkably beautiful eyes."

"The twins have amazing eyes of amethyst, and you expect me to think my boring brown eyes compare to theirs?"

"There's no need to compare. Yours are beautiful in their own right. Perhaps I'm biased, because you are one of the women who blew me away when I arrived in Exeter. Sure, your eyes are gorgeous, but they are merely a small part of a spectacular whole."

Although she turned her face to hide it, her cheeks glowed again. Imagination was unnecessary to realize how powerfully his revelation affected her. Quickly, though, she recovered her composure. "Oh, you're good. They warned me about you, you know."

"Warned you? About what?"

"That you'll charm a girl's pants off. And smooth, too."

Chuckling, he said, "They told you that?"

"Totally." She also laughed, although hers was out of discomfort.

"Do they tell you everything?"

"Pretty much."

Still with a smile, but his eyes hardened. "What else did they tell you about me?"

"Nothing, really. The usual. Nothing too bad—promise! Even when they talk about you being a womanizer, it's not a criticism. Just describing the way you are, the way Lique is a flirt—take it or leave it—and Josette can be a sarcastic bitch."

"Like that isn't critical?"

"It's true, and you know it, but I still love her like a sister."

Chin propped on a hand with his elbow resting on the table allowed him to give her a side-glance. Someone might think him relaxed. "It's true what I said about you. The moment you walked into the wake, trying not to look sexy but unsure how to turn it down, I felt an instant attraction to you. You're one of the most beautiful women I have ever laid eyes on."

"Stop it!"

"The funny thing is, you know it's true, no matter how much you hate it. You loathe what you can't control, no more than you can control the alluring color of your skin or the fact that you were born in a crappy little town in the middle of nowhere, Rhode Island. And you hate that guys only see your beauty and don't give a shit about your brain."

"I'm going to fucking kill those two!"

"They didn't tell me. Didn't have to. It's as obvious as your eyes. Try with me. Look into my eyes and tell me what you see. Or tell me what they said about me and pretend you can read it on my face."

"Okay, this should be fun. Let's see." Elbows planted firmly on the table in a two-handed version of his position, she peered into his face. "Blue. Sapphire blue! That's what I see."

"Come on, you can do better than that. Try harder."

Face locked into a mock-serious expression, she gave it another go. "Dangerous blue. I don't know, what am I supposed to see? I see a guy who's cute, but somehow comes across as hot, even though he's not. It's more attitude than looks. Like your cousins, I guess; although they are identical, if you asked a thousand people, every one of them would say Angelique is more beautiful."

"It's simple if you put your mind into it. The same way I can tell so much about you by looking into your eyes."

"How do you see more than that? They gave you the full rundown and you're just screwing with me, right?"

"I've got some bad news for you: they don't talk about you as much as you apparently believe they do. At least not to me. Then again, Josette sensed right away my attraction to you, so they might avoid the subject with me."

"Yeah? Well, same must go with me. Oh, shit! I did not just say that out loud!"

"You did. Good, at least we are being honest with each other."

"I don't like you anymore. You're like Perry Mason. I confess!" But she reached over, allowing her fingertips to touch his arm, a casual, subconscious signal.

"You know what we should do? Someday, when the weather is hot and sticky, we should go up to Yawgoo."

"You want to take me to the water park?"

"Sure. Why not?"

"Like a date?"

"Call it whatever you want."

"What do you call it?"

He let out a long exhale. "Aren't the most memorable first dates when you do something fun, maybe a little exciting? Movies don't allow much opportunity to get to know the other person; dinner is nice, but too stiff. More on guard, worried about making a good impression. Trying not to spill food on your shirt."

Her tone more a statement than a question, she said, "While your cousins are home sick, you want to date me?"

"They won't mind."

"Don't be too sure about that!"

"What's between me and them is totally casual. Nothing life or death, just some good, clean summer fun."

"Are you sure it's clean?"

"Well, mostly. Did you know your eyes are even more enchanting when you smile?"

"I suppose getting me out of my clothes and into a bikini never entered your mind."

"Of course not—but now that you mention it..."

Again tilting her head as if examining him from another angle might reveal the truth, she asked, "Tell me the truth: are you just looking for sex, or something else?"

"To be honest, something else."

"Have you slept with either of them? Because if you have..."

This time, it was he who reached out, taking her hands in his. "Let me assure you, I have not made love with either Lique or Josette."

"Remember, I told you I'm not judging."

"Do you believe I'm the kind of guy who would cheat on my cousins with their best friend?"

"You want honesty? Yes! Maybe what I saw in your eyes is a blue-eyed devil."

"Call them. If you don't believe me, ask them yourself."

"They will strangle me when they find out."

"We won't go behind their backs; I'll tell them up front. They'll be cool with it."

More obvious than actual gears turning in one of those clear, plastic heads in biology class, the pregnant pause while she worked through the permutations in her mind lasted a brutally long time. "This isn't because of you, because if this was only between us… but it's not. Fly as you are, I need a man-tart in my life like I need a hole in the head."

Nonplussed, he asked, "Man-tart? That's what you think of me?"

"As you've already noticed, I was born with eyes. And if you believe my two best friends don't talk to me about *every*thing," she emphasized it as if the word had four syllables, "then you are a space cadet."

"Honest, they're totally cool with it." While his eyes held hers captive, he took the end of one curly lock dangling low on her shoulder and twirled it between his fingers. "Talk to them. Then, let me know. You know where to find me."

"Sure do." He turned to go, but Abby stopped him. "All that talk about eyes made me remember something. Have you noticed anything strange about Lique's eyes?"

"Well, they are purple, same as her sister's. Strange might not be the word I'd choose for eyes of such unique beauty."

"Normally I'd agree with you—those girls have the most beautiful eyes I've ever seen. What I'm talking about is now. The other day when I dropped by, there was nothing beautiful at all about hers. Something was wrong with them. I've never seen anything like it."

"Tell you what—when I get home, I'll check them out for

you and let you know when we go to Yawgoo."

Making a good exit is a true art form, and he turned to make his before more questions came to mind.

LIKE A VIRGIN

Tim Maloney had no clue what to do. This was his first time he set foot inside a police precinct, and the moment he walked into the Providence Police Department, doubts hit. He had plenty of those. What seemed like a big deal back at home now felt ridiculous, even to him. The desk officer acknowledged him with a nod of the head.

"Hello, I'm not sure who to speak to about this, but I have something that might help your investigation." Tim placed a videocassette on the counter.

Again motioning with his head, this time at the VCR tape, the sergeant asked, "Which investigation?"

"Not sure about that, either. It's about a girl in the park. I knew nothing about it, but a friend of mine who lives a few blocks away said something happened in the park across from his house. Police, ambulance, fire department. I slept through the whole thing, but when he told me about it, I checked my tape, and he says this is the same girl."

"Okay, take a seat. I'll see what I can do."

†

He found the twins on the couch with a light blanket pulled over them, staring glassy eyed at a Madonna video playing on MTV.

"Oh-oh, this looks bad. What's wrong?"

As he reached for the remote control, Josette narrowed her eyes and her brow furrowed into a scowl. "Don't you dare turn that off!"

"What's the matter?"

"You know exactly what's wrong, and you are the only one who can do anything about it."

With a weak grin, Angelique explained, "She's having a rough day."

"What about you?"

"Oh, I'm okay."

"Meanwhile, I'm literally dying over here, and you aren't doing anything about it. Even worse, you promised me!"

"Well, that's what I wanted to talk about. Angelique, you don't mind if I borrow your sister for a few minutes, do you? Alone?"

"Depends on what you plan to do with her."

"Nothing that she doesn't want done to her."

Eyes lighting up, Josette said, "You mean…"

One of his greatest regrets was to deny another woman the same dying wish as Josette's. Regret has its own immortality. "Why don't we talk about it upstairs? Your mom and brother won't be back before dinner, so if you don't mind being left to your own devices for a while, I made a promise to Josette—and I honor my promises."

"Seems like I remember a promise you made to me, too."

He offered a hand to her sister while winking at Angelique. "And I intend to keep that one as well."

"Don't do anything I wouldn't do," Angelique's wicked grin followed them.

†

Detective Higgenbotham leaned one elbow on the far end of the long counter in the lobby while Tim Maloney related the story. With his other hand, he fidgeted with the tape, tapping the case against scarred linoleum. When the helpful citizen finished, he continued tapping.

"The thing is, there is no case. This incident is a textbook suicide attempt. While technically illegal, most times we don't charge people for failing to kill themselves. This case was no exception."

"Look, the footage is grainy, but when I showed it to Jim, he swears that is the same girl he saw laid out on the ground. According to the timestamp on the video, she walked by my house about a half hour before all the sirens woke Jim up."

"Why do you video the sidewalk in front of your house?"

"A few months ago, someone tried to break in. Check your records—I reported it. I'm a jeweler and sometimes keep valuable things inside my house. It's no surprise a jeweler's wife has plenty of fine jewelry, and when I attend shows, I often keep my display items or anything I purchase there in my home overnight. After the break-in, I installed cameras: one in front, one in back. In front, I aim it so it films the street. Never know when I might need to know what car someone came and left in."

"Listen, I will take a look at it, but I am not sure why it matters if a half hour before a disturbed student slits her wrist, she walked down the street with friends."

"Well, Jim said nobody was there with her. By then, her friends had vanished. How far could they have gotten in that time?"

"If they walked to a nearby car and drove off before the girl tried to kill herself? Pretty far."

"You're right, it's probably nothing. Maybe it will turn out to mean something, but if not, go ahead and keep the tape."

"Thanks, I will." The detective held the box up and gestured with it. "You never know."

†

Two red streaks raced down Eddie's chest, curving under his pectoral muscle and following along the contours of the ribs beneath it. In seconds, Josette set onto him, hands bracing against his shoulder and stomach a millisecond before her lips and tongue reached the leading drop of the quicker of the blood trails.

"Mmm," she moaned, lapping it up, smearing one cheek in the process.

"As much as you need," he said, running fingers through copper curls. "I fed last night, so drink. Take from me." Seconds later, he fell back onto the edge of the bed, holding himself up while steadying her head as his knees gave out. The pleasure the twins gave greater even than that of their mother, for reasons mysterious to him.

The secret of Josette's blood was no mystery. Virgin blood. No blood was redolent as the blood of a beautiful virgin. His youngest sister, Hope, told him on his deathbed a story an old man who had seen vampires as a child told to her. The blood of the innocent and the beautiful, he said—that is what vampires seek. Hope mentioned it only in passing as she struggled to accept her role in what they did to Lena, but it stuck with him. Lena was a virgin, too. When the illness first struck Eddie, so was he.

Josette's honied blood was sweet as any he had tasted. A shame if fulfilling his promise took any of its sweetness, but he gave his word. But Angelique's was magical, and she freely admitted to her lack of sexual innocence. Celeste's, too. Perhaps the allure of blood which shared his curse was the most powerful. If not, he owed her. More than that, as a woman, her appeal to his baser nature took more willpower to control than he possessed.

He stared, unable to pull his eyes from her beauty. Even emaciated as she was, in his twelve decades, he may never have seen a more perfect woman,

After a moment, he pulled up her tee-shirt. This morning, she'd dressed as she felt, perhaps the least sexy thing he'd seen her wear, but if attempting to hide her beauty, she failed miserably. White cheeks concave from energetic suckling on his nipple relaxed, allowing her to yank her head through the hole, her mop of curly hair pulling through last. The instant her arms were freed, she lunged for his wound again, muscles rippling under diaphanous, translucent skin, beneath which ribs and each bone of her spine stood out. The emaciation her illness caused did nothing to dim her beauty.

Crouched down on the floor between his knees kept her plaid flannel PJ pants out of his reach, so his hands around her waist lifted her onto the bed beside him, and she willingly came. If she noticed him pulling down her pants, she did not let on until, reaching her knees, she lifted to help him. Despite the many times her sister had bared her body to him, this was the first time Josette had allowed him to see hers gloriously nude, and for a moment he allowed himself to drink in the vision as she drank his blood.

"Slow down—there is no hurry."

"I'm famished!"

"I know. Take your fill—you'll need the energy."

His words must have allowed his reason for bringing her to her bedroom to intrude back in her mind, pushing aside an instinct so primal it cast aside all other thought, enough for her to reach down and touch him. Angelique enjoyed giving him this type of pleasure while he was already in the throes of blood passion, but she never did.

"Don't." He smiled as she glanced up. "Today is all for you."

"You don't want...?"

"Only if you want."

As though a veil lifted, Josette's focus on feeding diminished. "If you are just doing this because I made you promised me I won't die still a virgin..."

"I want to possess you in every way, and for you to possess me any way your little heart desires."

"This is all real, isn't it?"

Puzzled, he asked, "What do you mean?"

"This. Us. Everything. Sometimes I expect to wake up from the strangest dream of my life, where I'm drinking blood and you're in love with me. Once awake, though, I'll still be a virgin and you won't be a vampire. Like we were."

"Sometimes I wonder the same. Do you want to feed some more?"

"Maybe that's enough. Now all I can think of is..." She kissed him, and he lay back, pulling her on top of him. For a long time, they kissed, longer than they ever had before, and he caressed every inch of the back of her body from her shoulders down far as his reach allowed, her uppermost thighs. Closing her mouth over his, she exhaled into him, sharing her breath again as he shared his blood to keep her alive.

Her passion, conveyed in those kisses, told him when she was ready.

"We do not need to do this, Josette."

Confused, she asked, "What do you mean? Don't you want me?"

"We already share an intimacy surpassing sex. What we've given, what we have taken, is greater than sex. Sure, when I drink your blood and you drink mine, a vulgar mind might consider that sharing body fluids, but it is much more. I offer you my life essence and you allow me to partake of yours."

"But in sex, don't you put your life essence inside me?"

"No, that's very different. It is not my life essence, it is the essence of a life which may come into existence only after it is inside you. My potential child's life essence, not my own. That cannot happen now, not with us."

"What does that mean, not with us?"

"The dead cannot father children," he said. "Besides, if I could put a life inside you, in nine months you will no longer be alive."

"When you consume my blood, you take from me what I need to survive, something that does not happen during sex. In fact, drink too much and one of us will kill the other. And while a woman may take some of the man's essence into her during sex, a man cannot take from woman the equivalent of what he puts into her body. He takes nothing from her but his own pleasure."

"But isn't the pleasure the point?"

"Of course, but the pleasure I have shared with you is far greater than you will get from sex."

"Am I supposed to just take your word for it?"

"Not at all. After experiencing the pure bliss of feeding, it's just that sex might be a slight let-down."

It started as a giggle, but in seconds was laughing so hard her knees curled her up in a ball and she hid her face with her hands.

"What? Did I say something funny?"

When she regained her self-control, she caressed his face. "Do you know what I love about you, Eddie? Intelligent as you are, you make an adorable airhead."

"What did I say?"

"Okay, first of all, I have more faith in your ability to satisfy a woman than you do. Second..."

"Hey! I'll have you know; I can satisfy a woman."

"Second, excuse me." She held up a palm like a traffic cop stopping traffic. "A woman's first time isn't about physical pleasure. Everyone knows how painful it is, which my sister took great pains to warn me all about—and that girl's pain threshold is as low as mine. It's emotional, the act that transforms a little girl into a woman; late as it may be in my case."

He avoided her eyes, head down with the expression of a foolish boy reprimanded by his teacher for flunking the easiest test of the year.

"In my case, there is something else. Have you ever wondered why I hung onto my cherry for so long?"

"It has crossed my mind."

"Years ago, I decided not to give it up until I fell in love."

"Oh, I see."

"Yeah, well, I'm not entirely sure if I love you or if you have simply hypnotized me into believing I do so you can kill me and turn me into a monster without me bitching about it too much."

"And take your virginity."

"Right, and take my virginity."

"I have never hypnotized you. I give you my solemn word. The only time I did that to you or your sister was when I came to you while you slept."

Sincerity in his eyes convinced her he spoke the truth. "Good, although that means I can't blame any of this on you. Then there is the minor detail that I don't even know who you are. We are related—I get that—but what am I to you? I shouldn't ask, should I? Because you are going to give me some screwed-up answer that is going to make turning into a vampire the most normal part of this whole thing, aren't you?"

"Pretty much."

"You're him, aren't you—the original Edwin Brown? Mercy Brown's brother."

"Yes, I am."

Her hands shot up to cover her breasts, then realizing what still lay exposed to him, covered her crotch with one while making use of her forearm to hide herself. "Goddamn it! I knew it! Then you're my great-great-grandfather."

"Three greats."

"Eddie, that is totally messed up!"

"Not really. Thank about it: five generations back you have 32 grandparents, which means I'm about 3% related to you. Your parents were first cousins four times removed. Technically, that makes them more closely related than us."

Her face glowed the deepest crimson color her skin had achieved in her entire life. "I'm in love with my grandfather. I am lying naked in bed with my grandfather. Why? Because I want my grandfather to..."

"Great-great-great-grandfather."

"Whatever. Because I want my grandfather to make love to me, so when he kills me, I won't still be a pathetic virgin! Does that about sum it up?"

"Yup. Sounds worse than it is, though."

"Okay, I need some air. Breathe!"

"Here, drink this." She pulled up the sheet up to cover her lower half so one hand and arm would cover her breasts and still allow her to hold the wineglass he offered, so far untouched. In her rush to guzzle it, a drop fell from the corner of her lips and landed on her cleavage, bunched up under her forearm like she was wearing a medieval bustier. She handed the empty glass back to him. "Are you okay?"

"Better. Trying to process all this. In the back of my mind, I think I knew this all along. It's easier to pretend, to tell yourself it's not as heinous as it really is. Whew!" Her free hand fanned her face from inches away. She took the glass when he offered it refilled, while he allowed reality to sink in.

"How old are you?"

"120."

"Do you suppose any other woman in all of history has ever slept with her great-great-great-grandfather?"

"Probably not."

"Please tell me that's a little hot."

"I may be biased, but if it wasn't hot, would I be here with you right now?"

"Did you kill my father?"

Her sudden change of subject was brilliantly played, timed to throw him off balance expertly as a Perry Mason cross-examination; unexpected as Roger Clemens throwing a knuckleball on a 3-2 count. "Yes."

"I knew it! Is it because of what he did to Angelique?"

"What did your father do to Angelique?"

Josette turned and spoke toward the far wall. "We were only eleven, twelve maybe. I knew, of course. She didn't tell me, but I knew. Twins always know things. I put a stop to it. Threatened him, swore I would tell Mama and everyone else. That's why we hated him."

"Did he stop?"

"Yeah. Yeah. She swears I saved her. Made us even closer. But we hated him for it."

"Makes me feel better about throwing him off that roof."

"You knew. Don't ask how, and maybe not the details, but I choose to believe you somehow knew somewhere deep inside."

"I guess it's possible."

"This isn't like that for you, is it?"

"No, of course not! Intellectually, I understand the details, and emotionally, we share a bond that comes from our blood, but I don't think of you as a granddaughter or anything. It feels like we are the same generation, though we are far from it. My son was born after I died and left Exeter, so I never knew him or any other descendants until your father, so to me, you are just some distant kin."

"It might be kinda hot to be the first woman in history to lose her virginity to her great-great-great-grandfather." Her smile was a relaxed one. "We won't need a rubber?"

"Vampires can't get a woman pregnant."

Josette crinkled her forehead. "Right. Because you are dead."

Eddie laughed. "Don't use the word *dead*."

"Why not?"

"It's not accurate. Am I dead? Was I dead when I drove you around in the car? When I drank your blood? Are you planning to make love to a dead man?"

"Oh, damn! What will that make me, a necrophiliac?"

"By the strictest technical definition."

"Oh, gag me with a spoon! We're a family of necrophiliacs!"

"Pretty much."

"Then what are you? Undead?"

"Better, but I don't fancy that too much, either."

"Then what should we call it?"

"Deceased."

"Deceased? No one uses that word. Not in real life. Doctors maybe. Undertakers."

"But that's what we are. Deceased. To cease means to

end. My life and your mother's ceased, then weren't ceased anymore. We de-ceased."

"That's clever. I like it! I'm going to use it, too." For a minute, she was deep in thought. "But I'm not a vampire yet, right?"

"It won't be long."

"Will it hurt?"

"Becoming a vampire, or becoming a woman?"

"Both, I guess."

"Yes. But I believe you will find the pain worth it on both counts. Are you sure you're ready?"

"When I was a girl, I imagined it being all romantic. Later, I can't tell you how many times I had to fight to keep it from happening in a car or in the bathroom at some party. I'm serious—half the girls I know lost theirs while drunk or stoned. Or worse."

"Wish this was more romantic?"

"How much more romantic can it be than losing it to a vampire after allowing me to drink his own blood to give me enough strength to enjoy it? I suppose most vampires would have just done it while I was asleep and they were feeding on me."

"Not sure there are any other male vampires. If there are, this must be your lucky day."

"Yay me!"

"I am here, and I am yours to use and abuse however you want."

"Will this be it? Our only time?"

"Depends. They say women enjoy it more the second time. Then again, we will have eternity together."

†

Despite piles of paper clogging his overflowing inbox, Higgenbotham sat in the interviewing room where he'd wheeled the TV and VCR cart. Unable to explain even to himself why, he watched the video Maloney brought him. Rewound to a few seconds before the part where the people entered the picture, just as the man explained, showed the static image of a front yard, street and sidewalks framing the top. Cars lined one side, parallel parked on this street built a hundred years ago, before there were cars.

Maloney was right, the black-and-white image was grainy. Manufacturers design VCR tapes to record four hours of video. To save money and allow recording a full night, this surveillance system crammed eight hours onto one tape, degrading the image for the sake of economy and requiring it to run on the slow-motion setting to view at regular speed. Although expecting it, the first several seconds were so still it startled him when figures emerged from the left side of the screen.

Right off the bat, he recognized the girl, Anne. Accompanied by a man dressed in black who towered over the petite brunette, his blonde hair the most notable feature in the grainy image. Half a second later, a woman followed close behind. Also blonde, and even with the poor image quality and the distance, this woman was a looker. Also dressed in black, hers a short black dress, early to mid-twenties, he guessed. The man was harder to pin an age on, roughly about the same. Nothing unusual, friends on their way home from the local bars. None of the telltale signs of intoxication cops know by sight.

Other than the head-turning looks of the blonde woman and the fact that the brunette slit her wrist a few minutes later, the video was wholly unremarkable.

Afterward, sealed in a manila evidence envelope, the VCR sat in his outbox destined for the records room with the incident report documenting a suicide attempt.

†

Legs, arms and fingers entwined, basking in the

afterglow, Josette asked, "Why did you kill our father?"

"By then, I decided I must try to transform your mom. She told me about the DKC, and since she could go at any time —your sister, too—I didn't want to dither in case something went sideways. Turning Angelique meant I had to take you with her at the same time..."

"Because I'd know."

"Bingo. Bernie is a kid, so I didn't worry much about him. But no way in hell was I taking your father! Just starting on his wife and two girls—well, it was big a risk. He had to go. Didn't seem anyone would shed too many tears, either."

"So you had to kill him to save Mama and my sister?"

"That's part of it."

"What's the other part?"

His finger followed the line of her collarbone. "I've lived 120 years. Everyone I know dies. Everyone. It gets wearisome. I tried everything, but nothing worked. My last hope was the answer lies in our genes. Luckily, it does. Before we met, I worried you might be a boring bunch..."

"Boring is one word no one has ever used to describe us."

"No kidding." He struck her hip, too soft to be considered a slap. "So much could go wrong. Before traveling here, I wrote out a list. Dumb as bags of sand, boring, super religious—not sure how that might have worked out. We're not talking about spending a week on vacation together. This is long term. Very long term. I'm not ashamed to admit another possibility terrified me."

"What was that?"

"What if all of you were butt-ugly?"

"Oh, you are such a pig!" Their bodies, still wrapped together, shook with mirth.

"Guilty as charged, your honor. Imagine if the ugliest guy you ever saw showed up and invited you to spend eternity with him? *No thanks, dude—I'm good.* Seriously, scared the hell out of me."

"Glad we didn't disappoint you."

"In my 120 years, I've never seen three women who compare to you. Josette, you are an astonishing woman. There is no one else I'd rather spend forever with."

†

Downstairs, Angelique turned to the sound of footsteps on the ancient wooden staircase. "How did virgin sacrifice ritual go?"

Her sister responded with a little dance down the final few stairs, and her sister rushed to meet her at the bottom with a hug, the two laughing until Josette reached for Eddie. "Get over here!" She pulled him to join in the hug with them. A tear ran down her cheek toward her upturned lips.

"This calls for a celebration!" Angelique returned with a fine bottle of Cabernet, which they drank on the couch with Eddie book-ended between two gorgeous redheads. "Tell me everything."

Eddie said, "Why don't we leave the details private?"

"You'll tell me later."

"Maybe," Josette responded.

"Is your sister always this nosy?"

"It's a twin thing. Those who aren't don't understand. Identical twins begin life as one person, but even after we became two, we are still one. We have no secrets from each other."

Angelique added, "Most of the time, we don't need to say a word. We already know."

"Good to know. I suppose you will use that against me?"

They giggled simultaneously, and said together, "We already have."

UNDER PRESSURE

How well he remembered days like this. Too weak to walk or even drag yourself out of bed to piss; too apathetic to care. Sometimes he loathed himself for subjecting anyone else to suffer through this—let alone these women he genuinely cared about. Years before, he thought he'd been cured of such pathetic empathy. Twice, at least. Any cure those tragic endings brought proved a temporary one, at best.

What he offered—what they stood to gain—more than compensated for any misery he inflicted upon these women. His own family. His blood. Unless Celeste was some freakish anomaly, these girls also would receive the same gift of complete freedom, and soon.

But their suffering weighed on him. Out of a sense of guilt, he carried Angelique's dinner up to her room on a tray. Josette still had the strength to make it downstairs on her own, thanks to the generous blood feast he gave before deflowering her. Angelique concealed her jealousy well, but her sister saw it. And so did he.

Tray balanced perilously on one arm, he tapped on the door with his free hand. "Room service."

To his surprise, the door opened. "Come in."

"What are you doing out of bed?"

"Try staying in bed all day every day; see how you like it."

"Oh, I remember. Don't forget, I've been where you are. Down the hall in your brother's room, but everything else is the same."

"I had to get up. Feels fine, if only in small doses. Here, put that down." She waved toward the bed while shutting the door behind him. "Where's everyone else?"

"Your mother is chauffeuring your brother—baseball practice, I believe—your sister is camped in front of the TV. I'll bring her up later." He placed the tray on the bedside table.

When he turned around, Angelique stood inches behind him. Much too close. So close, in fact, he nearly bumped into her—if he had, she hadn't the strength to stay on her feet, so he grabbed her slender hips. "Woah! Almost knocked you on your ass!"

Without a word, she struck. Lips of pink so light, deprived of blood as they were, translucent and unbearably soft, closed over his lower lip as arms encircled his neck. Her body smashed against his as her tongue forced itself into his mouth without ceremony.

It was an unusual kiss, and not in a bad way. Her tongue burned with a passion her body lacked the ability to deliver. Perhaps realizing this, in less than thirty seconds, her tongue slowed, her lips sealed over his, and she inhaled, drawing air from deep within his body into her own. Immediately understanding, Eddie gently exhaled into her, then took her breath into his lungs in return. Her tongue never left his mouth, but caressed his as their life breath passed over it.

Then she pulled away and stared into his eyes. He asked, "What was that about?"

"Thank you."

"Well, in that case, I'll bring you three meals every day and snacks on the hour."

"Not for that, dufus!" Narrow eyes and wrinkled brow convinced her that he missed her meaning. "My sister told me. About last night."

"What did she tell you?"

"Everything."

"Are you sure?"

"*Every*thing!" Arms pulling herself in tighter and her tiny, fragile body molding to his, she said, "When this is over and my energy comes back, I have some other ideas how to more properly thank you."

"Better than this?"

"Better," her face nuzzled his chest. "Much better. The way Josette thanked you last night, and a few she can't imagine."

"Listen, Darlin', being with your Mom and your sister will be complicated enough."

"Don't even start! It's poor form to deny a dying girl her last request—even if she won't be able to fulfill it until she's dead and gone." Again, she sought out his eyes. "Seriously, am I the only woman in this family you don't want to sleep with?"

"Trust me, that is not it at all."

"Do you have any doubt I trust you? I trust you with my life, and now I'm offering my body as a cherry on top. Okay, maybe not a cherry like my sister's, but—trust me—it will be worth your while."

"Oh, no doubt. It's just a lot for a simple country boy to take in. Maybe we'll have a family meeting to discuss this. Sounds like a high degree of difficulty, and we will need to all be together on this. The last thing we will need is conflict."

"Exactly. We all need to be together."

†

Reports such as this can slip by unseen and forgotten in Detective Higgenbotham's over-stuffed inbox. With his caseload, too many do. Chalk it up to divine intervention, but he read a BOLO for a couple of suspects wanted for kidnapping and assault. No names, no photos. An easy BOLO to ignore because, without those essential details, the memo might read *Watch out for bad people*.

This description, though. He'd heard it before. In fact, he'd seen them. Both blonde, early to mid-twenties, the young man tall and handsome, the woman petite and strikingly attractive. Similar M.O., too. This woman, however, did not nearly bleed out. Same absence of drugs in her system, nothing stolen. In the BOLO, the blondes took her home. When she woke up in the morning feeling ill, they had vanished into the night without a trace. The only thing doctors found wrong with her was a small, unexplained laceration.

The next morning, he began the day in Kingston. After that, he drove to Cranston. It wasn't fair—nothing in Rhode Island is. In less than a half hour, he pulled into the parking lot of the state Institute for Mental Health. Originally, some bureaucratic genius named it the State Insane Asylum, but by the time they completed construction in the early 1870s, calmer heads prevailed and it opened under the kinder, gentler name State Asylum for the Incurable Insane.

When an orderly brought Anne Carlisle to the meeting room in the administrative wing, Higgenbotham had an AV cart with TV and VCR player ready to go. "Hi, Anne. Have a seat, if you don't mind. Do you remember me? I'm Det. Higgenbotham from the Providence Police Department, and we met that night out at the park. You were pretty out of it at the time."

"Sorry, I don't remember you."

Today she looked much prettier, and they allowed her to dress in street clothes, although he took note the belt loops in her jeans were empty. "This is Det. Brenda Russo from the Kingston P.D. How are you?"

"They tell me I'm mental, but other than that...?" She shrugged her shoulders. The medication took the edge off her emotions.

Det. Russo picked up from there. "Well, I am investigating a case down in Kingston, and we think you may be some help to us."

"I haven't been to Kingston for at least a year."

"Don't worry, Anne—you aren't a suspect. We hope you might help us identify a couple of suspects. It might help your situation, as well."

"How can it help me?"

Higgenbotham said, "If you don't mind, can we show

you a video? A home CCTV camera took this; it's grainy, so sorry about that. Just take a look at it and let us know what you think."

The moment the man walking with her came into view, she leaned forward in rapt attention. A second later, the woman stepped into the frame. "That's them! Where did you get this video?"

"Someone brought it in several days after your attack."

"Those are the people who drugged me. That looks like when they were taking me to… where they found me."

Higgenbotham could not contain a grin. "Anne, Det. Russo has a similar case, and we showed this video to the victim of that incident before we came to see you. That victim identified these same two people as the ones who kidnapped and assaulted her."

"See? I told them I wasn't crazy, but no one believed me."

"Well," Higgenbotham said, "we have evidence supporting you now."

†

"Hey, how are my girls?" Abby found the twins under a blanket on the couch, snuggled together in front of the TV. She must have been worried about their continuing malady to have decided to again stop by unannounced to check on them. As usual, she let herself in through the kitchen door. Although able to control it well, for an instant after her eyes fell on them, her face conveyed the shock.

"We're okay," Josette said, rather unconvincingly.

"I sure hope you feel better than you look, because you look like death warmed over."

Angelique answered, "Well…"

Underneath the blanket, Abby may not have noticed her sister's elbow, which somehow hit Angelique in the boob to shut her up. "It's a slow process, but we're getting better."

"Please tell me you've been to your doctor?"

"No. Mama's fine now, so we know it won't be long until we are, too. Angelique's having a rougher time of it, but she's okay, aren't you?"

"So they tell me."

"This is loco. You need medical attention. Have you seen yourselves in a mirror? You were always too perfectly skinny, but now you look totally anorexic."

As she spoke, the theme music of the early news played, leading off with a robbery and car chase that began with a traffic stop in Narragansett and ended in a four-car crash somewhere in Connecticut. Just background noise, since no one paid much attention. Abby made sure of that, peppering them with questions, her gorgeous face twisted with sympathetic pain. Intrusive as her questions were, they usually appreciated their friend's concern.

This was not one of those days.

Josette snapped first. "Can't we save it for another day?"

Her tone shocked Abby. "It's your lives we're talking about. Can't you see I'm worried about you?"

"It's boring to talk about. We'll be fine. Can't we discuss something else?"

"Anything else?" her sister concurred.

In the momentary pause that followed, the news anchor said, "And police are asking for your help locating two persons of interest involved in a pair of attacks that left one Rhode Island resident hospitalized and another lucky to have escaped unharmed. Home surveillance cameras caught two persons of interest with the victim of one of those attacks. The man is described as twenty to twenty-five, six feet to six foot three, with blonde hair and blue eyes. The woman is twenty-five to thirty, five two to five four, also with blonde hair. If you recognize these people, call Crime Stoppers at (401) 322-..."

Abby's mouth hung open, head forward. "What the hell? Did you see that?"

Angelique asked, "See what?"

"Didn't you recognize them—the suspects? That was

Eddie and your mother!"

"I wasn't paying any attention," she answered, although Abby saw her staring straight at the TV screen the second the story ended.

"That was them! I'd recognize your mother anywhere, and Eddie came by my house—which is the reason I came over to talk to you."

Josette chuckled, "It's not them. The report said the woman they are looking for is twenty-five to thirty. That would make her eleven or younger when she gave birth to us."

"I don't care how old they say she is; did you see the video? That is her!"

"Why do you want to talk to us about Eddie?" Angelique's icy gaze startled Abby almost as much as her refusal to discuss something as serious as her mother and cousin filmed at some crime scene.

Her sister added, "Did you see this video before you came here? Is that what this is about?"

"No, I never saw that video before! I only came because Eddie asked me out. I figured it was a good idea to tell you before anything happened."

Now Josette's expression appeared identical to her twin's. "What do you think is going to happen?"

"Huh? I mean, he asked me out. And he's got something going on with your mother. I knew that before I saw them on TV with some woman who was attacked. Did they say where that happened?"

"We told you we weren't paying attention."

"Don't spaz out on me. What is going on with you guys? Do you know what those two are up to? Are you covering for them?"

"There's nothing to cover for," Josette said, her voice a low growl. "Did you say yes? Are you going to go out with him?"

"He's on the news—police are looking for him and your mom because they may have attacked some women. You think

I'm going out with him under those circumstances? What has gone wrong in your head?"

"You should," Angelique said. "He's sweet. And the last thing Eddie would do is rape a woman. Believe me—I've tried to get him to rape me, and nothing doing."

The twins giggled, which repulsed Abby. "That's not funny! Whatever you two've got, it's messed up your heads." She practically jumped to her feet. "The last subject I ever expected you to joke about is rape! Either of you. That is disgusting!"

As she stormed out toward her car, the twin's giggles exploded into a round of unrestrained, boisterous laughter.

†

Around another campfire out by the pond provided the necessary seclusion. In other circumstances, it might have been as fun or romantic as their previous evenings there. This time, the risk of Bernie overhearing made it necessary. Still, though far from prying eyes and ears, they held their voices to a whisper. Which was hard—perched on the edge as they were.

Eddie quizzed the twins. "How fuzzy was the picture?"

Josette answered, "Your faces are pretty blurry."

"If the two of you weren't together, I never would have noticed," Angelique added. "Mama, your head is turned, so it's mostly the back of your head. Your butt—it looks like butter in that dress, by the way. I doubt anyone will recognize you other than people who have seen you together and think, hey, wait a minute…"

"Good thing few people know me," he said, "but if Abby recognized me, someone else might, too."

"She said you just saw her, so you were fresh on her mind," Josette said. "She says you showed up at her house to ask her out a couple of days ago. When were you planning to tell us about that?"

"I planned to tell you if we go out. Does anyone have a

problem with that?"

Scowling, Angelique said, "As a matter of fact, some people I know just might. Depends on whether you are going out with her because you are hungry or because you are horny?"

Exasperated, he sighed. "Does it really matter?"

"It's true what they say about you guys: get what you want and then you are off on your next conquest," her sister said.

"Please, girls—chill, okay? That's hardly the biggest problem here. And you need to get over this jealousy thing. Funny, before my transformation I undoubtedly would be furious, but now little things like that don't matter. Eddie needs to feed and we can't always be hunting strangers on the street. Which gets back to the problem at hand, the one with the videotape."

"Thank you, Darling." He leaned over to kiss Celeste, a sumptuous kiss which may have been a message.

Brow crinkled up in mock disgust, Angelique said, "How do we handle this?"

Leaned forward on his elbows, he asked too calmly for comfort, "Will she tell anyone?"

"Good question," Josette answered. "Abby's a good girl, but she's also a good friend. If she decides to tell, I bet she will call first to give us a heads-up."

Celeste said, "She won't tell you in person?"

Oddly shaking their heads synchronized in perfect the time of Olympic skaters, Angelique spoke. "If she is convinced it's you, she is going to be terrified to come anywhere near Eddie. No, she'll call to let us know so Mama can do something. Maybe even to give you time to disappear."

"She'd do that for you?"

"Sure," answered Angelique. All this whispering strained her voice, setting off a round of coughing.

"Maybe," said Josette.

"Well, we can't take that chance, can we? If your mom

and I could turn into bats, the police showing up might not be a problem. Movie vampires have it so easy."

"Yeah, I've been meaning to ask about that," Angelique said, her voice raspy, then coughed again.

Josette picked it up for her. "We have some questions about that. Not necessarily bats—that part was always stupid—but some of the other things."

Her mother put an end to that line of questioning. "Now's not exactly a good time for that, dear. Not when we have genuine problems to deal with. Speaking of which, it's almost time for the eleven o'clock news. Let's head back to see if they are still showing the video."

As they stood, Eddie wrapped it up. "Girls, she can't know you spoke to us about this, okay? She's glued to the TV, waiting to watch the late news to convince herself she was seeing things. We're probably good for tonight, at least. That will give us time. Don't worry—I know how to handle this."

HOT FOR TEACHER

Eleven miles west of town, the car took the on-ramp onto I-95. An hour south, it exited the highway. Laid out like a wheel with spokes radiating from its center, they drove through the city center only a minute or two after leaving the interstate. Even after sunset, locating a more charming New England town may well be an impossible task, but to enjoy it, you must know the area well enough to take your eyes off the road. Instead, Eddie followed Celeste's directions.

"Okay, turn right here—I think."

"You think?"

"Hey, the twins were in elementary school last time I came here. Don't worry—you can't get lost in this town. If we miss it, we'll just park and walk a couple of blocks."

They missed it. A circle composed of right turns brought them back around soon enough, though. On their second pass, she pointed to a green and white awning protruding over the sidewalk from an otherwise nondescript two-story building.

"Toad's Place. Strangely, it has a ring to it."

"Oh, it's perfect," Celeste assured him. "U2 played here; so did Springsteen. It is *the* place in New Haven."

"Reggae, blues, jazz, hip hop, metal, dance," Eddie read off the awning, passing slowly in search of parking. "What are the odds it is metal night?"

"I hate metal."

"We didn't come for the music; we came for the food."

"You sound like a TV commercial."

"Missed my calling," he said.

"Are you sure you took care of the problem?"

"Reasonably sure," he answered with a calm smile. They did not ask, and he did not explain what he had done, merely assured them he took care of it and expected no more trouble from Abby. "The twins like her too much to make the problem go away permanently. Will be a shame if it comes to that. Such beauty should never be wasted. Besides, I genuinely like her."

She wrapped her arm through his and cuddled him close. "The girls will put a stake in your heart if you hurt Abby."

Two blocks away from the parallel parking spot Eddie found, they neared the club, arm in arm like any other couple on a date. Eddie started humming a tune. "What is that? I recognize it—from my childhood, maybe?"

"Peace Frog, by the Doors. Toad's Place made me think of it." Then he started singing the lyrics. "*Blood in the streets in the town of New Haven.*"

Celeste joined in a line later, after a couple hummed lines of forgotten lyrics, "*Blood is the rose of mysterious union.* I always thought that was a cool line, even though I had no clue what it meant when I heard it as a teenager."

Together, they sang the rest of the way to the bar. *Blood in the streets is up to my ankles, blood in the streets is up to my knees. Blood in the streets of the town of New Haven.*

As usual, heads turned inside when they made their way through the bar. Men, women, Yale students, laborers. Borrowed from Angelique, patterned black stockings hugged shapely thighs flowing from an oversized sweater. This one blood red, an identical match to the gold sweater she wore on their first hunt, a neckline so massive it hung off her bare shoulder down her bicep. Unbelievably sexy, although not overt. Then again, Celeste could have made painter's overalls look fine. A raised table with tall stools afforded a view over the crowd.

She nodded in the direction of one studly man in his thirties. In response, Eddie shook his head. "Not that one."

"Why not?"

"He's old. Do you want to look old? Because that will

happen if you take blood from someone his age. Choose someone young, innocent. Someone beautiful."

"We'll have better luck finding someone young and beautiful than innocent in here. Besides, he's younger than me."

"Two out of three ain't bad. Do you prefer looking twenty-five or thirty-five? Heck, let's go raid a retirement home."

She drew in a deep breath. "Can you imagine how easy it would be there?"

"Listen, we didn't drive all this way for easy."

She swirled her beer in front of her face, eyes sparkling above its rim. "Will drinking genius blood make us geniuses?"

"You know, that sounds like a theory worth testing out. One twin can feed from Yalies, the other can suck moron blood."

"How about I suck Yalies and you suck beautiful bimbos and we'll see what happens?"

"That's not the worst idea I ever heard." He ducked in time to miss being hit by a masterfully flicked coaster. "Dang, you are deadly with those things."

"It's been a while, but this is not my first time bar-hopping." She motioned behind him with a wicked grin. "What about them?"

"Jackpot! Scholarship nerds! From the looks of 'em, not a one has ever been laid."

"And what do you know—right next to the dart board." She flashed a coquettish grin. "Care to make a bet?"

"I may just be lousy enough for one of my shots to accidentally hit them. I'm sure you won't mind making sure they don't bleed all over their clean white shirts."

†

"This just sucks!"

Almost asleep, Josette pushed her head deeper between

two pillows. "What sucks?"

"Aren't you famished?"

"I'm constantly hungry."

"It's been two days."

"He hasn't fed all week; he has nothing to give us. That's why they're out hunting tonight."

"Doesn't make it suck any less."

"Stop whining and go to sleep! Let's hope they have some luck down there. They will share."

Ten minutes later, Josette did not hear the floor creak or the door close as her sister tiptoed down the hall.

†

The four made their way back to the car. Eddie held open the front and rear passenger doors for the women to get in. Celeste took the back seat; Stephen, a computer engineering major, climbed in the other side beside her. The small Asian woman took Eddie's offered hand to climb in front. Beth—from L.A. and in her senior year studying French literature—felt light as a feather, but was adorable, even if her hair, chopped off too short in complete disregard to style, was simply tragic.

Quality over quantity. He forced himself to remember to take care.

In the rear-view mirror, the unblinking kid following Celeste's every move. "Hey, Steve—how you doing back there?"

"Good."

Celeste leaned forward to whisper, "Is he?"

"Steve, remind me of your date's name? I forget."

"Oh, I don't... that's strange."

He winked at her. "See? Told you—you can do it. Beth, why don't we go back to your apartment?"

"Let's go to my apartment," she said.

Instead, they drove north, out of town, toward the Naugatuck State Forest. If either of the students noticed, it failed to reach the parts of the brain that control speech, movement or fear. Did they believe they were swept up in a dream?

One thing he knew is that he was not is a burglar. Better take them somewhere than to break in while some stranger is asleep. Long ago, he found this flawless strategy worked. Whatever memories remained were muddled, foggy, confusing—that much he knew. But often, he imagined himself in their places, walking down a street or riding to their doom in a stranger's car.

The Park proper closed at sunset, although roads passing through remained open. A dirt road ran behind a hill to the right. An ancient logging road, snaking twists which Eddie negotiated like a Florida retiree. Out of sight from the road, he stopped and switched off the lights. "Beth, why don't you undo the seatbelt?" Thank the stars or heavens or gods or whatever, this car did not have those infernal automatic seatbelts permanently anchored in the center. He tucked her short hair back behind one ear. "I want to kiss you."

A careful gash behind her ear bled delicious red; he drew his insidious meal.

In the back seat, an eager Stephen allowed Celeste to unbutton his shirt, and a small knife opened a slit through the pale skin of his skinny chest. The kid's head fell back, just like the woman in the front passenger seat.

In the cool, humid forest air, windows fogged with moans trapped within.

†

A glow appeared on the horizon. The car shot down an off-ramp at a nondescript exit. "Out of gas?"

Eddie shook his head. "Nope."

"Why are you stopping, then? We're only twenty miles from our exit. There is nothing at this one."

"There is the sunrise. And you are here."

Alongside an orchard of unripe apples ran a dirt road, a

perfect place to park. To their right, across a cornfield, the glow painted the sky brilliant oranges and pinks.

"I'm so glad it's not like the movies; I would miss never being able to see the sun."

"Me, too." He released her seatbelt with a click. "Race you to the back."

Although he jumped out fast, back through the rear door in seconds, she beat him by climbing over the seat. He smacked her bottom as she spun her leg over. "You wanted that little Asian girl, didn't you?"

"She is gorgeous, in an academic way."

"I thought about you the whole time I was feasting on Stephen."

"And I have been pondering where to stop since we left. Sunrise chose this spot for me."

A cotton sweater hit him in the face, momentarily blinding him, wrapping around over his shoulders as she laughed; he tossed it up front while reaching for her pants. She squealed and mimed an effort to avoid danger. Their lips and tongues met wild, her nimble fingers loosening his buttons. Once the last of their clothes were gone, Eddie pushed her head down to his chest, and she drank from him. When she mounted his lap, she turned her head, chin on his shoulder, and while they made love, he sucked the unhealed wound on the back of her neck.

This time, the sun's rays drove any fog from the windows. Sated on their shared blood and bodies, the sun had risen halfway before they dressed for the rest of the drive home.

†

Bernie was home most of the day, so the twins had to wait until nightfall. Once, in mid-afternoon, Angelique woke Eddie from his deep, post-feed slumber begging him to take her out to the pond, but he refused and let sleep reclaim him, impervious to her pleas. Only when Celeste roused to drive Bernie to Narragansett for some promised ice cream finally gave them a chance to feed.

"Slow down—oh, god! Slow," Eddie moaned as they sucked his life side by side. Beth lacked enough blood for three, but he allowed them their bloodlust, for it also took him. Afterward, Angelique's skin had a slight rosy glow, so while her sister snuggled again him, he took some back from her. Not much, only enough to avoid feed again too soon. Rhode Island might be too small for two vampires, even allowing for side trips to Connecticut.

Celeste and Bernie returned, doors closing downstairs, footsteps passing in the hall. Still weak, Josette slept, using his chest as her pillow while he and Angelique spoke in low tones.

"You didn't tell me when I can start hypnotizing people."

"Pretty sure that's only when your transformation is complete. For a month or more after mine, I didn't realize I had that ability. Might have saved me some trouble, but, then again, maybe it does not kick in right away."

"And you are who's supposed to be teaching us? Turns out I can teach you a few things."

"Did you try hypnotizing someone?"

"Nope. I didn't try—I *did* hypnotize someone."

"Seriously? Who?"

"Bernie. Don't look at me like that—it worked, didn't it?"

"What do you mean, it worked?"

"It worked."

"What, did you experiment over dinner? *Hey, Bernie, haven't you had enough pizza?* Or while he was playing Donkey Kong? You know the game hypnotizes him, right?"

"No, I tried it last night."

"What do you mean?"

"Well, I was starving, and you would not be back until today. I couldn't stand it anymore!"

Josette's head rolled off him limp as a rag as he jerked upright, grabbed her shoulders and lifted her to a sitting position beside him. "Tell me you didn't. Tell me you are joking!"

"No," she laughed, completely unintimidated. "Don't worry, it worked perfectly!"

Wrist clamped in his cinched fist, he jerked her to her feet and threw her robe at her, allowing just enough time to get it over her shoulders before hauling her behind him down the hall. Unable to tie the sash with one hand, she held it closed with her clenched free hand, down the stairs and out the door. Painful rocks tripped her, toes stubbing against them as he dragged her barefoot across the farm, past the Christmas trees, toward the pond. Only when they got there did he speak.

"You are NOT a vampire! You are a..."

"A what?"

"I don't even know if there is a word for it. You are becoming, but until your transformation is complete, you are not a vampire!"

Each word of the last sentence he emphasized by shaking upper arms now squeezed tight in both hands. Shook hard enough to send her hair flying back and forth. "Let go of me! You are hurting me!"

"Are you listening to me? This doesn't hurt. Hell, there isn't enough blood in your body to even leave a bruise. Want to know what fucking hurts? Seeing the vampire who made you killed because you were too damn arrogant to see this process through to the end! Do you want to see someone kill me?"

"No one is going to kill you!"

"Should anyone—*anyone*—get it into their head that there is a vampire around these parts, and they cut off my head and my legs and bury my torso with a skull and crossbones lying on my chest forcing me to spend eternity looking at useless legs knowing we aren't going anywhere ever again... How will you feel then? What will they do to you? Bernie says a word about you drinking his blood in the night, they will damn well rip you apart, too. They won't know you're only a nymph yet to transform."

"Nymph? Is that what I am?"

"What you are is a little kid who steals mommy's car for a joyride and wraps it around a phone pole because you don't know how to drive! You are dangerous, but you are still human! You're going to get all of us killed—me, your mother, Josette. If they come for you, they will kill her, too. Hell, they'll probably kill both of you just to make sure they got the right one!"

"Okay, calm down!"

"Calm down? I've seen it, okay? I've watched them cut a vampire apart. I have smelled the stench of a vampire's flesh burning."

"Wait, when did you see that? Were you there when they killed Mercy Brown?"

"Listen to me! Oh shit—how are we going to deal with this?"

"Don't worry, I'll talk to him."

"No! No you will not! That is the last thing we need."

"We'll have my mom talk to him."

"Can you hear the words coming from your mouth? Okay, go tell your mother what you did. Go ahead—I want to be there to hear that."

"Oh, damn! Right! She'll stake me."

"It's got to be me. Who else? It's either you or me, and it sure as hell cannot be you."

"What about Josette?"

"She cannot even know about it. Not until we know it's safe."

"Eddie, I'm pretty sure it worked. I hypnotized him; he won't remember a thing."

"You'd better hope so. That may be the only thing that saves all of us."

†

The next day was Monday, so Bernie left on the bus early, as normal. If he suspected anything, he never let on. Not that he ever displayed much interest or questioned anything that went on around the house. Waiting became so frustrating, Eddie went up to the state park and spent the day hiking and in contemplation. When he returned, he packed his things—in case the need arose to vanish into the night with only a moment's notice. Why hadn't he spent more time trying to break through that wall of disinterested aloofness to build a relationship with the kid?

It was all his own fault, and much as he wanted to blame Angelique, he was the one who turned her into a vampire nymph. As a teacher, he failed miserably. Sure, he was working on three simultaneously, but that was his fault, too, his own foolish planning. It almost exposed him that time he let them drain too much of his blood in his haphazard rush to transform them all at the same time. What surprises might an exam in the ER have uncovered?

Nymph. That made him laugh, a rare break from his current pit of self-loathing. Intended as the insect stage before the butterfly or mosquito emerges in adult form, it also describes the mythical creatures who appear as beautiful maidens. How well it applied to the twins, soon to emerge in even more beautiful form.

If she had not already screwed that up.

THE SWEETEST TABOO

Learning. Year after year. Decades dedicated to learning. Never in classrooms but with primal senses, with eyes and ears and that undefined sense called intuition. Honed sharper through errors, not success. His being there itself a testament to an innate skill and ability to learn. Once upon a time he still could count his mistakes, but long ago stopped trying to tally them all. All that mattered was to never repeat one to avoid exposing himself.

Then, he had been alone. How much easier for one to avoid foolish blunders than a for an entire group. The larger the group, the more inevitable the screw up. In his search for a companion, most important was finding someone he could trust. Now he questioned his judgment. The Brown women were only a desperate choice, but he held no illusions—in no universe were they his first choice. Perhaps Celeste, but although they looked the part and no man spending eternity with them ever could tire of their beauty or taste, the twins were his choice of last resort.

Orange hair should have given sufficient warning.

In all those years, he learned the solution to most mistakes boiled down to two options. Fight or flight. Death solved a plethora of problems, but killing Bernie was not a viable option. Nor could he run—not now, after transforming Celeste and so close to learning if lightning might strike twice more through the twins. Now, at long last, finding a companion and perhaps two more. A family. Something he had been missing since…

Why hadn't it occurred to him to ask Angelique for every detail? Another mistake, one that left it to him to ask the kid.

As usual, he found Bernie alone in his room, sitting on the floor, leaning back against his bed, mastering one of the hidden expert levels of another video game.

"Hey, can I ask you kind of a weird question?"

"I guess so."

"Do you ever have strange dreams?"

"What do you mean?"

"Back when I was your age—maybe a little older—I started having these wild dreams. During puberty, when hormones take over and, in my case, began showing up as dreams. About girls. Women. That sort of dream."

"No. I sometimes dream of fighting creatures, like I'm in a video game. Those are pretty cool."

"Yeah, that isn't exactly what I was thinking about. You do like girls, right?"

"Sure. I mean, I don't have a girlfriend or anything. Not exactly. Kelly Langford and I mess around sometimes, but nothing serious. At parties and such."

"That's nice. Good. Go for it. But no dreams about her or other girls?"

"No."

"Would you tell me if you did?"

He shrugged his shoulders. "I guess. Why not?"

"Look, for now, I feel like circumstances have made me the man of the house. I'm not—not really. You are, but since I am the only *adult* male, and I remember being your age, just remember, I am here for you, okay?"

"Sure. Thanks, Eddie." They shook hands, the way adult buddies do. Inside, he held onto a massive sigh of relief over Angelique's successful turn as a hypnotist. After saying goodnight, he was half out the door when Bernie waved for him to come back. The door clicked behind him.

"Do you remember something?"

"Well, it wasn't a dream."

"What was it?"

"This isn't going anywhere, right? If I tell you something —it's just between us. You won't go tell everyone else?"

"One thing I am good with is secrets. You can tell me anything."

"Well, the other night Angelique woke me up in the middle of the night."

"How did she wake you?"

"She was sucking my—no, I should not tell you."

Long ago, the word swooning went out of style. Now everyone calls it passing out, but the word popped into his head. Light as it felt, the word must have been rattling around all by itself in there. So this is the sensation a person experiences in the seconds before swooning. One hand steadied himself against the dresser next to the door. "You pretty much need to tell me; you can't leave me hanging like that."

"It was just so warped."

"Bernie, was she sucking your…"

"My knee. She was sucking my knee."

Somehow, he caught his laugh before it erupted, successfully stifling it. A powerful sense of relief radically changed his mood, but left Eddie lightheaded in a different way. Giddy, rather than panic-stricken. Perhaps the kid misunderstood. "Your sister woke you up sucking on your knee?"

"Yeah. We had a pads-and-helmets practice, and everyone just wore shorts. Chase Thornton shoved me off the sideline and I went down on the track." Lifting one cuff of his sweats revealed a nasty raspberry two inches wide just below the kneecap. Still raw, it had yet to scab over. Right in the center, it looked deep, almost punctured. "Hurt like hell when I went to bed. Funny thing, though—when she woke me up sucking on it, it didn't hurt anymore. Hasn't hurt since, either."

"What did you do when you, ahem... when she was sucking your knee?"

"Nothing. I mean, it was so screwed up. And it did feel kind of good. So I figured, if she wants to suck on my knee, why stop her? I pretended to be asleep and let her suck."

"How can you be sure you weren't dreaming? Because it sure sounds like a dream."

"No, dude, this was real. I mean, she must have sucked for ten, fifteen minutes. And she was way into it, too, moaning and shit, rubbing on my leg. It made me feel queer, but I figured she'd stop soon enough, and she did."

"Then she left?"

"Yeah. Never said a word. I lay here half the night trying to figure why she came in here to scarf on my leg."

No doubt, accompanied by other thoughts. "Do you want I should talk to her about it?"

"No, that would be really screwed up."

"Okay, well, if you have any dreams, let me know about them. Sometimes it helps to tell someone. And thanks for letting me know about Angelique. You know, she must have been sleepwalking or something. Who knows what that bug she has does to her?"

"Yeah, maybe that's it. Hadn't thought of that. I always tell her she sucks, so when she really did, I didn't know what to do about it. Didn't have anyone to tell about that. Can't tell my friends my sister came in and sucked on me; I'd never hear the end of it."

†

"You gave your kid brother a knee job?"

"I can't believe he was awake the whole time. He just lay there, quiet, not saying a word..."

"That describes how he spends every day."

"Okay, this is, like, so embarrassing."

"It's much worse than embarrassing—it is dangerous. Suppose he tells one of his buddies what happened? Worse yet—he's not dumb. What if he puts two and two together?"

"I've known him his entire life; believe me, he will tell no one in a million years. And I know him better than you, and he is that dumb." Meant as a joke, the way siblings love to take digs at each other like his at her, but she knew, Bernie might be quiet, but he was no fool.

"But he will lie in bed every night wondering when you are going to come suck on his knee again, and why you did it the first time."

"Oh, god, you don't think he got off on it, do you?"

"Did you?"

"I was starving!"

"Oh, hell—you did!"

"Yeah, well, that's the reason you won't feed on guys, because you know you'd get off on it."

"And you will do it again."

"No, I promise, it won't happen again."

Already exacting its toll on her, she trudged through the house more a weary old lady than a teenager. Each day, she slept more than twelve hours. He wondered if she weighed eighty-five pounds, her face gaunt with cheeks and eyes sunken in. Celeste looked so beautiful as her light faded, young and peaceful. Even her twin looked better than Angelique, although from her symptoms, Josette seemed further along.

He had seen this too many times before: Angelique was dying. Not the way a vampire dies as a necessary part of its transition, as her mother had and he so long ago. Dying as a victim of a vampire who is never coming back. Desperate, she fought to prevent her flame from being snuffed out by feeding as if she were a vampire. But she was powerless against the inevitable.

"Compared to what is coming, Angelique, what you have gone through so far is nothing. Your sensation of starvation will worsen, because you *are* starving. We can't watch you twenty-four hours a day. How am I supposed to trust you? If I was a junkie going through withdrawals and there was a kilo of heroin in the next room, how much would you trust me?"

"Will it be that bad?"

"When my end came, I understand nothing. Only that a hunger gnawed at me, but with no conception what it was. In my mind I saw blood and remembered Lena letting me suck on her wrist, but the pieces never came together with no one to explain things to me. With your knowledge, I would have..."

"Would have what?"

"Done anything. Absolutely anything. Desperation worries me."

"Then let me feed off you more."

"But feeding you will not help your transformation. I did not die until after she stopped feeding me. It had to run its course of slow torture before I died. It wasn't until I woke up in my coffin that I had any clue what was going on. I shouldn't have told you. That was my mistake."

"Don't worry—I'll be a good girl." For a second, she wore that angelic façade she gets, the one she uses to obtain what she wants. If she dies a human, it will be a terrible waste, for no one could make a more exquisite vampire.

"Angelique, you have never been a good girl a day in your life. I wish I could have seen you as a little girl, but we both know you were never good. A classic case of opposites attracting that draws me like a moth to a flame. Within you lies the power to destroy; resisting temptation will be impossible."

†

For hundreds of years, long before anyone dreamed up the concept of refrigeration, a moment of genius struck some farming family. Some inspired and long-forgotten inventor dug a hole into the earth in an unused corner of their field and realized, down under layers of earth, the ground felt cooler. Cool enough for the vegetables and fruit the land produced to remain fresh for a very long time. A simple storage hut constructed over it blocked the sun, kept the chill in and the produce fresh all winter. Neighbors noticed this family's health improving and dug their own. Before long, farmers everywhere shoveled out root cellars to store their harvest for the long winter. People dug them in cities, too, storing goods long after the harvest had been reaped.

Early in the 1800s, another genius of a subsequent generation invented a method for cutting ice from frozen winter lakes and rivers in the north in commercial quantities. Trains carried this ice far and wide faster than it melted, and the icebox was born. Affordable electric refrigerators replaced the icebox in most homes by the Second World War, so root cellars were largely relegated to a dusty remnant of the past. Obsolete technology, although farmers continue to rely on their large capacity in less-developed parts of the world.

No one remembered when the Brown family stopped using theirs, but the shed over it appeared to date from the 1930s. Now, it stored everything from spare parts for farming machinery to moldy, broken old furniture. Decades passed since it stored its last fruit or vegetable. After a thorough cleaning, Eddie set up four chairs down in the cellar.

The first time he invited others down, only three chairs were necessary.

Eddie paused for a moment, regarding the two women before speaking. "We agreed we are in this together. This will test that commitment we made to each other."

"Why isn't my sister here?"

"Because this concerns her."

"More the reason for her to be here."

Celeste nodded. "Josette has a good point."

"Listen to what I have to say," he continued, undaunted, "and if you still believe she should be here, we'll go get her. In any event, I plan to include her, but after we talk." That satisfied them, so he told the story. "Angelique has been feeding on Bernie."

"What?"

"No, that can't be."

Head bowed and holding up a hand in acknowledgment, he said, "I know, but when she confessed to me what she did, I went straight to him and asked about it. He confirmed everything. She assumed her power to hypnotize worked with him, but he was just being Bernie. Sometimes I think that kid could go a month without saying a word if nobody forced him to talk."

"Oh, my god!" Celeste rose, ready to run back up the steep stairs to the closed trapdoor in the cellar's ceiling. "Bernie knows what she was doing?"

"He knows what she did, but if he has any idea why, he isn't letting on. Before anything else happens, we need to decide how to handle this."

Her transformation into a deceased predator did not extinguish Celeste's motherly instinct. "Well, now that she knows she hasn't developed those powers yet, surely she won't do it again."

"Mama, have you met Angelique?"

"Exactly." Eddie sighed. "Hunger has already grown far beyond her capacity to control. She is much too impulsive. And feeding will delay her metamorphosis. It may even prevent it—I really don't know."

"Then what?" her twin asked. "She'll be stuck in this phase forever?"

He shrugged his shoulders. "Who knows? Possibly."

Celeste had a different concern. "What about Bernie? Will it turn him? Is she *trying* to turn him?"

"I suspect that is part of it. We will need to face that prospect one of these days, but this is not the time to worry about him. Even if she has the power, transforming three people at the same time? Turns out two is too much at once, so until you twins have turned, we can't consider him right now. And Angelique is not strong enough."

"We cannot consider Bernie at all! He is still a child, and I am still his mother. That decision is mine and mine alone. She has no right!" Josette took her hand to calm her. "What, is he supposed to spend eternity as an awkward teenager? Hell, at least wait until he's full-grown!"

"She's not going to turn him. Right?"

Both turned to Eddie for answers. Answers he did not have. "That is why we are here—and why she is not."

Celeste seethed with fury. "I swear, I could kill her right now!"

"That is one option." Both women turned to stare at him.

"I didn't mean it—not literally."

Josette broke the brutal moment of silence that followed. "Will feeding on Bernie harm her?"

"I don't know. In theory, it's possible. But what do we tell Bernie when she up and dies? Another fake coma like yours? It's my fault; I didn't think this through. A series of unexplained deaths in a family over time is one thing, but two or three in one summer? Or two strange, unexplained comas, both while refusing all medical treatment?"

"He'll know something is up. Worse, he will talk. Trust me," Josette said, "he talks to his buddies, even if he's a mute at home. It will slip out, even if he tries to keep it quiet. 'Hey, I need to skip practice tonight—my sister's in a coma or dead or something.' This is so messed up!"

The weight of their dilemma fell heavily on Celeste. "What are we going to do?"

"Well, I do have one idea, although I am afraid neither of you will like it." Although no one could hear them, and the floor above their heads would betray anyone entering the shed attempting to eavesdrop on them by creaking under even the slightest weight, the women leaned forward as he laid out his plan.

PART III

Fade to Grey

For blood and wine are red,
And blood and wine were on his hands
When they found him with the dead.
Oscar Wilde

NOBODY'S FOOL

"I changed into my nightgown and brushed my teeth. When I returned to my bedroom, the light was off. I assumed the bulb burnt out, so went to turn on the nightstand lamp. It was dark as hell, but I know the layout well enough to find it with my eyes closed. Even so, a little moonlight came in from outside, enough to see once your eyes adjust. I'd only made it a few steps into the room when the door shut behind me. Quietly, but I heard the click, and that's when I saw him standing there."

"But you didn't scream?"

"No. The moonlight was bright enough to see who it was."

"Most people might expect you to scream, *Get out!* when confronted by a man you claim to barely know standing in your dark bedroom in the middle of the night."

"I always expected the same of myself," Abby said with a sigh. "Every time watching a horror movie, I yell at the TV, *Get out of there! Scream! Do something!* When it happens to me? That's what I should have done. But faced in real life with a stalker in my bedroom, I didn't. Don't ask why. Maybe I froze, or maybe when I saw him... See, he asked me out a couple of days before that, and I was looking forward to it. We were planning to go to Yawgoo once this crappy weather clears up."

Detective Higgenbotham viewed her with a skeptical eye. "At best, a jury will assume you were expecting him to be there; maybe invited him."

"And at worst?"

"They will assume none of this ever happened."

With her face set with certainty, Abby held out her arm. "What about the scar?"

"What about it? An accident? Abortive suicide attempt? Heck, you could have done this yourself any time during the week between when you claim this happened and when you reported it." Despite the disappointed slouch of her shoulders and the pout his comments brought about—a very sexy pout, at that—he said, "Please continue. What did you do?"

"When I realized it was him, my first reaction was relief. In that half-second between seeing him and realizing who was there, my heart stopped. Literally stopped."

"*You scared the hell out of me*, I whispered, keeping my voice down so my parents would not hear. *What are you doing here?*"

"I knew it was Eddie, even though in the dark it was hard to see his face. Even before he spoke, his blonde hair, those eyes—you can't mistake those for anyone else's. *You know why I'm here.*"

"For a minute, the same thought any woman thinks when they find a guy in their bedroom, a guy who's broken in—that's what crossed my mind. Somehow, though, my instinct knew Eddie hadn't come to rape me. Maybe because he walked toward me slow as a shadow. A flash of lightning lit him, and his face was strange—a smirk or some weird kind of smile or something—hard to tell in that split second. The funny thing I remember is wishing I had worn a big tee-shirt or something. The nightgown I had on was a little too sexy, and right about then, the last thing I wanted to be was sexy."

"*Eddie, you're scaring me.*"

"*Well, isn't that a coincidence—you've been doing an excellent job scaring others.* By then I had backed up against the wall and he was close enough to feel his voice on my face. Despite the darkness, the blue of his eyes stood out."

"*Please, if you leave now, I won't breathe a word of this to anyone. It'll just be between us.*"

"*You aren't going to tell anyone.*"

"I won't say anything about any of this, I swear!"

"About any of what?"

"Eddie, I don't believe any of it, and even if I did, do you think anyone will believe me?"

"He must have known how terrified I was, because before he touched me, he said, *I don't want to hurt you, nor do I have to. Wouldn't you rather be with us?*"

"By that point, I had no idea what he was talking about. One of us? It made no sense, so I said, *What are you saying? That it's true?*"

"His hand touched my face. An icy hand, which freaked me out a bit, but his touch was so tender, like a lover, it gave a weird relief. He was close, and his eyes stared into mine like he could see through me. He said, *What I told you the other day, it's all true. I want you—have since the first time I saw you. Do you want me?*"

"Not like this, breaking in during a storm in at two in the morning saying shit like 'I don't want to hurt you.' That's messed up."

"The storm was close by then, lightning followed only a second or two by thunder that grew closer each time it hit. Close enough to shake the house. *Do you want me?*"

"Stop."

"But he didn't stop. With his other arm around my waist, he pulled me to him, lifting me a little, and that's when I wanted to scream, heart pounding in my chest—he must have felt it. When he kissed me, at first I didn't kiss him back. Don't know why, but I gave in. Maybe I assumed this was his bizarre idea of being romantic. It felt like something from a movie with the storm outside and all, and although sure not going to admit it to his face, I did want him. His arms felt so comforting around me."

"Then we were on the bed, sideways with my feet hanging off. He was on top; his weight pinned me down. Crazy as it sounds, my body desired his touch. And how he kissed! Screwed up as it sounds, in the moment—thunder crashing, lightning flickering every few seconds—it was romantic. I wanted him."

"Then he pinned my wrists against the bed, over my head, his weight heavy between my legs as he lifted his shoulders off me, eyes reflecting lightning brilliant blue—and he was gone! It was morning, and I was lying there curled up, still sideways across my bed. Had it been a dream? It must have been, because—I assure you—I had not had sex. I would have felt it and there was no... evidence. My panties were still on!"

"Later, when trying to remember every detail, one more thing he said came back to me. Not sure when, because this was hazy and faded even when it came back to me.

Det. Higginbotham waited for several seconds before asking, "What did he say?"

"Now you're one of us."

†

"Let me get this straight—do you believe your boyfriend is a vampire wannabe? Some sick role-playing fantasy?"

"A, he's not my boyfriend. But that is possible. And what if he is taking this one step further?"

"How do you mean?"

Abby looked down at the gash on her wrist. The exact spot a person slashes their wrist while sitting in a warm bathtub listening to Echo and the Bunnymen blaring from the stereo. The doctor said no stitches were necessary since the bleeding had stopped on its own, but offered no explanation why it showed no signs of healing. It more closely resembled an orifice than an injury.

"Maybe this is what you meant by wannabe, but what if he is actually drinking blood? Don't ask me why he might do that. The reason I wonder about that is those murders and the attack on that girl up in Providence, because it's obvious when you look at that surveillance video that's Eddie and Celeste. Seriously, look at that video and tell me that isn't them. Looks like them, walk like them—it *is* them!"

"Well, you know them better than I do. I knew Celeste well back in the day, but—granted, this video is grainy—this woman looks younger and thinner. She may have lost weight since I saw her last..."

"She lost ten, fifteen pounds when she was sick. That's how she looks now. It's her! Don't take my word for it—drive out to the farm and see for yourself."

"We will," Higgenbotham assured her. "Is that why you did not report this to us right away?"

"Now that the twins are missing, I'm terrified he has done something to them." Her exotic eyes turned from one detective to the other. "That night he came to me scared me. If breaking into my house is such a breeze, what else was he capable of doing? When he said I am one of them, he made clear he wanted me to keep quiet."

Det. Russo tapped the eraser of the pencil in her hand on the legal pad in front of her so many times it grated on her nerves. "What explanation has Mrs. Brown given about your friends?"

"That Eddie took them somewhere. On vacation, she says. Detective, you should have seen those girls! They are in no condition to go on vacation. They are so sick. At first, I wondered if Eddie gave them some drugs, but they didn't seem stoned. There were saying strange things, but not stoned. It's hard to explain. Now my imagination has gone wild."

"What do you imagine?"

Her expression grave, in a low voice Abby spoke the words haunting her, unspoken, for several days. "Did he poison them? Nothing else makes sense, and after what happened to those other girls, I wonder what he has done to them?"

"Why would their mother be covering up for him?"

"Why would she be with Eddie when he attacked that girl? Almost killed her! Nothing makes any sense. After her husband died, she changed. I'm pretty sure she was having an affair with Eddie, although the twins denied it. Then I see her with Eddie and that girl who almost died, and I know something is wrong."

"Have you gone out to the house to check on the girls?"

"Are you kidding? Not after what Eddie did to me—or tried to do to me. I don't know what he was doing, but now that the twins are missing, I am keeping my distance from their farm!"

†

Celeste laughed. "Missing? Who says they are missing?"

"We are just following up on a report," Det. Higgenbotham answered.

"But you are with the Providence P.D. Why is there a report on my girls up there?"

"It is in conjunction with another matter; right now, let's leave it at that."

"Well, I can assure you they are not missing. They missed their spring break while sick with that bug. All of us had it, except my son. With all the time they missed from school after their father died and then everyone got sick, they withdrew for the rest of the semester. Going somewhere warm and sunny seemed like a great idea until they get their health back."

"Sounds reasonable. Where did they go?"

"Wandering. No set destination. Camping, sightseeing, visiting the beach—wherever the wind takes them."

"How long have you known Eddie Brown?"

"Well, he's a distant cousin. We met him right after my grandfather's funeral and invited him to stay. Now, well—he's become part of the family."

Higgenbotham had known Celeste since high school, when they ran in social circles that often converged. Regardless of the rest of it, Abby Strong was right about one thing: he hardly recognized her. More gorgeous than he remembered, which was saying a lot, but this attitude was not what he remembered of her. Unconcerned is the word that came to mind, and if anything, back then, she was a bit high-strung. "Doesn't it worry you for your teenage daughters to go off wandering the country with a man you have known only a short time?"

"Not at all," she said, her expression almost convincing. "Eddie's a fine young man, a true gentleman. And I assure you, my girls are perfectly capable of taking care of themselves. It is nice for them to have a man along to protect them, though."

Nice for a young man, traveling with two beautiful teenagers, he thought, but the arrangement sounded anything but nice to the detective. Certainly not the sort of arrangement concerned mothers approve of. "How about your son—is he home?"

"No, he's up at the high school. Football practice. He made the varsity team as a freshman."

"Where were you on the night of the 17th?"

"The 17th? Can't say. What day of the week was that?"

"Saturday. Three Saturdays ago, to be exact."

"Here, I guess. Since I've been a widow, I rarely get out. Particularly with a house full of people. The girls were sick then, too."

"Was your cousin Eddie here with you, too?"

"Probably. Since I cannot remember that specific night, I can't be sure he was here with us. He doesn't know many people, so he sticks close to us."

"I suppose your family will be able to confirm you were home that night? Assuming we can locate them?"

"Why is there a need to confirm my whereabouts a couple of weeks ago?"

"A woman was attacked up in Providence. Video surveillance captured her walking with two people; one of them resembles you, and people say the other is a dead-ringer for your cousin Eddie."

"Are you accusing us of attacking that woman?"

"No, certainly not, Celeste. At this point, the people seen walking with her are only witnesses who we want to speak to, to find out what they saw."

"Well, I'm afraid I cannot help you with that. Had I witnessed anyone being attacked up in Providence, I would report what I saw. Is that all your questions, Detective?"

"For now," he said, rising to leave. Referring to his title, rather than his first name as she had when they hung out in the same crowd, made her position clear. "Here is my card. Will you let me know when Eddie and your daughters return? We would like to speak with him, too."

"Of course." She smiled as she held the door open, inviting him to leave. "May I ask what happened to that woman? The one who was attacked?"

"She is recovering. Bled half to death, but she pulled through."

Halfway to his car, realizing Celeste stood watch over him in the open door, Det. Higgenbotham turned back and pulled a Columbo. "Celeste, when is the last time you heard from your daughters?"

"Oh, they've only been gone a couple of days, Detective."

"But they haven't been in touch with you since they left?"

"I'm sure they are having too much fun to call and check in with their mother."

"Doesn't that worry you?"

"No," she lied. "Why would I be worried?"

Acknowledging her answer with a nod of his head, the detective turned and continued walking to his unmarked Dodge. She was lying, of course, although which portions were lies? Another realization nagged at him, as unwelcome as it was unprofessional. Since he last saw her perhaps a decade ago, why had age inflicted itself on him so much more harshly than her? She looked fantastic.

Why, indeed, was she worried? And why was she trying so hard to hide it?

I RAN

On paper, this thousand-mile drive should take sixteen or seventeen hours. Theory does not take into account New York City traffic, particularly when a wreck somewhere up ahead minutes before rush hour sends plans right out the window. In back, curled up on her side under a blanket, Josette drifted off in Connecticut and did not awaken through the stop-and-start of the city, continuing well into northern New Jersey.

Revitalized and full of the energy feasting upon her brother's blood provided, Angelique rode up front to keep Eddie company for the drive, full of conversation to ward of road hypnosis. "So, if you're a hundred years old, give or take, you must remember all those world events they made us study in school. The Depression, both World Wars."

"Remember them? I was there in World War One."

"What do you mean, there?"

"In France. First Expeditionary Division. Fought in the St. Mihiel, Meuse-Argonne Forest and a few other places. What, does that surprise you?"

In a sarcastic, lilting voice, she answered, "Yeah! How did that happen?"

"What, can't a vampire be patriotic? Signed up seventy years ago this year. Filled with perhaps too much arrogance, I assumed having an immortal warrior on our side is all we needed to turn the tide. Besides, it seemed like a good idea at the time. I needed new identity papers for a younger man—to match how my face looks—and being immortal and all, it sounded perfect."

"Was it? Perfect, I mean."

"Hardly. The papers came in handy for a while, that's true, and while the Spanish flu a year later killed so many of the men from my unit, it didn't bother me. Took only a few days to realize, though, while I may be immortal in theory, immortality is no match for a German shell with my name on it landing square on me and blowing me into a thousand pieces. And imagine trying to feed while in a trench surrounded by no one but your comrades in arms and the Kaiser's army across No-man's-land trying to kill you."

"What did you do?"

"I did what I needed to do. Which probably explains why, to this day, I only feed off men as a last resort."

The hum of the road filled the silence while Angelique absorbed this unexpected revelation. "What was war like?"

"Imagine the awful stories in your history books and multiply them by a thousand. Cold, wet, terrifying and miserable. People you care about dying around you every day. Bodies torn apart, gassed. And the stench of death and rot and shit—there is no way to describe it, and for years the horrible smell fills your nostrils. Sometimes I still smell it."

"Learned your lesson before World War Two?"

"Sure did. Joined the Coast Guard for that one. At least I stayed in the States and could feed when we got leave. Patrolled the Atlantic Coast hunting for German subs. My ship sank a few, too, although we only got credit for one. That was my job, firing the depth charges, so I'm proud of that."

"Don't tell me you went to Vietnam, too?"

"Are you kidding? Much as I could have used a new ID right about then, I wanted nothing to do with that shitshow. The anti-war movement was much more fun. Never had an easier time feeding in my life. I expected to find others like me there, but if they were, they hid it better than I did. Which reminds me, be careful not to feed off someone who has been doing mushrooms or acid. That crap will mess you up."

Head back, they drove half a mile with her cackling the

entire way before her face sobered. "I can't believe you are a veteran of both world wars. Somehow, that makes it more real, how long you have been around! What else have you done? The Depression—the Civil War?"

"How old do you think I am? Missed the Civil War by a few years. The Depression sucked, but it made for easy hunting then, too. Upheaval and desperation are boon times for those like us. Lost my shirt in the stock market crash, although I got it back and more during the Second World War. I was the only seaman in the Coast Guard getting rich off my investments while sinking U-boats, no doubt. Finally earned a college degree on the GI bill after the war. You two should finish your degrees. Believe me, you'll never find feeding easier than it is in college—unless the 60s return."

Twin lines of red taillights warned of another backup ahead. Once traffic snarls, it can take forever to clear up. Construction closing down the right lane as part of a widening project helped further slow the pace and burn through gas. Somewhere south of Wilmington, Delaware, Eddie stopped for a fill-up.

"We don't need anyone nosing around the car, not with Josette so ill; New Jersey does not allow self-pumps," he said, explaining why he waited to stop.

As he got out, Angelique turned to the rear seat. "Josette, pass his CD case up here so I can pick something new. Got any requests?"

"Depeche Mode is good for driving," he suggested. "Either that or metal to keep me awake."

Dollars dinged as they rolled by on this gas pump, the bell tolling almost once every time a gallon ticked by. As the eighth ding rang out, the front passenger door flew open and a bright-haired flash sprang out. At first stopping for a second at the passenger side door, she sprinted around to his side, leaping over the knee-high hose dangling from the pump to the car.

"It's Josette. She's not waking up!" She opened the rear

door next to him and leaned in, shaking her sister, calling her name.

Dings continued ringing, abandoned behind him as he knelt down into the floor space beside her. The girl's cold face told the story, but he touched her carotid to be sure. Her sister shaking her, trying to awaken her, made locating a pulse impossible, and when she ignored his raised hand, he pushed her against the back of the front seat. "Quiet! You'll attract attention. Let me find her pulse."

Despite knowing her heart had stopped beating—and judging by the temperature of her skin, some time ago—he let the seconds pass. Ten, fifteen, thirty. "Get in the car."

"No! She can't be! Wake up, Josette!"

Both crouched down, squeezed into the footwell inches apart, Eddie grabbed her, covering her mouth with a firm hand. Wild eyes bulged as she struggled against him, while his narrowed in response. "There is nothing we can do, but if you don't calm down, everyone in this place will come to see what is going on. And if I don't let go of you in about two seconds, someone's going to assume I am attacking you and call the cops. Now get in your seat—we are leaving. Okay?"

Tears had already reached his hand, pooling where her cheeks bulged from the pressure, but she nodded her understanding. He opened the driver's door for her to scoot over to the passenger side. Angelique reached behind her over the bench seat, but the distance was greater than her short arm, her sister's corpse a foot beyond her reach. "How did I not know? I should have known. Why didn't I sense anything?"

A flood of adrenaline caused him to push the gas with too much enthusiasm, lighting up a squeal of rubber chirping over painted concrete as the engine roared. A mile down the road, an empty parking lot beside a shuttered store beckoned, so he pulled in. Josette lay on her side in the foetal position, her face peaceful as if sleeping. Ghostly white as her skin had been the last few weeks, it changed little. Perhaps now with a trace of bluish gray; her lips, though, had lost their last traces of pink. Angelique cradled her sister's head in her lap as she sobbed. Eddie allowed her this indulgence as he scoured the map. The interstate highway ahead too dangerous now, with the chances of a wreck or truckers looking down from their high perch as they passed, not to mention the efficiency of state troopers eager to meet their quotas.

Once he had picked out an alternative route, he perched alongside her on the edge of the seat and held the grieving girl. "I wanted to be with her when she went over."

"You were," he answered in measured tones to comfort her. "This is how she'd want it—peaceful and with no one fussing over her."

"What if she doesn't come back?"

"Don't worry, she will—just as your mother did."

"Oh, shit! What are we going to tell her?"

"Nothing. Not now. Back roads will take longer, but we'll call her when we get there."

Highway 301's two lanes run through the Maryland side of the Delmarva peninsula, most of the way quiet and rural. The sun set before they reached the Chesapeake Bay Bridge-Tunnel. At least the darkness hid silent tears from stabbing his conscience, his greatest distraction as he drove. Along the dark, lonely bridge, miles from any lights except headlights of the other cars driving on Highway 13, she asked, "Mother was the first, right?"

"And Josette will be the second."

"How can you be so sure?"

Of course, he could not. In a century, only three had conquered death, including him. Certainty no more existed. Still nothing more than a theory, developed over decades. All the times he tried, ending in dismal failure. Josette may well end up the latest in that long line of failures, another doomed experiment to dispose in some unmarked grave during the black of night. After one success, greed and arrogance had taken over, the lust for companionship too irresistible. Add his gluttony and greed to his pride, and he had most of the seven deadly sins covered. Why had taking Celeste not satisfied him?

"She will awaken. You'll see." The only thing holding Angelique together in the seat beside him was hope, and he knew better than to extinguish it. What she needed was confidence—even if mere false hope. He must avoid admitting her sister lay dead under an old blanket, draped across the back seat, a pawn in a nightmarish experiment.

†

The lights of Norfolk illuminated the powder blue blanket covering the body in the rear seat, pulled up to cover her head but otherwise leaving her as she was. A chill swept up his spine, peering behind him, curves outlining the obvious shape underneath.

Highway 17 bypassed most of the city, heading down into the Great Dismal Swamp. Perfect. When the headlights lit the green sign marking the entrance to the Great Dismal Swamp National Wildlife Refuge, Angelique stared at it, then said, "You've got to be fucking kidding me."

"Yeah, tell me about it. But Park rangers are less likely to pull us over than county Mounties, so this route is best."

"I hate you," she said as they drove through the gloomy forest of cypress, tupelo and pine. Along this stretch of highway, other cars were a rare sight. After clicking on the dome light, she inserted the same Cure CD the three had enjoyed together in better times, and they rode without speaking most of the way through the appropriately named swamp.

Upon reaching the North Carolina side, the road bore west, and they burned away the next forty miles, in which they passed perhaps only a dozen cars heading the other way. Two-thirds the journey behind them, he allowed himself to relax.

Blue lights lit up the night behind them. "Oh, shit," he heard beside him, melancholy desperation making her voice waver.

"Stay calm and whatever you do, say nothing. Let me handle it."

A Martin County deputy shined a blinding flashlight on his face, then on Angelique, starting on her face, then following her body down to her legs. "License and registration."

"Did I do something wrong, officer?"

The deputy ignored the question. "Where are you two going in such a hurry?"

"Oh, was I speeding? I thought the speed limit was sixty through here."

"Uh-huh," the deputy answered, more an accusation than an answer. His light focused on the papers in his hand. "Don't get many cars from California 'round here."

With that, he returned to his car. Eddie watched him filling out a ticket under the interior light. "At least he didn't check in back," said Angelique.

A few minutes later, the deputy handed him a ticket and his documents. "Sign back there said 45. Slow down, beach boy."

Eddie squinted as the flashlight bore into his eyes. "I'll be more careful."

Once more, the light played over Angelique for another long look, then the officer turned to go. As he did, his flashlight trailed through the car's interior, shining across the rear seat, illuminating bright red curls spilling out from under the blanket of baby blue. His hand gripped the handle of his .357 Magnum. "What's under the blanket?"

"That's—that's my sister. She's sleeping."

The flashlight tapped the window above her head, a loud crack threatening to break through the glass. "Miss, are you alright back there?" His light trained back upon Eddie. "Hands where I can see them. Step out of the car. Slowly."

"Shit," he muttered under his breath before opening the door, hands open beside his ears.

"On the fender, feet out, shoulder width. You know the

drill." Once he assumed the position, the cop turned back inside the car. "You next. Keep your hands where I can see 'em." Across the car, Angelique took the same position on the opposite side of the hood, feet so far back her palms supported her weight. Once she also complied, the deputy patted Eddie down first, then went around and did the same to her, although on her, he took his sweet time. Eyes met across the hood as the deputy's slow hand followed every curve of her body. After groping her ass, he reached around to give each breast a lascivious squeeze.

"There's nothing there but me," she snarled.

"Keep quiet!" The deputy barked, returning to the driver's side and, keeping a close eye on Eddie, opened the rear door and pulled down the blanket. A quick touch to the clammy face and he jumped back, gun aimed square at Eddie, now shaking. "One move and I'll blow your goddamn head off."

Shielded behind the open door of his patrol car, he called it in over the radio. "Officer needs backup, east of mile marker 47. Send paramedics and get Sheriff Dawson out of bed and out here. There's a dead body in this car. California tag KA… what the hell?"

Brilliant orange hair flowed from the seat, brushing the ground bright in his headlights. The deputy dropped the mike onto the seat and rushed over, still pointing his gun at the two motionless suspects. Without doubt, the dead body had moved —that's the only way her hair could have spilled out of the car. Gun trained on the driver, he lit the body with his flashlight. From all appearances, she remained in the same position as he left her, but before the dead body had been lying with hair pinned underneath, and somehow it had gotten out from under her head. It made no sense. As he bent down to check more carefully for a pulse, her eyes opened.

Pale violet blinking eyes searched around. "What's going on?"

"Are you alright, ma'am?"

Squinting, she snarled, "Get your damn light out of my

eyes!"

Josette sprang with unnatural speed. A flash that gave no time to react. A shot rang out in Eddie's general direction as her mouth latched onto his neck. Although tipping the scale at ninety pounds, sheer force adding to the surprise, driving him over backward, sprawling onto the road and landing with a jarring thud. On him in a second, Eddie had his gun and wrestled his arm against the pavement while Josette hung on, neck tight in her mouth. His struggle lasted only seconds until his eyes stilled, staring straight up into a million stars bright in the country sky, and he lay immobile. Angelique stood over them, hands covering her mouth. A circle of light moved across the treetops as the flashlight rolled in an arc beside them on the asphalt until it came to a stop, illuminating the ditch between his patrol car and theirs.

Stunned, Eddie sat on the road beside them and watched her suck the man's blood. A black puddle expanded beside his neck, testimony to the damage her bite inflicted. A moment ticked by until his common sense took over and, realizing the urgency, pulled her away by the shoulders. When he did, her head reared up and snarled at him, wild, damp hair obscuring her face.

"Come on, Josette—he called this in. In five minutes, this place will be swarming with cops."

"Oh, my god, you're alive!" Angelique hugged her sister as she stood, helping yank her to her feet in the process. "I'm so happy to see you're okay! How did you...?"

In the starlight, Josette smiled, a satisfied, toothy grin. Even in the midnight gloom, the unmistakable sight shocked the other two. On both sides of her mouth, her two canine teeth extended down a half-inch longer than the rest of her teeth, ending in long, razor sharp points.

†

"How the hell does she have fangs? How do you have

fangs?" Angelique turned around in the seat next to Eddie to face her sister, sitting in back where her dead body lay a few minutes before.

"You think I have a clue? I mean, they are just there! How the hell am I supposed to know how they got there?" From her grin, she was not worried about how, but thoroughly enjoying her grand luck.

The road screamed by to the roar of the engine. So long as no headlights approached, he knew no one was around to clock him, and they needed distance—fast. The flashing blue lights faded until a bend in the road obscured them behind trees, and the only visible light came from their headlights bobbing along the highway and splashing the blur of trees on each side. "You were freakin' awesome back there!"

"Let me look!" Kneeling backward over the seat, Angelique ran an admiring finger over her sister's fangs. As she did, they began to recede. In seconds, they were gone, her teeth returning to normal. "Holy shit! Oh my god! Do you think I'll get fangs, too? I want fangs!"

"We're twins," Josette said. "If I have fangs, you will have them, too."

"Would you two stop that crap? Someone grab that map and tell me how to get the hell out of this county. We need to be heading a different direction before they round up a posse looking for us."

He saw red flashing on trees up ahead ten seconds before headlights came into view. Eddie eased on the brakes as an ambulance passed, heading toward the scene. The cop's flashlight lit up the map as Angelique inspected it. "Turn somewhere up ahead. Highway 64. Goes east and west. Looks like it's in a town."

"Nothing before that?"

"Not on this map."

He knew Highway 64, although he'd never taken it far enough east to reach this section. Further west, it runs through the mountains, a beautiful drive through the improbably named Transylvania County, North Carolina. How he relished the irony of taking a new victim to Transylvania for some camping or hiking, and while there, sated himself with her. Must have done it a dozen times over the years.

Now he fled toward Transylvania, to make his escape with a newly deceased vampire.

A right turn, heading west, led toward home; left led into sparsely populated farming country he was unfamiliar with. To the left would throw them off his true destination. The roads intersected in Williamston, at the only red light in town. The light took forever to turn green so he could turn left out of town.

He hung a right.

FOREVER LIVE AND DIE

The city of Atlanta's motto is Resurgens. To rise again. After Sherman burned it to the ground, from the ashes of buildings constructed of pine and oak rose a modern city of steel, glass and concrete skyscrapers sprouting everywhere like mushrooms. The city where the lost cause died in 1864 in a great conflagration, and from where it later rose from the smoldering ruins.

While the city's residents blame General Sherman for the torching of the city during the Civil War to this day, the accurate history is far more complex. During the months before the fire immortalized in *Gone With The Wind*, the Union Army destroyed much of the city during a six-week long siege. When the Confederate Army fled the city, the skedaddling rebels blew up a munition train, igniting one of the largest explosions of the entire war that leveled much of what remained standing. As he left, Sherman and his army took care of most of the remnants, leaving precious little behind to burn.

The complexity of its history has continued. The home of Martin Luther King Jr. also saw lynchings, and not only of former slaves and their descendants. Seventy-five years before, prominent members of local society lynched a prosperous Jewish businessman from up north for a murder of a young girl everyone now agrees he did not commit. Like almost everyone in the country at the time, Eddie followed the tawdry stories of that unseemly drama played in the newspapers from coast to coast. Today, elementary schools bear the names of the leaders of that lynch mob.

The city is so accustomed to hiding its secrets hardly anyone acknowledges their existence. Can things no one is willing to speak of truly exist?

In recent decades, the city reinvented itself as a young, vibrant destination, marketed as too busy to hate, erecting a new skyline of gleaming skyscrapers and major league sports stadiums. Leaders recently began whispering about hosting the Olympic games, and while no one took Atlanta's chance seriously, it sure sparked the imagination.

Nothing predating 1864 survives in the city, other than its ghosts.

Because of countless, massive building projects, ever-widening highways and industrial cranes sprouting from what once was oaken forest, the unofficial motto, spoken only half in jest, is that Atlanta will be a great city—when it is finished. Tony neighborhoods both in-town and springing up throughout the suburbs rival any city in America for their opulence. A few of these older neighborhoods date to the Victorian era, but most date only from the early 1900s.

Two sets of lavender eyes bulged in shock at the sight. Both twins scanned about at different paces, taking it all in, jaws slack. Josette spoke first.

"This... is yours?"

Eddie flashed an embarrassed grin. "Welcome to my home."

Awestruck, her sister said, "It's amazing! Why didn't you tell us you are rich?"

"I don't remember anyone asking."

Built in the 1930s of burned brick and dark wood, it had the look and feel of a British manor house. A gas station entrepreneur designed it, after an early investment in a local concoction soon to be known around the world as Coca-Cola made him a very wealthy man. He christened his home Amethyst, for reasons he took to his grave. After his mysterious death, the house sat abandoned for years until Eddie bought it for a song and back taxes.

Years ago, Eddie moved away, and for decades leased it to a wealthy widow rumored to have made a fortune running a bordello catering to wealthy clientele. When she died during the Gulf Oil Embargo a little more than a decade before, at some point, a young blonde man took up residence. None of his neighbors took notice when he arrived. Since then, he put over ten times the purchase price into renovations and antique furnishings.

"It's perfect! Dark and Gothic," Angelique said, still spinning around, soaking in its grandeur. Her eyes fell upon the word Amethyst carved into a limestone block above the main entrance. "You could make a movie here. It looks haunted —is it?"

"If not, it should be. Rumor has it the dead frequently roam the halls."

A woman entered, pretty if a bit plain, about their mother's age and wearing an outdated, conservative dress. "Oh, you are home. Why didn't you call?"

"Spur of the moment. Margaret, these are my cousins Angelique and Josette. Don't worry if you cannot tell them apart; you will learn. They will be my guests for a while."

"Very good. Where will they stay?"

"Perhaps the corner room—although they are to be given free rein of the house."

The matron examined them with a cynical eye. "Of course they are. Shall I prepare you something to eat?"

"Coffee—maybe Irish?"

With a nod, she left the entrance hallway toward the rear of the house. Angelique's jaw again hung open. "Is she a—servant? Or girlfriend?"

"She, my dear, is a bit like you. Some might describe her as under my spell. I keep her around because her blood is particularly sweet, and she is quite dedicated. Unlike you, though, she is nothing more than a servant. She has been with me since she was about your age, and because she remains mortal, she continues to age. Don't know what I'd do without her. Takes care of this place and asks nothing more than I neither kill her nor release her from her current state."

"That is fricking awesome! Will I..." shooting a brief glance at her sister, Angelique self-corrected, "will we be able to do that? Servants and all?"

"I suspect she already can. Come to think of it, Margaret could use some help around here; maybe we should find out."

Over coffee, sitting on a brick patio under a sprawling, fern-covered oak sipping steaming cups spiked with liberal pours of Jameson, Josette regarded her surroundings with an expression of distaste. "What about all you said, that we should not draw attention to ourselves? This house is quite the opposite, don't you think?"

"This is a quiet neighborhood. It's called Decatur, and most of my neighbors are doctors and executives too busy to worry about little ol' me. They somehow have the impression I am some eccentric who inherited money, and far be it from me to disabuse them of that notion. As long as I keep the parties under control, mow the lawn and trim the bushes, they hardly notice I am here. The good thing about Atlanta is so many new people are coming here, no one knows anyone else. Down in the basement, I can play music loud as I want and no one can hear a sound."

Arms stretched wide, he yawned. "Tonight, I will show you around town. After driving all night, I need some sleep." Directed toward Josette, he said, "I suspect your transformation will leave you tired for several days, so you must want to sleep, too. You are both welcome to join me, or you can sleep in your own room."

The whiskey had the effect of shutting down Angelique, kept awake this far by the excitement and adrenaline of her sister's own *resurgens*. "If you think we came all this way with you to a place for us to be alone only to shut us off in some guest room, you don't know us as well as we assumed you did." Her twin nodding in agreement, they ascended the oak staircase with his arms holding each one close to his side.

†

Providence has little on Atlanta. A bare quarter the size of the southern city, other than enormity, the crucial difference was the newness. Eddie cruised down Peachtree Street at twilight behind the wheel of a red 1971 Olds 442. By day, he kept the car in a garage the original owner called a carriage house. Along the way, he explained the local society.

Although they had been to New York and Boston, the twins' heads swiveled to take in this alien world. This city was different. Across the living skyline, cranes moved like some sort of ungainly prehistoric predators perched atop growing, swelling skyscrapers. Some brightly lit arms still swung this late in the evening. Deadlines are deadlines.

Even stranger was the layout. Like trees grow only along the banks of a river flowing through a parched desert, these impressive steel and glass towers sprung up along the narrow corridor fed by Peachtree Street. As he chauffeured them north along this famous thoroughfare, downtown gave the impression of a deep canyon with unclimbable vertical sides. This artificial gorge surged north like the leading crest of a tsunami. Then, reaching the abrupt line the tsunami had yet to hit, trees again lined the road, which twisted and turned past scattered small shops and shopping plazas and even a residential district.

With head-snapping suddenness, past a stretch of neighborhood bars and a business district bordering on seedy, more tall buildings sprang up around a massive shopping mall and its near-twin kitty-corner from it. Enormous cranes again pulled up tall buildings underneath them. This new section ended with the suddenness it began; after only a few blocks, an enormous Baptist church signaled the border of another residential district.

"Several competing cultures exist here in town," Eddie explained as they wound their way down a curvy, hilly street.

Lavish houses set on large lots filled with beautiful, ancient trees—many mature back when Sherman marched his troops from the burned remnants 123 years before—lined the road where Eddie turned at the Baptist Church. "There's the old Atlanta elite, which is hard to break into. Might not be a problem for two gorgeous WASPy women like you, though."

"Closely related is the religious culture. Then there are the young newcomers who make up much of the nightlife, ever-changing and anonymous. We're developing a decent subculture of music and artsy types, which is awesome and growing. They tend to overlap. Many of the churchgoing type spend their Saturdays carousing, then show up at church Sunday morning acting all pious. The key is to move between these groups so no one becomes too familiar with your presence."

Seated next to him on the wide bucket seat, Josette broke her attention from the lights and sights, the artificial canyon downtown still visible in the distance, when breaks in the trees allowed a glimpse. "Which are you taking us to see tonight?"

"The most fertile ground, if not the best source of innocent blood. But the blood there is beautiful and plentiful."

After a lengthy tour lasting an hour, he followed a floodlight fading into a darkening sky to the corner of a strip mall containing a Kroger grocery store. Despite the hour, the parking lot was packed. Eddie drove past a valet stand to park up near the road. "Never use valet."

Curious, Angelique answered, "Why not?"

"Don't leave any unnecessary witnesses to whom you leave with. And never—ever—leave a key to my house with anyone."

Josette had a very different question. "Why does a grocery store have valet parking, and why are we shopping on a Friday night?"

Instead of entering the sliding glass door of the market, he let them to a door beside the grocery. Dance music throbbed behind that solid door. A giant with shoulder-length hair pulled into a ponytail opened the door for them. Eddie said, "Welcome to the Limelight. Or, as we affectionately call it, The Slimelight."

Inside the sprawling club, colored lights and ear-splitting music assaulted their senses. Past a small entryway, the building spread out before them like a succession of low waterfalls, leading down to a sunken dance floor already half packed despite the clock not yet striking ten. "Wait until later," Eddie shouted. "It fills up."

A dozen men caught sight of two redheads wearing similar short dresses of form-fitting jersey knit. Both elbows extended, each twin took one and together they promenaded through, toward the bar overlooking the dance floor. The first strains of O.M.D.'s *Forever Live and Die* began. "Anyone care to dance?" In answer, both women pulled him toward the twisting masses on the dance floor.

"You dance pretty good for an old man," Josette yelled directly into his ear, leaving traces of brilliant vermillion lipstick around the rim.

Hard as it was to take his eyes off the provocative swaying of these two to the slow, driving beat, each set on outdoing the other, he often glanced past them to the bar. Angelique noticed. "What do you keep looking at?"

Motioning with his head and eyes toward a woman sitting at the bar, "Beautiful, isn't she?"

She rolled her eyes. "I suppose."

A light palm traced the line of her jaw, and he smiled. "Only two women here are more spectacular than her."

The DJ played Madonna next; halfway through the song, Angelique slowed. She cupped a fist to stifle a cough. His firm arm around her waist turned her toward the stairs. Her sister followed, but he waved her off. "Have fun—we'll be right there," so she continued dancing alone. Two guys jockeyed in before the other two made it to the steps.

Two empty seats were available at the bar. Eddie sat his weary cousin in one, then took the seat his attention had been on, next to a dark woman in a silver and black dress. "This wasn't taken, was it?"

"No, it's yours."

"I'm Eddie." He extended his hand. Up close, he realized he may have underestimated her beauty. Thick, straight hair of jet black hung just below her shoulders. Fair skin contrasted with exotic features and prominent eyebrows. Eyes dark as her hair gazed back.

The woman returned it, but with a loose grip for ease of extrication. "Aryana."

"That's beautiful. What does it mean?"

"It's Persian meaning utterly pure."

"Oh, I'm terribly sorry to hear that. Beautiful name, though quite difficult to live up to, I'm sure." She returned his smile. "Are you Persian?"

"How did you guess?" Since the Iran hostage crisis eight years before, no one identified as Iranian. Her accented English suggested the recent emigration of her family, perhaps fleeing the Iran Revolution. Calling herself Persian bespoke deeper, ancient cultural ties and opposition to the current regime. The form-fitting dress she wore might mean death at the hands of the regressive Islamic revolution.

"Just lucky, I suppose. This is my cousin Angelique." She flashed an insincere smile and offered another limp hand. Aryana explained she was in town for a job interview, so he asked where.

"Eastern airlines. I hope to be a flight attendant."

"How long will you be here?"

"Only a few days."

Whitney Houston rang out over the loudspeakers. "I wanna dance with somebody, and my cousin's a bit worn out; do you like to dance?"

"Sure your cousin won't mind?" The way she said it, her tone dripping with sarcasm, suggested skepticism of his story.

He pointed to the dance floor. "We'll send her sister to keep her company."

After a tentative and demure start, Aryana soon warmed up. By the time *Pump Up The Volume* played, they laughed like old friends or a couple having a fantastic second date. Worried about her health and wary of other forms of predator, Josette joined her sister and watched from there. "He's good."

"Think he's mesmerized her?"

Josette shook her head. "Not yet. He's a charming sonofabitch, I'll give him that."

"As long as he lets me feed off her, I don't care what he does."

"How do you feel?"

"Like death warmed over."

"Sounds about right. I'll go drag him away and make him take you home."

Leading Aryana by the hand, he took the hint. The Persian beauty accompanied them outside. "Mind if I drop them off? Better yet, I can show you my house..."

"How am I supposed to show you with my things in my room?"

Annoyed, Angelique asked, "Show him what?"

"Aryana has a job interview tomorrow; she wants my opinion on what to wear."

"I swear, I'm going to kill him," Angelique muttered to her sister.

As they got out at his house, Eddie said, "I won't be long. Aryana needs her sleep for her big day tomorrow."

Taillights sped off down the street. Angelique said, "While he's enjoying the fashion show, think he'll mind if I feed on Margaret?"

"Let's get you to bed. In our room," her sister answered.

†

"Honestly?"

"Of course." Her accent sounded more alluring in the quiet of her hotel room.

"It's a bit too—I mean, it looks incredible on you," he answered, and it did. Accentuating her sumptuous curves better than the silver and black dress which drew his attention at the Limelight.

"Not for a job interview?"

"Perfect for a second date, though."

She looked fantastic walking away, toward the garment bag hanging in the closet from which she took something with her into the bathroom. A minute later, she returned wearing a navy suit with a skirt two inches below the knee in acceptable corporate fashion, which on most other women would have appeared conservative. A cute spin allowed him a 360 view. She raised her eyebrows at the look this garment elicited. "No?"

"Maybe for a job as a corporate lawyer. Don't you have something in between?"

"My mother hates this one—says it shows too much cleavage. She's very traditional, but maybe you will like it." Five minutes later, the outfit was worth the wait. An oversize black and white hounds tooth accentuated with purple here and there, it showed some cleavage, but not too much. An amazing fit to her slender waist and hourglass hips. "How's this?"

"I'd hire you."

"Really? It's not too revealing?"

"No, that's the one," he answered, standing and walking close, those ebony eyes following him every step of the way. "Perhaps you should take it off so it will be pristine for tomorrow."

Was it a look of fear or apprehension on that stunning face? "What you told me, that you aren't interested in sex tonight..."

"That is true. What I want from you is not sex, but something more profound, far more intimate." She reached behind her to slowly unzip the dress. "Same as you want, isn't it? Intimacy? A bond unlike anything you have ever experienced?"

Fascinated and oddly detached, she nodded as the zipper

reached the small of her back and stopped. First from one shoulder, then the other, he slipped the dress free and held it for her to step out of, then laid it with care on the desk next to the TV—it would be a shame to ruin it. Then, turning back to her, he said, "Let me see you."

"You want me to take off..." she reached up to touch a bra strap. A brief head shake in response stopped her as she reached behind her back. "Promise me."

"No sex, I promise."

Compelled by a force even Eddie could not explain to her, when he stepped toward her, instinct drove her to back away. An animal stalked as prey. Yet she longed for him in some unfathomable, primal way. Not a mark marred her perfect body, one so mesmerizing that Eddie wished he had not made her a promise. But he had.

Pushing raven locks back behind her ear and caressing her face, he kissed her while lowering her onto the bed. Black lace lingerie revealed so much of her body, most of his usual feeding spots, and he hated to scar such perfection. Pinned beneath him, her body moved with him. Again, his hand went to her face and pulled back her hair.

Kissing her cheek, her ear, her neck, his tongue licked up behind her ear. Sweet-smelling blood filled his nostrils, savory with hints of floral. His tongue located the flicker of a pulse, quick from the excitement and fear, behind her ear. An agile slash, little more than a nick, and blood flowed from behind her ear across ivory skin.

Aryana sighed with an unexpected pleasure and her arms clenched him as her body quaked and Eddie drank.

"Eastern's training facility is up by Cumberland Mall," he said when dressed once more in silver and black. Hair covered all traces of her wound, and she stood with him at the door. "It's not far, maybe twenty minutes from my house. I'd like to see you again."

"Me, too," she answered. How she got back into the dress she wore out clubbing, she had no clue. It felt like she had blacked out, but even with the odd afterglow, she knew he had not molested her. Whatever happened, she enjoyed it—enjoyed him—and an intense longing overwhelmed her as he prepared to leave.

"Good luck tomorrow. I hope you come back, and even if you don't wish to see me, I hope you get the job. Funny—I have a sneaking suspicion you will."

"When I do," she said in that lovely accent of hers, "I want that tour of your house." One more kiss, and then he left, feeling her eyes on him as he walked down the hall. A click behind him as he approached the elevator told she closed the door before he turned around.

†

"How much was you and how much was—your power?"

Eddie sipped his wine before answering Josette. They sat in the basement, the music of Mercyful Fate playing at a volume low enough to not drown out conversation. "Who knows? It's not like there's a switch."

"When can I try?"

"Soon. I don't know how much you got from that cop, but you will need to feed before long." Giving her a long look, he said, "Your sister can't come with us. Tonight proved that."

"Can I feed her? To keep her going; she's so weak."

"Yes, but how long do you want to delay her transformation? Don't you want her to experience what you have, now that you are one of us?"

"It's not that. I can't watch her die. She's my twin—you can't understand."

"Not entirely. It isn't easy. At least you did it in your quiet style, without giving us a hint. We assumed you were just sleeping."

"She won't make it so easy on us." Then she started giggling. "All she cares about is fangs. Oh, please let her have fangs! Can you imagine how pissed she'll be if she doesn't?"

"She'll kill us, won't she?"

"Damn right! I mean, I'm dying to try mine out and all. I was out of my mind when I bit the cop, acting on pure instinct. This music is scaring the hell out of me."

"Good. It's supposed to." A pause, then he said, "Go ahead."

"What?"

With the intensity of a jeweler, he gazed into her amethysts searching for imperfections where there were none. As he did, without a flicker in his gaze, he reached up to twirl a lock of her hair at her cheek. "Try your fangs."

"How? On you?"

"Why not?"

"Can I? You want me to bite you?"

"Tonight is a good night—I'm flush and you need to try 'em out."

"Where, on your neck?"

"If you can control yourself a little better than you did with the cop—you nearly tore his throat out."

"You are a fool, you know that, right?"

"After witnessing what a butcher you are with those things, count me a fool, but I know you want me." A tilt of his head, offering his jugular vein, proved too much to resist. By the time she crawled onto the couch, onto his lap, menacing fangs sprouted and her eyes dilated crazily. First she kissed his neck the way he kissed Aryana's hours before, then to the brooding sound of *Don't Break The Oath* on the stereo came a sharp, hot pain as two needle-like fangs tore into his flesh.

And she drank from him.

†

"Let me see your neck!"

Eddie sat motionless on the edge of the guest room bed as Angelique leaned close, touching his skin.

"You let her bite you?"

"Sure did."

"I cannot believe you let her do that! You're an idiot."

"That's the general consensus."

"How can you trust her after she attacked that guy like a rabid wolf?"

"Immortality encourages taking stupid risks."

"She really fucked up your neck. You can't go out like that."

"Yeah, we didn't think it through. Good thing I heal fast."

"I'm going to bite you somewhere hotter." Her hand rubbed his upper thigh, suggesting one potential spot. "Bet you'd love that!"

"You can bite me there now, if you want."

"I'm so hungry I might chew down to an artery."

Her sister sat next to him. "Well, we decided I am ready. I want to feed you this time."

"Should I leave you two alone?"

"Oh, come on—we know you want to watch. Besides, we have no secrets. Maybe you can spare her a few drops yourself."

While Angelique fed from an eternally unhealing gash on her sister's thigh, Eddie unbuttoned his shirt and tossed it aside. He allowed both to feed from him, the pleasure the two gave going to his head, and he let Angelique take more than they planned. Did her sister use her new power on him? The three rolled around the bed, partaking of each other, and while it lasted, he frankly did not give a damn.

BIZARRE LOVE TRIANGLE

"Now batting: number eight, Dale Murphy!"

A roar rose from the crowd—decent-sized for a midweek game, with between ten and twelve thousand in attendance. Murphy was the fan favorite, the team's biggest star and two-time National League MVP. Atlanta loved him. In fact, scuttlebutt predicted he was destined for the Hall of Fame once his playing days were over—which no one in the crowd was in any rush to see happen anytime soon.

Josette and Eddie applauded along with the rest of the crowd at Braves Stadium; she even hollered at him, caught in the infectious spirit of her first Major League game. Murphy smiled in their direction. The electricity generated by the live crowd and the athletic bodies of the players swept her up. "He looks like he could whoop your butt."

"Well, he's got the advantage of a bat…"

"Oh, right; we don't get bats."

"Exactly."

"The bat thing is deeply disappointing."

"Yeah, I remember when *Dracula* with Bela Lugosi first came out—the least realistic part, but the one that made me the most envious."

Murphy stroked a line drive into left-center field, bringing everyone to their feet.

"Hard to believe this is so much fun!" Josette bubbled with excitement. "If I had any idea, I might have gone up to a Red Sox game back home. Bernie's games are so boring—I guess that's why I paid no attention to the sport."

"It is fun," he answered, "but don't forget—we aren't here for fun."

Totally ignoring him, with a mischievous grin, she said, "It's about time you took me on a date; I was beginning to believe you were ashamed to be seen with me in public."

"What are you talking about? We went dancing, and I was proud to be seen with a woman as beautiful as you."

"When we went dancing, it was the three of us—and everyone loves being seen with Angelique. This is the first time it has been just you and me."

He took her hand and squeezed. Insecurities survive the turning, a fact he sometimes forgot. One day, hers will fade, too, once she becomes comfortable with her new, superior form and abilities. "Is that what you call this—a date? Whatever it is, it will always thrill me to show you off to the world. Let's do it more often."

She stroked the back of his hand with her thumb with a sigh. "What else do you call it when a boy takes a girl out to a baseball game?"

He chuckled. "Are you forgetting? I'm not a man and you aren't a woman. Not anymore." While gazing into her eyes, he entwined his fingers with hers.

"Well, it's still a date. What else do you call it?"

He could have disputed her, but he was enjoying the game and being there with such a beautiful woman, so although technically not the reason he brought her, he supposed she had a point. "So, if it is a first date, do you think I might get a second?"

"Don't push your luck! It's only the third inning, so there is plenty of time for you to blow this one. Who knows, I may find out you turn into some kind of monster or try to take advantage of a girl."

This time, he roared. "Oh, you can be sure of that."

"Remember, nice girls don't put out on a first date."

"They don't?"

One corner of her mouth twitched upward as she gave him a long side-glance. "Lucky for you, I'm not a girl anymore."

†

Bill cussed as he ambled toward his car. Although he saved enough money to buy a beer by parking in a vacant lot between decaying shotgun shacks on a side street instead of the main parking lot across the street, now he had no clue on which street he left his car. The ramshackle homes all look the same. One thing for sure, it wasn't this far down. Behind him loomed the silvery rim of Atlanta Stadium that, in daylight, reminded him of the spaceship from *Lost in Space*, which he watched in reruns through junior and high schools. No, this view of the Robinson's spaceship was unfamiliar.

Too much beer did it to him. Still not old enough to legally drink, he watched the Braves win with some of his buddies from Georgia Tech, who were twenty-one and bought beers for him. He spun around like a weathervane in a whirlwind before deciding to backtrack and try the next block down. As he wandered, a couple of silhouettes followed half a block back, but after deciding to retrace his steps to Capitol Avenue to make his way to the next block, they were nowhere to be seen.

That worried him. Although having no hint of trouble before, plenty of stories of muggings down here circulated on campus. On the far side of the stadium ran I-75/85, but this side bordered a rough neighborhood where residents supplemented incomes by charging to park cars in their front yards. A chill ran through him, although it was still warm enough, hovering in the mid-70s. Summer in Hot'lanta never gets chilly.

As he walked, he scanned for where those silhouettes may have gone, but wherever they went, they left without a trace—no cars cranking up or doors opening on any of the houses nearby. Too distant from a streetlight to give a clear view, partially hidden behind a parallel-parked car, he had the distinct impression one was a woman, the only thing keeping panic at bay. Who mugs on a date?

Still, he remained alert as the five or six large beers inside him allowed him to be.

Soon as he turned the corner on the next block, he knew he'd stumbled upon the right street. Now he remembered the old Ford Falcon station wagon parked in a driveway on the left, the same yellow color as the one his parents drove when he was a kid.

Where the sexy redhead came from, he had no clue. When he turned back from the car that looked like his old family wagon, she was just there. Her hair sparkled from the light of a streetlight half a block away, which somehow also caught her eyes so they glowed an unreal, gem-like color.

"Oh, I'm so glad to see you!" Her voice was loud, followed by a whisper. "Please, can you help me?"

If he had ever met a girl this gorgeous, he forgot when. And he'd never forget meeting a girl this exquisite. "What can I do?"

"That guy over there is following me—don't look!" Bill looked. Half a block away stood an obscure, menacing figure in the gloom between streetlights. "He's my ex, and he spotted me at the game and now he's following me. Can you be a doll and walk me back to my car?"

Really amazing eyes, he thought, the kind that make a guy ignore how dangerous it is to get involved in situations involving a jealous ex. "Where's your car?"

"Just past where he is standing."

"Let's go," Bill said, gallant and full of liquid courage. As they walked, he asked, "What's your name?"

"Julie," she answered, but otherwise was quiet. Poor thing is terrified of her ex.

At a near-empty wildcat parking lot, nothing more than a vacant lot between two darkened houses with peeling paint, she said, "Here it is."

The guy was gone. At her car, they looked around and she stared up at him. "Looks like you ran him off! How can I thank you?"

"Well, I have a few..." before he could run through the list of ideas rattling through his mind, she reared up on tip-toes to kiss his cheek. Then she moved down and kissed his neck, followed by what almost felt like a nibble...

And everything went black.

†

The basement was the one place in this old house where Eddie found his greatest comfort. Dark oak under brick walls that swept into graceful arches of a vaulted ceiling and a wide fireplace lent an Old World feel to it, as close to a medieval castle as he had found this side of the pond.

It had not come this way. Over the years, he renovated, purchasing carved wooden panels from old homes being demolished to make way for new malls and office buildings, which he installed down here. Split into three sections, the smaller area beneath the front of the house he converted into a wine cellar, about ten by thirty feet. At the other end was a seating area near the rear, which opened into the backyard through a door; two windows overlooking the backyard let in some light from the outside.

In between, separated from the seating area by another door, the bulk of the space he considered his private sanctuary. His playroom. A Bang and Olufsen stereo with Bose speakers filled the room with sound when he craved music. Leather couches, an ancient desk and other antique furniture decorated the spacious room. Bookcases packed with leather-bound volumes lined one wall, separated by arches and a solitary door. Metal, industrial, a door normally found near a loading dock in back of a warehouse, the only thing in the room that felt out of place.

A lock and two dead bolts secured this door.

Margaret had never set foot down here. In fact, the only people permitted in his sanctuary were guests Eddie himself invited, and those were few and only when he accompanied them down. More than one never were seen leaving the basement.

Fingers of flame flickered on Josette's pallid skin, somewhat flushed with fresh blood. A blanket pulled coquettishly over her, concealed only portions of her flesh. Beside her, Eddie traced a finger over the exposed expanses of her skin. "How long?"

"Are you interested in me only for my blood? Or have you more noble intentions; my body, for example?"

"Only the most noble intentions—considering our circumstances."

"Whatever happened to losing interest in sex? Seems to me you have insatiable appetites now."

"I've wondered the same thing myself. I came up with a theory." His hand stopped where her hip and leg stuck out from under the blanket, eyes drawn to the delicate curve. "Until now, I could never be with anyone like myself."

"Like us?"

"Like you. After I became deceased, the act of taking my blood became more intense, more pleasurable. At first, it only took away pain, but during the process began giving more pleasure."

"It was the same with me, too."

"This seems similar. Sharing blood with another deceased is even more intense than when they are living. Perhaps human women suffice when there is no alternative, but because she isn't one of us makes it impossible for her to satisfy me. Certain members of our family will accuse me of being biased against humans. Guilty," he grinned. "I assume it is the same for you."

"Who knows? I've had only one lover during my life... and in my death."

"Someday you may have an opportunity to compare."

Rolling onto her stomach to mirror him, she no longer worried about covering up. "Do you think I will take lovers?"

"You may. One, two hundred years from now, who knows how sick you will be of me?"

"Or you of me."

Taking her hand and gazing at her in the firelight, where the flames reflected reminiscent of the night at the campfire when he first kissed her, he sought to assure her. "Ninety years alone has a funny way of teaching the value of equal companionship. You are what I spent decades yearning for."

"You in the plural sense? Because now you also have my Mama, and soon you will have my sister, too."

"And you have me. You singular."

"And plural."

"Yeah, I guess so. Don't allow yourself to feel jealousy; it is perhaps the worst flaw in our human form and serves no purpose now." His kisses were sweet, but with a taste of awaiting passion within.

"I'm not; not really. Sharing a lover with my mother and sister takes some getting used to."

"I can only imagine. Human morality is so deeply ingrained."

"As I can only imagine how stressful trying to please three demanding females will be for you. In a way, I should envy myself for not having that problem."

The only way to stop his laughter was by kissing him, she found. Then she pulled him to her thigh and fed him more of the drunk kid's blood. The pleasure of feeding him erased all notions of carnal pleasure.

U GOT THE LOOK

Atlanta's weather is predictably unpredictable. During spring and summer, the most violent weather first ravages Alabama, so when hail and tornadoes sweep across its western neighbor, Atlanta receives a few hours warning. Same in winter, when blizzards blow in from the west. But winter lay months away.

Reports began coming in first thing that morning. Tornadoes on the ground near Tuscaloosa and Birmingham, and the skies over Atlanta grew worse by the hour as the inevitable threat rolled closer. Meteorologists called for a rough evening rush hour, with worse to follow until late into the night.

Not that it mattered.

"Did you know amethyst was one of the five traditional cardinal gemstones?"

Angelique's forehead crinkled. "Cardinal, like the bird?"

"No," he answered, taking her hand, "the rarest, most precious and beautiful, along with diamonds, emeralds, ruby and sapphire."

"Like your house or our eyes? That's how you always describe them, as amethyst."

"Some might say your destiny is to live here. I doubt anyone with amethyst eyes has lived in Amethyst."

"Destined to die here?"

"Perhaps. Then to live here again, deceased like us."

Lids shut over her amethysts, too heavy to hold open any

longer. "It's a nice thought."

Gripping harder, he said, "It will happen. You will see."

"You did this to me. Remember that."

A steady wind blew, and outside it was dark as night hours before sunset. Angelique's body weighed ninety pounds —if that. Her alluring rosy lips were now discolored like a bruise, somewhere between blue and purple, and skin normally devoid of color, but the palest pink now turned ashen.

Josette followed close on Eddie's heels as carried her down the stairs. Angelique's arms wrapped around his neck as if holding on, but were too limp to provide any support, and her face nestled on his chest, so her lips rested on the side of his neck. Short, shallow breaths of air warm on his jugular vein.

"Where's Margaret?" her worried twin asked as they made their way to the basement stairs.

"I sent her away for the day."

In the basement, he stopped before the metal door. "The keys are in my front pocket; will you unlock the door?"

Ordinarily, Josette might have had fun fishing the key ring out, ensuring he enjoyed it even more. But watching a twin sister die before your eyes has a way of wiping baser thoughts from your mind.

Inside, walls of bare brick ten feet by ten feet enclosed a plain single bed beside a small table and two chairs. Eddie had made the bed with his finest linens, and the scent of roses filled the room from a vase on the table. A halogen bulb, recessed in the ceiling, flooded the interior with harsh light.

While Eddie returned upstairs ostensibly to write Margaret a note saying they would be gone for a few days, allowed the twins time alone. Angelique opened her eyes and gazed into the identical pair next to her. "Don't leave me."

"I won't. We were all together when I passed, and we will stay together with you."

"If I don't..."

"You will!"

"If I don't, will you stay with him?"

"You will be back, just like Mama and me."

Her twin nodded and closed her eyes. "Are you planning to give me last rites?"

"I don't suppose prayers will work." Josette laughed through the tears.

As the storm raged above them, down in the secret room in the basement, they heard only the nearest thunderclaps. The most violent. Otherwise, nothing outside the four brick walls existed. Eddie returned and locked them off from the world.

Her head moved on the pillow, motioning her twin to come close with her head and eyes. A thin voice asked, "Can I have music?"

"Of course. Eddie, bring your boombox. What do you want to hear?"

"Bring that scary one."

Head jerking back, Eddie asked, "Mercyful Fate?"

When she nodded, Josette asked, "Are you sure?"

"I want to be so terrified of Hell there is no way I will end up there. Heaven sure won't take me, so I will have no choice but to stay here." Translucent lips curled into a smile that would have been beautiful had they not been a pale blue.

Not long after, to the sounds of his *Don't Break the Oath* CD played at the lowest volume he ever played it, her twin and her killer each holding one of her hands, Angelique's chest rose for the last time as she drew in one final, agonized breath. Eddie felt her chest for a heartbeat, then her neck. A despondent Josette wept. No need to cover her, so they kept vigil with her, watching her face for any sign of her overcoming death's icy bonds.

Hours passed, the couple in mournful silence. Her face turned gray, then an even starker white than imaginable even for her. They closed her eyes when they became glassy and dead.

"I thought we were over emotions. We feel nothing when

we feed upon someone, when we kill them." Although her eyes were still red, her face was calm now.

"She is one of us. She is our blood—both from birth and literally from our bodies. Every drop of blood in her veins, she drank from your body or mine. We feel love for each other and we feel pain and loss. I suspect we will never lose our capacity to inflict pain on each other."

Josette wiped a tear away from red eyes. "When I died, did you feel this way?"

"Worse, I think—but only because then I was less sure. Your life ended with such shocking abruptness, and only your mother had successfully returned before then. She will come back to us, same as you did."

"It only took me a few hours?"

He nodded. "But your mother was three days."

"How long until you deceased?"

"Best I can figure, about a day. When I transformed, I couldn't really ask. By myself, terrified, escaping from that coffin must be how a zoo tiger feels when it finds the door unlatched. All I knew is I needed to get away; the rest took more time to figure it out."

"For me," Josette remembered, "the only thing I knew is you and my sister were in trouble. Well, that and feeling like I hadn't eaten for a month."

"Which you pretty much had not."

"That night you opened up your chest, and we saw that blood—it was like that, only not from the sight of blood. How do you suppose I knew I had fangs?"

He shrugged his shoulders. "Probably the same way I knew to escape rather than go home. I remembered dying, and when I awoke knew in an instant that I was no longer the same."

"I don't remember dying," she said. "Must have died in my sleep, like a dream."

"If you two don't stop that insipid babbling, I swear I am going to come over there and rip your throats out!"

Angelique's eyes were open, watching them with lifelike amethysts. A corner of her mouth pulled up in a smile and she lifted her head. Josette leapt onto her, screaming in joy, and a full smile spread over pale pink lips as she looked to Eddie through her sister's curls.

"Welcome back, my Love!"

One hand let go of her sister's back to cradle her temple. "Why didn't anyone mention the hangover?"

Eddie unbuttoned his shirt. "Let's get you some hair of the dog!"

Blood already trickled down his chest from his ancient wound when he bent over her, her tongue flicked it off with a long, sensual moan. Looking up at him, she flashed a toothy grin to reveal two long, vicious fangs. A sharp inhale from her twin, but she kept her eyes on Eddie as blood flowed over his chest.

A handful of his hair pulled his head; he tilted it to one side, offering his neck. With a suddenness that shocked all of them, she struck. Again, her sister inhaled, only this time in fear, remembering what she did to the deputy when she awoke filled with bloodlust. Eddie, though, showed no fear. Guided by the scent of blood, her incisors sank into his flesh, finding the vein flowing right below the skin from his brain on its way to his heart.

They collapsed onto the bed, where she rolled atop and drank deep of him, smearing some still flowing from his chest, staining her nightgown over her breast, until Josette began lapping it up to keep it from going to waste.

Angelique's moans vibrated against his throat as she experienced the fullness of pleasure for the first time. Soon they were moaning together, their blood mingling. So great was the pleasure, Eddie had to force himself to stop. Angelique required a gentle shove, but backed away soon as he did, and the three lay together on the narrow bed, legs dangling off the side. One started laughing, and the others joined in, and together they lay in each other's arms as one.

†

Bright stars danced in the sky when they emerged, the storm having passed during the night. Angelique lay dead about twelve hours, they figured. Soon dawn would break over their new world. Before long, she would require fresh blood, but they each fed her sufficient to fulfill her needs until they located prey for her. It was a heady time of celebration.

As typical for a weekday evening, Lenox Square teemed with life. Construction began on Atlanta's most popular mall three decades before, in the late 1950s as Atlanta entered its boomtown phase and enlarged several times since. A modern city deserved a modern place to shop. It's Peachtree Street location on the dividing line of residential area to the east and the booming business district stretching west to downtown made it a perfect place to stop on the drive home from the office.

The wealthy came to shop at Neiman Marcus and a collection of exclusive boutiques. Rich's and Davison's department stores—Eddie still called the latter by its old name, despite being bought out by Macy's a year ago—and clothing stores like Merry-Go-Round drew teenage girls by the thousands, who, in turn, drew boys to the mall. They came to see and be seen, as well as to shop.

"There's so much to choose from," Angelique said as they made their way through the wide and crowded two-story central promenade. "Pretty boy or pretty girl?"

"Your choice," Eddie answered. Boys and men leered as she strolled by, while girls eyed her with envy. "Plenty of options either way."

"Holding back is the hardest part," she said.

"And the most important part," he added. "Much as we need to feed, we must avoid being caught doing it."

So they continued wandering through stores, focusing less on the more traditional merchandise on shelves and racks, concentrating instead on living merchandise browsing alongside them. A brand-new Victoria's Secret store attracted her genuine interest, and she soon handed him a handful of lingerie she picked out for herself. At a table laid out with a display of bras in bright pastels, she sidled up to a pretty brunette.

"See any 32Bs in the bright pink?"

The girl eyed her skeptically, eyes falling to Angelique's chest. "Same size I'm looking for; might be small for you."

"I wish. Here's one—oh, lucky us! One for me, one for you!" She handed the girl a bra that looked far too sexy for her. She might have been a sophomore in high school. "It will look fantastic on you!"

"You think?"

"I'm positive. I'm Angelique, by the way."

"Sandy." Again checking Angelique's breasts, a mental size comparison in her head obvious, she said, "Maybe I should try this on. Thanks for finding them."

"Anytime!"

On another table, she picked out a super-sexy lace bra and panties set, then another identical to it. Eddie asked, "You like this one, huh?"

"Will look great on my sister, won't it? I need to bring her something. What did you think of Sandy? Cute?"

"Very. Maybe too young."

"Young and innocent—who is the vampire who told me that once? Besides, I want to share my first feeding with you."

"Aren't you in a generous mood? Better hurry, though." He nodded to the far side of the store, where a clerk was putting Sandy's pink bra in a black bag.

"Crap! Hey, be a dear and check out for me—I'll see where she's going. Buying lingerie won't embarrass you?"

"Not at all. Meet me in front of County Seat if I can't find you."

Her prey had disappeared into the crowd, and she turned in the same direction the other girl went. Another customer beat Eddie to the checkout counter, so he had to wait his turn. Well worth it, though—$200 may never have been better spent.

It took only a few minutes to track them down next to Waldenbooks at Camelot records, where he found the two flipping through an album bin together. "Oh, here he is right now. Sandy, this is Eddie; he's my cousin."

She giggled, which made the girl smile. Adorable in a suburban, somewhat mousy way, browsing through King Diamond albums which, if looks did not deceive, was as novel an experience as chatting with vampires. Pop music oozed from this girl's pores.

"She goes to Pie High."

"St. Pius High School," Sandy explained, in case Eddie was unaware of the local nickname. He was, though, and told her he knew of the school a few miles from the mall.

"I was just telling Sandy about this." Her eyes bespoke doubt in her powers, questioning whether her new abilities allowed control of this girl's mind, holding out her hands to make the point even clearer.

He whispered, "Suggest which one to buy—then you'll know."

"Here, buy this one." Angelique handed her an album. "Unless you want the CD."

"I'll buy this one," her victim answered flatly. While she paid, Angelique bumped her shoulder against him, violet eyes glowing and smiling. They led her to the huge parking garage outside; their prey followed, carrying her new album without question. The delivery vans were still in their corner of the near empty bottom level, two levels below ground, unmoved since a brief scouting expedition when they arrived. Eddie soon found the girls, after dropping their own bags in the car to avoid any loose ends in the event an unlucky interruption forced them to flee.

Angelique stood behind her, massaging the girl's shoulders, awaiting his return. "Isn't she the cutest thing ever?"

"She is." He stopped in front, cutting off any escape route. Angelique's hands slipped down Sandy's back, around her sides, holding her tender as a lover. Her head rolled back against Angelique's shoulder. "I think she likes you."

Sandy surprised them by answering, "I love her."

Slender fingers brushed her brunette locks back behind one shoulder, exposing a thin, supple neck, still kneading a breast with the other hand. Two sharp, white daggers drove through tanned skin, then pink lips enveloped the gaping wounds, and Angelique drank with a voracious appetite.

"Come taste her; she's delicious!"

First kissing a smear of blood from her upper lip, Eddie then ran his tongue from the bottom of the lowest running drop up to pinprick incisions in her neck, and he, too, drank from the girl. Sweet and untainted. Only a taste, though, because his protégé needed it more. Angelique drank lustily from her, deep and low moans of a lion emanating as she did, both hands caressing Sandy's body. The girl also moaned, hers softer.

Soon, her complexion growing pale and arms limp at her sides, Eddie told her it was time to go. Angelique continued feasting on virgin blood.

"That's enough!" Grabbing a handful of orange curls, he pulled her away from their victim. She bared her fangs at him and hissed a warning. In response, he torqued her head back and shoved her against the closest delivery van. With his free hand, he caught the girl and lowered her to the cement floor. Using direct pressure, he made sure the flow stopped before they left.

Neither spoke a word up the corner staircase, not until they reached the floor where they parked. There, Eddie snatched her arm and pulled her close, azure eyes alight. "When I say stop, you stop!"

She grinned, quite pleased with herself. "Why are you so worried about *her*?"

"What do you suppose will happen if she dies? One thing TV news loves is a dead, pretty high-school girl! The police will turn over every stone to catch her killer. If you kill someone, make sure it is a person no one will miss. The last thing we need is a manhunt like the Atlanta missing and murdered kids, and that's what we'll get if they start finding dead sophomores in parking garages around town!"

"You're right. I... I..."

"It's your first hunt." He released her arm, caressed it, then smoothed out her curls. "Learn to control the bloodlust. It is difficult, but you must master your self-control. That's why I am here with you. It is every bit as essential to us as feeding."

Then he pulled her to him and kissed her, the taste of virgin blood still on her tongue, and she molded her body to his, igniting the passion they shared.

WELCOME TO THE JUNGLE

Dozens stood in line leading toward a small shack in the shadow of a chunky, hulking building built from rough-hewn gray rock. High above the crowd, a head kept watch next to a small shack. So high, the twins expected to find the bouncer standing on a stool or wooden crate in search of troublemakers, but when the line inched forward, allowing closer inspection, it became clear he stood on the same ground as those lined up for tickets. Almost everyone in the queue stood a full foot shorter. Neither woman had ever seen a specimen this huge. Unlike most men approaching seven feet in height—if there is such a thing as "most" among such a rare breed—his body was not slender like a basketball player's. Shoulders broadened into an immense V, which his black, tight-fitting tee-shirt bearing the words *Masquerade Staff* emphasized well.

Ahead of them, four college kids pulled out driver's licenses and their five-dollar cover charge, and after the giant compared their faces to the photos on their IDs, motioned them with his head toward the building next door, from where throbbing bass somehow penetrated those massive slab walls. The gargantuan bouncer then turned his attention to Eddie.

"Those girls better have ID; they don't look a day over fifteen."

"Sure thing. I've got theirs right here. And you are way off," he said. Exchanging a worried glance, knowing neither carried a fake ID showing them to be the required twenty-one, the girls wondered what Eddie was up to as he pulled a $100 bill from his pocket. Holding the crisp edges, he pulled it tight with a snap. "Believe it or not, they are each fifty. Twins, in case you haven't figured that out."

Handsome in the most menacing way conceivable, the giant's harsh eyes narrowed and examined the twins. "I'd never have guessed. They look great for their age. Whatever you are doing, keep it up." Ben Franklin disappeared into his pocket.

"Kev, these are my cousins Angelique and Josette." Eddie took the massive hand the gargantuan offered in a thumb-shake, their hands slapping together.

Their tiny hands disappeared inside his when he then shook them. His voice was such a low bass it vibrated their chests the way a clap of thunder does. "Which one is the witch?"

Every kid his age rushed home the minute elementary school let out to watch *Dark Shadows*, and knew its characters by heart. "For crying out loud, Kev, I worry about your powers of observation—can't you see they are both vampires?"

His eyes panned up and down each one from hair to boots, starting with Angelique, of course—his powers of observation were spot-on. "I see. What threw me off: most vampires dress in all black and are nowhere near as hot."

Heightened senses were quite unnecessary. Not with the twins that night. Hair teased up big, their first experiment with this style for this occasion, caught every eye waiting up and down the line. Josette skipped curling hers, a change Angelique was considering, as well. Nearby men envied the tall blond in a black suit, shirt and tie accompanying them.

Kev was right, in part: while dressed in black, both wore outfits accentuated with plenty of color. Matching black spandex pants painted on, Josette wore a neon pink shirt under a black patent leather jacket. Angelique's black top with purple geometric designs was so tight, every detail of a fine gold necklace trapped underneath strained against thin fabric. So did every luscious curve it stretched over.

But the eye makeup they painted on each other proved to be the show-stopper. Angelique's eyes were highlighted by a long black rectangle that ran from each temple, razor straight to squared corners at the edges of her nose. Josette's was similar, only with rounded corners and pink circles around the eyes an exact match with the color of her shirt. They looked straight off either a Paris runway or an album cover and moved with a newfound attitude to match.

Kev could not help but turn to watch them pass, then stopped Eddie behind them with a massive hand on his shoulder. He closed his eyes and shook his head in disbelief. "Let me know if you need any help with them."

"If you weren't such a good man, I would take you up on it. Trust me: you'd never be able to handle them."

"Can you?"

A little roll of the eyes and shrugged shoulders. "Their mom loves me. Go figure."

"Don't worry—I'll be right here if you need rescuing," Kev called after him.

Angelique glanced back behind her. "That is the largest human being I have ever seen. There must be enough blood in him to feed us both for a month. How do you know the Colossus of Rhodes?"

"He's training to be a pro wrestler. We work out at the same gym. Great guy."

"No offense, but it looks like he works out much more often than you. And from the looks of it, he doesn't need protection from us. Seems you got that backwards."

"Wait until you discover the full extent of your powers; you may surprise yourselves."

No one remembers when it was built around a century before, what began its existence as DuPree Excelsior Mill producing packing materials until plastics rendered it obsolete after World War II now stood as a monument to Atlanta's existence prior to the war. Recently refurbished and launched as a concert and dancing venue after a brief stint as a pizza parlor, its industrial Gothic structure gave it an atmosphere incomparable with any modern building. Blackish paint slapped onto its wooden surfaces added to a sense of doom, as if the building had somehow survived being engulfed by fire.

Inside, the attention only intensified as the twins embarked upon their first hunt together. Their first hunt in a full pack. The way they strutted, if Madonna was with them, no one would have noticed.

Heavy wooden stairs led to Masquerade's three levels. The upper level, the large concert venue, was called Heaven; the basement, where industrial dance music blared down onto a massive dance floor, they named Hell. In between, a low-ceilinged level once housing offices where managers processed orders for excelsior now renamed Purgatory and served as an indie alternative artists and singer-songwriters venue. People below stopped to watch the three ascend the stairs.

Angelique stopped on a walkway where stairs led off in three directions toward each level. "Where to?"

They had long awaited this night. "Mercyful Fate won't play until midnight or so."

Josette gave a theatrical twirl back and forth between stairs on her left and right. "What until then?"

"Will you dance with me in Hell?"

Early as it was—just after ten—bodies already throbbed to the rhythm of a dark beat in a Hell lit only by flashing strobe lights. Eddie led the twins to what passed for a quiet corner. "This place draws in all kinds. Bikers. Hardcore. Goths. Maybe a drag queen or two. Tourists are your best bet. They stand out, easy to spot as a fish flopping on a dock: preppies, Georgia Tech students. Find me an Emory sorority girl and I'll be a lucky man."

Huddled close enough for burnished copper hair to tickle his face as he yelled between their ears, pressed-together, their nodding along made the tickling worse. The sound almost swallowed their soprano voices. “Will you come with us?”

“If you wish.” For an answer, Josette wrapped both arms around one of his, mashing one breast on a bicep. Angelique’s cheek pressed against his so he could hear.

“Find me before the show starts.” With that, she ventured alone into the mass of dancing bodies.

To avoid the mob to the extent possible, Josette stayed along the outer periphery of the dance floor, dancing self-consciously and without conviction. Not that anyone noticed —spectacular as she looked—every stiff movement possessed the power to mesmerize. Two bright sets of eyes scanned the mass of bodies surging as one to the hypnotic beat.

“How do you choose?”

“Innocence, beauty, vulnerability. Hard to find anyone too innocent in a place like this, but if you do, they will come hand in hand with vulnerability.”

“Vulnerability is the most important?”

“For you. Tonight.”

“And you?”

“Tonight, I’m hungry for beauty.”

“Should I be jealous?”

“Jealousy is a human emotion.”

“Maybe I’m still a woman.”

Heavy synthesizers drowned out his laugh. He pulled her close. Roughly. “No one will come between us.”

“Not even my sister?”

“Not even her.”

Still dancing seductively against him, she glanced around. “Why do I still hate crowds? Isn’t claustrophobia a human emotion, too?”

“Try waking up in a coffin. That’s where I transformed. No, to a certain extent, we will always be who we once were.”

Nearby, two men started scuffling and one dragged the other to the floor, so they danced their way to a safe distance. This early, they could afford to be choosy, so continued scanning the crowd, comparing notes of potential targets. A couple next to them started making out. Building in intensity, the DJ spun a hypnotic mix of beat-heavy, industrial music. A throbbing song came on that lit Eddie's eyes.

"Front 242! This is a great song!" He danced with abandon, as if he was invisible, even though everyone was watching his contagious enthusiasm.

"I've never heard any of this music in Rhode Island," she shouted, "or seen anything like this place."

One hand caressed a velvety cheek, down to her neck, thumb applying slight pressure over her windpipe, then pulled her close. Red and blue flashed on his face. "We have barely begun—the wonders I will show you, the experiences we will share."

Faster and faster her heart raced. Excitement. Intimidation. Eagerness. A tinge of fear, and not only from being packed into a crowd of a thousand people dancing too close in a deafening, dark basement called Hell. Among this crowd, not part of it. They were no longer who they once were and—alien as this place was—this now was her element. Accepting this may prove more difficult than feeding on human blood.

A giant shadow approached from one side, almost completely eclipsing one bank of throbbing lights. Towering half a head taller than Eddie, a stunning black woman sashayed over to them as titanic in stiletto heels as the bouncer Kev, hair a remarkable platinum blonde coiffed into a bouffant and wearing a tight sequined yellow dress slit up the front to her waist. Almost nothing could have shocked her more in this place.

"Honey, where did you find this magnificent creature?" Her voice penetrated the music like she had hijacked the DJ's mike.

"Had to go all the way to Rhode Island for this one."

Confused, and a little terrified of this flamboyant behemoth two feet over her, Josette sidestepped away. The woman stopped dancing, bent forward from the waist and gave Eddie in a polite friend hug. “Ru, meet my cousin Josette.”

Turning to her now, she examined her like a specimen of some sort, beaming the whole time, took her hand and kissed her knuckles. “*Enchanté.* Is she your boo?”

“Believe it or not, she is one of a matched set.”

Her expression changed, in an instant menacing to match her enormous size. “You aren’t planning to challenge me as the undisputed queen of the Atlanta night, are you?” Still holding onto her hand, grip tightening as she tried to retrieve it.

“No—nothing like that!”

“Oh, sugar, I’m just playin’ with you! Do a spin so I can get a look at ’cha!” Holding her hand high, she guided Josette through the slow pirouette of a ballroom dancer. “Funny, this light does amazing things to those gorgeous eyes of yours. They look like two jewels.”

“The strobes have nothing to do with it. Her eyes are amethyst, same as her sister’s, and every bit as perfect in daylight.”

One hand fanned up and down in front of her neck. “Catch me if I swoon, Edwin. I refuse to believe two visions of such perfection are walking the same earth as me until I see it with my own two eyes.”

“She’s here somewhere, but if you can wait, she’ll be back.”

“Hon, are you the kind of boy who keeps all his girls waiting? Although seeing two of her might just be worth the wait.”

Perhaps seeing this natural wonder dancing with her sister and Eddie lured Angelique to get a closer look, or it may have been nothing more than a coincidence, but she appeared alongside before the end of the song, hands clasped overhead and performing a seductive dance-walk over to them.

“Meet Angelique.”

“Oh, my stars! You do speak truth, Edwin!”

“Have I ever misled you?”

“Not yet—but I never give up hope!” Ru turned to the twins. “May I steal these family jewels from you?”

“You may borrow them, but if they aren’t back by the time the band starts playing in Heaven, I will come looking for you—and you don’t want that!”

“Trust me, I won’t mind that at all! Come, ladies—I have some big plans in store for you!” One in each hand, held by dainty fingers on hands extended waist-high—shoulder height for the twins—Ru led them off into the crowd, Angelique dancing alongside as they walked; Josette turned, looking back over her shoulder pleading for her cousin to rescue her. Eddie finger-waved and winked.

Then he set off in search of prey.

Sorority girls stand out. Their wardrobes of whites and bright colors are dead giveaways. Four danced together in a square, three trying hard to get into the unfamiliar rhythm, the fourth appearing uncomfortable as Josette. He took the space next to the latter, dancing, smiling to the girl on each side. All four grinned, inspiring the dancing trio to put more energy into their moves. Eddie leaned toward the fourth, a gorgeous brunette with shoulder-length hair, a white shirt and dark eyes too large for her face. Tall and waif-ish, yet with soft breasts that seemed borrowed from a heavier girl; her body reminiscent of Princess Di.

“I’m Eddie.”

“Emily,” she shouted. “Are you here alone?”

He turned and pointed to the far end of the dance floor two hundred feet away, where three figures danced atop the bank of speakers. How Ru got herself and the twins up there, each in their heels, he hadn’t a clue. It was her favorite place to dance, for which she developed a secret method. “RuPaul borrowed my cousins.”

“That’s RuPaul?”

“The one and only. You’ve heard of her?”

“She’s famous. You know her?”

"We go way back. First time here?"

"It's that obvious?"

"Maybe a little. Let me guess: Emory?"

"You always this good at guessing?"

"No guessing involved." He pointed to one eye. "Observation."

Only swaying now while her friends continued dancing, although keeping eagle eyes on him, she asked, "What else can you observe about me?"

"Nothing much. English major? Emphasis on Emily Dickinson? No, too obvious with your name... one of the Brontë sisters. Definitely not Emily."

"Charlotte."

"Should I keep going?"

As she leaned close, touching his arm which she self-consciously pulled away a second later. "No. Proved your point. I'm a terrible guesser—tell me about yourself."

"Not much to tell, really. Just a creature of the night, alone, abandoned by his family for a celebrity. You here to see Mercyful Fate?"

"Who are they?"

"A band. Playing in Heaven later."

"What kind of music?"

"Gothic metal."

"Hey," she yelled to her sorority sisters, "are we going to see a band tonight?"

All three shrugged their shoulders better than if they choreographed it.

"Can I entice you with sex on the beach?" Her eyes bulged. "I prefer gin, myself, but shooters are fun."

"Shooters are trouble."

"Then let's get a couple."

†

An emaciated woman, her right arm an extravagantly

colored tattoo sleeve, strummed an antique acoustic guitar. Her beautiful soprano rang like a bell. Much more Josette's style than the throbbing industrial beat in Hell, Eddie tracked her to a table for two in Purgatory, alone. Most came to the Masquerade to dance or—on a night like this—to see a band playing a unique style of music, so the room was a third full; much like its namesake, Purgatory felt like an afterthought.

"What happened to that girl you found?"

"She may join us for the show."

"What if she doesn't?"

"If not tonight, then another night; she gave me her number."

"Hopefully she won't blow you off so you can focus on helping me hunt."

"You have my full attention. Too bad she is so skinny; I bet she doesn't have enough blood left in her body to feed you, too."

"Wait, what? You already fed from her?"

"Well, you were up on that speaker dancing so long, opportunities that great can't go to waste."

"So, she's already under your spell? Then she will show up."

"I doubt it. I didn't leave her enchanted for more tonight. Sorority girls like her aren't into metal. Figured spending time with you will be more fun."

"Really?" Fingertips absently wiped condensation from the sides of her cup. "Let me ask you a question."

"Shoot."

"What are we to you?"

"What do you mean?"

"Are we both your girlfriend? Another one, like Aryana?"

"Why do you feel a need to label it?"

"Everything has a name."

"Not everything."

"Sure it does. Are we lovers? Some sort of vampire coven? An incestuous undead family who screws each other's brains out?"

"Your problem is not everything falls within the construct your mind has yet to embrace. We are all of those things, yet that barely scratches the surface; we are none of those things, because we are no longer among the living."

"So, you're saying we're horny corpses who hang out and drink blood together?"

"We're that, too." A momentary chuckle before he penetrated her eyes and what passed for her soul. "We are one, neither living nor dead, sharing this secret no one else can comprehend. Like it or not, blood and fate wove us together in ways beyond anything I could have contemplated a few months ago. If your sister is hungry, she can feed from me. If I am in danger, you will kill for me—as you demonstrated once already. A hundred years from now, a thousand, we will be together. By then, we will be even more to each other."

"We might hate each other by then."

"True, but we will still hold each other's secrets, so even if we learn to hate one another, our need for each other will continue. And I hope we will never become enemies."

"We won't, you and I. Nor will our mother, I suppose. My sister, on the other hand…"

"Yeah, she is a different breed."

"The two of you might end up hating each other. You'll still be screwing each other, of course, and you'll probably be drinking blood from that heart you carved and she'll be sucking on your nipple, giving each other vorgasms…"

"Vorgasms?"

"What else to call it? Everything must have a name. Anything as powerful as that sensation drinking blood gives deserves a name. Vampire orgasm—vorgasm."

"I like it. Funny, I can picture you being right about your sister and I, although we can hope it will never come to that. If it does, I suspect it will not be my decision, but hers. When it happens, we will screw like mink, feed each other, then try to find some way to kill each other."

"And you wonder why I never wanted to fall in love. Before..."

"Don't confuse this with love. Love is a human emotion; it has no power over us any more than does death. What binds us together is far more powerful than love or any other emotion. It is pure, primal need. I need you; we need each other."

"So, you don't love us?"

With a wry grin, his eyes sapphires reflecting every bit of light, he took her hand and stroked her fingers. "Compared to what burns in my dead, beating heart for you, love is a very feeble emotion. Call it love, for lack of a more accurate term, but I have been in love and—trust me on this—it cannot hold a candle."

"You know," she said, then sipping her blood red wine, unblinking eyes burning into his, "I believe you. Maybe because I am a twin. Sometimes I hate my sister, yet we have a bond that transcends all. Now I feel something like that with my mother—and with you. Not the same, but frighteningly similar. I chalked it up to love. Maybe it's need." She shrugged her shoulders.

"Well, right now, I have a need of a different kind."

Perplexed and intrigued, she asked, "What do you need?"

"I need the most beautiful woman in this building to accompany me upstairs before the band starts their set."

†

Angelique arrived with a young, nerdy guy in tow soon after the band launched their tantalizing first set. Or, perhaps more accurately, this dude came wrapped around her finger. From the lost-at-sea look on his face, no woman in her league had ever paid him much attention. Arriving BYOB freed her sister to cuddle with Eddie during the show, and they took full advantage—his arms around her, holding her to his chest. A Valentine's card image of lovers. Inspired by the couple swaying to the music alongside, the kid—Steve something or other—tried the same thing, but Angelique danced just beyond his reach.

Lips and tongue brushed her ear as Eddie leaned down close enough to whisper. “Thirsty?” His eyes motioned behind her and she nodded almost imperceptibly, the corners of her lips curling up. In his arms, her sister swayed to the beat, vying for attention.

Onstage, the band’s singer, King Diamond, wailed into a microphone attached to a pair of human-looking femurs lashed by leather into a cross. Crosses painted in the black and white paint covering his face created a demon mask crying black painted tears. His voice rose into a haunting falsetto. “How do you like them?”

“They’re awesome! Hypnotic—scary, too! Are you having fun?”

A hand slipped up over one breast and pressed her body tighter against his. “If only I could sing along. This is way beyond my vocal range.”

“I will give you something to sing about,” she promised.

An hour later, when the band wrapped up the show after two encores, Josette shouted at her sister’s numbed and ringing ears, “See you in Hell!” Eddie’s firm hand in hers, she dragged him toward the door hustling to beat the crowd. Behind them, much of the audience followed, drawn *en masse* to an already packed Hell.

“How can I drink blood yet still loathe being in a crowd?”

“Remember, traces of who we once were remain—which is kinda great, because you were pretty darn awesome when we met,” Eddie answered.

Downstairs, her eyes flashed dark and wide in the pulsating light, searching wildly for something in the throng. Colorful lights played across her face, one side bright red, the other blue, her entire face in orange, then deep purple on the right like a half moon. Now more tightly packed. A man’s elbow hit her. Crowded against Eddie, their feet overlapping, leaving them too cramped to sway, a woman behind backed into her. Eddie caught her against his chest, colors flashing across her face and enormous eyes. A stout push off his stomach propelling her into a spin and she fled through the dancing masses. Eddie watched, then began following before she disappeared.

At the door, Josette took the stairs at a trot, fast as her heels allowed. A couple descending into Hell ducked out of her way, watching Eddie taking two stairs at a time to keep up.

"Josette, wait!"

She ignored his pleas.

Upstairs, Josette sprinted past two guys on the walkway, Eddie ten yards behind and—unencumbered by high heels—gaining fast. The two watched the petite stunner and her bobbing mop of orange pass, then one stepped into Eddie's path.

"Let her go, dude."

Both significantly larger than the man chasing the girl, these good Samaritans expected the thinner man to give up the chase, allowing her to escape. Neither expected the pursuer to plow right into the one man with sufficient force to bowl him over onto the wooden planks with a resounding thud. The impact slowed his momentum enough for his buddy to grab hold of Eddie's wrist, spinning him to face the other man, who failed to comprehend his mistake.

A shove hit the interloper's chest, powerful enough to lift both feet off the walkway and send him flying against the rough stone wall five feet behind him. A sickening crack rang out as his head struck gray masonry stone. A frantic Eddie turned and leapt over the prone figure of the first guy. After seeing what happened to the gallant men who tried to protect the girl by intervening, others who stopped to take in this excitement stepped aside to clear him a path.

Midway down the walkway, where the stairway descended from the upper floor, Angelique came into view, her puppy still close behind. "What's going on?"

"Your sister freaked out." he slowed and turned without ever quite stopping.

"Where is she?" Pointing, Eddie continued his pursuit; Angelique joined in the chase, her plaything bringing up the rear.

Making use of the head-start his little dustup with the do-gooders provided, Josette continued running until she made it to the parking lot across a two-lane side street. Then, safely away and in the cool, calming night air, she stopped, turned and waited for the others to catch up to her.

"Are you okay?"

"I'm sorry! Oh, I can't explain what just happened." Her sister ran up and swept her into a protective hug. Close behind trotted up her puppy dog.

"Hey, buddy. Is she okay?" Based on his preppy clothes, Emory University. Sophomore, maybe, packing a fake ID and thrilled Angelique plucked him from the minors for a shot at the major league.

"Crowds aren't her thing," Eddie answered.

The four walked to the car. A twin wigging out in public is less a cold shower than an opportunity to console or help in some nebulous way, keeping Steve's hopes alive. Halfway across the packed lot—by day a vacant expanse of crushed granite gravel through which patches of grass tried to survive—Angelique swapped places with Eddie, allowing him to escort Josette and lead the way.

"Why am I such a spaz?"

"Now we know mass gatherings are not your preferred hunting grounds. No worries—there are plenty of other options. Besides, it's probably better this way. Remember my rule about not drawing attention; not a soul in that place missed the two spectacular redheads."

"Especially the one who ran screaming from Hell."

"You're much better at attracting attention than avoiding it."

From behind, a noise drew their curiosity. The soft thud

of sheet metal giving, a person sitting on a flimsy car hood, a door or fender popping when someone leans too hard against it. A sound so unexpected, Eddie turned.

Sprawled across the hood of a brand-new red Eagle Talon they had just passed, Angelique had pinned her frat boy. Curls spilled across the kid from his chest to his longish, gelled-back dark hair, and for a moment, he thought they were making out. Out to his sides, though, languid hands flapped on the hood, resembling pectoral fins of some fish desperately trying to swim through air. Hands that, if kissing such a beauty, should be caressing her back or waist, if not groping more desired parts of her body.

"Oh, shit!"

"What?" Josette turned to see what the fuss was.

Oblivious to her, he said to her sister, "Not here! What are you doing?" Hurriedly searching through rows of parked cars, at least no one else could be seen in the lot. Her face turned toward them, white in the streetlight's glow, red smeared around her lips. A pinkish film covered half-inch fangs. Ignoring him, her eyes locked onto her sister.

"Did you feed?"

Her twin took one step forward. "No."

"Not here," Eddie said. "Come on, let's get him to the car."

Instead, she ran into his elbow in her rush toward the supine kid, who stared up into a moonless sky. Angelique moved to the side and returned to his neck, from which two ribbons of blood ran toward the car's hood. When Josette joined in, this time her hair mingling with her sister's covering the boy's face as she bent toward the other side of his neck.

"This is not happening," Eddie said. Blood lust had taken them both. The only thing for him to do was stand guard, for he had no interest in fighting two vampires off their victim amid such blind frenzy. The only thing going for them in this open expanse—the entrance was visible and, past it, so was the exit from Excelsior Mill across the street. After a couple of minutes, girls moaning with pleasure the whole time, a group of five exited together, laughing and yelling, drunk and happy.

They were heading this way.

"Come on, we need to go!"

Still taken by feeding, the vampires ignored him, so he tugged on Angelique's shoulder. Rather than yielding, her head spun, and baring fangs at him, hissed a warning. Her sister turned, as well, showing sharp, identical incisors, but Josette growled. Growled! At him! Totally out of control, what sort of screams or curses might erupt if he tried forcing them to abandon their prey?

Across the road now, the group—two women and three men, one wearing a new tee-shirt as a concert souvenir—made their way down a row one over from where the kid was being drained of lifeblood. When they were fifty feet away, despite all the noise the twins were making, Eddie squatted down below the rooflines of the cars and whispered to them, "Quiet—they'll hear you!"

Without parking spaces marked out in the gravel, drivers parked at an angle in this row, but the row of cars the others walked down were all lined up straight. When the five concertgoers reached the gap between cars directly across from them, one woman turned in their direction, listening. Crouched down behind a square K-car like those the Atlanta Police drove, Eddie peered around the rear pillar, holding his breath while, behind him, the girls continued moaning.

The woman burst out laughing. "Hear that? Someone's screwing over there!"

"Where?" The other four turned in their direction, looking for the show.

"Damn it—shut up!" Eddie spoke loud as he dared, he hoped quiet enough to not carry the fifty feet to the group searching the darkness for a public sex show. As luck had it, from where they stood, the Talon's roof blocked any view of the three spread across its hood.

One guy called out, "Hey, get a room!"

He and his friends all found that joke hilarious. At last,

hearing this voice ringing out jolted the twins to reality and quieted them. Bored, one woman started walking off, and unable to determine where the sounds came from, the others drifted away one by one. All five squeezed into a nearby Cressida. Brilliant lights flashed on, illuminating the K-car shielding Eddie, forcing him to duck down lower. It backed out, beams swinging across the red Talon, but the car drove away. Somehow, they must have missed the horror two car-lengths away.

"Alright, you two are through!"

Engorged and returning to sanity, the twins stood. Boy toy Steve slid limp down the sports car's sloping hood like water disappearing over a waterfall. His head thumped against the bumper before landing on dusty gravel. Already glassing over, his vacant eyes stared lifeless.

"Damn it! This is why we take them."

"Our mother told us she killed some guy behind a bar in Providence."

He waved his hand by their faces. "This guy just left with two women everyone in the bar saw, with big, orange hair no one inside missed. Was he here with friends?"

Angelique wiped blood off her cheek with the back of her hand. "He said so, but I saw no friends. He might have made them up."

"Did they see you? Did he leave long enough to brag by pointing you out to some buddies from across the room?"

"Chill out! He went to the men's room once, but nobody was around."

"Alright. Help me load his body into the trunk; we'll worry about what to do with it later. Right now, we've got to get outta here!"

NEVER LET ME DOWN AGAIN

Only two keys to the basement door exist. One belonged to Eddie, of course. Despite her years of faithful service and the trust built up over that time, Margaret did not have the other. When Angelique lay dying upstairs, he gave the second key to her sister in case he was down there when she needed to get to him right away.

Soon as they arrived back at Amethyst House, he took the twins with him down to his sanctuary and locked the door behind them. Neither had ever seen him in such a state of pure, unbridled fury. He paced the basement floor, ignoring when they spoke, so they talked to each other and ignored him back.

Angelique knew he directed his rage at her. Unfair as it was, because she never intended to screw up their night's fun. She needed blood, and after tolerating Steve's pathetic shadowing long enough, her bloodlust simply surged beyond anyone's capacity to control. When he stopped pacing, distracted, lost in thought, she went to him and rubbed his arm while trying to establish eye contact.

"I'm sorry for upsetting you so much. The thought of spending another moment with that kid was driving me nuts, and once we were outside and away from everyone, all I could think about was my hunger."

With stunning suddenness, he spun and grabbed both of her arms, eyebrows twisted low into an unfamiliar scowl. His eyes glowed with a beautiful icy light. "When we are together, we are *together*! Your impudence put all of us at risk—most of all, your sister."

"I wasn't thinking."

"Precisely my view of the problem! No one can tell the two of you apart. Sometimes I still confuse you. Anyone who witnesses what you do will take one look at Josette and blame her for your actions. I'm just imagining a police sketch of you on TV, in the papers."

Josette defended her sister. "Is it really so bad? She made mistakes, but no one saw what she did—then we got him out of there."

"You," he turned to her. She shrunk back as he raised his hand, but surprised her by caressing her cheek. "You disappointed me more. Did you know that?"

"I'm sorry; it was like a panic attack."

"That is not what upsets me. Your betrayal was worse than hers. You growled at me like you forgot who I am. You were out of your mind, same as her. At least she has the excuse of the thrill of first kill. What is your excuse?"

Betrayal. The word stung her sister, although Angelique considered it a stretch. Certainly not intended to betray him. His overreaction surprised her. Oddly enough, his anger excited her in ways as difficult to understand as anything she experienced since her transformation.

"I'm sorry," her sister apologized again, weak and cowed.

Eddie stopped in front of the fireplace—an unnecessary decoration this time of year—pulled out his wallet and removed his driver's license from it. "So long, Alfred Dalrymple."

The license flared up in the small flames, darkened and its edges curled.

"What are you doing?"

"Who is Alfred Dalrymple?"

"Until tonight, he was your lover. I've used his identity for several years. Time to say goodbye. Let them look for Alfred; good luck finding him."

Angelique snickered. “Isn’t that a bit overly dramatic? If anything, they will be looking for us, not Alfred.”

“I may have killed a guy, too.” To their shock, he recounted the two fools who jumped in to save Josette from what they assumed either a crazed lunatic or jealous ex. “So, if they are searching for anyone, let them look for Alfred.”

Angelique asked, “Are you sure he’s dead?”

“Have you ever heard a coconut smashed against a concrete floor? That’s what his head sounded like.” With a chuckle followed by a sigh, he said, “Death row scares me more than anything else.”

“Why?” Josette asked. “If you are immortal, they can’t execute you.”

“They can try. It won’t work, but I can guess the electric chair is no fun. After two or three tries, they probably will give up, figuring I have some strange immunity to electrocution. Worse, though, I can only imagine the boredom of several lifetimes in a prison cell. How long will it take until they turn me into a science experiment? 100 years? Two centuries? Eventually, they will try to figure out why I won’t die, why I never age.”

Josette cupped his cheek as he cupped hers a moment before. “You were protecting me and they tried to get in your way.”

“No mortal will come between us.”

“Nor will we allow it, will we, Angelique?” Her lips took his, and he pulled her toward him as her twin came from behind to kiss his neck. Fangs brushed his skin but did not penetrate him. Not yet.

“If they are coming for us,” she looked up to see her sister’s lips and his inches away, “let’s make tonight one we will always remember.

On the floor, flickering firelight dancing across pallid skin, casting shifting shadows of the three engorging themselves on each other. All three having fed, they feasted upon each other purely for their mutual pleasure, sharing the lifeblood flowing in their bodies with each, giving their bodies fully and completely. This unique combination of anger, fear, need and whatever it was they confused for mortal love, brewed an intoxicating aphrodisiac. A bloodlust so deep no one wished would end.

Eventually, though, post-feeding torpor overcame them and the threesome fell into deep slumber before the dying embers of the fire, their bodies and fates as entwined as they had been in the midst of their bloodlust. And they slept unmoving while the sun outside rose and set again.

†

Unrecognizable under a baseball cap pulled low with hair tucked up inside, Angelique followed his directions south of town, past the suburbs and into stark countryside. Driving one of his other cars, the sleek convertible he paraded them through town on their sightseeing tour when they arrived, Josette followed at a respectable distance. Although she kept the written directions on the seat beside her, she tried to keep the car in sight, only losing them for a short while in city traffic until she caught sight of them again at a red light.

In the middle of the night, only the shape of their distinctive headlights and tail lights identified them, but the generic K-car she followed resembled thousands of others on the road. Half of them cops.

The mythological Griffin has the head and wings of an eagle set on the body of a lion. Endowed with the characteristics of the kings of both sky and beasts, it fights to the death to protect its territory, whether in the form of precious treasure, living creatures or royal lines. Formed into wine goblets, its eggs have the mystical power to prolong the life of those who drink from them. These virtues held particular interest for Eddie since he became deceased.

The town of Griffin must be named for a person with that surname, for it is among the most unlikely of places to bear such a noble creature's name. Other than the towering brick courthouse downtown, this seedy, poor cousin of Atlanta smelled of desperation. A sprawling junkyard loomed alarmingly close to the center of town. After a few words from Eddie, a guard held back a tiger-striped, snarling pit-bull and opened the gate to them. An elderly, heavyset black man with a shock of pure white hair met them somewhere inside the maze.

"How much?"

"Two hundred."

Eddie slipped him three crisp C-notes. Within minutes, a massive, aquiline claw descended, penetrating the K-car's wet toilet tissue roof, hoisting it into a massive, coffin-like industrial machine. Two loud minutes later, this machine spit out a cube little more than a square yard in size, steel flecked with remnants of the midnight blue paint, all that remained of what began the night as a working automobile. Somewhere inside that blue metal cube, Steve or whatever was left of his crushed body lay forever entombed.

"One problem solved." Josette offered him the keys to the Olds 442, which he refused.

"Are you forgetting who burned their driver's license? The last thing we need is for me to get pulled for a rolling stop. Police here will not pull over a pretty white girl driving a muscle car through town, though."

†

When they ventured downstairs the next day, the twins found Eddie scouring a stack of newspapers spread across the kitchen table, leading Josette to ask an obvious question. "What the hell is going on here?"

"Oh, glad y'all are up." He waved toward the counter. "Margaret grabbed me copies of all the papers from the last few days. Help me look to see if there are any reports about that guy I may have killed at the Masquerade. Or Steve. It probably happened too late to make the following morning's *Constitution*, so I am starting with the *Journal* from that afternoon. Then we have yesterday's copy of each and this morning's paper."

At the counter pouring coffee into two matching dark mugs the color of green marble, Angelique laughed. "For a Rhode Island Yankee, you sure sound like a southern boy. *Y'all!*"

"If you can turn your focus away from how southerners cleverly overcame a glaring oversight in the English language when some idiot decided to use the word *you* as both singular and plural, we have a stack of papers to go through. Look everywhere: front page, local section, police blotter—if he's still alive, it might be buried somewhere in a one-sentence notice somewhere."

Unimpressed, Angelique asked, "Why are you so worried about that guy?"

"It's not rocket science," her sister rolled her eyes while turning at Eddie. "If the guy's dead or lying brain-dead in the hospital, the police are looking for Eddie. And unless he plans on playing it safe by staying in the basement for the next few years, it might be nice to know if he can step outside."

"Thank you! And, if the police start digging, they might notice a missing Georgia Tech student who was last seen with either the same redhead the suspect was trying to protect, or her twin."

"And then they will start looking for us," Josette completed the thought for him, much the way the twins trade off in the middle of a conversation.

"Whatever. I'll help you go through these newspapers, but I think you are making too big a deal out of this. If they are looking for you, we will deal with it; if they aren't, they aren't."

It took longer than anyone expected, but they finished with that morning's paper almost an hour later.

"Looks like you're in the clear," Josette said, all three grinning in relief.

Angelique winked. "Told y'all!"

†

A nightgown of lavender satin Eddie bought for her flowing in her wake, accentuating and matching the tint of her eyes, Josette tiptoed down the stairs. It was dark, but vague light created shadows below. On the couch, Eddie lay with his feet up, reading a book, the only light on in the basement a small swivel lamp on the table, its low-intensity bulb angled toward the open pages in his lap. "Where's Angelique?"

He lay the book open on his chest. "I figured she was with you."

"I assumed she was down here with you, so I left you alone for a while."

"How considerate. Perhaps she is doing the same, assuming you are down here with me?"

"Well, I am. What are you reading?"

"*Gaiour* by Lord Byron."

"Never heard of that; what's it about?"

"It means *infidel* in Turkish. It's about a woman named Leila, who is in the king's harem and is in love with an infidel. It's about love, death and the afterlife."

"Sounds intense. Reminds me of something." She grinned. "Should I let you finish, or..."

"There's room here on the couch," he tapped the edge, only wide enough if she snuggled tight against him, "we can read it together, if you like."

"I've never read poetry with a guy—outside of class," she said, curling into his arms with her head on his chest where she could see the pages as he flipped back to the beginning.

†

Weeknights are slow—at least the ones without a big-name headliner. Usually Kev only worked weekends, but Mike called in sick, so he volunteered to help by filling in.

Even dressed in casual clothes, hair pulled back in a ponytail and wearing only a trace of mascara, she was unforgettable. "Which one are you?"

"Angelique—the witch."

"Right. I suppose you forgot your ID again."

"Oh, I brought it with me tonight. Don't need it, though."

"Oh?" In the quiet, no boisterous line waiting to get in, his voice sounded even deeper when he murmured. "This should be interesting—what did you have in mind?"

"I'm not going in—I was just driving by and wondering about that guy who got hurt that night when we were leaving. Happened right near us. My sister said he looked dead, but I said he's going to be okay. So, figured you are the perfect person to tell us which one wins the twenty dollars."

"Gambling on death—gotta love it. Turns out the guy can take a good bump. He was out cold for a few minutes. I hear he took about twenty stitches but is going to be fine. Looks like you win the bet."

"Good! That should pay my cover this weekend."

"I'll try to remember that you showed me your ID tonight. 1966, right?" Twenty-one years ago. The latest a person's birthdate could be to gain entry into a club serving alcohol in the state.

"Thanks for examining it so closely," she said, blew him a kiss and sauntered away with an exaggerated swing of her hips, giving him an excellent opportunity to scan the pocket of her skin-tight Calvin's, snug enough to make out the rectangle of a driver's license still tucked inside the right rear pocket.

Kev watched that booty all the way until she crossed the street and disappeared from view, shaking his head in awe the whole time.

†

"Don't be so upset; I bring you good tidings. That good

Samaritan you tossed like salad against the wall? He's fine. Busted his head open, but when he woke up, all he needed was a few stitches."

"Where did you get that information?"

"Returned to the scene of the crime. Talked to your gigantic buddy Kev, and he gave me the 411."

He came close and said, "Thanks," followed by a long, tender kiss.

"Always thinking about you, my love." The next kiss was longer and slower. When they broke for air, she asked, "What would you do without me?"

"You two need a room." Josette walked past them to the coffee. "Where were you last night?"

"Out exercising my private eye skills, making sure we are not harboring a fugitive."

Their facial expressions told the story. "We're not?"

"We are in the clear," Eddie said, squeezing her twin close.

While blowing across the top of her cup, Josette said, "I guess you earned a reward. Maybe I'll leave the two of you alone here today. I may do some exploring at the mall."

After delivering such good news, no one thought to ask what time she came home.

†

The only time Eddie turned on the news was when storms were heading their way. Immortal or not, a fortress for a basement made a perfect place to ride out a tornado warning, and the papers predicted a front coming through, bringing with it severe weather. Channel 11's anchor, a gorgeous redhead, made the choice of which channel to watch an easy one on those rare occasions he overcame his general loathing of local news. Besides, missing men rarely stay in the news more than a day or two; it's missing white women who garner weeks of top story status, the stories he avoided, and he had not been involved in a woman's disappearance in this city since spring.

He never made it to the weather.

"This is Terri Merryman, and we have powerful storms heading our way later tonight, but before the storm warnings, there are recent developments on the body discovered this morning behind the Kroger on North Avenue in Midtown. Atlanta Police have not released the identity of the victim, described only as a fourteen-year-old boy. Police sources say he apparently bled to death from wounds to his neck, and due to an absence of blood at the scene, suspect the murder took place at another location and the unknown killer later dumped the body behind Kroger..."

The room spun crazily around him. These are the very stories Eddie sought to avoid. Each time reported the same way, with the same breathless excitement, although this was the first one describing anyone other than a female victim. Never a fourteen-year-old! Josette had been with him all night. He knew this Kroger—it was only a few short blocks from the Masquerade, the very place Angelique admitted visiting that same night.

He found the twins upstairs, sitting on his bed listening to music on his boombox without a care in the world. "Angelique, is there something you care to tell us about last night?"

Her sister looked puzzled, but she answered with confidence, "I suppose you mean, did I feed last night? And I suppose you already know the answer, so why not just ask me?"

"The kid behind the Kroger?"

"How do you know? Oops, I didn't take too much blood, did I?"

"He's dead," Eddie said, his face twisting into a snarl, "but I suppose you already know that, don't you?"

"It's no big deal. Nobody saw us—I made sure of that."

"No big deal? Murdered kids are the biggest possible deal

in this city! Nobody here has forgotten fishing dozens of kids out of the rivers here a few years back. Another dead kid is going to bring every cop in the state into the manhunt, and they will leave no stone unturned!"

"Trust me, there is nothing to worry about. I was careful."

Josette stared wide-eyed at her sister. "What were you doing going out on your own, anyway? After the nightmare last weekend, we decided we would feed together—at least until the two of us have enough experience to try hunting on our own!"

"I was hungry!" On her feet now, she rushed over to Eddie, who backed away. "Listen, I didn't plan it. I only intended to go to Masquerade, but on the way home, I saw him and just *needed* to feed. It's been days! You know how it goes."

"Didn't I make it clear to you? *No kids*! It's too risky and draws way too much attention. First, you ignore me and kill a guy in the middle of a parking lot; your next kill is fourteen. Why not turn on a red flashing light and holler *I'm killing someone over here* for your next trick?"

"It's not that bad!"

"It *is* that bad," her sister said, still wearing a look of disbelief. "A fourteen-year-old kid?"

"He looked a little older than that. Look, I don't know what you are so pissed about."

Eddie had heard enough. His hand moved too fast to see, wrapping around her slender wrist before she could react. Dragging her along, Angelique kicked and screamed down the main staircase and all the way down to the basement, where he stopped before the metal door.

"No!" she screamed as he groped for his pocket, and blocked his hand from reaching the keys inside while trying to grab them herself. In the struggle, their shoulders slammed into the door with a hollow thud. She might only weigh a few pounds over 100 after feeding, but had already grown strong —greater than when he was a young man strengthened from working his father's farm.

Books fell from shelves as they bounced off the bookcase. Angelique's eyes glowed, and her fangs had sprouted at some point during their struggle. She bared them, making feral sounds.

A hand shot down his pants pocket while both of his were occupied wrangling her, and he felt the keys pull out.

"I've got the door," Josette said, her voice an odd calm.

Bent over, Eddie drove his shoulder into Angelique's stomach and hefted her over it when he stood. When he reached the bed inside, he dropped her onto it and pointed one finger at the center of her chest, only inches away. A pale light came from his eyes in the darkened room. "Don't move—don't make me do something I will regret."

His voice had a similar calmness to Josette's, that menacing kind of calm unbefitting the situation, something neither of the twins had ever heard. From him or anyone.

The door slammed shut, and in the darkness, a key turned with a clicking sound. Then a light turned on.

No sound penetrated that door or the brick walls, so Angelique did not know when they went upstairs, leaving her alone down there.

†

"She did what?"

"You heard me. It will make the national news in the morning, after all those kids from a few years ago."

Celeste sighed into the phone. "Were you involved with that, Eddie?"

"Of course not!"

"I didn't think so, but since that guy they caught never seemed right, I had to ask. That's how it will go, though, isn't it? If someone like us isn't careful?"

"Yes," he sighed into the phone, having experienced it before, "that's how it goes."

"How long will you keep her there?"

"I don't know. A hundred years? The heat should be off by then." He took a deep breath. "Maybe when she calms down."

"Mama, she was a wild animal," Josette said on another phone, the one upstairs in his bedroom. "She's lost it."

"Okay. I'll be on the next flight down. I'll find someone to look after Bernie for a few days. I can tell people she's had a relapse of her illness and needs her mom—everyone will buy that."

"Is that really necessary?"

"Well, you said we are all for one, the Four Sangreteers, if you will, and if there is one time you need her mother and her sister there to sort this crap out, it is now. Am I right?"

She was, which they both conceded.

After they hung up, Eddie said, "I need a drink."

"I think I'll join you."

WITH OR WITHOUT YOU

While certainly qualifying as a dungeon, this was as good as dungeons get. The temperature stayed in the pleasant mid-70s, the bed comfortable, as was the armchair. Atop an antique table, a pitcher full of water and tumbler were set out for her. Without a clock, time did not exist as it does above ground. However many hours she had been down there was anyone's guess.

Angelique was lying in bed when the lock clicked in the door and on her feet by the time her twin slammed it behind her. "Hey, I came to see if you are hungry or need anything."

"I'm going to kill that sonofabitch when I get out of here!"

"Okay, stop. You aren't going to kill anyone. The only reason you are here is because you did kill somebody, and now you need to take a chill pill while we figure out how to handle this."

"Handle what? Me? I tell you, Josette, the minute I get out of here, I am going to kill him!"

"He's the one who wants to set you free."

Shock tempered the flames for an instant. "You? You're keeping me here?"

"Angelique, we're protecting you! You're going to get yourself killed! You'll get all of us killed!"

†

Alone. That's what tortured her. As a twin, she had not been truly alone since days after conception, before she and Josette split from one into two. Their whole lives spent together, and the rare times they were apart Angelique spent surrounded by others. Hours passed by—at least, it felt like hours. A watch would either be nice or worsen her torment, but she'd take her chances with one. It had to be better than seconds which dragged long as weeks.

She paced the room to have something to do. How do prisoners in solitary confinement spend their days? Other than go completely batty?

Hours later, the lock clicked again.

"Word is you want to kill me, so I figured the only way for you to accomplish that is if I come down to see you." Eddie smiled, that cute, boyish smile of his, locked the door behind him and took a seat in the chair across from where Angelique sat on the bed hugging her knees to her chest, which she found more enjoyable than walking in infinite circles.

"You're an asshole."

"I assure you, people have accused me of far worse." That got a grin even from his prisoner. "I'm actually wanted for murder, you know. Dates back to late forties, but since there is no statute of limitation on murder, I suppose it's still active. Hasn't bothered me much for years because, well, they are looking for someone in their late sixties, so I feel reasonably safe these days. My fingerprints are still out there, so I want to avoid that. Too many questions if there's a match and I really don't want to see how that might play out."

"Can I be a witness at your trial? Because I have seen you kill people: my Mama, my sister… me! I'm just getting warmed up."

"Don't know how much a jury will listen to a ruthless killer such as you."

"Josette said you want to let me out; is that true?"

"Are you cool? If we let you out, can we trust you not to

put us or yourself in jeopardy the way you did? Will you listen to us and work with us rather than against us?"

"Will you believe me if I agree to be a good little girl like my sister?"

"Depends how convincing you are when you say it." There was that adorable half-grin of his.

"What if I tell you I hate the two of you for locking me down here?"

"Understandable. Honest, too. Far as I'm concerned, you needed time to cool off. Tell you the truth, so did I." His hand caressed one of her knees with a firm yet gentle grip. "Let's get out of here."

As they walked free, his arm around her shoulder holding her to his side, he said, "Oh, I escaped from prison once, too. Not sure what the statute of limitation is on that..."

†

Less than an hour later, Josette ran down the stairs.

"Where's my sister?"

"Isn't she up there with you?"

"If she was up there with me, would I be down here asking you where she is?"

Together, they searched the entire house and yard—Angelique was nowhere to be found. He asked, "When is the last time you saw her?"

"Ten minutes ago—fifteen tops. She's still pissed at me—at us. I said something that set her off and she stormed out, but I figured she came down here to bitch about me."

"We need to find her—pronto. Hopefully, she just went for a walk to cool down..."

"But...?"

She followed him out the front door to the street, searching both ways. No one was visible far as they could see. "You go right, I'll go left. Meet back here in fifteen minutes."

"What if we don't find her?"

Eddie set off without answering.

A block away, a man shaping a bush framing a brick mailbox waved as Eddie approached. He recognized him not as a lawn service worker but the neighbor who drove the blue Mercedes and hoped the neighbor did not also recognize him.

"Excuse me, I'm looking for a redhead..."

"Isn't everyone?" the neighbor answered, nodding.

"Well, in my case, a specific one. She went for a walk and I'm trying to catch up to her, but I'm not sure which way she went."

"You aren't a stalker, are you?"

"No, I live down the street and she's my..."

"Just pulling your leg. The old Calhoun house, right?"

Damn it! "Yeah. Well, if you..."

"Sandy Grey." The neighbor removed his right glove and extended his hand.

"Alfred Dalrymple. Good to meet you. Listen, my cousin does not know her way around the area and I'm afraid she will get lost."

"Don't worry, she seems to have found you." Sandy nodded, indicating to turn around. There, about a hundred yards away, Josette was heading their way.

"The other one looks just like that; they are a matched set."

"You don't say. Twins?" Eddie forced a grin and nodded, trying to think of a way to extricate himself from this conversation. "Well, I'll be! Then how can you be sure this isn't the one you are searching for from this distance?"

"The other one is wearing a blue top."

"I'll keep an eye out for your missing earring." Another forced grin acknowledged the comedy act, but the returned expression must have showed his puzzlement. "What good is one earring? If I lost one of my ruby earrings, I'd search heaven and earth for the other, too."

"Well," he turned to make his escape, "if you see her..."

"You'll be the second to know," Sandy promised.

Josette asked, "Well?"

"She didn't come this way. My randy neighbor would never miss her," he answered. "See, this is what happens—now a neighbor knows more about us than he needs to. Let's turn around; she went another direction."

At the corner, they split up again, each taking a different direction. Although the sun had nearly set by then, that did not matter. Human vision may worsen at twilight, but they were no longer human. In fact, his eyesight seemed to improve in the dark. Of course, there were plenty of places to hide —if she had not broken into a sprint the second she set foot outside. A possibility that became more plausible every minute. In that case, she might be miles away on foot—and what driver stood a chance of passing a hitchhiking Angelique without stopping to offer a ride?

At the next corner, he turned left toward the main street. A car passed, driver waving as the headlights illuminated him. Eddie's hopes dimmed with each step.

It happened in a flash, with no time to react. One second he was walking on the sidewalk, the next he slammed hard on grass still fragrant from a fresh evening mowing. Above him, Angelique's bright fangs stood out despite the dim light, visible as she laughed.

"That was easier than I imagined," she said, hovering inches above him, her fingernails digging into his neck. "You know I could kill you right now."

"Well, good luck. Give it your best shot."

"Aren't you supposed to have super powers of observation?"

"No match for your super power of sneaking up on me. Are you going to chew my neck off? If not, put those fangs away before someone comes along."

Nails dug into his flesh. "Will you lock me up again?"

"If you don't let go of my neck, I will brick you into that room and you can stay there until someone demolishes the place two hundred years from now."

With a suddenness matching hers, his hand wrapped around her swan-like neck with enough force to throw her onto the grass, reversing the position lightning fast. Angelique laughed wildly, fangs still prominent.

"Look what you did to me—you did this!"

"Calm down, okay? People can hear us."

"You locked me up because I did exactly what you made me do. This hunger, this compulsion—did I ask for any of this? You wanted me to be your plaything, your companion into immortality, and the minute I show a mind of my own and give in to the bloodlust **you** gave to me, you lock me up in a fucking dungeon!"

Possessing strength and speed no ordinary man—let alone woman—could match, she bucked and scratched and tried to throw him off, fury increasing with each unsuccessful effort. But Eddie was not an ordinary human, rather one endowed with strength and speed equivalent to hers in a body nearly double hers in weight, with much longer arms and legs. Faced with superior strength in his bulkier frame, she slashed at his face, using fingernails as claws.

In his attempt to subdue her, after capturing one wrist, then the other in his grip, her fangs lunged at his face and neck.

"Angelique... don't make me... hurt you," he grunted, astonished by the rage and force in her slender body. Her answer was to slash the fangs at the right side of his vulnerable neck. A quick pull-back got him out of her limited range. "Please. Stop."

"Go ahead, rip my heart out! Feels like you already did when you locked me up like that, so why not do it for real?" His body relaxed and, under him, so did hers. One wrist still in a vice-like grip jerked her onto her feet and began dragging her home. "If I wanted to leave, you'd never see me again."

"What was this, a demonstration?"

"I needed air to clear my head."

"Didn't think telling us might be a good idea?"

"Speaking with the two of you was not high on my agenda at the time."

"Let go of her! I've called the police!" On the porch beyond the lawn they turned into a wrestling ring, a middle-aged man stood holding a Colt .45 automatic at his side.

"It's okay," Eddie called. "We're just fooling around."

"I said let go of her. Police are on their way."

Angelique scowled up at him, faint eyebrows dropping low over slits of eyes. But she nodded, and he released his hold on her wrists and, holding up empty hands at head-level, stepped back. Still facing Eddie and away from the man, she suggestively wiped grass from her bum, slower and several more times than necessary. Then her head spun so fast the motion flung her curls out and, when turned enough to face the homeowner, those locks carried across her face to her far shoulder, forming a copper veil covering the lower half of her face.

A low, guttural growl came from deep within her body and she sprang like a cat toward the man on the porch thirty feet away.

"Jesus Christ!" the neighbor yelled as his body jerked backward against the white wood siding beside a bright blue front door. Her move equally surprised Eddie, but he was close enough to wrap one arm around her stomach and powerful enough to halt her, momentum swinging her legs off the ground, waving in the air as she jerked to a stop. The wide-eyed man shouted, "What the hell is wrong with her?"

Eddie waved his free hand. "We're good," then wrapped it across her chest to hold her body against his

"Seriously? You're feeling my boobs right now?"

"Not intentionally."

"This is why I don't want to leave you; you're even kinkier than I am."

"Are you coming with me?"

"Not yet—but you're off to a good start!"

"Don't come back here!" The terrified neighbor moved to

the porch railing to shout after them. "I'll remember you. You hear me? I don't want to see you around here again!"

Angelique giggled, innocent as a schoolgirl. "Are you going to come kill that guy tonight, or are you going to let me do it?"

"Flip a coin?"

"Deal," she said as he jerked her in the direction of home, fingers dug so firmly into her wrists it would have left welts on a living person.

On the way, they came upon her sister still searching the streets; she followed a couple of steps behind, just in case her twin broke free of the fleshy handcuff before they made their way home.

†

"Oh, crap," Eddie groaned.

The twins broke into a sprint, and he let loose of Angelique's wrist to allow her to run free. Remnants of grass still clung to the back of a grass-stained shirt, stains so deep they might have to toss it. High-pitched squeals in stereo pierced the near-dark. Celeste held arms wide to hug them, almost bowling her over as they plowed into her.

From between the two copper mops, she watched him climb the porch stairs. "I assume you did not get my message."

"No, we were out for a walk…"

"I made the flight I was wait-listed for. I had to take a cab."

"Sorry."

The twins held onto their mother and looked, for a moment, like little girls.

"Where are your bags?"

"Someone named Margaret took them inside."

"She's my… we have some catching up to do."

"My girls told me your place is nice; they didn't do it justice."

"Come in, let me show you around."

Taking one look at Angelique as they turned, Celeste swatted her back. "What did you do to this shirt? It's ruined—is that grass?"

"Grandpa got fresh, then some guy with a gun wanted to kill him, but it's all good now."

Inside, he told Margaret, "We'll be downstairs and we aren't to be disturbed."

She chuckled. "Looks like you've been disturbed enough for one night."

He rubbed the woman's shoulder. "If you only knew the half of it."

†

The four walked together upstairs long after midnight and a few bottles of some of his best wines, Eddie and Celeste leading the way arm in arm, the twins following a couple of stairs behind. Their arms were also locked together, and they drew each other close.

"Well, goodnight, Eddie," Celeste said, standing before his bedroom door, staring into his eyes.

"Where do you think you are going?"

"To my room."

"We have not seen each other in months; do you really want to stay there?"

"I hoped you might offer a better alternative. I didn't know who... what may have transpired between you since you've been gone."

"Nothing has changed, has it, My Darlings?" He turned to the twins.

"We expected you to stay with him," Josette answered, her expression impossible to read.

"Good; I am glad to hear that." Celeste leaned forward, toward Eddie, rising high on her toes. Her fingers gripped his arms right below his shoulders and pulled him to her, although he needed little encouragement.

Their lips met and Celeste opened hers wide while brushing them against his. Her tongue flashed out, penetrating his mouth, and his welcomed it with a slow, evocative kiss. He knew what she was doing, and his eyes turned toward the twins, who stood gawking. From there, they had to see their mother's tongue reaching into him this way, yearning for his.

Vampires surely are capable of love, he knew in that moment, and he loved this woman. Loved her for such a masterful display of dominance over her daughters as well as for her passion. Without speaking a word, she had seized the alpha female role from her daughters. She did not ask, nor did she care that her daughters also loved him, or that he loved them. They were one and belonged to each other. Celeste owned Eddie as he owned her daughters. As she belonged to them.

"Goodnight, girls," she said to her daughters.

"Goodnight," they answered.

"Night, ladies," Eddie said to them before he opened the door to his bedroom and led their mother inside.

Later, the sounds of animalistic lovemaking or feeding echoed through the upstairs hallway and, two doors down, giggles came from the twins' room, rising to the occasional burst of full laughter.

†

"Honestly?"

Two emerald cabochons encircling onyx jittered back and forth, searching his glowing blues, both sets of pupils still dilated from passion and blood. "They take good care of me, as I do for them."

"But?"

"Josette is your daughter in every way. Angelique is harder to tame."

"I warned you—that one is not be tamable! If you can't do it, then it cannot be done."

"She is fun and makes me laugh one minute, and the next I see in her eyes she is still feral."

"Does she worry you?"

"Why do you think I asked you to come?"

"I thought it possible you may just miss me. Or I underestimated how I could compete with beautiful twin teenagers who can fulfill your every desire." Her hand crept down his stomach, gentle fingers trailing behind as nails scratched his skin. Even their wild romp had not quenched his own feral nature. Those fingers caressed him before settling in on his inner thigh.

"I did miss you. Now we are complete."

"Will they be jealous that I have taken their place tonight in your bed?"

"Angelique still has some jealousy—of course. Would she be Angelique without it? Recently I have weaned them by bringing only one here for the night. Maybe Josette hides it better."

"How does Angelique handle it?"

"When it's her turn, or when she joins us after, she does her best to impress me."

"Oh, no!" Celeste burst into laughter. "I can so see her doing that! Can you imagine?"

"Imagine what?"

"That we are discussing any of this? About you and my daughters?"

"Are you jealous?"

"Don't I hide it as well as Josette?"

He chuckled. "Sometimes I am glad there is only one of me."

"Sometimes I wish *you* were twins. One of you could have stayed with me."

"I'm glad you are here." He pulled her face against his neck. "Angelique is dangerous."

IF YOU LEAVE

Overnight, another storm blew in. The morning skies were overcast, heavy, menacing. Josette greeted her mother and Eddie with the smell of coffee and some fresh pastries. "I stopped by that cute bakery over in Virginia-Highland. Mama, they make the best cinnamon buns; muffins aren't to be laughed at, either."

She kissed her daughter's forehead. "Where's your sister?"

"Sleeping. Couldn't rouse her. It was like after feeding, that blood coma you get."

Eddie grinned. "We had quite a tussle yesterday. Guess she isn't near full strength yet, although you couldn't guess from the fight she put up."

"Wow, you weren't kidding about these cinnamon buns," Celeste agreed. Josette did a face-palm and giggled. Eddie sidled up next to her, leaned over and his lips enveloped the tip of her nose to suck away a glob of icing.

"Mmm, delicious!"

"Are you two going to act like this the whole time you're here?"

"Honey," her mother answered, "you've had him all to yourselves for a couple of months—I'll only be here a couple of days, and then I will be out of your hair and you can get back to normal."

"That's what I figured," she said, and tried to look judgmental, but a corner of her mouth refused to obey and flickered up.

Later that morning, as Eddie and Celeste left for

some sightseeing around town, an approaching car from the opposite direction stopped with a series of manic honks, a hand waving from the open window, so Eddie slowed. "Oh, damn!"

"You know this guy?"

"Sandy Grey. We met yesterday when your daughter went on her walkabout."

The cars pulled to a stop with open driver's side windows a couple of feet apart. "Hey, did you find your friend yesterday?"

"Yes, thanks. She got herself lost back in the neighborhood."

"Whew! I've been thinking about you since I heard the news."

"What news?"

"About Doctor Owen."

"Who?"

"He lives in the neighborhood, a couple of blocks down. Well, lived—they found him this morning when he didn't show up at the hospital for surgery. They say someone murdered him last night. I just came from there, but everyone is mum. Can't get near the place; police have the entire block shut down."

Had he been standing, Eddie may have fallen over. The last time he had been so lightheaded, he face-planted in the A&P. He forced panic from his face. "Where did Doctor Owen live?"

"You know that white house with blue shutters and that wide porch on Ridley Circle—right over where you were heading when you were searching for your lost redhead? So, of course, I was worried something had happened to her, too."

"Um, no, she's—ah, we found her. She's fine."

"That's my daughter," Celeste leaned over to smile at him. "She's home now. That's so thoughtful of you to be worried about her!"

"Listen, Sandy," Eddie stammered, "we're running

late...."

"Sure. Make sure to lock your doors until they find whoever did this. Terrible!" The tires of his Mercedes chirped as Sandy roared off toward the safety of his home.

"Goddamn it!"

Celeste jerked her head back. "What's the matter with you?"

"That's him! That's the guy who came out on the porch when Angelique and I were fighting in his front yard. When we left, we were joking about which one of us was going to kill him. She did it, Celeste!" He maneuvered the car into a three-point turn and roared back to his house faster than Sandy Grey had sped off for his.

They found her still deep in her coma, and Eddie took extra care not to rouse her, reaching for her sleeping body slow as a lengthening afternoon shadow.

†

The vault door opened and Eddie slipped inside. Angelique must have been awake, rushing toward him before the door slammed shut, wildness in her eyes. He moved to block the door, but instead of trying to slip by, she veered straight toward him. Despite her tiny mass, she struck him hard enough to drive him back by her force alone, one foot stepping out necessary to maintain his balance. $E=MC^2$. Arms wrapped around him, caressing his body, pressing her breasts against his chest. Her face nestled into the hollow at the base of his neck.

"I am so glad to see you!" Fangs glinted below her full, vermillion lips.

He held her, too. "How are you holding up?"

When she looked up, her lips brushed against his neck. Those magnificent eyes could not be any more beautiful. "All those scary stories as a girl, the Grimm's Fairy Tales and monster movies, and not once did I expect to find myself locked in a real-life dungeon—for a second time, no less."

Her fangs were a hair-breadth from his skin, breath cool on his neck.

"You must be starving."

"I am. How long have I been down here?"

"A few days. We can't let you feed."

"I know."

His hypnotic jugular vein bulged with the blood flowing through it. Its sweet scent pulsed, as well. "It's hard for me, too, you know. If I could, I would let you take your fill from me."

"Really? Would you?"

"You know it's true. Have I ever lied to you?"

"Yes." His eyes narrowed and brows wrinkled. "*Cousin* Eddie."

"Oh, that."

"Are you here to kill me?"

"Not now."

"Will you tell me if you are?"

"Maybe."

She gripped him tighter and nuzzled her face against him. "What can I do to convince you? You know you can do anything you want, take anything from me. Anything."

"Including kill you?"

"Maybe. Not now." He held her tighter, too.

"I love you," he said.

"I know."

"We all do."

"I love you. I didn't think it was possible, not after what you made me, but I do."

He kissed her, first the top of her head, then her lips when she offered them. Her fangs were gone, and his tongue traced the edges of smooth, human-like teeth. Her tongue tasted of hunger. He pulled away.

"If I didn't know better, I'd believe you have the power to enchant me."

"Would I do that to you?" Her face bore the most

innocent expression, a Norman Rockwell painting of purity. But her eyes twinkled. They laughed, and she pressed her forehead against his chest to hide them. "Any enchantment is the same as you do to me."

"Then why do you do these things?" Holding her at arm's length, he leaned forward until his face was inches from hers. "Will it satisfy you when they kill us, leaving you alone as I was for 95 years? 95 years! Finally, I have a family again, closer and more intimate than I dreamed possible in my century of solitude, literally sharing our life, our blood—everything—and you put it all at risk!"

"I never asked for this. Okay, maybe I asked for you, but I expected at most a fling, maybe some good sex." Again her eyes glanced up, less-than innocent. "Okay, I expected *fantastic* sex. Not for you to come in here so I can smell the blood in your veins and need that from you, too!"

"How could I allow DKC to kill you and your mother too young when I possess the power to keep you alive forever?"

"Sometimes I forget that part."

"Would you have agreed before you tasted my blood?"

"Just the mere hint of anything like that, and I'd have assumed my poor, deluded cousin was off his frickin' rocker!"

"The whole consent thing has tormented me for almost a century. It's one thing to ask a woman to sleep with me, quite another to ask her to let me take her blood or to kill her and—hopefully—bring her back transformed into something new and superior. Honestly, I owe you an apology. I accept full responsibility."

"Look, I get it. Sounds like an awesome way to end up locked in a loony bin." her eyes scanned the corners of the room. "Or a dungeon."

"If I had offered to cure your DKC, and told you what the cure was, what would you have thought?"

"*This is the most creative way a guy has ever tried to get into my pants*. Oh, and that you are crazy as a sprayed cockroach. But I never would have bought it, even for a second."

"What are we going to do with you?" His hold loosened so they could lean back from the waist to soak in the other's presence and beauty. "The most important thing we must have is trust. Once it is destroyed..."

"Don't you trust me?"

"How can I after you chewed that doctor's head off?"

"That's an exaggeration. The papers have blown this all out of proportion. Sure, I bit him—he struggled too much, that's all."

"Are you intentionally missing the point? How you killed him or why is unimportant. The easiest way to get caught is to shit where we eat, and a butchered body blocks from this house does nothing but draw attention. More importantly, though, the reason you did this behind our backs is because you knew we never would have agreed. What we agreed on is to be in this together, and despite violating our trust only a few days ago, once more you sneak out to kill someone while everyone is asleep, to keep us clueless."

"Don't worry so much—nobody saw me. If they did, I wore that sweatshirt with a hood, a baseball cap inside to hide my face. If anyone videotaped me like they did you and Mama, all they will see is somebody walking down the street. They won't even be able to tell if I was a man or woman—sometimes these tiny boobs come in handy. Sometimes besides when they are in your cold, dead hands."

"If it was such a great idea, why not brag to us about your plans? Because if there is one thing I know about you is your incessant need for approval and praise."

Although desperate to hide how much his criticism stung, she failed, her face wrinkling and sour from his rebuke. She stepped back from him, perhaps realizing for the first time how seriously she had miscalculated their reaction. His reaction. "What are you going to do to me?"

"That is one question I cannot answer. Remember what we all agreed? It's not my decision—we are a democracy."

"No, you are a jury."

†

Housing Angelique in the dungeon—a term they never spoke aloud yet, in their minds' depths, all thought of the room as now—created an additional problem. Although they suspected the sounds of their voices in the other portion of the basement could not penetrate the brick walls or steel door, no one could be sure. For all they knew, a water pipe or air duct hidden in the ceiling might carry their words straight to her.

Up on the third floor, an unused room provided perfect privacy. Squeaky boards in the floor added an additional layer of security. Trustworthy as Margaret might be, no one outside their circle must know.

"We don't need to decide anything tonight," Eddie said. Which relieved all three, since two hours had passed and they were no closer to a decision than when they began.

Splayed fingers pushed carnelian curls back in frustration. "Those are our only options?"

"That's the whole point of this exercise, honey," her mother answered.

"Give me a third or fourth—hell, I'd love to have ten choices," Eddie sighed. "We haven't thought of anything else since we started, have we? And this is all we've come up with."

"Well," Josette sighed, "she's my twin, something neither of you will ever be able to understand. We're inseparable, so I cannot shun her and I will never—EVER—vote to kill her."

This stone wall pushed her mother too far. "Then you come up with another way to control her. You seem to forget she is my child. I gave birth to her and raised her. This isn't easy for me, either."

"I never said it was easy, but you're talking about killing your own daughter!"

"We're only discussing options. Right now, we have two which, I agree, both suck."

"The fact that we're even sitting here discussing this is

so fricking weird," Josette said. "How can we be doing this, calmer and more rational than deciding to put down Jimmy?"

Eddie jerked his head back. "Who's Jimmy?"

"Our cat—*my* cat. He had feline leukemia last year. I know it's a stupid name for a cat, but we were only ten when we named him. All of us were crying and yelling at each other, yet now we are sitting here discussing this the way normal people talk about what color to repaint the den. What's wrong with us?"

"This is life and death to all of us," her mother answered.

Eddie added, "And we aren't normal people; not anymore."

"This is what it does to us? Makes us willing to consider killing one of our own family members?"

A humorless smile flickered on his face. "Six months ago, try imagining yourself killing a kid on the hood of a car in a bar parking lot. Face it: we have changed. Things which not long ago would have seemed crazy are our daily lives now. Someday I will tell you about how it almost destroyed me. We need to consider the fact that some people might not be able to handle this—certainly not while working with others and protecting them. We may need to separate ourselves from her. If so..."

"If so, how?" Celeste looked to each of them. "From my perspective, I am not sure I can trust her again, can you? If so, do you trust her in the same house with you, or even the same world as you? Because that is the question we need to decide. I hate it as much as you, but it boils down to that."

†

Margaret answered a deliberate knock at the door to find two men in suits. From the look of them, she knew who they were before they introduced themselves.

"Is Eddie Brown home?"

"Who?"

"Eddie Brown," the one wearing a fedora repeated.

Merely as a formality, she asked, "Who's asking?"

While both wore suits, only one also wore a hat. Twenty years had passed since anyone put a fedora on their heads, with one glaring exception. The Atlanta P.D. homicide department's famous Hat Squad.

Homicide detectives earn their hat by solving their first murder case. Stephen Romero earned his three years before, when a male hooker was gunned down in a drive-by shooting near Piedmont Park. Typically, male prostitutes garner little attention from the police, but Romero treated it no different than if the victim was a female streetwalker. Or, for that matter, a teacher or nurse. A dogged search for witnesses produced a sufficient description to track down an F-150 owned by a guy who despised Atlanta's growing gay population. Sodomites, he called them. Currently, he was serving a life sentence down in Riedsville, and Romero took immense joy in imagining him being cornholed on a regular basis in prison.

"Detective Romero, Atlanta Police. This is Detective Higginbotham from the Providence, Rhode Island Police Department, looking for a person of interest in a crime up there."

"Well, you have the wrong house. No one named Eddie Brown lives here, and the only man here is the owner."

"Mind if we have a look around," Det. Higginbotham inquired.

"Do you have a warrant?" If nothing else, Margaret was sharp.

"No. ma'am," the local detective said.

"Then we mind very much. Now, if that is all your questions, I have dinner on the stove. Sorry y'all wasted your time," Margaret said, directed toward Higginbotham, "especially after traveling all the way from Rhode Island. Good luck finding your man."

Desperate for more information, Det. Higginbotham slowed the door from closing by asking, "What is your name?"

"Not Eddie Brown." The door slammed shut and the solid deadbolt clicked into place.

Through cracked blinds, she monitored the officers' animated discussion for a couple of minutes until they turned and walked back the way they came. The Yankee detective could not help himself, turning to look back twice before they reached the wrought-iron gate at the end of the walkway, where it intersected with the sidewalk.

Once they left, she rapped on the basement door. This is the sort of news Eddie did not mind being interrupted for.

†

"Can you do this to me?"

"We all agreed in our first conclave to obey the decisions of the family."

"So if they want to get rid of me, you will stand by and allow them to do that?"

"What would you have me do?"

Seductively rolling out her most powerful weapon, she crossed her arms behind his neck, nestled her body against his and gives him a most remarkable kiss.

"To save yourself, you would do this to anyone if I told you to, and with the same sincerity in your eyes, convince him you mean it."

"How can you think so terribly of me?"

"Because I died a hundred years ago, and have done what I needed to survive for a century."

"What can I say or do that will convince you I am with you? Because I am, blood and body and soul—or whatever. I realize how much of a pain in the ass I can be, but I promise—I'm worth the effort."

"Angelique, someone with your intelligence knows that is not it." With a deep sigh, he drew her close. "You shattered our trust. It's gone."

"Won't you miss me?"

"I'll still have your mother and sister."

"So you will look at Josette and pretend she's me. Pretend you are possessing me while you are shagging her?"

"It is an unusual scenario. Few men lose a woman with her twin to console him."

"You love her, don't you?"

"Close as I can come now."

"But you love me?"

"That is not important."

"It is the most important part."

"We all love you. In my life, I've lost everyone I ever loved, every woman I cared for. It numbs you. What's another one?"

"Especially when you have an exact double who you can pretend you are holding, feeding with, screwing… satisfying your every desire with."

His effort to hold back a chuckle failed. "It will help make things more bearable."

"Much as she resembles me, you know Josette cannot offer you what I can. Cannot satisfy your darkest desires. She may look like me, but she isn't me."

"We cannot trust you, Angelique. Our survival is more essential than my desires."

She loosened her jeans and began wiggling free of them. "Feed from me."

It was a true shame, because her potential abilities were unlimited. Even he was powerless against her seductiveness, and knowing that, still he allowed her to peel off his shirt and loosen his pants as he fed from her bloody heart. Together, they rolled across the floor, aware they may be sharing their bloodlust for the last time.

Somehow, she retained the power to push him away. "Save some for later. Let me show you what my sister can never give you, for she will never be me."

The way she crawled across the floor, she reverted to that first night of bloodlust, once more a tiger stalking its prey. The pleasure left him ready, but her soft lips kissed him, over him as she eased his pants down his legs.

"Can Josette give you this?" Lips that moved against him as she spoke, looking down at what she held in her hand. She then raised her eyes, glowing with violet light, and her mouth opened. Two fangs flashed for a fraction of a second before she took him into her mouth. Those needle-like fangs, smooth ivory save for their razor tips, rubbed firm against his flesh on both sides. Trapped this way, with her over him and hair falling over his lap, fingernails of one hand digging into a thigh as the other held him in an icy, pleasurable grip, made escape impossible. Still, he squirmed in terror, feeling those fangs straddling him. Since he awoke inside a coffin almost a century before, he had never been so vulnerable.

Expecting at any second those fangs to pierce his flesh, ripping his source of mortal pleasure as easily as those teeth shredded that doctor's neck only hours before, Angelique's cruelty had never been so insidious, so complete.

"Please, Angelique, don't do this!"

She answered his plea by biting down. Not hard, only enough to serve as a warning, and only with the four human teeth between the fangs. Those vulpine incisors pinched him in between, tight but not piercing his skin. The longer he feared what fate awaited him, the more complete her revenge.

"Angelique, I will kill you!"

"And you know how, don't you?" Speaking allowing him an excellent view of the fangs on either side of his flesh. "Rip out my liver, my heart? Burn them? Reduce them to ash?"

"I will, and you know it!"

"And you know I will never hurt you. Or Mama. Even less Josette." Now her teeth freed him, but her lip caught on the end of his manhood and he wondered why he refused to wither from her. Fear, though, is a powerful aphrodisiac. "I will never hurt you, Eddie. You have my word."

Her fangs did not fade, either. Not the whole time she continued until, with those freakish teeth scraping his length, she finished giving him his most human form of pleasure. He yelled when blissful release came—with as much unrestrained passion as she ever heard him make from the pleasure of feeding.

Angelique kissed her way up his body, tongue flicking his skin like a viper's, up to his wounded nipple, which she licked and sucked, but made no effort to feed. Her fangs were gone by the time she kissed his lips and his tongue savored her mouth, relieved to find teeth returned to normal.

Her face pressed against his chest, the way he loved, and she lay on him. She shared his love for it, the pair close as twins. It may have only been imagination, but they knew the other's thoughts.

CATERPILLAR

Why do they think no one can see them?

The degree of arrogant stupidity on display brought a silent chuckle, despite himself. The reddish Crown Victoria parallel parked four houses down from his was impossible to miss. Ford called this color Cabernet, but if someone dared to serve Eddie a glass of wine this color, he would send it back without risking a sniff of its bouquet. No more transparent than Margaret's *nobody's home* ruse. Proving her story false required a search warrant, though, and whatever evidence the police may have in their possession must be insufficient to persuade a judge it reached the level of probable cause necessary to issue one.

Score it Margaret 1, Cops 0.

Of course, it was possible they intended to be visible. If convinced no one was home, perhaps they hoped to provoke a chase when the missing suspects returned. Not only would fleeing provide probable cause for arrest and a thorough search of the car and its occupants, it might get them a warrant for inside his home, as well.

Through narrow gaps in the wooden blinds up on the third floor, he made sure they were alone and had not brought backup. No, they were on their own. Every other car on the block were regulars, recognizable as belonging to neighbors. Margaret identified one of them as the Rhode Island cop who reentered her life to inquire about Eddie, so the dead surgeon a few blocks away unlikely to have inspired their interest, although it must seem much more suspicious than a curious coincidence.

"Are they still there?"

"Yes, and it is insulting to our intelligence, believing we won't notice a cop car in front of the Stevenson's house."

"Still only the two of them?"

"That's it. So far, so good. If they had any inkling Angelique killed that doctor, this place would be lousy with cops."

"Are you going to feed," Celeste asked him as went out the back door.

"I need to clear my head, and for that, solitude will help. A houseful of people is still alien to me."

"I suppose that means you won't be taking me with you?"

The skin of her face was satin against his palm. "Next time. They won't stay there forever."

Twilight arrived earlier each day, bringing with it the relief of cool air after still scorching days. In a half hour, it will be dark. The neighbors living behind him were not yet home from work, judging by the darkened windows. Better still, they hate dogs. Eddie hopped the fence with the ease of a gymnast, one hand braced on the upper rail.

Little Five Points was only two miles from his house. He kept to back streets, two-lane roads lined by homes similar to his, avoiding like the plague main roads police were more likely to take. The neighborhood reminded him of his own, although the houses were a decade or two older. Although confident they would not patrol this route, he checked over his shoulder when he heard the approach of a car. A pre-sunset escape was a brilliant plan, for once twilight descended, distinguishing oncoming cars by headlight shape alone was sure to ruin his pleasant stroll.

This was the first time he'd been out alone since his road trip down with the twins. A sense of calm settled over him. He missed their company, their mother's too, but relished a few moments by himself. Old habits and all.

If Atlanta has a mecca for *avant-garde* culture, it is Little

Five Points. College students and artists of all types come to buy used and vintage clothing, hand-tied bracelets and necklaces or simply to browse quirky stores and restaurants with quirky names like The Junkman's Daughter, Euclid Avenue Yacht Club, and a bookstore named A Cappella. The place to buy new and used albums, comic books and subversive magazines was Criminal Records. No one bothered the homeless there, a true sanctuary for freaks, oddities and those who appreciate them.

He stopped long enough to grab a burger at Zesto, a burger joint trapped in time, unchanged since its opening twenty-five years before. One of his favorite guilty pleasures in the years since, Zesto proved delicious and gourmet are by no means synonymous.

Still early for Little Five, as its regulars called it, most of whom did not make an appearance until later in the evening, perhaps an hour before local bands took the stages at its several bars, he wandered around as the last purple faded from the sky. A couple eating nachos watched him through the window table at the Euclid Avenue Yacht Club, miles from the nearest body of water capable of floating a yacht. The table was little more than a counter facing the window, allowing a view of passersby outside along the far side of the table, the man far more suspicious than his girlfriend, who smiled through the pane of glass.

A couple of doors down, a young woman pulled inexpensive sterling earrings mounted on two-inch cardboard squares hung on a rotating rack just inside the door of a jeweler. She had to step aside when he entered, and when her eyes the color of milk chocolate met his, she dropped a pair onto the floor.

"They're good quality."

The brunette's face was crimson as she retrieved the card with two tiny turtles mounted on it. "Are they?"

"It's real sterling."

"Do you work here?"

Eddie laughed. "No. Just shopping like you. I come here often."

At the counter ten feet away, he asked the jeweler to show him a tray of 18-karat single earrings. She was watching, but he pretended not to notice, picking up a few from the tray, one at a time, examining each with a buyer's interest. Stories of some vampiric aversion to gold were as fanciful as those of their failure to cast a reflection in mirrors. Good thing, because gold worked so well with Celeste's complexion. The twins, too.

"We offer free piercing," the jeweler said, noting his virgin earlobes.

"Thanks, but two or three women I know will be furious if I deny them a chance to stab me in the ear." Lifting a golden crucifix to his left ear, he turned to the brunette still going through the motions of perusing the rack, raising his eyebrows and shoulders. She giggled and shook her head. Next an ankh; the girl wobbled an open hand from side to side, so he put it back and picked up a gold ring and inch in diameter. "Does it make me look too much like a pirate?"

"Dread Pirate Roberts, maybe," she giggled.

"Who?"

"Haven't you seen *The Princess Bride*?"

"Must have missed that one."

"It just came out. You look just like Dread Pirate Roberts."

"Is that a good thing?"

The jeweler, herself a woman of about thirty, smiled. "A wonderful thing. He bears a striking resemblance, doesn't he? Just needs a tiny mustache."

The three chatted for a few minutes, the brunette reversing roles and asking his opinion of a few items off the rack. A bag at her feet fell over when she turned the display, so she moved it to the counter next to the tray of gold earrings and held up another pair Eddie made a face at. "Maybe if I knew your taste more. What's in the bag?"

Emblazoned with Criminal Records and the size and shape of an album, the question delved into her musical taste.

"Oh, it's..."

"Wait, don't tell me. Let me take a stab at it." He examined her, starting down at the black Chuck Taylors on her feet, up her incongruous black and white checked pants and a top with vertical stripes either intended to make her appear taller or minimize a few extra pounds from her voluptuous frame. "The Bangles—no, wait, the Cure."

Those chocolaty eyes grew to an enormous size. "It's *Kiss Me, Kiss Me, Kiss Me*. How did you know?"

"A lucky guess," he brushed it off, pointing to a pair of tiny silver inchworms, curled up into a mid-step arch. "Dust my lemon lies with powder pink and sweet."

"*The Caterpillar*! I love that song."

"I'll be Dread Pirate Roberts if you are Caterpillar Girl." He extended his hand, which she shook. "How much?"

"Yours is $90, hers are $15. Tell you what, make it an even hundred." Eddie slipped a hundred-dollar bill on the counter.

"Let me pay for mine," she said.

"Tell you what, you'll owe me."

"Owe you what?"

"Filling up my hopeless heart, oh never never go," he again recited lyrics from the song.

A pretty thing, the kind who would attract attention on her own, but strolling down Euclid Avenue with him, the couple received plenty of attention. A block past the store and across from Criminal Records stood a high school, empty this time of night. On a bench, they sat chatting about their shared interest in music. Cindy was a DJ at the Georgia State University radio station, and he dazzled her with his knowledge and taste.

"I suppose you don't let guys you just met kiss you, do you?"

"I've never kissed a dread pirate before."

Her kisses were hungry, the kind intended to impress. The kind men respond to. Soft, full breasts filled his hand. He kissed her neck.

"Ouch!" Her hand flew up behind her ear, just beyond his nose.

"What's the matter?"

"Felt like something stung me!"

"Let me look." He pulled her forward, enough to see a trickle of blood behind her ear. "Let me kiss it and make it feel better."

With each breath, her breasts rose and fell against him. Her body fell limp across his lap. While she still breathed and with her skin still warmed by blood remaining in her veins, he pulled his lips away and rearranged her hair a bit to conceal the wound. Careful as if she was a newborn, he lay her across the bench. A distant streetlight lit her enough to see her lips—lipstick now kissed away—had a pink color. He lifted her feet onto the bench.

"You'll be okay." He kissed her forehead. This girl deserved a chance to live a long, full life. When he stood, her hand slipped to the ground, flopping alongside the bag with her record inside. She was still in this position when some passerby woke her around eleven.

Confused and still dizzy, Cindy made her way to her car. She drove home, not understanding why she had fallen asleep or how she had made her way to the bench.

WANTED DEAD OR ALIVE

After a day's unexplained absence, the following day, the burgundy Crown Vic still sat parked up the street, under a steady rain.

Behind a locked basement door, Eddie invited Celeste and Josette to sit while he unlocked the metal prison door.

"What are you doing?"

"She deserves to know cops have followed us from Rhode Island." Only the slightest squeal came from its well-oiled hinges as he closed himself inside.

Angelique was on her feet and one hand caressed his chest as she nuzzled against his neck. "You smell as good as you feel."

"I'm well-fed." His chin lifted and turned. "Taste me."

"Is this a trick?"

"Not at all; you must be starving."

Two fangs sank into his flesh with precision, penetrating his jugular vein. As he stumbled back against the wall, he took her bottom in both hands and pulled her tight against him. Smaller now, her bum filled his grip, round and delicious. Slender legs coiled around his waist, squeezing serpent-like to support her weight. She moaned first, a deep, lascivious moan of pure satisfaction. Together they slid down the wall until he was sitting and she lay atop him, sprawled out in a mutual blood orgasm.

Angelique pulled her lips away and licked the last traces

of blood from his skin. "Did I pass the test?"

"What test?"

"Don't treat a girl like an idiot after giving her the best vorgasm of her life," she said, using the term her sister coined. "You wanted to know if I can control myself." Her hand caressed the rigid bulge in his pants. "As if not biting this thing off when I had the chance didn't already convince you."

"We can't be sure unless you know we aren't testing you."

"Then let me prove it to you."

Rather than answering, he asked, "Did you draw enough blood to manage a conversation with your mom and sis?"

Shock showed on their faces as he escorted the prisoner into the main section of the basement, who took a seat in a chair near one pillar supporting the vaulted Gothic ceiling. He revealed everything to her, including the continuing surveillance on their home. Tense arms crossed over her chest pushed her breasts up in a way that might have been sexier had she not spent days locked in a dungeon. The family so smug, so comfortable after spending who knows how long locked up made her blood boil.

To relieve them of uncomfortable questions, Eddie offered an explanation. "Now that the police are sniffing around creates an issue which concerns all of us and is a more immediate problem than the issue we planned to discuss today."

From her spot in the corner, Angelique asked, "Whether to kill me?"

"That issue. Hardly seems important now."

"It's fairly important to me." Confinement had failed to rob Angelique of her snark.

Her twin blurted out, "Well, we all know we weren't going to kill her anyway, so let's stop pretending we were."

From the disapproving glare her mother cast on her, any clarity on that point existed only in the mind of the accused's sister.

"Listen, the cops are here because your mother and I were fricking sloppy. Let he who is without sin cast the first stone."

Pushing up her cleavage with a tighter clench of her hands under her armpits, Angelique scoffed. "Seriously? The Bible? Are we even allowed to quote from that?"

"He's got a good point," her mother agreed. "The police must have followed me down; I led them right to you. While certainly unintentional, I refuse to vote to punish one of us when I am the one who put us in mortal danger."

"Capture by the police will be the end of us. Since my last arrest ages ago, technology has increased exponentially. They'll subject us to a medical exam, which makes me shudder to contemplate what that will show. Prisons will be much more difficult to escape from now."

Sounding like her sister, Josette said, "*Unsolved Mysteries*, here we come."

"Particularly if they dredge up my old fingerprints from the 1940s and match them with my mug shots from back then. Technically, I am still wanted for escaping from prison."

"What were you in jail for, Eddie?" asked Josette.

"Well, they accused me of murder."

"That sounds like our Eddie, alright," Celeste squeezed his knee.

"Let's just say I was feeling jaded at the time and thought it might be fun seeing their faces when they tried to electrocute me. Having three other people who rely on me offers a slightly different perspective."

"We all need to protect each other," Celeste added.

Angelique glared, but held her razor-sharp tongue. Her eyes followed the conversation, focusing on each one when they spoke, but both facial expression and body language conveyed contempt. When she screws up, she literally ends up in a dungeon, but when others screw up, hey, kumbaya, we're all in this together.

So, while they discussed what to do about the ongoing

police stakeout and how to feed while the cops sat watching from their unmarked car, drinking from a thermos of coffee, she half-listened. Angelique was making some plans of her own.

†

In a house this expansive, staying out of sight is quite a simple proposition. Perhaps already accustomed to Angelique being out of the picture, locked downstairs in her temporary prison, her absence went unnoticed all night. Not so the comings and goings of the police officers outside. The unmarked car remained in its spot, too dark to see more than its general shape and some dim reflections off the chrome of the bumper and grille. However, rather than leaving, once the rain let up, the detectives walked past in clear sight. To avoid giving them an opportunity to flee should both detectives leave for even a few minutes, they each made the long walk to the nearby drugstore for toilet breaks and coffee to fuel the next one.

When Josette's voice echoed through the house at 5:30 in the morning, though, the others did not miss that. "Damn it! What have you done?"

They found her in the kitchen holding a sheet of Eddie's fine cotton stationery. "What's the matter?"

She thrust the note toward them. "Read for yourself."

Hi, bitches!
What did you expect? I need a break and some space. I know you are leaving soon as you can find a way past the sentries, but figured I'd get a head start. Don't worry—I know you will—but just try for once to trust me. When I'm good and ready, I'll come find you if you don't track me down first. That means you, Josette. I am sure our connection will survive and you will know where I am and what I am doing before I know it myself.

It may take some time to get over my own family locking me up while trying to decide whether to kill me, but apparently the one thing we have unlimited amounts of now is time. So, watch over your shoulder as I will be watching my back for one of you to try sneaking up on me. Maybe by then I'll be able to deal with those who turned their backs on me.

To show there are no hard feelings, I left you a little going-away present. I suggest you pack up your shit and get ready for a road trip the moment the opportunity arrives. You are welcome, BTW.

Hugs, kisses and licks—and happy hunting!

Angelique

What came after, though, was the *pièce de résistance.*

Below her signatures, sketched in pencil, were three portraits. Quick sketches, unpolished, but each capturing superb likenesses of the subjects. Facial features, expressions, the tilt of their jaws—all were spot-on. But it was more than that. The essence of her mother, her twin and her maker jumped off the page more accurately than a photo, as if she put the last traces of their souls in gray graphite onto the paper. Their eyes were so alive, using pencils the colors of emerald, amethyst or sapphire would have added nothing. In fact, the lingering impression was that their eyes were in color, not the gray which she drew on the page.

The portraits took their breath away.

Eddie stared at the other two while Celeste reread it for the second time. "What the hell does this mean?"

"It means she's more pissed than usual," the artist's doppelgänger explained.

The letter half-crushed in her hand, her mother said, "But warning us to leave? And a parting gift—I don't have a clue what she's going on about."

"Is she telling us to follow her?" Eddie asked.

Her sister sighed. "No, pretty sure it's the opposite. She knows I will, but she's telling me to back off. Don't ask me about the rest of it—it's too cryptic even for me to make any sense of. Unless..."

Josette ran up the stairs, calling her sister's name. "Okay, you've made your point. We get it! Angelique? Stop screwing around."

Angelique was not screwing around. They searched everywhere—even the last place they expected to find her, back in her dungeon. Because she knew they would look everywhere else first.

Angelique was gone. An orange glow hinted the arrival of another day, one without their fourth. Some of her clothes were missing, as was a backpack. She must have slipped out during the night, in all likelihood following a similar path to the one Eddie took to go feast at Little Five Points.

"If anyone can make it on her own, it's her," her mother said through hopeful, red-streaked eyes.

"She will do better than I did." Eddie hoped it was true, holding inside doubts about her ability to keep her impulsivity and rashness under control for long. Her departure raised the stakes for them, though, and she was right about one thing—they needed to disappear. At least for a while and before she did anything to attract more attention to herself. Soon as someone saw her feeding on some kid, the police would show up at Amethyst House with a search warrant and a SWAT team to serve it.

The house must be empty when they arrived.

Hundreds of early autumn birds created a melancholy song, the only sound that made the early morning tranquility more peaceful than if it were quiet. It seemed just another beautiful southern day was dawning until that tranquility fractured like glass. A scream pierced the neighborhood, one of pure horror and grief.

What had she done? Had she found a way to end herself? Or maybe tried and left some horror-movie failed attempt outside for a neighbor to find? From upstairs, they searched through tree branches still full of leaves, although some had started to turn as they began their beautiful annual death. Those trees blocked too much to locate the source, but a growing commotion of other voices outside raised the panic level higher.

"Wait here!" It was not a suggestion; Eddie's expression made that crystal clear. From a window, they watched him run down to the sidewalk, Celeste still clinging to what now felt like a suicide note. For a second, he stopped at the street, then sprinted off to the left, out of sight.

Sprinted toward a scene which, indeed, came straight from a slasher film.

A crowd was gathering around the unmarked police car, but no one dared touch it. Several people were wearing only their robes and slippers on their feet. A jogger had found the gruesome scene, and she might have passed by without paying too much attention because everyone had seen the cops by then and tried to ignore their intrusion on this fine neighborhood.

But the morning sun caught a smear of red on the passenger window, and the hapless jogger saw Det. Higginbotham staring out the blood-stained window up at a still-lit streetlamp. His mouth hung open and his face was the color of Elmer's glue. Beside him, slumped over in the driver's seat, the Atlanta detective's head rested on the steering wheel. His pants were at his ankles, and blood had dripped all over one naked thigh.

It does not take a detective to correctly identify two murder victims in a parked car.

So immersed was the crowd in this grisly crime scene, none of the neighbors noticed Eddie flying back home. If they did, they assumed he had either run to call 9-1-1, as several others had, or to puke his guts out in private. As several others did, too.

"Grab your stuff and throw it in the car!"

Celeste bounced down the stairs with her daughter a step behind. "What's going on out there?"

"Angelique's going-away present. Foolish as hell, but it just might work."

"What is it?"

"She killed the dicks. Don't ask me how—they're dead in their squad car, no doubt about it! A damn evil genius, that girl of ours! If she was still here, I would kiss her or seal her in that dungeon with bricks. Freaking brilliant if it works!"

The two women had never seen Eddie so excited, and he became much more animated in his motions and facial expressions than they could have expected. They had no time to be picky, sirens were already closing in, so they threw what they could gather into the car and Eddie backed slow as a Florida retiree down the driveway, merely a nonchalant commuter heading to work who had made it out of the house ten minutes earlier than usual to avoid the normal rush.

Two white Dodge K-cars with ATLANTA POLICE in bold, blood-red letters roared by, skidding to a stop just past their house. Eddie turned the direction they had come, toward Ponce de Leon, the main street leading to the Interstate.

Sirens came from everywhere. Nothing brings cops faster or in larger numbers than a call of 10-999: officer down. Police cars tore by going a hundred miles an hour down this narrow, curving residential street, sirens wailing and lights flashing. None paid any attention to the car with the gorgeous blonde and redhead car-poolers heading in the opposite direction, piloted by a slow and cautious driver.

Blue lights flashed far as the eye could see in both directions when he stopped at the intersection, interspersed with some red lights now as the fire department and ambulances started arriving with them. He let them pass, paused at the stop sign waiting for a break, knowing the last thing police expected of a fleeing cop-killer was for them to yield to flashing blue lights.

Technically, they were not cop-killers. Well, Josette was, but that was weeks ago, in another state. But her twin had killed the two detectives, fed off their blood—after mesmerizing one into dropping trou, no doubt expecting something very different than two fangs in his throat. What the police saw was two women car-pooling to work with a man behind the wheel who thoughtfully obeyed the law by stopping while emergency vehicles responded to the most dreaded radio call there was.

When a break came, Eddie turned right onto the main road. Toward town—not the direction he'd choose on a workday, where the traffic already was backing up on the major streets and highways, but it would do.

A cassette sat ejected from the tape deck. When he pushed it in, the sound of dark guitars filled the car as The Cure played *The Blood,* their neighborhood dwindling in the rear-view mirror.

Only a few minutes after that first scream, once free from the neighborhood confines, like Angelique, they simply disappeared among the living.

THE END

ACKNOWLEDGMENTS

When I began writing a book based on a true story in which the main characters not only died by their deaths were the climax of the book, I did not expect the journey to continue, let alone to lead to a third novel.

But, since *The Last Vampire* was about a girl who history records as cheating death as a vampire, these sequels should have been obvious from the start. Only after completing the first novel did the idea begin to germinate. Eddie Brown was the fourth member of the Brown family to die of the mysterious illness that took his mother and two of his sisters, and the last to die from this scourge. Despite dying mere months after his more famous sister, Mercy Lena, they had not desecrated his body like the 3 before him. Most notably, although he died only weeks after his part in immortalizing his sister as the last vampire, despite the same illness claiming him, his family handled his death entirely differently than his sister's.

It is likely the Brown family died of natural causes. Indeed, it is highly probable they all died of tuberculosis passed from one to the other. But… what if?

DECEASED was the first of the sequels which I wrote. Returning home a century later seemed a logical place. And the late 1980s seemed a perfect time. During that decade, everything changed. It was sexy and fun, yet also haunted by a new form of mysterious death, the emergence of AIDS. The pace of change into the future accelerated with such alarming speed that people began looking back at earlier times. Goth music and lifestyles developed. And the interest in vampires increased. In fact, after decades of being relegated to B-movies, vampires began to take a place in the modern culture they have occupied ever since.

But, as I wrote this book, the concept of covering what Eddie had gone through at a midpoint in between took form. Thus, *Red Dahlia* came later to fill in the gaps and help explain how Eddie became who he is by the time of this story. I intended each to be a stand-alone story, so the reader does not need to read all three to enjoy the experience, but if you enjoy the journey, I hope you will enjoy the others, as well—despite each one being written in a different time and reflecting those historical periods.

My great fortune came in finding the model who graces the cover. The bright red hair which I have given the twins is more than a distinctive characteristic or part of their allure. It becomes a major plot point, as their hair makes them stand out—an unwelcome trait when trying to go unseen to prey upon hapless victims in a modern society. Their beauty and that remarkable hair provide perhaps the most vivid mental image of the story. This was the image I wished to capture for the cover, but finding a model who captures the combination of innocence and dangerous beauty with such alluring golden curls is no easy feat.

Thanks to Dawn Fowler, who I have known since the time captured in this book, and who introduced me to her daughter, Caroline. She did more than capture the mood of Josette and Angelique—she *became* them during the cover photoshoot—minus the lethal consequences. So on one steamy summer day, Caroline and Dawn endured a sweltering sun, mosquitos and injury with smiles on their faces and a willing spirit to produce the stunning images which became the beautiful face of this novel. For that, I will remain forever indebted to them!

Thank you!

Whether Eddie, Celeste, the twins or any other characters will continue their journey remains unknown. But I have enjoyed the journey they have taken me on, and hope you will, as well!

ABOUT THE AUTHOR

T.A. Bound's debut Young Adult adventure, SHARKANO, was published in 2020 by Solstice Publishing. In 2022, he published THE LAST VAMPIRE: The Strange Legend of Mercy Brown and its first sequel, RED DAHLIA. An attorney by trade, he has also published a non-fiction book on insurance claims. Raised on the Gulf Coast of Florida, after attending college and Law School in South Carolina, he moved to Marietta, Georgia, his current home. There he lives with his wife and their adopted dog Maksim Gorky, named after the Soviet author, where he enjoys cooking, writing and reading: history, biography, horror and thrillers—particularly historical fiction.

He is currently working on additional sequels to *The Last Vampire*, as well as other stories.

www.ingramcontent.com/pod-product-compliance
Lightning Source LLC
LaVergne TN
LVHW010536160826
845677LV00013B/2894

9798985393651